DAVID EBSWORTH is the pen name ~~~~~~~ former negotiator and workers' representat~~~ ~~ British Transport & General Workers' Union. He was born ~~ ~~~~~~~ Liverpool but has lived in Wrexham, North Wales, with his wife, Ann, ~~~~~ ~~~~~ ~~~~~.

Following his retirement, Dave began to write historical fiction in 2009 and has now subsequently published twelve novels: political thrillers set against the history of the 1745 Jacobite rebellion, the 1879 Anglo-Zulu War, the Battle of Waterloo, warlord rivalry in Sixth Century Britain, and the Spanish Civil War. His sixth book, *Until the Curtain Falls* returned to that same Spanish conflict, following the story of journalist Jack Telford, and is published in Spanish under the title *Hasta Que Caiga el Telón*. Jack Telford, as it happens, is also the main protagonist in a separate novella, *The Lisbon Labyrinth*. The third of his Jack Telford novels, *A Betrayal of Heroes*, takes Jack into the turmoil of the Second World War but through a series of real-life episodes, which are truly stranger than fiction.

Dave's *Yale Trilogy* tells the story of intrigue and mayhem around nabob, philanthropist (and slave-trader) Elihu Yale – who gave his name to Yale University – but told through the eyes of his much-maligned and largely forgotten wife, Catherine.

The eleventh novel, *The House on Hunter Street*, is a mystery set during the political turmoil of Liverpool in 1911 and, more recently, Dave has published a non-fiction guidebook of Wrexham history, *Wrexham Revealed*. It was his research for the guidebook which inspired him to write his twelfth novel, *Blood Among The Threads*, and this, its sequel, *Death Along The Dee*.

Each of Dave's novels has been critically acclaimed by the Historical Novel Society and been awarded the coveted B.R.A.G. Medallion for independent authors. He is also a member of the Crime Cymru Welsh writers' collective.

For more information on the author and his work, visit his website at www.davidebsworth.com.

Also by David Ebsworth

The Jacobites' Apprentice
A story of the 1745 Rebellion.

The Jack Telford Series
Political thrillers set towards the end of the Spanish Civil War and beyond.
The Assassin's Mark
Until the Curtain Falls
(published in Spanish as *Hasta Que Caiga el Telón*)
A Betrayal of Heroes
(published in 2021)
The Lisbon Labyrinth
(an e-book novella, set during the 1974 Portuguese Revolution)

The Kraals of Ulundi: A Novel of the Zulu War

The Last Campaign of Marianne Tambour: A Novel of Waterloo

The Song-Sayer's Lament
Another political thriller but this time set in the time we know as the Dark
Ages, 6th Century post-Roman Britain

The Yale Trilogy
Set in old Madras, London and northern England between 1672 and 1721
The Doubtful Diaries of Wicked Mistress Yale
Mistress Yale's Diaries, The Glorious Return
Wicked Mistress Yale, The Parting Glass

The House on Hunter Street
A mystery set during the political turmoil of Liverpool in 1911

Blood Among The Threads
A Victorian crime novel set during Wrexham's "Year of Wonder", 1876.

Wrexham Revealed
Non-fiction. A walking tour with tales of the city's history

DEATH ALONG *The Dee*

A WREXHAM & CHESTER VICTORIAN MYSTERY

DAVID EBSWORTH

SilverWood

Published in 2024 by SilverWood Books

SilverWood Books Ltd
14 Small Street, Bristol, BS1 1DE, United Kingdom
www.silverwoodbooks.co.uk

Cover by Cathy Helms at Avalon Graphics

ISBN 978-1-80042-287-2 (paperback)

British Library Cataloguing in Publication Data
A CIP catalogue record for this book is available from the British Library

Page design and typesetting by SilverWood Books

For Tony

Author's Note

The Victorian era was, as Dickens might have said, the simplest of times, the most complex of times. And this novel, therefore, set in that same period, is a wee bit similar. A historical fiction, a basic Victorian crime novel, but with all the events and incidents forming its background either historically true or, at the very least, based heavily upon sometimes astonishing fact – as detailed in my notes at the end of the book. It is also, as our long-distance friend and fellow-author Californian Patricia Bracewell has said, another "love letter to Wrexham", my home now for many, many years.

DEATH ALONG THE DEE

Chapter One

'A murder?' said her husband. 'No, Superintendent, I fear you must find somebody else. If I remember correctly, you previously warned me against involvement in such matters.'

'That was eight years ago, sir,' Wilde replied. 'A different matter entirely. In this case? I simply need your professional opinion. There's nobody better qualified, after all.'

Ettie could see that the police superintendent's seeds of cultivated flattery had fallen upon fallow ground. And Neo – Alfred Neobard Palmer, Neobard being his mother's maiden name – was not a man who would succumb easily to propagated blandishments.

'Might I, at least, offer you a cup of tea, Superintendent?' she said, easing herself from the relative comfort of her armchair. And there it was, the pain again. After all these weeks. The pain. The foolish sense of guilt.

'That would be kind, Mrs Palmer. My thanks, ma'am.'

Mrs Palmer? She had still not quite settled to the title, either. How long, she wondered, might it take?

'And you're perfectly correct,' she said. 'There is nobody who understands the chemical properties of Wrexham's water quite like my husband.'

As she had hoped, Superintendent Wilde turned his head in Neo's direction, away from her, and she seized the opportunity to glower at her husband, lifting her hand, rubbing the tip of her thumb against clenched fingers, dramatically and silently mouthing the word "Money!"

It was water which, in so many ways, had carried them both to this point in their lives. Or, rather, the income from her husband's fathomless understanding of its properties.

'My wife is correct,' said Neo, and offered her one of his most infuriating smiles. 'But, I fear, I simply have too much business on my hands just now. And, seriously, Superintendent? If the fellow drowned, and you discovered his body on the banks of the river, can there truly be any mystery about the location of his demise?'

Ettie lifted the old kettle from its trivet and slammed it back on the hob. He could be so infuriating at times. Almost child-like in his obstinacy.

'Yet, did I hear you say, Superintendent,' she innocently asked over her shoulder, 'that his clothes were entirely dry?'

'Precisely our conundrum,' he replied, and shifted himself on her prized carver – Welsh oak, and beautifully etched with ancient designs. Wilde had changed little. A touch more grey in his whiskers but still tall and ramrod straight. Still the same Shropshire accent. Still the same resemblance to those daguerreotypes of poor Abraham Lincoln. Still the same – now unfashionable – stovepipe hat balanced upon his knees.

'A conundrum, indeed,' said Ettie, as she passed into the scullery.

'And it was remiss of me, Superintendent,' she heard Neo say, 'not to congratulate you on your promotion. Well deserved, sir. Well deserved!'

He was dissembling, naturally. Attempting to change the subject. They had, after all, hardly seen eye to eye during their previous encounters. Still, swept under the bridge, she hoped, and finished arranging the China cups and saucers on her finest tray.

'I could return the compliment,' said Wilde. 'Your own business. Fine premises, Mr Palmer, if you don't mind me saying so. A pleasant house. Pleasant.'

She had taken some persuasion to move from the house on Ar-y-bryn Terrace, a house purchased with the money left by her father, when they'd settled in Wrexham. Their first proper home, after sharing accommodation, initially in Chorlton, then with Palmer's father in Thetford.

But here? Yes, pleasant enough. L-shaped, the shorter side taken up, behind Neo's office, by the dining room, narrow entrance hall and staircase, while the longer portion contained her comfortable back parlour with its cosy fireplace oven – she liked to call it her breakfast room – and, beyond, the scullery. In the angle, between the two sides, the yard and privy.

She opened the caddy. Barely sufficient for this pot, and she made a mental note to add Benson's on the High Street to her shopping list, in the hope that maybe one of Neo's clients might soon settle their account.

'I was far from certain,' came Neo's reply. 'About the business. But two years at Zoedone. Two more at the steelworks. It seemed to me there was a gap in the market. That this fine town had great need of an independent analytical chemist.'

'And an equally analytical chronicler,' Ettie called.

She reached up to the shelf on which the pot itself nestled among the rest of her tableware. Another stab of pain, and she clutched at her abdomen.

'Great heavens,' she whispered. 'Will it never stop?'

'Kettle, my dear – it's boiling,' Neo shouted, above the further congratulations Superintendent Wilde heaped upon her husband.

His first published work, a pamphlet based on an earlier paper, *The Towns, Fields and Folk of Wrexham in the Time of James the First.* But little might the policeman understand how its publication had increased their financial difficulties.

She carried the teapot and caddy back into the room and saw her husband's affectionate grin turn instantly to a grimace of concern, a narrowing of his rheumy eyes and fingertips worrying at his carefully trimmed beard. Ettie realised the pain must show on her face. But now she deliberately straightened herself, forced her own lips to fashion a smile. She shook her head at him. It was nothing. Nothing at all.

'And already a figure of celebrity,' said Wilde, as Ettie warmed the pot with a little of the boiling water.

'The lectures?' Neo replied. 'Though I fear the *Advertiser* may have entirely distorted expectations.'

It was her husband's current obsession – the way the paper had so inaccurately reported his appearance at the Wrexham Scientific and Literary Society, insisted on recording the subject matter as... *in the Times of James the Second.* Absurd, Neo had raged. Sixty years separated the reigns of those two Stuart monarchs, and how – *how* – could anybody confuse them?

'Still, sir,' said Wilde, 'making a name for yourself as a chronicler of history – an antiquarian, indeed. The very reason I believed you might be intrigued by our discovery of the deceased.'

She poured the warming water carefully back into the kettle and brought it to the boil once more.

'I fear, Superintendent,' said Ettie, 'that my husband shall not rise to your bait.' She counted each heaped teaspoonful of the precious Darjeeling leaves into the teapot. Four. 'But I, for one,' she went on, 'am intrigued. The poor fellow was found where, precisely?'

'Esther!' scolded her husband. Her Sunday name. Reproach enough, without need of a further word.

'You have made your position plain, my dear. How can it possibly harm to learn a little more? Simply to satisfy my curiosity, if not your own.'

Neo flapped his hand at her, a gesture of surrender.

'Very well,' he said. 'Very well. If we must...'

'Besides, it was the *Advertiser*, Mr Palmer, which caused me to think of you. Your intention to extend your interests – encompass even so far as Holt, it seems.'

Ettie filled the teapot and left it to brew. She would not leave it for too long. Nothing in the world less supportive for the soul than stewed tea or an absence of spirituality.

'Holt – the banks of the Dee, then?' she said,

'Yes, ma'am,' said Wilde. 'The Dee. Just across the river. On the English side. Farndon. That's actually where they found him. But whether he drowned there, or somewhere else...'

'You know the fellow's identity?' said Neo, though without any real interest, she thought.

'Not yet. Some connection to the breweries, we think. A dispensing bottle in his pocket – filled with yeast, it seems. The bottle with a Wrexham marking on it.'

'And hence...' Neo began.

'My own involvement? Quite. My colleagues over the border only too happy to be shot of the paperwork. And forgive me, Mrs Palmer, but wild animals have made the identification – what shall I say? Difficult.'

If Wilde expected her to be shocked, he would be disappointed.

'Yeast?' Ettie hurried into the scullery once more to bring the tray, and the jug of milk from the larder's cold slab. 'In a dispensing bottle?' she shouted. 'Would that be normal?'

'Another mystery, ma'am. Yes, another.'

'Well?' she said to her husband, after they had bidden farewell to the superintendent. 'Are you not intrigued?'

'Not in the slightest,' Neo told her, and reached for his kerchief. Another bout of coughing. Though in general he was no longer so afflicted as he had been in Manchester. Yet she saw that his features had settled again into that troubled expression he wore so often – his bloodhound look, as she liked to call it.

'And here,' he said, taking the tray of cups from her, 'allow me to wash those.'

'I cannot believe, Neo, that you have no interest in this puzzle.'

'But you must – believe it, I mean. For I have neither the time nor the inclination for anything other than the success of our various enterprises – and, of course, the care of my sweet girl. I worry about you, Ettie. Still in pain?'

'Are we not both – still in pain?'

'My dear,' he said, and pecked her on the cheek, before heading for the scullery, 'there shall be more babies.'

She bit back a tear and summoned for him a smile of reassurance, a quick nod of her head – though she knew with absolute certainty that there would be no more.

No. There would not.

Chapter Two

Palmer discovered the anonymous note when he opened up for business the following morning.

Let SʃEEₚIng DoₚS LiE

It was posted through the door of his business premises just around the corner in Chester Street. In truth, the house – as well as Palmer's office and small laboratory – were part of the same three-storey property. Though there was no direct access, one to the other.

So, this morning, after breakfast, he had left Ettie busy in the scullery and closed their front door – number 34a – behind him, picking his way around the puddles of the coaching lane to reach Chester Street itself.

Thankfully, the rain had stopped, and Palmer had stopped as well, before turning left to open the office door of number thirty-four. They had been lucky to get the place. It was the last property on the right side of Chester Street heading north out of town – at least, the last property before the wall, the railings, the shrubs and the poplar trees hiding the Coopers' house – named Bodhyfryd – from the prying eyes of passers-by.

It was the stables, the coach house and their other outbuildings which Palmer could see from his rear upstairs windows – and which prevented him spying any further into their grounds, their allegedly elaborate gardens. All the same, the tops of the Coopers' fruit trees, in the orchard beyond, offered a pleasant enough perspective.

Pleasant, Palmer had thought, smiling to himself, as he glanced back up the lane. For, was that not how the name translated from the *Cymraeg? Bodhyfryd.* Pleasant. Lovely, perhaps. For this was the pure joy of Welsh – the variety of possibilities flowing from any single adjective or noun.

Across the street, the old Baptist Chapel and the elegant, porticoed Griffith mansion. Palmer's house was no more than a five-minute walk from Roseneath, William Low's residence, where Palmer had lodged eight years earlier – though Mr Low himself was now living in London.

And so, unlocking the office door, the piece of paper was wafted across the black and white floor tiles by the breeze from outside.

He had left the house in a good humour, having reassured Ettie once again that she should try to set aside her disappointment about their loss – though he had not broached the question of its cause. For his own part, he thought it might be connected to her strenuous activities in the Wrexham Cycling Club. It seemed a more likely possibility than some of the other commonly accepted reasons for such misfortunes, since Ettie had neither suffered a tooth extraction, nor been foolish enough to partake of sea bathing. That left two other commonly cited etiologies – excessive happiness or the excessive use of a sewing machine. The sweet girl was undoubtedly guilty of both, but Palmer's scientific mind dismissed each as feeble fallacies and, despite the seriousness of the subject, he could not help being amused, as they were always mutually amused, by the use of the word. For she was, indeed, his Ettie. So, what better word to define a cause for her ailments than etiology?

Still, he was certain that, with less cycling and a little care, there would be no similar difficulties in the future. It was the image which had filled his head as he'd opened the door – himself surrounded by little ones and their playful laughter. Such joy! The image evaporated like steam from the kettle as he retrieved the note and studied the letters cut so carefully from some broadsheet or similar publication, then pasted onto a strip of plain writing paper.

'Let sleeping dogs lie?' He read the words slowly and shivered. What was the saying – like somebody stepping upon one's grave? What did it signify? His thoughts went immediately to the talk he had delivered to the Scientific and Literary Society and those difficult questions hurled at him in the aftermath. About whether he might be attempting to stir trouble against landowners in the area? And, of course, he had not. Though he had been surprised by the venom of his interrogators – themselves two very significant freeholders and, as such, hardly likely to stoop to anonymous letter-writing.

In any case, he should be thankful to them, for they had sparked an interest. After all, had the landowners' harsh response to their tenants' rights not helped to spark the so-called Rebecca Riots only a few decades earlier? And were there not still many of the same problems remaining? The Welsh Land Question, as Palmer's friend, Edward Owen, called it. And, in collaboration with Owen, he was working on his next volume. He already had the title: *A History of the Ancient Tenure of Land in the Marches of North Wales.*

There remained only one problem – how to raise the funds, or gather sufficient subscriptions, to cover the cost of its publication. And how to broach that subject with dear Ettie.

He studied the note again, tempted to go back around the corner and share the thing with her. But his concerns about her health remained and he feared some relapse should she become agitated on his behalf. In any case, he had the samples to finish for the Lager Company, and his promise to Mr Wassmann that he would deliver his findings to the brewery's office before it closed, this being half-day Saturday.

But the note – what was he to make of the note?

He sat at his desk, still wearing his coat and hat, and took a pinch of snuff from the silver box which had once been a gift from Esther.

'The superintendent's visit yesterday?' he said to himself. Could that be the other issue to which it might relate? And what was it, precisely, that Wilde had wanted from him? Analysis of fluids from the lungs of the deceased. Palmer swivelled his chair around and surveyed the contents of his modest laboratory. He was no magician. And how could anybody possibly have known about the policeman's request for his assistance? No, the note must relate to something else. Or, perhaps, some jest that he could not yet quite fathom. The note and Wilde's visit simply a coincidence, surely.

He turned back to his report, dipped his pen and began to write.

'Though it is one of the few things I share with the fellow,' he murmured, 'that neither of us believes in coincidence.'

*

It was, indeed, no coincidence that Palmer's route to the Lager Beer Company's offices led him directly past the infirmary and he decided that it could, after all, do no harm to pay a quick visit – only to see, naturally, whether the good doctor, Edward Davies, might perchance be there and about his gruesome business. For Superintendent Wilde had left him with that information, a *post mortem* examination to be conducted this very morning, in time for Tuesday's inquest at the Nag's Head.

It was innocuous enough, surely. It did not imply that Palmer would take any protracted interest in the matter. But it was hard to ignore the note entirely and he must admit that it had helped to pique his innate inquisitiveness. Yet, piqued sufficiently for him to endure the horrors of the infirmary's mortuary?

He was escorted there, with the blessing of the senior house-surgeon, by an obliging nurse who remembered him from the time he had spent there as a patient. Remarkable, for it had been eight years earlier. And the mortuary itself – when they had passed through the main corridors to reach the rear gardens and yard – was something of a disappointment, little more than a large brick-built shed. It was depressingly small, barely room for a slab in the centre, upon which the deceased lay entirely covered by a blood-stained white sheet. Beyond, a grey stone sink at which the doctor's assistant washed the tools of their butchery. Above the sink, a set of wooden shelves with bottles large and small, each containing the repulsive and preserved internal organs of those who had passed through this place recently. Palmer wondered, not for the first time, about the conundrum of resurrection for no longer entirely whole.

'Welcome to the dead-house, Alfred,' said Doctor Davies, looking up from writing in his journal. 'Wilde told me you would be paying us a visit.'

'He did?'

The absolute nerve of the fellow. Policeman he might be, but...

'Indeed,' said the doctor. 'You plan to analyse some of the bodily fluids, I understand.'

'I had not specifically agreed to do so, Edward. Though, since I am here, do you have any results?'

'Well, Mr Roberts?' Davies said to his assistant. 'Do we – have results?'

The man turned to face them. He was old. Impossibly old, with flowing sideburns like clouds of cumulus. Like the doctor, his suit was protected by a long leather apron, though his own so worn and stained that Palmer wondered why he had bothered.

'Results?' croaked the ancient. 'As we say hereabouts, sir, that *remains* to be seen.'

He cackled with laughter, though whatever the jest, Palmer failed to see it.

'A grim business, Alfred,' said the doctor. 'Without a little levity, I fear we should all go mad.'

'Levity,' Palmer repeated. He was still less than certain they were quite on the same page. 'I suppose you must be right.'

They were old acquaintances, of course. The doctor was William Low's son-in-law, married to Low's eldest daughter, Alison. And the Palmers had been their dinner guests on more than one occasion in the Davies's happy residence at the bottom of Grosvenor Road. They had named it Plas Darland, though the *Plas* spoke more of Edward's aspiration than to any actual palatial resemblance, the house being comfortably large but simply semi-detached.

'And Esther? Fully recovered, I hope?'

He had attended upon Ettie following her mishap.

'I have insisted she should rest,' said Palmer. 'And encouraged her to abandon further involvement with the Cycling Club.'

'My dear chap,' Davies began, 'I hardly think… Anyway, to business, I suppose.' He glanced at his pocket watch. 'And Superintendent Wilde has insisted on a mask maker and a photographer. They should be here shortly.'

A death photographer. Macabre. Ettie had suggested having such a remembrance of the babe, but he had demurred. It had hardly even been recognisable. But he quickly set the memory aside.

'He attaches such significance to the case?' he said.

'For all I know, Alfred, it may be his standard procedure.'

The doctor read aloud from his notebook, a somewhat tedious account of the *autopsia* findings, plainly a rehearsal for the forthcoming

20

inquest. Inhaled water in the alveolar spaces of the lungs. Pulmonary oedema. Page after page.

'Wilde mentioned a dispensing bottle upon the fellow's person,' said Palmer, when the doctor seemed to be at the end. 'Filled with yeast.'

Davies shrugged his shoulders.

'I know nothing about it,' he said. 'But the salient details? By way of conclusion, you understand. Drowning. Though no signs of immersion except his head. Contusions around his neck and shoulders. Lacerations as well, doubtless caused by some clawed scavenger – a dog, perhaps.' He paused, glanced at Palmer. 'Though it must have been a large one, Alfred. Large, indeed. Have you seen the newspaper reports?'

Palmer nodded. Last week's *Advertiser*. Another sighting at Marchwiel of the so-called Corpse Dog, the *Cwn Cyrff.*

'Superstitious nonsense,' said Palmer.

Dr Davies gave a shrug of his shoulders, as though he might not entirely agree. Then he returned to his notes. 'No obvious means of identification – except...'

He beckoned for Palmer to follow him and they joined Mr Roberts alongside the slab. The old man lifted the sheet and pulled forth the dead man's pallid left arm where, above the elbow, was an ornate tattoo. A crown, sitting above what must surely be a series of mountain peaks.

Palmer pondered its significance all the time he spent at the Lager Company and, later, as he hurried home, anxious to tell Ettie about the anonymous note. But, back in the house, after hanging his coat and hat upon the hall stand, he found her considerably distressed.

'My dear,' he said, 'what is it?'

Chapter Three

Ettie knew she should have commented on the note, but as Neo waved the thing in her direction, he had seen her stricken features and gently lifted this week's copy of the *Advertiser* from her hands. At the same time, he set a neatly wrapped parcel down upon their occasional table.

'What is it, my dear, that disturbs you so?' he said.

She had been staring at the newspaper for – how long? She had no idea. It was not one thing alone which had so upset her but several.

'Ah…' said her husband as he found the paragraphs which had most immediately affected her, the words now burned upon her brain.

MYSTERIOUS CONCEALMENT OF BIRTH AT SUMMERHILL
Another body discovered in an ashpit.

'How?' she sobbed. 'Stillborn they might have been. Miscarried, according to the inquests. Yet…'

'Abandoning the poor mites like that,' Neo murmured, crouching beside her chair and taking her hand. It was warm, reassuring.

But she could conceive of few worse sins. To dispose of one's babe as though it were some piece of garbage. An ashpit. Denied a Christian burial. What was the matter with people these days?

'And somebody,' she said, 'must know the creature responsible.'

'I think we must assume,' he replied, 'that the balance of the poor woman's mind would have been seriously disturbed. Or that there is some element to the history here we do not understand.'

She felt his gentle squeeze of her fingers. And somehow it angered her.

'Must you always be so open-handed, Neo? It is sinful.'

She pulled her hand free, snatched the newspaper back from him and pointed at the bottom of the page. The same page. The very same.

'And this!' she said. 'From a medical practitioner, of all people.'

Some doctor on trial at the Cardiff Assizes for attempting to cremate the remains of his dead infant.

'And acquitted, my dear. The practice, it seems, is not technically against the law – though I never heard of a case before this one.'

'Barbaric,' she said. 'Are we all to become heathens now? What sort of doctor does not believe in the resurrection?'

It was, after all, her own single consolation. She thought of the unadorned cross upon the cemetery plot they had themselves so recently purchased.

'I cannot believe it shall become commonplace, sweet girl. And I was more astonished that this Dr Price had named the child Iesu – Iesu Grist, in fact. One must assume the doctor to be a Christian, and yet...'

And yet, and yet – with Neo there was always some *and yet*. Why *did* he have to be so damnably reasonable?

'Do you think the same of me, Neo?'

She threw down the broadsheet.

'The same – as what, my dear?'

'The balance of my mind – disturbed?'

'Esther,' he said to her, as he stood and took the snuff box from his jacket pocket, 'I can imagine no person upon the Almighty's good green earth whose mind could be more in equilibrium than your own.'

She knew he was dissembling. She felt it within. Something missing. And not just the babe, of course. No, this felt as though some drought had caused the waters of her life to slow, to become a mere trickle where once there had been a flood. Still, she was grateful for his attempt to humour her, and she stood to embrace him.

'I do not deserve you, Alfred Neobard Palmer. You must have had a tiresome day. I shall make us a cup of tea.'

'Indeed, you shall not,' he insisted, and gently pushed her back into the chair. 'I shall do it. Oh, and I almost forgot...'

The parcel upon the side table – the table which had once belonged to her father. Octagonal. Useful pull-down shelves at each side. She touched the carefully polished wood and remembered him.

'You brought cake.' She forced a smile. 'I recognise the ribbon. Kendrick's.'

It brought her a flicker of light to the darkness in her soul. For it had not been the newspaper alone which had dimmed her day. Though that could wait – for now, at least. Perhaps until he brought the tea.

She watched him pick up the parcel and turn it, this way and that, teasing her. He still had the note in his other hand and, again, she knew she should have made some comment.

'And was it?' she said, as he carried the precious cake into the scullery. 'A tiresome day?'

'I finished my report,' Neo shouted, above the clatter of crockery, 'on the samples for Mr Wassmann. He's a delightful fellow, my dear – for a German.'

I suppose I should count our blessings, she thought, as Neo continued his preparations for their afternoon tea and recounted his visit to the Lager Beer Company. Her husband's contract with them provided a modest retainer. But only thanks to Neo having worked for Silverstein before – in Manchester, as an analyst for Silverstein's dyeing business there. And shortly after she and Neo had moved to Wrexham, Silverstein had appeared here also, this time as one of the major partners in his new industrial adventure – brewing German lager, of all things, in a town so renowned for its traditional ales. It had been Silverstein's offer of the contract which had caused Neo to leave his most recent steady employment, at the steelworks, and set up his own business.

'Still,' she said, when he returned and set down a delicate slice of princess cake upon the table, 'I remain surprised that your passion for temperance might allow you to so readily work for the brewing industry.'

He now stood at the fireplace, somewhat flushed by his efforts, unbuttoning his jacket with one hand, holding the kettle – its handle wrapped in a cloth – with the other.

'I have explained already, my dear,' he told her. 'The lesser of two evils. The alcohol content so much lower in these lager beers that we should welcome their introduction. Though I am less certain about the brewery itself. The next page in the *Advertiser* – have you seen it? I have to say I would be happy to join the protest. And I told Mr Wassmann so.'

Neo's complaint to the brewery's manager would, she decided, have been so polite as to render it entirely ineffective. Still, they had a point. The noise of the brewery hooter was indeed hideous. The beginning and end of shifts, night or day. Surely it must be unlawful, to terrorise people in this way. Though it was not the hooter which had caused her own terror this day.

'Bad enough here,' she murmured, still searching for the right moment to tell him. 'But right behind the infirmary! It must be a nightmare for the sick and infirmed.'

'Which reminds me,' said Neo, as he filled the teapot, 'I called there to see Edward – Davies, of course. You remember Superintendent Wilde mentioned he might be performing his *post mortem* examination this morning?'

She was suddenly filled with still greater dread.

'You went, Neo. You had set your head against it, remember?'

'Indeed. But I decided to heed your advice – about the money. We are so badly in need, as you say.'

Yes, it was so. The cost of the premises here. No regular income. Neo's literary ambitions – and, of course, she knew he had already commenced working on the next one. But the expense.

'Still...' she began, but the fear gripped her, a black dog of her own, and prevented her from pouring out the story.

'Do you know,' said Neo, 'the rogue had arranged for a sample of the fellow's lung fluids to be left for me? The sheer impertinence.'

'He would have known that your curiosity would get the better of you.' She took the proffered cup and saucer from his hands – her own now shaking so badly that she spilled some of the tea onto her pinafore.

And we all know where curiosity leads, she thought to herself.

'Anyway,' said Neo, 'I shall do this one small thing – so long as they do, indeed, pay me for the service. But after that...'

'After that, you shall have nothing further to do with it, I hope?'

'Absolutely, my dear. Though – well, I should show you this.'

She watched him delve into his jacket pocket again and produce that same piece of paper. Once again, she knew it was remiss to interrupt him, but there was the curse, like Lord Tennyson's *Lady of Shalott*.

> *Out flew the web and floated wide,*
> *The mirror crack'd from side to side.*

'My love,' she cried, almost choking on her emotion, and unable to hold back the wave of alarm any longer, 'I have had the most dreadful vision.'

Chapter Four

His eyeless, decomposed corpse had been fished from the river. From the Dee. Esther had been certain it was the Dee, though she'd not recognised the specific location for her vision. It was surrounded, she had simply said, all about by flowers. White blossoms.

'And how,' he had asked her, 'could you be so certain this was, indeed, the River Dee?'

She had simply known. Intuition.

'But this corpse,' he had reasoned with her, 'so badly corrupted, yet so easily recognisable as my own?'

Again, she had simply known. More intuition.

'Perhaps,' he had suggested, 'merely some warped reminder – you remember? That time when our lives were indeed endangered. The Menai Straits?'

That, she had reminded him, was – how long? Eight years ago?

'I think you are mistaken, Neo,' she had said. 'Do you think I am not familiar with the difference? A nightmare recollection of the past, or this form of prescient foreboding. No, I tell you, my dear, you must take this as a warning.'

It kept him sleepless most of the night and plagued him, this morning, on the way to his place of worship. He had walked Esther across to the Baptist Chapel, sheltering her beneath his rain napper from the light drizzle, in time for the morning's Sunday School class. She would teach there, delighting in providing some supplementary religious education for the children. Much-needed these days, they each believed.

Palmer himself, however, remained enmeshed in his own strictly Wesleyan beliefs. He was fortunate, for Wrexham boasted two Primitive Methodist chapels and now warranted its own Circuit. But his choice fell, as always, on the farthest, on Talbot Road – the chapel once located at the top end of Farndon Street. Tomorrow was Market Day, of course, and therefore the Lord's Day was disturbed by the drovers herding their cattle through the town's streets, ready for the following morning's auctions. The lowing of the beasts, the clatter of their hooves on the cobbles of Bridge Street, and the stench of dung mingling with the usual heady odours emanating from the town's tanning yards and many breweries.

He was greeted in the chapel's doorway – if greeting it might indeed be termed – by the familiar bent form of Bethan Thomas.

'*Felly – rydych chi yma eto, ydych chi?*' Oh, back then, are you? She peered up at him, scowling.

'Bethan,' he replied, also in Welsh. 'The same question every week. Where else should I be?'

During Palmer's short stay in Wrexham for the memorable Art Treasures Exhibition, they had worked together – himself as curator of Mr Low's museum and Bethan as his assistant. They had almost become friends, and he had ensured she should become curator in her turn when Palmer returned to his work in Manchester. The museum still existed, on the ground floor of Low's Westminster Building on Hope Street, now serving more as an art gallery.

But, since his return, things had soured again. First, he had foolishly – though innocently – enquired why she had converted to Wesleyanism from her previously staunch Welsh Presbyterianism. He had also once questioned her on a point of Welsh grammar – simply because he was keen to learn. Yet she had taken his honest queries, first, as a challenge to her faith and, second, as a criticism of her own use of the phrase in question. Ever since, and despite his several attempts to explain, he had been dismissed as some *Sais* misogynist – a damnable Englishman – a nobody, hardly worth even an acknowledgement. When she did acknowledge him, it was now only ever in Welsh. And, even in Welsh, he was surprised at the way in which their exchange developed.

'Investigating, I suppose. Isn't that what you do?' she snapped at him. 'Analyst, like, you call yourself?'

The chapel was small but already packed with worshippers, some of whom turned at the sound of this modest altercation.

Palmer smiled and nodded reassuringly at the faces of the curious. 'Investigating?' he said.

'This Tobin.'

The Circuit's superintendent, Reverend Howcroft, beckoned urgently to him since, once again, Palmer had been invited to preach, then lead the discussion after the communion service.

'Tobin?' said Palmer, waving a finger towards the reverend. Just one minute, he mouthed, then returned his attention to Bethan. He had a bad feeling about this.

'Drowned, wasn't he?' she said. 'Found at Holt?'

He had been under the impression that the fellow's identity was unknown. But he might have guessed that if, over the weekend, some new information had come to light, the whole town would now be aware of it – at least, the whole town apart from himself, it seemed. Though he had no intention of admitting this to Bethan Thomas.

'Tobin,' he murmured. 'Yes, indeed. Though actually found on the Farndon side. From the Lager Company, was he not?'

Her bird-like neck stretched out, her head turning sharply, up and around. She stared at him.

'Know, do you?'

There was surprise in her voice and he was not about to reward her by admitting he had merely guessed as much. He had spent much of Saturday evening analysing the samples from the mortuary – after swallowing his indignation at Wilde's audacity.

'Of course,' he told her. 'But now, Bethan, if you will excuse me...'

He made for his place near the simple lectern and all through the service he rehearsed the report he must, tomorrow, deliver to Dr Edward Davies and to the police. It would, he knew, have to be sufficiently authoritative to avoid him having to appear before Tuesday's inquest in person. He edged his way to the harmonium, competently fingering the keyboard while also raising his voice to the Heavens.

At Jacob's Well, a stranger sought
His drooping frame to cheer...

How strange, he thought. *Jacob's Well*, indeed. Ettie would surely have read some mystic meaning into this choice of closing hymn.

The liquid taken from the dead man's lungs, stomach and duodenum contained traces of sand and plant seeds which, Palmer believed, could only have come from one place – ground with which he was somewhat familiar due to his studies for *The Towns, Fields and Folk of Wrexham*. Yes, he was certain, the fellow had drowned at one of the streams feeding the Gwenfro and rising west of Maesgwyn, almost certainly the Pant-y-Golfen spring. And that had given him his first clue about the brewery – for those same waters, as pure as those of Pilsen itself, also fed the Wrexham Lager Beer Company Limited.

The second? According to Wilde, they had found a dispensing bottle filled with yeast. Naturally, the connection might have been to any of the town's breweries. But this link to the spring. It wasn't conclusive, though Bethan seemed to have confirmed his opinion. *Da iawn*, Bethan. Very good.

Yet, if Tobin – supposing this was, in truth, the victim's name – had drowned, or *been* drowned, so close to town, how had he been discovered six miles away, at Farndon?

He found himself at the lectern and recalled that he had deliberately chosen, as the theme for his sermon, that verse from Isaiah, 12:3. *Therefore with joy shall ye draw water out of the wells of salvation*. He preached about the boundless nature of God's beneficence, without limit, like the oceans of the world. For Palmer had the gift. The ability to see the beauty of redemption through God's eyes. Still, he was surprised by his unconscious choice for his closing text.

Proverbs, 5:15. *Drink waters out of thine own cistern, and running waters out of thine own well.*

Was this not simply another way of saying the same as that anonymous note? Let sleeping dogs lie? And this reminded him – he had still not shared the note with Ettie. Perhaps tonight, their usual Sunday evening constitutional stroll, weather permitting, promenading with their neighbours up the road and Acton Hill.

It should be a fine one, for he had carefully checked the barometer against the rise and fall of the glass over the past few days. He had consulted his Illustrated Almanack against the colour and quality of dusk and dawn, against the moisture in today's air, against the brightness of last night's stars.

Yes, a fair evening. Though, perhaps, given the present state of her mind...

The day's discussion fell quite naturally to the subject of temperance, and the next planned march of the Blue Ribbon Army, around town in just a few weeks. So many had now taken the pledge and wore the blue ribbon with pride. Bethan, as it happened, had been busy with a new banner. But when Palmer tried to congratulate her – *llongyfarchiadau, Bethan* – she had turned to one of the others and spoke in English.

'Ask him, then,' she'd said. 'If he's so keen on abstinence, how come he's working for this Lager Beer Company?'

It was the same criticism Ettie had levelled against him. There were those in the congregation who also seemed shocked, though Reverend Howcroft was quick to support him.

'My friends, we have had this discussion before. The inferior of two evils. Preferable that those not yet convinced by abstinence should at least partake of this less intoxicating product.'

It was true. The alcohol content in lager was significantly less than in more traditional ales and since the Lager Beer Company was now, at last, in full production, the various temperance groups had given it a cautious welcome as one small step towards the eradication of the demon drink from society entirely. Though there were those – Bethan Thomas among them – who saw this as, rather, a step towards damnation. Zealots, and to Palmer it seemed the world was presently full of them.

'And how,' he said to the gathering in general, 'might we, as Primitive Methodists, show affinity with workers and their struggles yet deny those same workers what they see as a simple pleasure in the interim before they finally see the light? I think we all know what Wesley himself would have thought.'

'Proverbs, twenty,' said Bethan to those around her. 'Verse one. *"Wine is a mocker. Strong drink is raging. And whosoever is deceived thereby is not wise."* Right, that is.'

'Yet, we are not discussing wine here, my friends,' Palmer reminded them. 'Nor gin or other strong liquor – but beer. And it was not so long ago that water available to working families was itself so foetid that beer was the only acceptable alternative.'

'And we are blessed,' said Reverend Howcroft, 'that here in our fine town, the Waterworks Company maintains such a supply of clean water to our fountains and pumps, to so many of our houses. For, without water there is no life.'

The debate swung back and forth. And debate it was, rather than the gentle discussion Palmer had intended. It was almost as though Miss Thomas, in her conversion, had somehow failed to grasp the main principles of Wesleyanism – its respect for the views of others.

'Says he's only testing it, he does,' Bethan sneered to one of her neighbours. 'Checking, like. Always the same with him. Curiosity, see? But we all know where curiosity takes us.'

She had confronted him this way soon after he had returned. Perhaps if he had left well alone, she'd said, there would have been fewer deaths. And he could hardly deny it. To some extent, he and Ettie had exposed those guilty for some heinous crimes though, on the other hand, the guilty had died in the process. These eight years later, it still plagued him. The sanctity of life, of course, the most sacred of God's gifts.

'The Dee,' she murmured now. *'Afon Dyfrdwy.* Waters of the Goddess, they say.'

'Miss Thomas!' Reverend Howcroft scolded her. 'This House of God is surely no place for such heathen beliefs.'

The others seemed to agree with him. Though Bethan simply shrugged the criticism away. Palmer's studies, however, had taught him much about the myths, legends and traditions of his newly adopted homeland. He held them in high regard. And might she have hit upon something important? Some connection between mythology of the Dee and the discovery of Tobin's corpse. It seemed unlikely, but perhaps the possibility should be explored.

'Aerfen, she's named,' said Bethan, more loudly. 'Dangerous, like. The goddess – and the river, both. Curiosity, see. Dangerous, like I said.'

She finally looked up at him.

Could it be? Perhaps it was his reluctance to think ill of anybody, but he was suddenly struck by the thought that all today's animosity from Bethan Thomas might be some form of mummery. Concern for his safety? Yes, perhaps she deserved the benefit of the doubt. And tomorrow he would make sure to speak with Wilde about this fellow Tobin. The superintendent would be bound to be there – for the next day would be a memorable one. For the town, and for Wrexham as a whole.

Chapter Five

'Fenians?' Ettie asked Superintendent Wilde. 'In Wrexham?'

A jet of yellow flame spat in the general direction of the Butchers' Market entrance, just behind them, from the mouth of a fire-eater in the midst of the High Street's procession.

'In my experience, Mrs Palmer, wherever Irishmen gather, there you shall find Fenians.'

Wilde turned his attention to Neo.

'The analysis complete, sir, I trust,' he said. It was a statement, an instruction, rather than a question.

'Indeed,' her husband replied. 'Though I still resent your presumption, Superintendent. And did you say you now have further demands upon my time?'

'Are you not too busy, my dear?' she asked, for she had now lost her appetite for further involvement in this case. The premonition more pressing than the paucity of income.

Neo smiled at her, reassuringly while, behind the fire-eater, a juggler, dressed like one of the Little People in Irish tales – and spinning no less than five red and yellow Indian clubs, up and around without falter.

'The yeast pot,' said the policeman, ignoring her. 'My sergeant was foolish enough to taste the contents. He has been violently indisposed ever since.'

There, she thought. I knew it. This thing already has too many complications.

'Well,' said Neo, 'I shall be at the Racecourse this afternoon, and will leave my report on the way to the game. Perhaps I shall collect this deadly yeast sample at the same time.'

The exchange continued, with Neo's reassurance that, yes, he would also deliver a copy of his report to Dr Davies in time for tomorrow's inquest. And, all the while, she felt her spine tingle with trepidation, as the juggling leprechaun was followed by a troupe of tumblers. She glanced around, unable to stop herself, twice-anxious now with this mention of the Irish troubles. For, here they were, in the midst of these celebrations in honour of St. Patrick. Gypsy caravans and folk in all manner of outlandish regalia, of green flags, of bagpipes, flutes and fiddlers. And the Market Day crowds thronging the pavements as spectators.

'Fenian,' she said to neither the policeman nor her husband in particular. 'Yet difficult to reconcile these scenes of joy with word from the newspapers.'

It was only March, and these past months alone, bombs at London's stations. Last year, the same. So many bombs, so many places. And the year before? Goodness, that fellow with government responsibility for Ireland and his undersecretary – both stabbed to death in Dublin. Phoenix Park, was it not? Though, perhaps, butchered would have been a more accurate description.

'Interesting origins, though,' said Neo. She saw him remember to angle the umbrella, to better protect her from today's intermittent showers. 'Fenians,' he went on, by way of qualification. 'The heroes of Irish legend. The Fianna – followers of Finn MacCool, you know?'

So typical of him – to quite lose the horror of some disaster or tragedy by wandering into the more comforting depths of his passion for historical detail.

'And this Tobin,' she said. 'You are certain he was one of them, Superintendent?'

'Pamphlets in his lodgings,' Wilde replied.

He had already explained that Mr Wassmann, manager of the Lager Company, had reported one of his overseers missing from duty and, early this morning, had identified the dead man – though with difficulty, due to the claw marks and bites about the fellow's head and face.

'McDermott's Building,' he clarified.

The policeman brusquely waved aside an ancient tinker trying to sell Esther a new kettle from his handcart.

'But not…' she began, somewhat vexed that Wilde had not given her the chance to decide about the kettle for herself.

'McDermott?' he said. 'Gracious, no. Pillar of the community.'

He was, indeed – of the town's Irish community, anyway. A considerable tenement building bore his name, on Yorke Street alongside the Black Horse, just around the corner from where they presently stood under a sky so mournful that even this festival affability could provide little amelioration.

'And, speak of the devil…' said Neo, adjusting the rain napper yet again.

Here came a long brewer's cart, pulled by a pair of magnificent Shire horses decked out in green ribbons and rosettes. Upon the cart, a tableau of characters from Irish history behind placards bearing their names: St. Patrick and St. Brigid surrounded by cherubs; the pirate Anne Bonny; and the warrior High King, Brian Boru, in all his shining armour. Along the sides of the cart, decorated with shamrock images, two colourful advertising boards, one proclaiming *McDermott's Irish Shop, Tuttle Street, Wrexham,* and the other *McDermott's Beehive Foundry, Mount Street, Wrexham.*

'And the gentleman himself, I assume,' she said as, behind the cart, strutted an enormous but elderly fellow in a tweed suit too tight for his frame. His red face beamed, and he waved to the crowd on either side from beneath an umbrella held above his head, she supposed, by the fellow's wife. They were surrounded by a dozen children of all ages, the smallest in a baby carriage pushed by a girl of perhaps fifteen – and the sight of the baby carriage caused Esther's abdomen to cramp once more. Without thinking, she squeezed Neo's arm.

'Is all well, my dear?' he said. 'If this conviviality is too much…'

She shook her head. Indeed, convivial though it seemed, she could not help but sense some other tension beneath the surface – evident when a few of the younger men, plainly somewhat inebriated, came just a little too close, shouting loudly.

'*Faugh-a-Ballach! Faugh-a-Ballach!*'

Ettie recoiled from them. Though neither Wilde nor her husband seemed to notice.

'The slogan they're shouting?' she said, when the men had passed. 'I've heard it before – their weddings at St. Mary's.'

Their weddings, she thought to herself. Now, why did I say that? But it was, she supposed, a foreign tongue, after all. And Neo was already speaking the words slowly for her, pronouncing them carefully in his gentle Norfolk accent.

'Fog-a-bolla,' he said. 'Erse. It means "Clear the Way!" – or so they tell me. Though it seems now to have lost its bellicose meaning. A little like the old Prussian battle-cry *Huzzah*. Now an expression of joy, of course.'

'You're maybe too young to remember, ma'am,' Wilde shouted over the chanting. 'But less than twenty years since the devils tried to attack Chester castle. A thousand of the rogues? Maybe more. If it had not been for the army...'

Her father had told her – enraged that so many of the Fenians had travelled there from Manchester, as well as Liverpool, Preston and Halifax. The plot, if she remembered correctly, had been to capture Chester castle's substantial cache of weapons to arm an insurrection in Ireland itself. The plan may have been foiled – but only just. And the rebellion had gone ahead regardless, in Dublin and elsewhere. A failed rebellion, of course. Yet the whole episode had left its mark.

More young men on the street now, singing at the tops of their voices. A song she knew – *Mrs McGrath*.

Now up comes her boy, without any legs
And in their place there were two wooden pegs...

The terrible result of war. And poor *Tada*, she thought. Six years and she still missed him. He had died just before their wedding and within weeks of Neo's mother. It had cast such a shadow over the ceremony. He had always believed Neo to be unworthy of her, of course. Yet, what might he think of her husband now? His own business – even though it was unlikely to survive for too much longer.

'This Tobin,' said Neo. 'A Fenian with a crown tattooed upon his arm?'

'Most of this lot – their families, anyhow,' Wilde told them, 'would have come to escape the famine. The streets of Wrexham – Mold and Holywell, too – paved with gold.'

Ettie had learned about the Irish famine at her father's knee also.

'My husband's friend, Mr Reynolds – God rest his soul – placed blame for the Irish famine squarely upon the shoulders of those who continued to profit from the export and sale of Irish crops to England, while those who had worked the land died from starvation following the potato blight. It is wicked, sir.'

She knew, of course, that this was precisely Neo's view as well, and she watched as three of the young men – each of them built like an ox – moved on, waving a huge flag, green and with a yellow rising sun, its rays stretching out like spread fingers.

'True,' said Wilde. 'They already hated us for the famine – but come here they did, anyway.'

'Then find there's no fortune to be had, after all,' said Neo.

'So, their sons join the army,' she said, 'there being little else for most of them.'

'Don't like the way they're treated in the army either,' the policeman smiled.

'Or come back crippled?' she suggested, recalling the story of *Mrs McGrath*.

'Hate us even more,' said Wilde. 'But we'll find out about this Tobin in due course. I suspect the tattoo has some link to the army. Now, listen – you see?'

The procession had slowed almost to a halt as the carts and gypsy caravans made the difficult turn at the Town Hall into Hope Street. The men with the flag had shifted to a new song, one she had not heard before.

High upon the gallows tree swung the noble-hearted three.

'There it is,' said Wilde. 'I might have known. New anthem. Those three Fenians hanged in Manchester after the insurrection in '67. Martyrs now, they say.'

"God save Ireland!" said the heroes;
"God save Ireland" said they all.

The song, it seemed, occasioned a degree of agitation among some of those in the procession, a couple of older men remonstrating with the singers and soon Mr McDermott was bustling back towards them. She could not hear his words, but his hand gestures and the angry expression were enough.

Superintendent Wilde also seemed affected by the song, for he raised himself up onto the toe-tips of his boots, waving across the High Street. To the other policeman sheltering in the entrance to the

Overton Arcade? No, she saw, it was the woman beside the constable, was it not? A tall woman with a face like a hatchet, who merely nodded her head just once and then, with a word to the policeman, disappeared into the darkness of the arcade itself, towards Temple Row. A woman! What, on earth...?

Agitation, too, further along the High Street, where more young men outside the Royal Oak, had begun to shout abuse at those in the procession.

'*Fenian bastards.*'

She heard the words distinctly. And she heard the words Wilde spoke to her husband.

'Perhaps you should be about your business, Mr Palmer.'

The tension she had sensed, now rising like flood waters – surprisingly fast, one minute a mere trickle, the next...

Strangely, she thought of that old saying favoured by her father. "*Carry thou me, and I shall carry thee.*" Something about coracles, was it not? And that thought, in turn, conjured up her dream again – Neo drowned in the Dee. Her fears returned. She had been desperate for him to accept the work, the fee. Yet this nightmare had somehow changed her mind, caused her to want him to turn his back on this case entirely. But Neo was alive, here, and had turned to her.

'Come, sweet girl,' he said, glancing over his shoulder. 'Time for a cup of tea, I think.'

She followed the direction of his glance. More men emerging from the Royal Oak, a glimpse of cudgels. And they were singing, as well. But a different ditty, to the tune of *Lillibulero*. The words...

Tell me my friends, why are we met here?
Why thus assembled ye Protestant boys?

Beyond the Royal Oak, more policemen appearing. More than belonged to Wrexham alone, surely. Their new headquarters along Regent Street was more substantial than the old Bridewell, certainly, but these numbers...

'In a moment, Neo,' she said, and pulled her arm free of him.

'But, my dear...'

The words of *God Save Ireland* had been taken up by others in the procession. By some others, at least. Elsewhere, there was consternation, confusion, the beginnings of chaos.

'Please, Esther,' he said, more urgently, 'if I am to get ready for this afternoon's match...'

Fighting had begun. Yelling and cursing from those involved in the brawl, screams from women among the onlookers, the procession disintegrating.

'And back for tonight's performance...'

He was desperate now, concern etched into his face, dragging her along the pavement, away from the fanatical hate-filled violence.

'But the police!' she shouted.

Wilde had disappeared, but she could see that the phalanx of constables was now fully engaged, the officers laying about them with their truncheons – though, so far as she could see, only against those involved in the procession.

There was blood. As Neo hurried her around the corner into Chester Street, she could see it. Blood!

Chapter Six

'I forbid it,' Wilde told him, and slammed Palmer's report down onto the deep crimson leather inlay of his desk. 'If there are Fenians involved, this is now a matter for the Special Irish Branch.'

The Special Irish Branch? Palmer had no idea what that might be. And the mysterious woman Ettie had claimed to see at the Overton Arcade? No connection, surely. And no more than the sweet girl's imagination, perhaps.

'I simply wish to visit the place where the body was found,' he said, unbuttoning his coat and settling his hat on the desk. 'At Farndon.'

There was a commotion outside in the courtyard. Cursing and vile oaths, protests of innocence and outrage. The superintendent swivelled in his chair and went to the window, from where he was able to survey his fiefdom.

'Ah, they have them. Excellent.'

Palmer stood as well, at the other side of the desk and joined him. Below them, across that inner cobbled yard, was the entrance passage through which he had so recently been admitted to this inner sanctum. And, in that passageway, a scuffle – three of the young men Palmer recognised from the procession, those who had sung *God Save Ireland*. He recognised them from their size alone. Now they were overpowered by a dozen or more constables, each of the three men with a bloodied pate.

'Most distressing, Superintendent. The procession...'

'Always a handful who cause the trouble,' said Wilde.

'And yet I see no sign of the troublemakers themselves – those who began the fight.'

'I think you must be mistaken, sir. We picked up the culprits. Those three. After something of a chase, I must admit.'

'But all those constables,' said Palmer, scratching at his beard in feigned bewilderment. 'Not just your own force, I collect?'

'We were warned there might be trouble. And the Branch drafted in some reinforcements from Chester and Birkenhead. Just as well, too. Could have turned proper nasty.'

'I find it hard to fathom.' Palmer took the silver snuff box from his pocket, offered it to Wilde, knowing the policeman would decline in favour of the fellow's own pipe. 'This propensity for violence. Partisan violence.'

'Human nature, I'm afraid,' said the superintendent, between puffs of lighting his pipe.

Palmer remembered the distress Ettie suffered as they had returned to the house, insisting she was simply too upset to even consider attending the night's performance at the Public Hall – despite him having already purchased the tickets. All that blood, she had said, time and time again.

'There were two sides involved in the brawl,' he said. 'Were there not?'

'Mr Palmer,' said Wilde, as though Palmer were a simpleton, 'do you not understand? Those others – Irishmen, indeed. But loyal Ulstermen. And you will excuse me for a few minutes while I see those Fenian rogues safely to their cells.'

Palmer was about to protest. There was the match to attend – and his arrangement to meet others at the Turf beforehand. Yet it was too late. Wilde had marched from the office, his studded boots drumming a tattoo upon the terracotta tiles.

Well, thought Palmer, now alone and glancing around at the green and cream walls, this is certainly an improvement on that dismal den he occupied at the old Bridewell. Maps of the town, naturally, and several *Wanted!* posters.

He turned again to the window, in time to see the superintendent cross the yard in a cloud of pipe smoke, as the last of the three men was finally restrained sufficiently to be dragged through an arched doorway. A postern gate, Palmer decided. For the place – until recently the Militia barracks – was indeed like some medieval castle, all buff-coloured Cefn Mawr sandstone, a circular turret at each of its four corners – and each turret complete with mock arrow slits.

The sides of the courtyard were formed by substantial two-storeyed buildings, with stables, kitchens, offices and an armoury on the ground floor with, above, on one side, living quarters for the married men and, on the other, the courtroom for the Petty Sessions.

And here I stand, Palmer smiled to himself, in the castle's keep from which Wilde is king of all he surveys. There was a gentle tap at the half-open door and a woman entered. Familiar.

'Mr Palmer,' she said. 'Delightful to meet you again. My husband reckoned as 'ow you might like some tea.'

Of course, Wilde's wife – though it was a few years since he'd last seen her. After that occasion, Ettie had remarked that if Wilde so closely resembled Abraham Lincoln, then here, surely, was Lincoln's wife. Pleasantly rotund, with a prominent chin, tiny eyes, her lips thin and straight. Martha Jane, if he remembered correctly.

'I hate to seem ungrateful, Mrs Wilde, but I was hoping to make a speedy departure. The football, you know.'

But she refused to take no for an answer and Palmer had the sense that he would not have been allowed to leave in any case.

'You have quarters here, ma'am?' he enquired politely when she returned with a tray and two brown earthenware mugs. But before she could answer, the superintendent himself was back.

'As befits my new station,' said the policeman.

And substantial, Palmer imagined, remembering the size of their brood even when he had last seen them. Now? Well, goodness knows how many more she must have birthed. Children, he thought – what joy they must bring. But with the tea poured, and Mrs Wilde returned to her family duties, it was back to business, the superintendent behind his desk and Palmer invited to take his own seat again.

'Now,' said Wilde, 'if you don't mind, can you explain this?' He picked up the manila folder containing Palmer's report again and waved it in the air. 'You found – what, precisely?'

He flicked over the pages, just three of them.

'Stag Spring Hawkweed – or, if you wish me to be precise, traces of the seeds thereof. They are distinctive, as I discovered from the available herbaria and botanical references.'

Wilde set down his pipe and sipped at the tea.

'And from this you've made some assumption that Tobin must have drowned at this spring you mention?'

'This particular form of Hawkweed was, apparently, first identified where the Gwenfro rises – just south and east of Bwlchgwyn, Superintendent. Its name is Ffynnon y Ceirw, the Spring of Stags.'

Palmer lifted his own cup, amazed that Mrs Wilde had managed to produce a beverage which, in colour, so accurately matched the deep shade of the muggen receptacle in which it sat, as well as the Brown Betty pot from which it had been poured.

'Rare, then?' said Wilde.

'Rare, indeed. And the records show that it can be found nowhere closer to Wrexham than another spring feeding the Gwenfro. At the Pant-y-Golfen spring. Of course, it is possible the fellow drowned further upstream.'

'But the nearest to the Lager Beer Company, Mr Palmer?'

Palmer set down the mug, deciding that such a strong brew would be less than kind to his permanently sensitive digestive juices.

'I assume, Superintendent, that you spoke with Mr Wassmann about the yeast?'

'Poor Sergeant Jones. He did no more than dip his finger into the pot – then licked the finger. Which reminds me...'

He slid open a drawer and produced a glass dispensing bottle filled – or almost filled – with tiny grey-brown granules. Wilde passed it over the desk.

'We're just praying he recovers quickly,' said Wilde. 'Only two weeks until our match against the Fire Brigade.'

'Jones – yes, of course.' Palmer examined the bottle, noted the embossed lettering running vertically down the front, *J.F. Edisbury & Co*, and the peeling dosage label on the back. 'Jones, your goalkeeper.'

The contents – Palmer had no doubt that these were, indeed, yeast granules – also plainly exhibited traces of blue-green mould. Interesting, he thought.

'You're going to see today's game?' Wilde asked him.

It was a wonder, Palmer decided, that the precision of language could, by mere intonation, make it so plain that Wilde would have wished to see the match himself but, at the same time, knew his duties would prevent him from doing so.

'I am,' he said, apologetically. 'But Wassmann – did he have anything to say about Tobin?'

Their brief moment of shared affection for football vanished in an instant and Wilde's features settled to the texture of cold Welsh slate – though Palmer reminded himself that the policeman was, in fact, a Salopian, born and bred in Shropshire.

'Police business, Mr Palmer.'

'Can it harm? And the more information I have, perhaps the easier shall be my analysis of the yeast sample. I assume you still wish me to explore – at least for the benefit of poor Sergeant Jones.'

He tapped his coat pocket for effect, and Wilde studied him a moment. Palmer could almost hear the calculating machinery of the policeman's brain.

'Very clever, sir. But Mr Wassmann could tell me very little – only that he found Tobin to be furtive. That was the word he used – furtive. Seems he'd previously worked for the Broughton Brewery. And you might not know this, Mr Palmer, but there's no love lost between the two companies.'

No, Palmer did not know specifically. Common enough knowledge, however, that Wrexham's brewers in general had hardly welcomed the arrival of yet more competition – and German competition, too. Lager beer.

'Enemies, you would say?'

'Not especially. But why should you ask? I've already advised you, Mr Palmer. Police business.'

Palmer gripped the lip of his cup between thumb and middle finger, turned it slowly round and round, the tea so thick it barely moved in the process. It was a good question. Why should he ask? None of his business. And he had not even wished to be involved in analysing the fluids from Tobin's lungs. But now...

'Why?' he said. 'No significant reason, Superintendent. Yet, I wonder if I might ask you a different question?'

Yes, he decided. The cogs of your calculating mind. Your pieces of the puzzle the same as my own. Contaminated yeast and rivalry between breweries. Tobin drowned at the Pant-y-Golfen spring – the same clear waters which supplied the Lager Beer Company. Why drowned, and by whom? Accident or cold-blooded murder? His body discovered beside the Dee at Farndon. Again, why? To mask the fact he had been killed elsewhere? Or the opposite – to draw attention to the killing, to create the mystery itself? Fenian pamphlets in the dead man's lodgings? Tobin furtive, in what regard? And the arrest of Irish Republicans on this, St. Patrick's Day. Finally, the bite marks – along with the apparent reappearance in the area of the Corpse Dog.

'If I am able, Mr Palmer,' said Wilde, wearily. 'If I am able.'

'Then, those three now in your cells – what shall become of them?'

Wilde drained the final dregs from his own cup and loudly licked his lips.

'They shall go before the Beak here,' he said, 'and from thence, I am sure, to the Assizes. A lengthy spell of Welsh hospitality and hard labour at Ruthin gaol for their reward.'

'Yes,' said Palmer. 'I had assumed as much. But, tell me, my wife believes that, among the constables so conveniently on hand when the brawl began, there was a woman. A woman who seemed to be directing them.'

No reply. And the policeman spent some time gazing at the maps upon his wall before finally pushing himself to his feet again. He picked up his pipe and carried it to the larger plan of the district stretching far beyond the twin settlements of Wrexham Regis and Wrexham Abbott, this town of two halves. Wilde used the pipe's mouthpiece tip to trace a line from their own location, on Regent Street, out along the Mold Road and a little southwards.

'Here, is it not?'

He tapped at the map, though from where he sat, Palmer could not see the details. He stood as well, and joined Wilde at the map. Ordnance Survey, but not entirely up to date. The Lager Beer Company, for instance, had been carefully added, a neat piece of draughtsmanship, in ink.

'Yes,' he said. 'Here. This depression or hollow in the land. No more than a shallow valley. *Pant*. And *Golfen*, or *Colfen*? It translates as bough or branch, does it not? Perhaps the Vale of the Bough.' The joys of the *Cymraeg*, he thought yet again. 'But Pant-y-Golfen. And the spring in question – why, waters so pure they match those in Pilsen itself.'

'Germany,' said Wilde, as though this might be significant.

'Bohemia, in fact. Plzeň, in the local tongue, I think.'

'You know, Mr Palmer, that I do not believe in coincidence.'

'And nor do I, Superintendent. The word implies almost an occult or astral conjunction of otherwise unrelated events, does it not?'

'Whereas, we both know that seemingly unrelated events coming together at the same precise moment do so either by the hand of man...'

'Or God,' said Palmer. 'And in this case, sir?'

Wilde regarded him with some suspicion, perhaps reading Palmer's thoughts. For Palmer had now determined that he must visit not only Farndon, but the Pant-y-Golfen spring also. Wilde had forbidden him from doing so, of course. But how could he be forbidden from visiting these two pieces of common land? And English Farndon was not even within Wilde's jurisdiction. Wilde knew it as well as Palmer himself. But still...

'I have said, Mr Palmer,' Wilde said quietly. 'A police matter. But let me say this. If there *was* indeed a woman – I should warn you, do not interfere with her business, sir. No, indeed not!'

Chapter Seven

Ettie screamed, and would have felt worse about doing so had Neo not tensed beside her at the same time. The sheer terror engendered by the first shocking apparition of Evelina's ghost in the performance.

'How *do* they do it?' she whispered. 'I have seen it six times – seven? And still…'

'Superstitious nonsense, as well,' he murmured. He had been somewhat less affable than normal since his return from the football. Wales defeated by England – though it was only a game, after all.

But true enough. Who, in this enlightened age, still believed in the existence of ghosts? Ghosts, no. Though she was her father's daughter, raised on tales of the *Tylweth Teg* fairy folk, who stole babies and left changelings in their place; raised on tales of the malicious *Pwca* goblins; raised on tales of the *Llamhigyn y Dwr* giant limbless reptiles which preyed upon wandering sheep – or wandering fishermen; and yes, raised on tales of the *Cwn Cyrff* Corpse Dog, the Underworld Hound. But ghosts? Of course not. Though, somehow, *The Castle Spectre* had been shocking audiences everywhere for more than eighty years. Astonishing.

'But look,' she said. 'Does she not resemble…?'

'Resemble, my dear?'

She remembered that he had not seen the woman. The woman with the hatchet face. Yet he had been quick to recount Superintendent Wilde's warning.

'Nobody, really,' she said. 'I was simply being fanciful.'

A rumpus further along the row sliced through her conundrum. A lady had entirely fainted away from fear, such was the realism of Alice Parsonage's portrayal of the phantom. And such was the professionalism of the troupe that they carried on regardless, while smelling salts were fetched and gentlemen wafted the casualty's face with their kerchiefs, or called for water.

'You were thinking of that other phantom,' Neo spoke softly into her ear. 'Your mysterious *agente provocateuse*.'

Did he mock her? Not in his nature, of course. Though, since the loss of the babe, she knew she had become more prone to taking offence. Peevish. Testy.

'At least, the superintendent seems to have admitted that she exists. But who might she be, Neo?'

'I have no idea. Not yet. But – gracious, not another!'

All heads were turned towards one of the private boxes, a loud gasp of distress. A shout and the thud of yet one more audience member stricken by the horror of it all while, on the stage, Evelina's ghost loomed over poor Angela, imprisoned within the grim chamber of evil uncle Earl Osmond's isolated castle until she was forced to marry him.

'My love,' she laughed, barely glancing up, 'have you ever seen this drama performed without at least this many victims?'

'I hear,' Neo replied, 'that on the London stage, before the prologue, there is always an announcement, a warning for those of a nervous disposition.'

He looked around again, up at the box in question.

'Oh, heavens!' he gasped.

She followed his gaze back towards the crimson-draped box, up and to their right. Near enough for her to recognise, without question, the tall figure of Denbighshire's Lord-Lieutenant, Major William Cornwallis West. In profile, the absurdly pointed and upturned nose, the waxed Imperial moustache and oiled hair. Still sporting clothes, she could see, more appropriate for a gentleman half his age.

'And that must be…' she began, her view of the woman bending at his side masked by the gilt-decorated front of the opera box. Also in the box, a clerical gentleman, gesticulating wildly, arms flapping as he moved forward to help lift another lady from the floor – to help the major's wife get her mother back into her seat.

'It can be no other,' Neo groaned.

Yes, now she knew them. Irish aristocracy, of course, the two women. And the two most glamorous ladies in all Denbighshire and Flintshire combined. Yet, the older one, the mother, now in her seat again, had been disgraced in her youth and forced to marry some country parson beneath her station – presumably this same clerical gentleman – following an alleged liaison with the queen's own husband. And the daughter, more recently, shamed and forced to marry the major in the aftermath of a similar intrigue with the queen's favourite son, the Prince of Wales. Each of them enmeshed in the circumstances which, eight years earlier, had almost cost Neo – and she, herself – their lives.

'Prison,' said Neo, as they climbed the steps towards the refreshment room. 'I think of that threat hanging over us each time I see their names mentioned.'

There had been matters of state secrecy in those same circumstances, both of them sworn to silence by agents of the Crown upon pain of imprisonment for treason.

'Then, perhaps we should have stayed in our seats, my dear.'

The interval had come, as usual, at the end of the Second Act. The audience had participated admirably and so traditionally in the *Megen-Oh* song as a joyful antidote to the scares they had endured during the first half.

'I believe they left,' Neo replied. 'Otherwise, I should have agreed with you. For I have no wish to ever encounter Mrs Cornwallis West again. Indeed, I should probably not have bothered so hard to persuade you to change your mind about coming.'

It was true. After the procession, she had set her heart entirely against attending. But Neo had purchased the tickets, and she had decided it might cheer him after his football disappointment. Then, when they had arrived at the Public Hall, she had felt somewhat privileged to be here. So many in the queue waiting to enter that they had missed most of the opening act, the laughable farce *Paddy Miles*. So many people turned away, the performance entirely sold out. Not only the seats but the standing spaces filled to capacity, also.

'I suppose we should have expected them to be here. They are Irish, after all.'

And this was, after all, the town's major event to mark St. Patrick's Day.

50

Around them, in the press and general hubbub of those trying to reach the tearoom, she could hear a few people still singing the repeated one-line chorus refrain.

Sing, Megen-oh! Oh! Megen-ee!

During the play, it had been the perfect accompaniment to Mr Beirne's admirable solo, but now, all this noise…

'Such a shame,' she said. 'For poor Mr Murch.'

The local Irish tenor, left upon the stage below, in the limelights, with the unenviable duty of providing the interval entertainment, a rendition of *The Dear Little Shamrock*. Few, however, were paying him any attention.

There's a dear little plant that grows on our Isle,
'Twas Saint Patrick himself, sure, that set it.

'A shame, indeed,' said Neo. 'But at least we shall now be refreshed.'

They had finally reached the front of the queue and were served their tea with astonishing alacrity. They exchanged greetings with a few neighbours, various people they knew from town and, of course, old friends.

'Alfred,' cried Dr Davies – Edward. 'And Esther!'

Alison, his wife, all Titian curls and elegance, greeted them with equal enthusiasm. Ten years older than Ettie – and the good doctor ten years older again – but close friends, they had all been together for dinner two months earlier to celebrate her fortieth birthday.

'Too long,' said Alison, her accent rich with the heather and honey of the Scottish Highlands. 'It has been too long, my dears. And have you tried the *bara brith*?'

'I had expected to see you, Edward,' said Neo, as the doctor's wife demanded two portions of the fruit loaf from a waitress. 'At that deplorable excuse for a game this afternoon.'

'It was as bad as we've heard?' Alison replied, and handed Ettie a plate.

'When Neo came home,' Ettie laughed, struggling to balance plate, cup and saucer, 'it took a good half-hour before he could even speak about it.'

'All seemed fine at the beginning,' Neo told them. 'A goal down after six minutes. But the lads playing as well as they did during the Ireland match.'

The previous month. Ettie recalled the celebrations. The first ever British Home Championship and such a victory for Wales. Six goals to nothing. Even she had felt the exultation. Still, she had been surprised at the depths of passion displayed by her husband. She listened to him now, between nibbles at the confection, giving a blow-by-blow account of the match.

'And young Arthur?' asked Edward.

Ettie knew this much at least. Arthur Eyton-Jones. Their neighbour. And aspirations to become a surgeon.

'Almost scored in the first half,' said Neo. 'But in the second – oh, dear. It felt like they'd all fallen asleep. And then three goals in the final quarter of an hour. Appalling.'

Neo was usually so rational. Usually so scornful of zealotry in all its forms. Yet, since they had settled in Wrexham, his fervour for the Wrexham Football Club, and for Welsh football in general, seemingly knew no bounds. Simply part, he often explained, of settling into his adopted new homeland – almost as important as his mastery of the language.

'Still, I'm sorry I missed it,' said Edward. 'But Wilde sent for me. One of his prisoners from this morning. Fell down some stairs, it seems.'

Esther did not wish to be reminded of the morning's events and she certainly had no desire to think about whatever might have happened, in reality, in those cells.

'Alison,' she said, as the warning bell for the second half sounded, 'shall we take back the cups?'

A further balancing act as they collected the crockery and left the men to their gossip.

'How are you now?' Alison asked her.

Ettie tried to pass her own cups and plate over the counter but could not reach.

'All water under the bridge, as they say.'

She had the sense that Alison wished to explore her condition further, but this was not a matter for such a public environment. In any case, there was a fellow at her side, trying to catch her attention.

'Excuse me, but can I help you, miss?'

The accent was foreign – American? But without waiting for her answer, he relieved her of the burden and, with his longer reach, handed the crockery across to another white-pinafored waitress.

'Esther,' said Alison, 'allow me to introduce our newest neighbour.'

'Esther?' said the stranger. 'Jiminy Christmas – enchanting.'

The voice was impressive, booming from within the depths of an excessively long and bushy beard. Ettie experienced that almost epiphanous sensation – encounter with a total stranger, yet some instant mutual recognition, as though perhaps one had met them in a previous existence, some alternative life. And she could not shake free of the thing, felt herself blush.

'And this, Mr Jackson,' Alison laughed gaily, 'is *Mrs* Palmer.'

'Married?' said Jackson, and held her gaze with his piercingly small black eyes. 'Bless your heart – but so young.'

She searched hard for a riposte, something to put the rogue in his impudent place, but no words would come forth. Simply a foolish grin.

'Mr Jackson,' said Alison, 'is Canadian, Esther.'

The second warning bell, and Neo was at her side, with Alison's husband.

'Canadian, did I hear?' said Neo.

There were further introductions, Edward explaining that Mr Jackson had mining interests, investment interests, and was lodging next door to Plas Darland, with the Morrels. But Ettie heard barely a word, beguiled by Jackson's frank admiration and his pleasantly swarthy features – at least, those few that could be seen for the beard.

'Well, Esther?'

She felt Alison touch her arm and realised she had missed a question.

'I'm sorry,' Ettie stammered. 'I was thinking about – never mind. You were saying?'

'A whist drive,' said Neo. 'This Friday. What do you say, my dear?'

Whist? Ettie thought to herself. How can I think of card games in the midst of all this confusion? A confusion which had entrapped her as surely as poor Angela's imprisonment by Earl Osmond.

Chapter Eight

'She has not been herself since…'

Palmer found that he could not complete the sentence and instead stared through the rain-streaked window as the Wynnstay's crowded omnibus bounced its way past the first of Holt's outlying dwellings. Six miles from Wrexham. It would have required a conveyance of some sort, of course, to bring Tobin's body all this way. But Wilde had made endless enquiries, it seemed, without finding a single witness to any suspicious vehicles before the body was found.

'And this fellow,' said his friend, Edward Owen, 'Canadian, you say?'

'For goodness sake, Ned!' Palmer lowered his voice to a whisper – or as much of a whisper as might allow him to still be audible above the clatter of the horses' hooves, the creak of the springs, and the ceaseless chatter of the tightly packed passengers. 'I understand her,' he went on. 'Or, at least, I hope so. Esther is your own age – and I, ten years her senior. But this rogue is yet older still. Fifty, if he's a day.'

'And flirting with her?'

'Indeed. Yes, indeed.'

A week ago. It had been a week. And, in all that time, he had thought it simply some temporary aberration. But then, on Friday, there had been the cards party at the Davies's house. The fellow could not keep his heathen eyes off her. She had not responded, of course. Not openly. But it was plain that she was flattered by Jackson's attentions. Despite his age, the Canadian seemed to have all the enthusiasm and energy of an adolescent.

'This Jackson,' Palmer went on. 'Is it possible you might be able to use your good offices? To find out anything about the rogue? He apparently has mining interests in Arizona.'

'My dear friend, I am employed in the India Office. And while I am certain there are also Indians in Arizona, I fear they are an entirely different breed from those with whom I am more generally concerned.'

'Still...'

'And you know what they say about flirts, Alfred?' Ned glanced around at the vehicle's interior and Palmer shook his head, dreading whatever further jest might now be forming on his friend's lips. 'That their hearts,' Ned grinned at him, 'are themselves like an omnibus. Always room for one more.'

Palmer groaned. Yet, it was also entirely apposite. Ned had arrived from London two days earlier, staying at the Wynnstay. He had travelled north so they might further develop their collaboration on the next book. But, as soon as he heard the story, he had insisted that, of course, they should visit the banks of the Dee at Farndon – and, perhaps, at some stage, also the Pant-y-Golfen spring. Palmer had already finally decided against doing so. Nothing really to do with Wilde's warning. What was the point? There had also been the note. *Let sleeping dogs lie.* Besides all that, this conundrum with Esther.

But Ned Owen would not be deterred. He had booked the Wynnstay's omnibus for the journey. Just the two of them. Yet, in the way of these things, with the hotel posting flyers announcing the trip, word had spread among all those who suddenly remembered or discovered that they, too, had business in Holt, or across the Dee's bridge, in English Farndon. So, this morning had found them, not alone as they'd planned, but in a queue for seats. Worse? It was raining, with nobody wanting to use the open upper deck.

And at least one of their companions seemed to find Ned's humour to his own taste. A rough-looking man with rain cape and bowler hat. Palmer remembered him from earlier, jostling past them as they had tried to board.

'Don't you just love 'em?' the man beamed. 'Omnibus whimsies, now.' The accent was Irish. Palmer decided to ignore him but Ned – dear affable Ned – was always happy to chat with total strangers.

'There are plenty of them about,' Ned replied, and Palmer prayed that he would not encourage the fellow. But at least they had arrived at the Cross, and their terminus. And now began the scrimmage, the conductor attempting to keep some order.

'One at a time now, see?' he cried, somewhat in vain.

'Have you heard this one?' shouted the Irishman with some delight, over the heads of others trying to disembark. 'A gentleman gets on the busy bus. Bit like this one. And he shouts out, "All full inside?" And some wag up at the front says, "Well, I don't know about the rest, but that last piece of oyster pie did the business for me!" What d'yer think, lads?'

He guffawed loudly and was still laughing as they finally alighted onto the muddy grass of the village green. And yes, Ned agreed, a good one. He even shook hands with the man, while Palmer opened his rain napper and started up the lane past the snorting horses, shouting thanks to the dripping driver clambering down from his box.

'Let's eat at the Swan,' he suggested, as Ned joined him beneath the umbrella. 'And let's hope this rain goes off while we're inside.'

The Irishman was eating there, too, and waved at them from his own booth.

'Do you not find it strange?' Palmer murmured into his napkin, while chewing on a piece of under-cooked potato. 'Another Irishman?'

'Another, Alfred?'

He felt a fool. Ned was right. A full week since St. Patrick's Day and he could not have attested to any other connection in all that time – and despite Wrexham's significant Irish community. So, he quickly changed the subject. A thwarted attempt to discuss the football – something about which Ned had absolutely no interest.

'Please, not football,' said his young friend, and called for a further beer, rather offending Palmer's temperance sensibilities. 'But Alfred, the water sample I understand. Yet, the yeast?'

Palmer wiped gravy from his beard and patiently explained the wonderous functions of yeast in the process of brewing beers.

'It must, of course, be correctly cultivated yeast. Domesticated yeast, you might call it. And each domesticated for its own purpose. The strain for German beers, for example, different than for British ales.'

'And for baking, I presume.'

'Oh, entirely. As different as a Chinese panda from a Patagonian alpaca. Well – more or less. Yet, the brewer's worst nightmare? Not that their particular cultivated yeast should be mistaken for another domesticated strain but, rather, that it should be invaded by one of the wild and entirely unpredictable varieties.'

'Whoever would have guessed?' said Ned. 'The world threatened by savage yeast.' He made an annoying face, bared his fangs and, worse, when he collected himself, it was with an even more irritating smirk. 'And such you found in the sample?'

Palmer had no idea what might have been so amusing but decided to press on regardless.

'Under microscopy it is easily possible to distinguish one yeast from another. And Mr Wassmann – did I mention, the manager at the Lager Beer Company? Well, Ned, he allowed me some healthy samples for comparison. Yet, this was not the worst of it.'

'Not then,' Ned grinned, 'the yeast of our troubles?'

'How long have you been nurturing that one?' Palmer snapped at him, then realised the big Irishman was at their table.

'Gone off, lads,' he beamed at them, and setting the bowler back upon his head. Palmer wondered how he knew – about the yeast – then realised too late that the fellow was speaking of the rain. 'God speed, my boys.'

Ned echoed the farewell while Palmer fulminated about being called "lads" and "boys".

'The worst?' Ned reminded him when the Irishman was gone through the door.

Palmer explained that, apart from the strain of wild yeast in the bottle, there was also the fungal infection which, undoubtedly, would have caused Wilde's sergeant his sickness.

'And if it had found its way into Mr Wassmann's brewing process,' Ned suggested when settling the bill, 'I suspect it would have been the end for them.'

Yes, Palmer agreed. Without doubt. But was that enough to account for Tobin's death?

Outside, the downpour had indeed stopped, and he hoped that today might at least prove more useful than their walk to the spring after yesterday's communion service. Another confrontation with

Bethan Thomas and then a desultory trudge through still more rain out past the Racecourse and across into the woodlands and yellow gorse-strewn grazing grounds, the shallow undulating lands beyond the town. Nothing. Except some abandoned ruins.

Now, they wandered past St. Chad's, dodging endless puddles, to the end of Holt's Bridge Street.

'And yesterday,' said Palmer. 'Your opinion about the note…'

Yes, he had shared the note with Ned. Though he had still not summoned the courage to do so with Ettie.

'It was merely a suggestion,' Ned told him.

They reached the ancient, many-spanned sandstone bridge and waited for several carts to pass before they began the crossing.

'But you seriously think the books…?'

'Was it not the point? What else was your pamphlet than a thinly disguised piece of propaganda about land ownership? And the new one – do we have a title yet?'

'We do. It is this, I think: *A History of the Ancient Tenure of Land in the Marches of North Wales.*'

'I suppose I should be thankful you did not settle upon *How the Present Robber Barons of Wales Acquired Their Ill-Gotten Gains.*'

'You are being foolish,' said Palmer. 'But even so, you believe there shall be a furore?'

Suddenly, he could see it as well and stopped, leaning upon one of the abutments, to gaze down into the turbulent waters of the river. Turbulence without end. Turbulence in a permanent state of metamorphosis.

'Seriously,' Ned laughed, 'you think Sir Watkin will be rushing to purchase a copy for his personal library?'

Palmer could never think of Sir Watkin Williams-Wynn without being reminded of Samuel Pickwick, though he was – besides being Denbighshire's Member of Parliament – without doubt, the wealthiest landowner, certainly in North Wales, and possibly beyond.

'I doubt he will be rushing anywhere,' he replied. 'Rumours the old fellow is seriously ill and may be near his journey's end in this world.'

Yet, simply the beginning of another, he thought. Like this racing river, on its way to the sea. And then…

'Alfred,' Ned gripped his arm, 'we have discussed this before. There will be others who will see the book as a threat. After all, are we truly so far from the Rebecca Riots? Tenants' rights at the very heart of the crisis. Then, less than twenty years since Welsh landlords evicted tenants because they had not voted as instructed in the parliamentary elections. And you must know – talk of an Anti-Tithe League being formed here in Wales. You seriously think the new book will not be seen as inflammatory?'

'I think you exaggerate. Or might it be wishful thinking?'

He pushed himself from the abutment and they continued across the bridge.

'You and your London Welsh friends, Ned. Dreams of self-government?'

Ned fell silent and Palmer experienced a surge of guilt. They had been good friends for six or seven years. Strangely, Ned had contacted him after Palmer's misadventures on the Menai Straits – Ned himself born and raised at Menai Bridge, where Palmer was somewhat renowned. Despite Ned's relative youth – only just thirty – he was already a noted antiquarian and the first Welshman ever to enter the Civil Service through public examination. The very first.

'I suppose I should rule out no possibilities,' he offered as a peace token. '*Let sleeping dogs lie*? The book and the land question. Yes, perhaps.'

'Now you are being condescending, sir.'

Ned turned to look back across the bridge.

'Something depressing about the place, don't you think?' he said. 'Seen better days.'

Palmer agreed. The ruined castle. The gasometer beyond.

'Of course,' he said, 'you are literally correct. From my reading, the town once prospered. But now they are even due to lose their corporation status.'

Beyond the bridge, where the road climbed into Farndon, Palmer led them to the left, the track along the farther bank of the Dee, heading north and west beneath a low, stratified cliff, the same sandstone as the bridge itself.

'Thank heavens for the inquest,' said Ned, taking a folded page of a newspaper from his pocket. 'And the *Telegraph*, of course. Let me see, "…*at the site of an old jetty, much favoured by local fishermen, who discovered the remains of the deceased.*" This must be the place, don't you think?'

Palmer studied the tumbled line of ochre-red shaped rocks extending out into the waters.

'The only jetty on this section of the river, it seems,' he said. 'And just as Esther reported.'

She had attended the inquest. Out of curiosity, she had said. So, Palmer had enjoyed her account of the proceedings. And the inquest jury, having heard all the evidence, had no hesitation about their verdict on the demise of Francis Tobin esquire. *Wilful murder, by person or persons unknown, but no evidence to confirm the identity of the perpetrator.* A statement from the local constabulary confirmed the location where the body of the deceased had been found and, on Saturday, Palmer had visited the reading room at the Liberal Working Men's Club to study the various newspaper reports. The *Advertiser* had covered many of the local details, naturally, but the case had also filled columns even in the main London broadsheets – including this lurid piece in Thursday's edition of the *Telegraph*.

'But do you imagine,' said Ned, 'that Tobin's demise would have achieved such notoriety had this simply been a Welsh incident?'

Palmer hardly heard him and found himself gazing across to the Welsh side. Something about the form of the land there. Seemingly geometric shapes to the ridges and gullies. As though the ancient jetty were a finger pointing towards them. Indeed, he began to wonder whether this was indeed a jetty at all. Perhaps the foundation of some other, larger structure. It happened to him at times. A sixth sense. And he imagined, for just a moment, that there, on the farther bank, there might be men in armour, crested Roman helmets.

'Could it be?' he murmured.

'Could it be?' Ned repeated, quizzically.

'No matter,' said Palmer. 'Though, perhaps there is more to Holt than we give credit. One day, I shall investigate…'

His musings were abruptly halted by a dark shadow rising over in the distance from those same careful green and brown folds of the water meadow. The shadow formed itself into the shape of a dog. Yet, a huge dog, black as the hobs of hell. It stood upon the highest ground and raised its enormous head to the sky, letting forth a howl which froze Palmer's heart.

Ned Owen had been studying the ground, crouching in the rain-soaked grass, but he started also, springing to his feet, as the hound bounded forward, jumped down into some hollow and disappeared from sight.

'What the...'

'You saw the thing?' said Palmer.

'Something,' Ned stammered. 'A hound, Alfred? Dark...'

'*Cwn Cyrff*,' Palmer murmured. The Corpse Dog.

Chapter Nine

'Cycling?' Neo demanded from the far side of the breakfast table. 'He also has some interest in cycling, now?'

He had not seemed quite himself since yesterday's journey with Ned Owen to Holt and Farndon. Nor, indeed, since his arrest, as he preferred to describe it. Still, she was sorry she had mentioned Mr Jackson and the cycling. It had been, she realised, an ill-judged attempt to lighten his humour.

'Eat your porridge, Neo,' she told him. 'And this Irish fellow you encountered. Police force?'

'He would not say. But I remembered Wilde mentioning some Special Irish Branch and – well, he was Irish. Besides, he had somehow summoned a carriage of his own. For all the world like a prison van, a Black Maria.'

'Though, this one green, did you say?'

His spoon halted halfway to his lips.

'Is there something amusing about this story, my dear?'

'Far from it, husband. But I am more troubled by your sighting of the *Cwn Cwrff.*'

Her father had frightened her as a child with tales of the Corpse Dog. Always told in the *Cymraeg*, of course, even though they lived in Manchester. Yet, she was more concerned today with avoiding further discussion about cycling – and Jackson.

'He forced us both into the back of the van – demanded to know what we had discovered.'

Neo had already related all this, but she decided against telling him so.

'Though, in truth, you had discovered nothing at all,' she said.

'That is not entirely the case, Esther.' Her Sunday name again. He had plainly taken her words as a criticism. 'I may well have discovered some Roman connection to Holt. I could sense it as strongly as – well, as the aroma of the bacon I now suspect to be burning.'

He wrinkled his nose and she turned to see smoke curling from the frying pan. She leapt from her chair and crossed to the range. The two rashers were, indeed, now no more than incinerated slivers. How had she not noticed?

'Curse this stove!' she cried and tossed the blackened remains into the fire itself. They were beyond redemption.

'Out of the frying pan...' Neo laughed, and the laughter brought upon him a fit of coughing. His health had indeed been much improved since their move to Wrexham, but there were times...

She set down the smoking pan and went to his side, rubbing his back.

'Still,' she said, 'it is good to hear you laugh. The first time for too many days. But we can ill afford the waste. And there, the guilty look again. You think I don't know how much this new book of yours will cost us?'

'I have thought to abandon the idea. But Ned...'

'You shall not.' She patted him firmly on the shoulder and took herself into the scullery, for bread and toasting fork, leaving him to study today's *Western Mail*. 'You have a talent, Neo,' she shouted back to him, 'for shining a light into the darkness of history, yet making it seem like no more than a merely academic study. Important work, my dear, and we shall find a way.'

'I have been afraid to share it with you – the cost. But Ned is convinced we shall find subscribers. Subscribers and, he fears, a few enemies.'

Ettie was back at the fireplace, bread impaled on the fork's tines and she kneeling on her tapestry-topped footstool, as though in prayer – that the pain would remain at bay.

'Landowners – yes, so I had supposed,' she said.

He stared across the room at her.

'Why should you look surprised, Neo? From the little you have read to me it was plain from the first chapter. And my father, God rest his soul, made enemies of his own in his younger days for speaking out about the way certain landlords treated their tenants – and not simply their tenants alone. Entire communities at times. It was the thing which principally drove him to leave Caernarvon.'

If she were a man, she often thought, it would be a cause she would espouse. The land. Welsh land. Farmed by tenants who spoke the *Cymraeg*. Tenants who were Calvinists, Wesleyans, Baptists or Quakers. Tenants with natural leanings towards Liberalism. But tenants under the thumb of landowners who, for the most part, were English-speaking, Anglican, Tory squires and aristocrats. Still, there were voices. In the Welsh papers, at least. Stirrings. And, perhaps, there would be a place for women in this cause, after all. Perhaps she might forge such a place.

'Yet, enemies or no enemies,' Neo was saying, 'if the book is ever to see the light of day, I believe I may need to abandon this Quixotic dream of my own enterprise and find more regular work again.'

'I fear you may be right, my love.'

'I have already been approached – did I say?'

'You did not.'

'By the Leather Works, among others. And McDermott, of all people. The foundry – you know? Though, why he should need a chemist is somewhat beyond me. He did not seem pleased to see me, either. He was at pains to prevent me seeing some of the designs, plans and the like, on which he must be working. Still, perhaps this way I shall once again be able to bring it home.'

It was, perhaps, the mention of Mr McDermott, a reminder about St. Patrick's Day. The other thing which had been troubling her, so that she entirely missed his cue.

'The bacon, my dear,' he said. 'Bring home the bacon. You see?'

She watched an anticipative grin vanish from his face, without quite understanding why it should have been there in the first place.

'Neo, you truly think there are Fenians in Wrexham?'

She had been thinking about those other newspaper reports. Again. Bombs at the London stations. Could it happen here?

'There will,' he said, 'undoubtedly, be many with leanings towards an independent Ireland. But Fenian rebels? I have my doubts.'

'Yet, Superintendent Wilde said there were Fenian pamphlets found in Tobin's lodgings, did he not?'

The toast was done and she set it down on his plate as he reached for the butter dish. He reached for her hand as well and gave it a squeeze.

'He did,' said Neo. 'Though I never had the wit to ask him what he meant, precisely. The substance. I suppose there could be a perfectly innocent explanation. So, you must not worry. And I shall ask him.'

'You are due to see him?'

'After we were accosted by that Irish fellow – policeman or no policeman – I went straight to Wilde. To report the thing, you understand? But he refused to listen. Reminded me of his previous warning. And then, impudent rogue, he had the temerity to ask whether I might go with him, tomorrow, to the Broughton Brewery.'

'The yeast sample?'

Neo studied the buttercup yellow spread on the tip of his knife.

'The yeast sample. Quite so. I wish he would make up his mind, Ettie. Does he wish me to be involved or does he not? It is all one to me, of course.'

She watched as a mask of innocent indifference settled upon his face. But she knew it was all a pretence, knew he was already committed to the chase – knew that, from this point onwards, Tobin's death would shape their fates.

Neo had gone to his work seemingly having forgotten entirely about the cycling. About Mr Jackson, also. Goodness, her husband was jealous. How hugely amusing. Bless him! And when she was dressed for the morning's meeting, she spent perhaps longer than usual checking her appearance in the hallstand mirror.

She straightened the dark green collar and cape of her coat. How wonderful it would be to afford the cost of a true Ulster, but Mrs Pine had tailored this wonderfully in the same style, though at a fraction of the price. Would he be there, after all? The Canadian? Or had he simply been practising upon her?

'It seems we have a shared interest,' he had said during the cards evening at Edward and Alison's. 'Would you welcome another Cycle Club here in Wrexham, Mrs Palmer?'

But he had refused to explain further, teasing her. Perhaps, this morning, she would find out more.

She turned her head, this way and that, trying to decide whether the beige silk bonnet was quite right, her ringlets and feathers neat and tidy. She glanced through the window, watched the still leafless branches of their neighbours' fruit trees swaying in the wind. A nuisance, she thought – the wind. But at least the rain had held off. Yet, her hair. What had Mr Jackson said about it on Friday night when they'd arrived, wet and windswept.

'Like a hurrah's nest, Mrs Palmer. As I live and breathe, a hurrah's nest.'

What did that even mean? And she had always imagined Canadians to be somehow less flamboyant, more – unobtrusive. Phlegmatic.

A last glance in the mirror. She remembered Neo had once teased her also. Her eyes dark and mysterious, he had said – though too widely spaced. The mouth cherry-ripe – though a little too pursed, a little too small. The eyebrows delicate like slender crescent moons – though a little too high upon her forehead. She had to agree, found her image staring back with that annoying permanent expression of surprise. And eyes with a sadness not present until her recent loss.

For an instant she imagined her reflection holding the babe, the infant whose name only she knew. Here she was, not yet thirty. And now she would never be a mother. So, what value Neo's prohibition of her cycling? How could he understand her triple deception? The first, her insistence that she was only attending today's meeting because she had promised to help organise Saturday's event. No more than that. The second, this futility of his concerns. The third, her plan – that, come Saturday itself, she would remind him how he had been reluctant to marry, his fear that marriage might consign his beloved to a role of subjugation, and her own persuasive assurance that she would never, ever, permit such fears to become reality.

He would be shamed, she knew. But he would reluctantly bow to fate when she once again borrowed Alison's tricycle and took part in the event itself.

And tricycles proved to be very much at the heart of today's meeting in the Temperance Hall at the corner of Theatre Road.

Yet another attempt by certain members to have them banned from Saturday's gathering.

'Yet, have you so readily forgotten?' she argued. 'The very reason we changed the name.'

Indeed, it was Esther who had proposed the rule change.

'How foolish must we have seemed, styling ourselves as a bicycle club when so many of us cycle upon three wheels rather than two.'

And so, after bitter debate, they had become, more simply, the Wrexham Cycling Club. It had been one of many schisms. The worst? The split which occurred after the argument about whether cycling for diversion and personal pleasure should be encouraged on the Sabbath. She had swamped that particular meeting with biblical verse after verse. Exodus and Isaiah. How could one deny so many strictures against "*finding thine own pleasure*" on a Sunday? A simple stroll up Acton Hill, or a few tunes on her concertina, singing with Neo, those were one thing, but the almost sinful intoxication of cycling velocity – that was quite another. As bad, surely, as that other form of insobriety yet, at least here in Wales, it was now illegal to sell the demon drink on Sundays. How could the same logic not apply?

So, another rift – the heretics meeting as the Wrexham Star at the Talbot and, openly, shamefully, regularly still cycling on the Lord's Day. It had all raised great emotion. Neo had made mockery of it, naturally, as only a Primitive Methodist might do. It was one of his favourite sermon subjects – how the most fanatical passions are so often merely self-made inventions. Myths made fact, he would say.

Well, fanaticism or not, might there be some suspension of hostilities this coming Saturday – the Star and the Club settling their differences temporarily for the sake of the cycling procession? There had been no conclusion, the matter left unresolved when she headed for home. Yet, by the time she had said her farewells and, the last to leave, ventured out of the Temperance Hall's front doors – once the doors to the old theatre – it was raining heavily yet again, a gale threatening to turn her rain napper inside out at each attempt to deploy the infernal thing. And, in her struggles, she was aware of a van waiting in the lane, across from the Beast Market's animal pens.

A dark green van, plain, with no insignia or markings.

At the horses' heads, a stocky bruiser in a bowler hat and wrapped in a rain cape. She remembered Neo's description of the Irishman who had accosted him – and she was suddenly afraid.

Ettie spun on her heel and, in doing so, her boot went over. She twisted her ankle and cried out, then felt herself caught in a strong embrace. But she, in turn, caught the smell of rubber from a waterproofed mackintosh. It was a smell which, since she lost the baby, she strangely associated with the infirmary – with death. She tried to stand and free herself, but the arms still held her tight, and she found herself staring into the face of the hatchet-faced woman she had seen on St. Patrick's Day. Malevolent eyes, shadowed beneath the dark brim of a flat-crowned riding hat.

'Shall we not get out of this weather, Mrs Palmer?' said the woman. Irish also, of course, though – to Ettie's ear, at least – the somewhat harsher accent she associated with Belfast and Ulster.

'Let me go,' she shouted, and looked around for help. But there was no help to be seen, the only people still on the lane too far away, too bent upon their own struggles with the wind and rain. She thought about the umbrella as a weapon, tried to jab it at the woman's foot.

'We just need a wee talk, so we do,' said the woman and hauled Ettie towards the back of the van, where the ruffian in the bowler hat was now opening the rear door.

'My husband shall hear of this,' said Ettie, feeling useless and unable to conjure a better threat.

'It's your husband we need to chat about, Mrs Palmer,' the woman hissed in her ear. Ettie was pushed up the step, glimpsed the varnished interior, a desk and chair and, at the farthest end, the iron bars of a small detention cell. 'Unless, of course, ye've no concern about becoming a widow so young.'

Chapter Ten

'So, Mr Steward, you intended to poison the whole town?'

Wilde had chosen to simply ignore the repeated denials by the Broughton Brewery's manager. He was a small fellow with stubby red features – nose, chin and cheeks, a bald pate, though with fiery ginger sideburns.

The superintendent could, as Palmer knew only too well, be formidable – a veritable Inspector Bucket – yet today the insolence of these men seemed to have diminished him. Their insolence and the police officer having been offered only a small stool while they towered above him, both perched on the farther side of the counting room's tall Davenport double desk.

Steward's face was made even more crimson with rage and he almost jumped down from his swivel chair. But his employer, Thomas Morgan, Viscount Broughton, eldest son of the earl of St. David's, set his hand firmly on the manager's shoulder, pushing him back into the seat while, at the same time, silencing him.

'How many times, sir?' said the viscount. 'You have presented not a shred of evidence.'

Palmer had seen him once or twice before, though they had never spoken. But the viscount was renowned as a local eccentric. Somewhat older than Palmer himself, with a Van Dyke beard and waxed moustache, and here today with his small daughter.

'Clemmie, my dear,' he said to her, 'find Bilby, won't you? Go play with the horses, perhaps.'

The child skipped away, scattering images of might-have-beens in Palmer's imagination. Then the office door slammed behind her, and Palmer was left with his more immediate problems – Ettie's strange behaviour today, as well as his recollections from Monday –

so that he remained only partially aware of the conversation taking place around him. Partially aware, and left standing in the far corner of the room – playing with the hat in his hands and unbuttoning his coat – for there was no further furniture on which to sit.

'Evidence?' said Wilde. 'How much must we provide, my lord? Tobin formerly in your own employ and found with a sample of toxic yeast. Can it have been for any purpose other than malicious damage to the Lager Beer Company?'

'And you have concluded, Superintendent,' said Viscount Broughton, 'that because we have been critical of those German rogues and their alien processes, we must have intended this act of Luddism? It is absurd, sir.'

'Industrial rivalry?' Wilde suggested. 'Threat to your profits? I have frequently come across more slender motivation for the criminal mind.'

Palmer's sense of being isolated from the discussion made him somehow more aware of his surroundings, the wood-panelled walls, the flickering gaslight, the cobwebbed fireplace, the shelves of dusty, red leather-bound account books, and the heady ale aroma which threatened to intoxicate without him imbibing even a drop.

'Profit?' The viscount sneered at the policeman. 'Twenty-five thousand acres in Sussex alone. Then Pembrokeshire, St. Asaph – and Broughton, of course. Profit, you say? I consider the brewery a mere *divertissement*, sir.'

He laughed, but Wilde turned back to the manager.

'Yet you, Mr Steward. Presumably you have a little more to lose than his lordship?'

'And how, Superintendent,' Steward replied, in his angry Scottish burr, 'do we know that this particular yeast has anything to do with our own brewery? Indeed, whose authority do we have that this yeast is, indeed, contaminated or dangerous?'

It was the accent, rather than the words, which recaptured Palmer's attention. Scots. For some reason, he had expected Irish, though he could not have explained the reason. He spoke now for the first time, and Wilde had not even named him.

'I believe this might be the reason Superintendent Wilde invited me to be present.'

Both Steward and the viscount turned towards him at the same moment, as though realising for the first time that he was even in the room. He wondered for a second whether he should introduce himself, then instantly decided against doing so. Let them ask, he thought. Let them ask.

'I need hardly explain any of this to you, gentlemen, but yeast is, of course, mostly our friend. In terms of their taxonomy, all yeasts belong to the Kingdom of Fungi, the Genus *Saccharomyces*.'

Palmer saw the puzzled look on Wilde's face.

'It means *sugar mould*, Superintendent. Their natural purpose...'

'Wait,' said the viscount, who had been listening all this while with his mouth hanging open. 'Now, just wait. Am I to be subjected to a lecture on yeasts, here in my own brewery? By...' He waved his dismissive hand in Palmer's direction. 'By...'

'Mr Palmer, lordship,' said Wilde. 'He is...'

'Palmer? You mean the fellow who writes about land tenure? *That* Palmer?'

Palmer imagined he detected a hint of admiration in the viscount's words. Not entirely the reaction he might have expected. And eccentric? Somewhat outside the norm, Palmer thought. Moving in an orbit which does not quite have the earth at its centre, as Ptolemy might have put it. I suppose on that basis, he decided, the rest of us must be considered as concentric?

'Merely a paper or two at this stage, my lord,' he said. 'But yes, land tenure is a subject close to my heart.'

'In the time of King James?' The viscount advanced from behind the Davenport.

'The *first* King James, sir, to be precise.' Palmer wondered whether his lordship might have read the piece in the *Advertiser* and now be under some misapprehension.

'Well, really, Mr Palmer?' Viscount Broughton stretched out his hand. 'Not King James the *Second*? The first – well, enough said, eh?'

They shook hands. As it happened, Palmer held some admiration for that first King James. Certainly, a monarch with many flaws, but he had, almost uniquely, ruled over a period of uninterrupted peace and low taxation. Whereas King James the Second...

'And Sir Watkin,' the viscount pressed on before Palmer could state his opinion, 'has spoken of you many times – though perhaps with more animosity than I believe you deserve, sir. For you are correct, of course. So many of our great landowners have no true right to the lands over which they hold sway.'

'I am sorry to hear that Sir Watkin remains indisposed, my lord.'

'Are you? There is no need, Mr Palmer.' The viscount wandered back to the desk, leaned against its tall side panel and lit a cheroot. 'The old fool will not be long now for this world, I think.'

It was heresy. In this part of the world, Sir Watkin Williams-Wynn was simply part of the air which one breathed. The Prince *in* Wales, as he was so universally known. But he was rarely seen in public any longer. Some injury to his foot, complications, then an infection of his lungs. Bulletins in the newspapers which significantly, in Palmer's opinion, failed to say very much at all. Rumour of amputation. Rumour of a relapse. Indeed, the bulletins were very much the same as one might have expected to read if the queen herself were infirmed. No more than might be strictly necessary to maintain the mystique of royalty.

'This is interesting, gentlemen,' said Wilde, 'but now we're done with the introductions – you were saying, Mr Palmer, this yeast fungus...'

But the viscount was in no mood to be silenced.

'Fungal infection,' he said. 'Is that not precisely the illness which now afflicts this nation? Only five years since our humiliation at Isandula. Now General Gordon besieged at Khartoum. And doomed. Mark me, gentlemen – doomed.'

Difficult to disagree, Palmer thought, fumbling for his snuff box and taking a pinch. Yet, he suspected that he himself, as well as his radical friend in London, newspaperman George Reynolds, would have had an entirely different perspective on the causes of the nation's problems. Oh, how he missed Reynolds's wisdom.

Still, he determined to press on regardless.

'If I may, sir,' he suggested, as soon as Viscount Broughton drew breath, 'I was saying that they serve a natural purpose as decomposers, feeding on dead and decaying matter. In use for millenia, but first named as *Saccharomyces* in 1837, though Dr Pasteur only demonstrated the chemical process by which yeasts function eight years ago.'

'Yes, Mr Palmer,' the viscount shouted. 'Yes. But the relevance, sir?'

Palmer reached into his coat pocket, produced the offending bottle.

'Like you, my lord,' he said, 'I am not entirely certain about relevance. But we are fortunate indeed that there has, over the years, been such studious investigation into the methods of generating yeast and especially into its wilder varieties.'

Mr Steward slammed shut the ledger on which he had been working.

'Bletherin' fool,' he murmured.

'As a result, Mr Steward,' Palmer said, with determination, 'it is easy – for those who have the necessary reference sources – to identify this particular strain, and the fungal residues you see here, as that which was first identified by a certain Reverend Mason – though it still lacks a scientific name – and which, in your industry, is known as Killer Yeast, for the toxins it secretes.'

'And you think,' Mr Steward growled at him, 'you be qualified to tell one type of yeast from another? I've been in this industry…'

'By studying the morphology of this particular sample, Mr Steward,' Palmer interrupted him, 'the size, shape and position of the vacuole, there is no doubt whatsoever. Killer Yeast, sir.'

'But poor Sergeant Jones, lordship,' said Wilde, 'discovered this without the aid of Mr Palmer's microscopes.'

'Then let us suppose, Superintendent, for one bizarre moment, that this Tobin was indeed acting as our agent, intent upon the preposterous business of adulterating our rival's production. And let us recall that the inquest's verdict was one of wilful murder. Might you explain precisely why we should have murdered our own agent?'

'Before we get to that, sir, might either of you have seen this before?'

Wilde had delved in his own pocket, stood from the stool, and produced a photograph. Palmer had seen it earlier, as they'd walked here, past the Willow Brewery, to this office building on Salop Road – with, behind, the usual mix of malt house, hop room, sugar store, brewhouse, fermenting room, cellars, cooperage, stables and all the rest.

The superintendent handed the photograph to Viscount Broughton. A fine picture indeed, produced from a wet collodion negative, Palmer guessed, for it was especially clear, tinted in the slightest shade of purple, which highlighted the edges of the image it portrayed.

'A tattoo?' said the viscount, taking the photograph from Wilde. 'The significance, sir?'

Palmer noticed that he barely even glanced at the picture. And he passed it to Steward rather too quickly, as though it had singed his fingers. His manager, conversely, spent just a little too long shaking his head and examining the image minutely.

'You're not sure, Mr Steward?' said Wilde. 'I would have thought you'd either recognise it – or not.'

'Well, I don't,' the man snapped, thrusting the photograph back across the desk.

'Now, William!' The viscount made a mummery of scolding him. 'The superintendent is merely doing his duty.' He turned to Wilde, lifted his head imperiously and twirled the end of his waxed moustache. 'But you see, sir, sadly we have nothing further to add. Not on this matter, at least. Though you, Mr Palmer, must dine with me. And with some other friends who share our passion for history. Yet, for now, you must swear to me, gentlemen, that you shall let me know as soon as you have further intelligence about this dastardly yeast affair – and about poor Tobin, too, of course.'

It was strange. For it was precisely the same promise forced from him this very morning by Esther in her new and more insistent agitation.

Chapter Eleven

She found herself hurtling at breakneck speed towards imminent disaster – in more ways than one.

Most immediately, this was supposed to be a procession, rather than a race. Had it been the latter, they would have held the event at the Wynnstay Park's purpose-built cycling track at Ruabon. She supposed it must result in part from the unexpected arrival of so many other clubs – from Mold, Holywell, Chester, and as far away as Denbigh and Rhyl – but also the participation of their rivals from the Wrexham Star, so that competition, rather than communion, had become the order of the day.

Such a press of them all as she pedalled furiously from their starting area towards the end of Argyle Street, past the few still surviving remnants of the Art Treasures pavilion and towards the corner, where she must try to make a turn to the left without either a spill or a collision with the other cyclists. It was almost too much to think about. And the distractions, the words hammering in her head.

'I insist that you reconsider, Esther,' Neo had told her, even as she had adjusted her skirts and mounted the Triumph, then hastily blown him a kiss that he did not deserve.

'I shall be fine,' she had shouted back to him as she stood on the pedal and pressed the machine into its first forward motion, bouncing its way over the new cobbles. Yet, she did not feel fine. The weight of the world upon her shoulders, so that she needed this cycling excursion to escape from it all – if escape were possible – even for just a short while.

And the exhilaration! This sudden propulsion caused the wind to catch at her bonnet, forcing her to risk lifting a hand and keep it in place, so that she barely heard the polite applause of so many onlookers

– and the scowls of just a few. Those, she imagined, who had written in such outraged terms to the *Advertiser*. Those insisting that cyclists were a hazard to other road users. Those incredulous that women should be cycling at all, regardless of the queen's own enjoyment of the activity. And those simply scandalised by the sight of an exposed ankle, even when it was enclosed so securely in a fine rendition of Mrs Bloomer's fashionable reformers, her jersey knickerbocker trousers.

'But you are forbidden cycling, my dear!' The words floated after her, though lost in the rattle of frame and chain, the satisfactory thrumming of pneumatic tyre on stone, like a corps of drums, beginning with a gentle *patter, patter, patter*, but rising to a percussive crescendo. A crescendo pierced by other remembered words.

'It's your husband we need to chat about, Mrs Palmer,' Hatchet-Face had said. 'Unless, of course, ye've no concern about becoming a widow so young.'

She saw again those awful eyes, caught the smell of rubber once more – though now, of course, from the friction of so many tyres.

She had lain awake all Tuesday night, fretting over how she might tell him about her encounter with that terrifying woman or, indeed, whether she should tell him at all. But then, over breakfast on Wednesday morning, her infuriating husband had finally decided to inform her about the note. *Let sleeping dogs lie.* After all this time. And he had even asked her opinion.

'What do you think, my dear?' he had said. 'The most obvious answer is that it relates to this Tobin murder. But then Ned put the thought in my head that it might, rather, relate to my writings – the land question. Some irate landlord, perhaps, troubled about my stirring up potential animosities.'

Ned Owen was now back in London. Otherwise she might have sought his advice. Should she have confessed? That the note had simply been her own handiwork? A jest, almost. But one intended to produce precisely the result it had achieved. To incite his interest in the case, so that he might accept the work, earn some much-needed income. Oh, she thought, what tangled webs we weave...

There was a scream, and she turned to see two gentlemen in tweed suits and knickerbockers – she recalled that they had brought their tandem tricycle all the way from Pontblyddyn on the back of a carriage – tangled hopelessly in the large wheels where they had taken a tumble in their attempt to turn onto Rhosddu Road and, at the same time, negotiate their way around a Hansom travelling in the opposite direction. Indeed, she felt the wobble in her own steering as she helmed her way around the corner, almost colliding with a young boy on a wooden velocipede.

Duw Annwyl! Like a Roman chariot race. She recalled those edifying episodes in the book. It had left such an impression. *Ben-Hur: A Tale of the Christ.* Yet another distraction. The Canadian, Jackson, and his connection to Arizona. For, was Arizona not a neighbour to New Mexico? And had the author not been the governor of that distant territory? Indeed, had Governor Wallace not also had involvement in the tale of some notorious outlaw? Bonney – William Bonney? As the trees of the Llwyn Isaf parklands flashed past to her right, she wondered whether Mr Jackson might ever have encountered the governor – or, indeed, the outlaw.

And there it was, the guilt once more. Guilt at the number of times the Canadian came to mind. Guilt about the lost babe. Guilt about the note. And guilt that she had not told Neo about the woman. She half-expected to see her along the route, here among the next batch of spectators perhaps, clustered on the corner of King Street, beyond the orchards. But, instead, she merely heard the words, over and over again.

'Fenians, Mrs Palmer. Here in Wrexham. And one in particular.'

Ettie had been torn between fear of the woman and outrage at being hauled so unceremoniously into the police van – if, indeed, the vehicle did belong to some constabulary or other.

'If you know the fellow,' she'd said defiantly, 'why have you not arrested him?'

'Ach, nothin' but a *nom de guerre.* Number One, they call him. But, believe me, he's here somewhere.'

Recollection of the woman's cold manner still sent a shiver down her spine.

'Involved in this killing?' she'd asked, dreading the answer.

'Maybe, or maybe not. But this hallion's killed before. And if yer husband gets too close to the truth, I'd not give tuppence for his chances.'

'And if he is warned, he will not stop,' Esther had murmured almost to herself. The guilt again. The note. Point made, of course. She'd stared around the pine-panelled interior of the van and its iron bars, wondering whether the woman intended to incarcerate her pending her acquiescence.

'The only way we might protect him, Mrs Palmer, is if we know precisely what he knows.'

There'd been something about the way she spoke her name which Ettie found particularly hateful. *Paaarmer.*

'Then, why should I not tell him – encourage him to share his discoveries with you directly?'

It had seemed the obvious solution.

'Because we're not sure where the loyalties of your fella might lie. Are you, Mrs Palmer? Friends o' his with dangerous views.'

Ettie couldn't help it. Her thoughts went straight to Mr Reynolds, the newspaperman. She'd never met him while he lived, but the opinions in his Sunday columns had, she recalled, been very plain. Support for an independent Ireland. Other revolutionary notions. But her excessively affable Neo? How could anybody doubt him? Had he not already proved that the nation's security was safe in his hands? But the moment to defend him had passed.

'An' if ye warn him,' Hatchet-Face had said, 'we'll not be responsible for the consequences. Cooperate and we watch over him. Keep him safe.'

What to do? She had no idea, but now almost collided with an old fellow on a high-wheeler as they all careered left onto Grosvenor Road.

'Have a care, madam!' he yelled. 'Have a care!'

Yes, she must. In more ways than one.

For the second time this afternoon, she risked lifting a hand from the steering arm, this time to wave at Alison, standing with her children on the steps of their house – the very place where this machine was normally stabled.

'Is the creature behaving itself?' Alison cried through cupped hands.

Ettie nodded her head vigorously.

'Indeed,' she yelled back.

Behaving perfectly, she thought. The latest model, with the larger front wheel. A true wonder!

There had been another whist party, yesterday evening, here at Plas Darland. Neo had regaled them all yet again with the tale of his visit to the Broughton Brewery, his encounter with the viscount and Mr Steward.

'An ancient and honourable name,' Alison had explained. 'You'll know its origins?'

Neo, of course, had known.

'Walter Fitz-Alan of Dundonald, Third High Steward of Scotland,' he'd explained, as he proudly took the winning trick in their game against Mr Jackson and Alison's neighbour – the Canadian's landlady – Madame Morrel.

'Adopted the title for his surname,' he had continued, savouring his superior knowledge – for he plainly saw Mr Jackson as a rival. 'So became Walter the Steward – or, equally, Walter Stewart. The two things mean the same, d'you see? And when his great-grandson had married the daughter of Robert the Bruce, the Royal House of Stuart had been founded.'

'And the rest,' Mr Jackson had smiled, 'is history, is it not?'

'Indeed, sir,' Neo had replied, triumphantly lifting another tab on the score marker. 'Ruled Scotland, and more latterly England as well, for almost four hundred years.'

'And you say this fellow spent a spell studyin' the tattoo?' Jackson had stroked his bushy beard thoughtfully, while Madame Morrel dealt the next hand.

Neo had been certain. Steward had recognised the thing. But now? Should she relay this information, also, to Hatchet-Face?

It troubled her the whole length of Grosvenor Road, where she was slowed behind an omnibus. But grand villas on either side, each with its name sculpted into tall stone gateposts. The very symbol of Wrexham's considerable wealth. Perhaps, one day – one day, when they could afford to buy her a cycle of her own... But Fenians? Here? Why? This was not London, nor Liverpool or Birmingham.

Ahead of her now, the grandeur of St. Mary's, the left turn onto Regent Street, past the police barracks, past the towering height of St. Mark's spire – one of the wonders of Wales – the lesser, though still significant spire of the Bryn-y-ffynnon Wesleyan Chapel, and past the twin towers of the Seion Chapel. Onwards, onwards, the field thinning somewhat as the cyclists pedalled down towards Hope Street.

The thoroughfare was busy with other traffic, and she was forced to weave somewhat erratically to avoid the heaps of horse dung in the road, earning her the curse of several carters. Ahead of her, another tandem, a man and his wife she recognised from the meetings, and a stranger all in stripes on a monocycle. Safety bicycles, Ordinaries, so different from the boneshakers of her youth. She had priced them. Fifteen shillings for a decent model – though still beyond her reach. Indeed, beyond the reach of any working man or woman. A shame, because her own club, like all the others, was dedicated to the principle that cycling would help to improve society in general, to civilise its less liberal tendencies.

Less liberal? What was it that Hatchet-Face had said?

'We know about yer husband, Mrs Palmer. May look timid, so he does. But gets a thing between his teeth, won't let go, now, will he? So, if we warned him – if you warned him – told him to leave it alone, ye think he'd do so?'

'My husband has been loyal to the Crown...'

'I know the story, Mrs Palmer. Yer husband an' all...'

There he was, outside the Argyle Arch where, eight years ago, the turnstiles for the Art Treasures Exhibition had stood, and the other side of which had been the starting point for today's adventure. Neo waved, his poor face still stricken with concern. For the third time she managed to steer one-handed, offered him a quick salute and her broadest smile. Then she had left Neo behind and was heading down the gentle slope. Gentle, but enough for the machine to begin gathering speed. Faster. Faster. The Talbot flashed past and, in front, the tower of St. Giles. More immediately ahead, the town hall on the right, the Sig-Ar-Ro store on her left, and the point at which she needed to make her next manoeuvre – the turn onto the High Street.

Too much speed, she thought. Too much.

No choice. She must back-pedal. Ettie did so and came to such an immediate stop that she was lifted from her seat, almost catapulted over the steering bar. She barely saved herself.

'Who are you?' she'd asked Hatchet-Face. '*What* are you – military intelligence?'

'Special Irish Branch, Mrs Palmer. It's all ye need to know. An' you just tell us all the *craic*. We'll try to keep him safe.'

She was on the move again, heading past the Butchers' Market, another left turn coming up. Chester Street. She'd be riding past her own home in a few minutes. Then the last leg, towards the finish, beyond the Four Dogs Gate, in the Acton Hall parklands.

'And you're sure?' she had said. 'This Number One – he's here?'

'Ye've heard of the Invincibles, Mrs Palmer?'

'The murderers from Phoenix Park?'

'The same. Murdered those two poor men like a butcher sticks a squealing pig. Well, this Number One, he's the fella behind the scenes, like. Responsible, even if he doesn't hold the knife, if ye get my drift. And responsible for my husband, too.'

'Your husband?'

'I was just a police matron, Mrs Palmer. Ye know about police matrons, do ye?'

Ettie had known. The wives of serving police officers, living in police stations – doing the daily chores.

'But your husband…'

'Well, I'm not just a matron no more, Mrs Palmer. No, not no more. Stationed at Ballingarry, we were. Sixty-seven, it was. Burned it down, Mrs Palmer – the Fenians. My man still inside.'

Chapter Twelve

'You'll be glad to know we made the arrest, sir,' said Wilde, and stretched out his hand to help Palmer up onto the passenger seat of the covered gig.

'Arrest?'

Palmer was glad to accept the lift. The weather was fine enough – and this morning's study of the Illustrated Almanack told him it should remain so – but his chest had been troubling him and he'd not relished the climb up Acton Hill. Besides, since his encounter with that Irish bruiser – policeman or otherwise – he had tried to avoid being alone in places where he might again be ambushed.

'Steward, Mr Palmer,' said the superintendent. 'From the brewery.'

Wilde clicked his tongue twice and flicked his driving whip.

'Walk on, girl,' he said. 'Pull on.' He urged the grey mare up the first stretch, the harness jingling, the estate wall off to their right.

'Confessed to the murder, Superintendent?'

Palmer felt in his coat pocket for the snuff box.

'Murder? No, but we pressed the rogue hard. Oh, hard indeed. So hard he coughed to the yeast.'

'Tobin was acting for them – for the Broughton Brewery?'

'For Steward, at least. As I suspected, a simple enough scheme to harm the Lager Beer Company. But swore on a stack of bibles the plan was nothing to do with his lordship.'

As *Wilde* suspected? It was not quite the way Palmer remembered things, though he bit his tongue, while the superintendent eased back on the reins.

'Woah!' said the policeman, and gave way to the last of the cyclists struggling with the slope, or even pushing their machines towards the summit. Overhead, crows wheeled above the trees on either side.

'You believe him?' said Palmer.

'Seems to me it might be politic to do so, yes.' Wilde urged the horse forward again, the mare struggling in the traces with the uphill start.

And politic? Heaven forbid that the constabulary might challenge the son of a peer.

'But there is motive, surely. Perhaps Tobin had decided to tell his new employer. To come clean, as you might say. Perhaps he even told Steward he intended to do so – and Steward decided to silence him.'

'Speculation, Mr Palmer. And hardly seems the murdering type, does he?'

They had reached the crown of the hill, where the gateway to Acton Hall's estate stood – a great neo-classical monument, ostentatious in Palmer's opinion. Four life-sized sculpted greyhounds – the symbol of the owners, the Cunliffe family - sat upon the top, high above the ground, keeping guard. The gates themselves were open, though with liveried servants on watch at the lodge. They waved Wilde and his gig through, into the yard beyond, where two stable hands took charge of horse and carriage, the yard itself already being full.

'Is there one?' said Palmer. 'A type, I mean.'

'Indeed, there is, sir. But Steward doesn't fit the bill.'

'And the tattoo?'

'Insists he was simply curious.'

A little way along the tree-lined driveway, the various cycles from the day's event were either abandoned where they stood, on the grass verge, or leaned against the chestnuts just coming into leaf. Further again, and a large tent, the erection of which had been organised for the occasion by Sir Robert Cunliffe himself. The fifth Baronet, Palmer recalled. And Member for Denbigh Boroughs, as opposed to the County of Denbighshire itself – still represented by Sir Watkin, of course.

From the marquee came the sounds of music and merriment, and Palmer exchanged pleasantries with late arrivals joining them on the way to the tent's entrance.

'What will happen to him?' said Palmer when they had once again separated from the cyclists. 'To Steward.'

Wilde stopped at the marquee's entrance.

'Attempt to cause a poison to be administered,' he said, 'regardless of whether or not bodily injury might be affected – felony, sir. Borough magistrate on Monday morning.'

In that case, thought Palmer, I shall be sure to get a detailed account. From Alison's husband – Dr Edward Davies usually presiding over such sessions as the town's leading magistrate, as well as its most prominent general practitioner.

'The Bench may decide to treat him leniently, of course...'

Palmer doubted it, knowing Edward as he did.

'And if not?' he said.

'Discretion of the Court in any subsequent trial. But felony? If found guilty, no judge could sentence him to less than three years – and it could be life.'

Palmer heard – or imagined he heard – a wolf-like howling from away across the parklands stretching into the distance. Trees. Deer paddock. Great fishing lakes. All surrounded by high boundary walls, the perimeter of which he had walked with Ettie. Two miles, he had calculated. Probably more.

He knew these lands had been taken from the Welsh, as part of the conquests by King Edward Longshanks and given to one of his English barons to form part of the Lordship of Bromfield and Yale. By the time of King James – King James the Second, of course – four centuries later, this particular ground was in the hands of the Jeffreys family, then the High Sheriffs of Denbighshire. That was before it came into the possession of the Cunliffes, naturally.

From where they stood, he could just see the rooftops and many chimneys of the hall itself, on the highest ground, but mostly hidden by the trees. He had never seen the house at close quarters but it was said that Sir Robert had made significant changes to the exterior's facing – and not particularly changes for the better.

'Life,' he said. 'A strange description, is it not, for a sentence designed to deprive a body of that very thing?'

'The law, Mr Palmer. The law, sir. Would you simply set such felons free to act again?'

'I think, Superintendent, that I should devise some system whereby felons might repay their debt to society in a more constructive manner.' It was another viewpoint he'd shared strongly with George

Reynolds. Revolutionary, he supposed. 'But I am not in a position to influence such things, and shall we step inside?'

They did so, almost immediately encountering Viscount Broughton himself, holding court with several of the cyclists and also, to Palmer's annoyance, with Jackson. The ubiquitous Mr Jackson, he thought. The garish yellow coat of which he was so fond. The absurd beard in which an entire host of sparrows might nest with perfect security. He found himself scratching at his own modest whiskers, trying to spot Esther but unable to locate her, his vision somewhat unclear and his eyes watering as they were wont to do.

'Well, gentlemen,' the viscount beamed, peeling himself away from his audience with polite apologies, to greet them. 'I'd not expected we might all meet again so soon.'

To Palmer's surprise, he seemed delighted to see them, Viscount Broughton extending his hand. Palmer shook it politely, the superintendent with more caution.

'Lordship,' Wilde murmured. 'Sorry we had to arrest your man, but…'

'Please, Superintendent. No cause for such distance, I can assure you. Simply doing your duty – a quality I admire. And Mr Steward shall have the best of representation when he appears before the magistrates. The very best. I am certain they will plainly see his innocence.'

Palmer watched him turn his head this way and that, twisting the end of his waxed moustache as he did so. Looking to see if he was overheard? And some indication, perhaps, that his confidence might not match his words.

'Despite a confession?' said Palmer, but looking for Ettie once more and wiping away the rheumy moisture. She often said he resembled an adorable bloodhound. But he still could not spot her, his gaze settling instead on the musicians at the far side of the tent. A fiddler, a fellow with a banjo, and a whistle player. Merry Irish jigs to accompany this noisy assembly tucking into a curiously misnamed 'at-home tea' of finger sandwiches, pies and pastries, fancy cakes.

'Confession?' The viscount laughed theatrically. 'A confession that Tobin had confided some hare-brained plan to him, but poor

Steward had not believed him. Of course, he should have alerted me earlier but – a sin of omission only.'

'That is not the way I recall the confession, sir,' Wilde replied.

'Then, we shall see what Monday brings, Superintendent, shall we not? But I wished to speak with you about an entirely different matter. A peace offering, shall we say? For I have a mind to introduce a new dining club to the town. The Cycle Dining Club. Might you be interested in joining us, gentlemen?'

But before either of them had a chance even to consider this somewhat strange and unexpected offer, Jackson had joined them.

'Did I hear the Dinin' Club mentioned?' he laughed. 'I fear I may have confused your dear wife, Mr Palmer.'

The Canadian looked over his shoulder to one of the tables now visible after his group of former companions had broken up. He waved – and Palmer saw Ettie wave back, then notice her husband and flashed a smile at him. As always, Palmer felt his heart lift and swell an inch or two, despite his irritation at Jackson's presence.

'Confused?' said Palmer, returning Ettie's smile.

But the discussion had moved on, Viscount Broughton introducing Jackson to the superintendent.

'In all my born days,' Jackson was saying. 'Has anybody ever told you about the resemblance, sir?'

'President Lincoln?' Wilde replied. 'Just once or twice, Mr Jackson.'

'Old Abe, large as life. Oh, my Lord.'

Wilde began to ask the predictable question – what brought the Canadian all the way to Wrexham? But Palmer knew the answer already, having been forced to sit through the insufferable fellow's explanations at least twice at the Davies's whist parties. Some family business bringing him to England and the town's mining expertise bringing him here, a consultation with mine engineering and quarry owner associates of Alison's father.

'Perhaps you would excuse me, gentlemen...' he began. But then a young girl ran up and grabbed Viscount Broughton's arm – the same girl, his daughter, who had been with the viscount at the brewery.

'Papa,' she shouted, 'might we have a photograph? Oh please, Papa!'

She pointed across at the team – Palmer recognised them as Mr Cogan and his son Joseph – arranging photographs, table by table.

'My dear, you must wait a moment,' said the viscount, then turned again to Wilde. 'You already met my daughter, of course.' It sounded like an apology. 'Clementina,' he reminded them. 'Now, Clemmie…'

'Clementina Sobieska,' the girl corrected him, curtsied precociously, then skipped away again.

'Children! And since her poor mama…'

Palmer had troubled to learn a little more about the viscount since their first meeting, the fellow's young wife dead from childbirth. Yet, he was keen now to be with his own sweet girl.

'Please, forgive me,' he apologised once more, gave them a bow and crossed the wooden flooring of the marquee, easing his way between the nearest of the tables. All gentlemen here, a conversation about today's big match. Wales against Scotland, in Glasgow.

'It's to be hoped they do better than the England match,' said one, and Palmer could not have agreed more. He supposed, being Thetford-born, that his sympathies should lie with the English team. But Welsh football had become something of a passion for him, as had all other Welsh matters and the *Cymraeg* itself.

'Don't worry, gentlemen,' he said as he squeezed by, 'Tom Burke and young Eyton-Jones will save the day.'

Two Wrexham players in the team and both of them excellent.

'Let's hope so,' said another of the cyclists. 'Let's hope so, indeed!'

It was, Palmer decided, the way that men engaged in debate. Each in turn, the conversation usually dominated by one in particular, usually the most boorish.

At Ettie's table, on the other hand, the ladies' discussion about the past week's entertainments at the Public Hall had all the vibrancy and excitement of an operatic ensemble, each voice shining individually but, together, their harmonious assertions and comments intertwined in a perfect symphony, each of the ladies expressing very different but entirely complimentary viewpoints at precisely the same time.

'My dear,' said Ettie, standing to kiss his cheek, 'these are my friends…'

Each was named in turn and Palmer invited to join them.

It was a pleasant interlude. And he was able to nod and smile politely in all the appropriate places while, in the other half of his brain, a fairground carousel of questions went around and around to the background strains of a calliope playing Irish ballad tunes.

Who had sent him the note? *Let sleeping dogs lie?* And if Mr Steward had not, indeed, drowned Tobin, then who and why? He was certain that Steward – and the viscount also – had recognised Tobin's tattoo, had they not? And why was Tobin's body found in Farndon, of all places? Then, the Fenian connection? The Corpse Dog?

Yet, it was Jackson to whom his questing mind kept returning, and when they were finally leaving and alone, he summoned the courage to ask her.

'Ettie, my dear. That fellow Jackson – when I encountered him earlier, he said he had confused you. Might I ask...'

'At Alison's whist party,' she replied. 'Do you not remember? He spoke of joining a cycling club – or so I thought at the time. But now it seems...'

Now he understood.

'Of course. This Cycle Dining Club. Our esteemed Viscount Broughton mentioned the same thing. Yet, is it not strange, my dear?'

He watched as she tucked some stray strands of hair back beneath her bonnet. It was one of those moments when he was aware of the difference in their ages. Sometimes, she seemed so young.

'Harmless enough, I suppose,' she said, as they reached Alison's tricycle and she began to wheel it towards the lodge. 'One more society for gentlemen alone. Precisely what the town needs.'

Just her little jest, he thought. But then there were hoofbeats out on the lane, beyond the estate walls. A rider, galloping through the gateway towards them. A policeman, red of face, charging past, and reining to a halt outside the tent's entrance.

'Great Heavens,' he said. 'Should we...?'

He stopped, curious. Though Ettie had already gone on alone, regardless.

'Absolutely not,' she shouted back over her shoulder. 'I am exhausted. And we have yet to return the machine.'

'Still...' he began. But he saw that it was hopeless and hurried to catch her.

'That view!' she said. Ettie had halted, finally, out beyond the gateway, gazing down, over the treetops, to the town itself. 'You see? Oxford might be the more famous, but on a misty afternoon like this, from up here, is Wrexham not also possessed of its own dreaming spires?'

She was right, of course. And it was a discussion they'd had before, on other occasions during their Sunday constitutionals up Acton Hill. Matthew Arnold, Palmer decided, would concur.

'It does, sweet girl. It does. But now – home?'

He needed to think. All those puzzles. A pot of cha would surely help.

'It would be easier to ride, Neo.'

'Were it a tandem, perhaps I could be tempted. Though, this...'

She laughed.

'Look,' she said, pointing to the A-frame supporting the rear wheels. 'If you set your feet here, and place your hands on my shoulders, I'm sure we shall be perfectly safe.'

'All the same...'

The sound of somebody running towards them caused Palmer to turn his head. Studded boots crunching on the driveways gravel. It was Wilde.

'Mr Palmer, sir,' Wilde yelled. 'A moment, if you please.'

He was carrying a sheet of paper. Palmer could see it was a telegraphic dispatch.

'It seems,' said the superintendent, waving the telegram in the air, 'we just had a message from our colleagues in Flintshire. Another murder. And this one, Mr Palmer – well, it seems to involve you directly, in a manner of speaking.'

Chapter Thirteen

Neo remained obdurate. He wouldn't look at her, continued staring through the carriage window at the Balderton sign.

'I still believe this is a mistake,' he insisted, as the train slowed through the station – a station built specifically to serve the Eaton Estate, the needs of the duke of Westminster, his family and occasional visiting royalty, and hence no reason to stop here today.

A full week had gone by since the superintendent had brought them the news.

'And how,' said Neo, finally deigning to look at her again, 'can Wilde possibly know there's any connection? With Tobin's death, I mean.'

But Ettie knew – though she could not tell him.

It had been a busy week. Monday, and she had joined other curious members of the public at the magistrates' court. Mr Steward had been closely questioned about his previous involvement with the deceased. Yes, he knew Francis Tobin was Irish and been employed at the Broughton Brewery since his arrival in Wrexham. From Ireland? No, from Chester. Sixteen years earlier? Seventeen? No, they had not been closely connected. No, he had no knowledge that Tobin might have been a Fenian. And yes, Tobin had left them to work for the Lager Beer Company just twelve months before.

'Do you know,' she said, 'that they barely mentioned the yeast again?'

'He stuck to the story?'

Indeed, he had. A contaminated batch from last year, while Tobin still worked for them. Steward had claimed he'd given Tobin the task of destroying it. So, his confession to Superintendent Wilde had been accurate – he *had* given Tobin the Killer Yeast. Though not for the purpose of felony.

'He was extremely contrite, Neo. Desperately apologetic that he had not spoken up sooner, once he heard of Tobin's death. It was a wonderful performance. And Edward's associates on the Bench swallowed it hook, line and sinker.'

'Or were bribed to do so?'

Edward's displeasure had been evident but, despite this, Steward had been acquitted.

'Had you been there,' she said, 'you might have drawn your own conclusion.'

The train's whistle blew and, out in the fields, there were cows, all lying down beneath the trees. Rain on the way? Probably, but regardless of any bovine meteorological foreknowledge.

'Too much work,' he told her, his mood lightening, it seemed. 'As you well know.'

It was a blessing, she supposed. A veritable silver lining. For, since this had all come to light, Mr Wassmann at the Lager Beer Company had insisted on more stringent analytical checks and Neo had been further engaged accordingly. Every batch of yeast. Regular sampling of the water.

'In any case,' he went on, thoughtfully kneading his bearded chin, 'the crucial question, sweet girl, is this – if money changed hands, if palms were greased, from whose coffers did the silver emanate?'

Could there be any doubt? But it was plainly a rhetorical question. They had discussed Viscount Broughton many times since their previous encounter with the man.

'Perhaps you could accept his lordship's invitation to join this dining club – just ask him the question outright.'

She was pleased to see him smile.

'Yes, perhaps,' he said. 'Though, I am equally intrigued by the name of his daughter. Clementina Sobieska? I must check the origins – when I eventually have time.'

'And yet,' she said, 'on Monday afternoon, you found time to attend the Racecourse.'

Neo took a pinch of his snuff.

'In the line of duty only, my dear. I told you so. Poor Sergeant Jones.'

It had, she recalled, been a match between the fire brigade and the police, with the sergeant in goal for his team. Still suffering, Neo had told her later, from the effects of tasting the Killer Yeast – as well as from smoke inhalation. For there had been a fire on Crispin Lane, smoke so thick that neither side would even have been able to find the opposing goal, but then the entire match abandoned anyhow, of course, so the firemen themselves could attend to the more pressing duty of extinguishing the flames.

'And the superintendent,' she said, 'did not impart anything further?'

When he'd brought them the news, after the cycling event, Wilde had known only the fellow's name. Connor O'Donnell. Another known Fenian, according to the Flintshire constabulary, who had been keeping an eye on the man. Another Fenian murdered. Coincidence? Naturally, the superintendent had not believed so. And Neo's involvement? Well, that was the reason for today's excursion, was it not?

'I cannot share the details with you, my dear,' Neo told her. 'Too awful for words.'

But Hatchet-Face had possessed no such sensibilities.

'A second grin,' the woman had told her. 'Throat opened up from ear to ear.'

She'd materialised from the shadows within the Butcher's Market as Ettie had picked up their weekly piece of gammon. And Hatchet-Face had imparted a strange tale.

'Ye understand?' she'd said. 'The sort of hallions we're dealing with, Mrs Palmer? Deadly killers. See now why your husband needs our protection?'

A strange tale indeed.

'Told ye about the Rising, I did. In '67. My poor husband. But ye'd be too young to remember that, over here, they had a plan to attack Chester Castle. For the guns, like.'

Wilde had also thought she'd be too young to remember. And while she'd been happy to correct the policeman, tell him how her father had regaled her with the story many times, she'd had no intention of sharing this with Hatchet-Face. Still, the woman's revelation that both victims, O'Donnell and Tobin, had been involved in that plot – strange, was it not?

'Involved – but not arrested?' Ettie had asked.

'Only the ringleaders, Mrs Palmer. But the one we were really after – this Number One fella – well, we was hopin' some of these small fry might lead us to him. And now, see how yer husband keeps getting' himself wrapped up in all this?'

Yes, Ettie had seen. Or had she? Two Fenians murdered? It made no sense. Were the Fenians not supposed to be desperate killers, rather than victims? And what on earth might Neo be able to discover that could put him in danger – or, indeed, be any use to Hatchet-Face?

Her husband's voice returned her to the present.

'There is still time to change our minds,' he said.

'We should at least find out what she wants, Neo. So urgent a summons.'

'Precisely my point, Esther.'

A summons, indeed. It had arrived on Wednesday. A telegram. But even, given the nature of such telegraphic messages, the language was especially curt.

EARLIEST CONVENIENCE STOP
VISIT STOP WARREN HALL STOP

Once again, Neo had insisted he was too busy – though it had been obvious he was intrigued. For there had been the final three pieces of knowledge Wilde had imparted to them. First, that O'Donnell's murdered corpse had also been found on the banks of the Dee. This time at Saltney's Upper Ferry. The second, that this body had also suffered damage from some scavenging creature, probably a fox – though it had been enough to stimulate more of Neo's nightmares about the Corpse Dog. And the third, that Neo – both of them, in fact – were familiar with O'Donnell's employer. Actually, more than just familiar.

'Is it far?' she said. 'Warren Hall?'

They were passing the signal box, pulling into Saltney station and they both stood, Neo recovering his hat from the seat opposite.

'From here?' he said. 'Four miles. With luck there shall be a Hackney. Though why we have come…'

Why? Curiosity, perhaps. And something else. That frisson of foolish excitement when one knowingly steps into the lion's den. They had each dressed for the occasion, she in her finest purple wool-silk walking skirt, matching coat and bonnet. For she would not permit herself to be daunted. Neither by Hatchet-Face, nor by this other woman who had, eight years earlier, almost been the death of them.

Chapter Fourteen

Eight years, thought Palmer, and still deadly.

It was the eyes. Hooded, like a bird of prey. Falcon-brown silks and black lace. She was sleek, proud, sixty or thereabouts, but still possessed of that same sensuous allure he had noted at their previous encounters – first at the opening of the Art Treasures Exhibition, then at the premises of Mr Williams the tailor in College Street. It seemed like yesterday.

They had, of course, seen her more recently. The evening performance of *The Castle Spectre*. The private box. And then, as now, he had wondered at how a lady encased in such a carapace of aristocratic breeding could be pierced to the point of fainting by a mere moment of theatrical drama.

And strange, he thought, that I still have no true idea whether she was, or was not, responsible for the dangers we faced, myself and Ettie.

'Well,' said the woman, with the same genteel Irish accent he also remembered, 'the ubiquitous Mr Palmer.' She had referred to him this way once before.

'Indeed, ma'am,' he said, 'though we thought we had arrived in error, such was the delay at your lodge.'

He found he was still somewhat vexed at the length of time it had taken for the gates to be opened, the questions about their business there, and only truly satisfied when Palmer had shown the telegram to the loutish lodge-keeper.

'In this day and age, I fear,' said the woman, 'one can never be too careful.'

Not even an apology! Palmer opened his mouth to comment but she had already turned her attention to Esther.

'And you, my dear. Welcome to the Warren. Our humble little Warren.'

Palmer considered that the name was apposite. Though, the adjectives entirely misplaced. Once they were finally admitted, a substantial tree-lined drive had led the cabbie, his vehicle and its passengers past the hall's façade – Italianate in style, many windows, an entrance porch with classical columns and double doors – and around through a winding maze of stables, barns and farm buildings to reach the yard and a rear entrance almost as grand as the front. There, the suspicion-filled glances of stable hands, a begrudged greeting from a liveried manservant and another serpentine route of panelled and picture-hung passageways, through the house itself, to reach the wide central stairwell. Around the two long sides of the stairwell, an arcade, each archway leading to a separate door and, in this case, to a well-appointed reception room with French windows looking out upon landscaped gardens, with parterres and fruit trees. A warren, indeed, though neither humble nor little.

'We were somewhat surprised to receive your...' Palmer was still uncertain how to describe it.

'My summons, Mr Palmer? Is that how you saw it?'

She dismissed the manservant with an instruction that afternoon tea should be served, then turned to the room's other occupant, the same man of the cloth they had seen at the performance, leaning casually against the wooden Jacobean surround to a stone fireplace – Tudor, Palmer decided, from its sculpted foliage spandrels and great size – with logs burning in the hearth.

'You see, Frederick,' said Lady Olivia, scornfully. 'I said, did I not? We could easily have dispatched a letter.'

The fellow puffed steadily upon a Meerschaum and the ceiling's elaborate rosettes, its cornice conceits, were already half-hidden by a fug of tobacco smoke. He was tall and athletic for his age – older than his wife, Palmer guessed, and from the mischievous smile he flashed in Ettie's direction, still fancied himself something of a ladies' man.

'It might not,' he said, 'have conjured quite the same level of urgency.'

Palmer had expected the Reverend FitzPatrick's inflection to also have some trace of the Irish. Indeed, he and Ettie had discussed the husband during their journey, both of them knowing, at least, a little of his background. Yet Palmer was now surprised to detect Welsh undertones to the voice. He raised a quizzical eyebrow for Ettie's benefit as they sank into the cushions of the sofa to which Lady Olivia had directed them with an imperious wave of her hand – but the woman had obviously noticed their silent interchange.

'I see,' she said. 'The name. Frederick, you had better explain how we come to be in this backwater.'

'I was born here,' replied the clergyman, with disdain. 'In this backwater, as my dear wife likes to call it. Bryn Edwyn, to be precise. But educated in Holy Orders at Trinity College. And afterwards, doing God's work in Ulster. But when I retired...'

'Retired?' Lady Olivia laughed. 'The truth,' she told Ettie, 'is that he was an embarrassment to the diocese.'

Palmer knew this much about him – a country parson whose duty to his impoverished parishioners and to the Almighty frequently took second place to his passion for hunting to hounds.

'Yet, the invitation,' said Palmer, desperate to get things back on track. 'It was, indeed, a surprise. And might we enquire, ma'am, about the rest of your family?'

He had been determined not to ask, but he also needed to know, and now found the words tumbling from his mouth before he could prevent their escape. Even worse, he wished he could have bitten off his tongue when the woman's response caused Ettie to stiffen at his side.

'You have none of your own as yet, I understand.'

Palmer felt as though they had been specimens, scrutinised through a microscope.

'Not as yet, ma'am, no,' he said. 'But...'

He squeezed Esther's hand.

'Time enough, I suppose,' said Lady Olivia. 'And then you shall understand the tribulations that children inflict upon us. But if you mean my daughter, Mr Palmer, why, in the name of Heaven, do you not say so? She is well enough, sir, though of no concern in this particular matter, if that is the thing which troubles you.'

It was just a little too vehement. But Palmer hoped it was true – the part about her not being part of the reason he'd been summoned here. For the daughter had been very much at the heart of the affair eight years earlier, so he had no desire to renew the acquaintance.

'And we read in the newspapers,' said Esther, quickly, 'that she is now more often in London.'

It seemed to Palmer that husband and wife scowled at precisely the same time. Though, possibly, each for entirely different reasons.

For Lady Olivia FitzPatrick, perhaps, the recollection that, as Olivia Taylour, young and beautiful daughter to one of the most powerful men in the House of Lords, she had once been a lady-in-waiting to the queen herself – until a certain indiscretion had caused her to be dismissed from that service, effectively banished back to Ireland and a forced marriage of family convenience to a mere country parson. Her own daughter's notable role within high society must surely have rankled.

For the Reverend FitzPatrick, almost certainly the memory that his past good fortune at having been married into Ireland's aristocracy must now be somewhat overshadowed by their daughter's most recent behaviour.

'The Langtry woman,' said Lady Olivia. 'An entirely bad influence.'

It seemed to be an open secret that Lillie Langtry was the latest conquest of the Prince of Wales, but her friendship with the FitzPatricks' daughter was equally remarked upon. Photographs of the two women together, shamelessly modelling the latest fashions, Ettie had told him, in *Town Talk* and *Vanity Fair*.

'Yet we are kept informed,' said Reverend FitzPatrick. Though, he seemed more interested in the pipe. For, it had now burned itself out. He took it from his mouth to examine the bowl. 'The queen is far from amused,' he murmured. 'Her Majesty...'

'Her Majesty,' snapped Lady Olivia, cutting across him, 'has instructed that they should desist, forthwith. And our poor son-in-law. How must such frivolities reflect upon a gentleman who is, after all, Lord Lieutenant of Denbighshire. The queen's own lord lieutenant, for pity's sake.'

Mercifully, tea arrived, with cucumber sandwiches and fruit scones. Ettie, in her usual indomitable way, accepted the refreshments with relish. Palmer himself politely refused all but the beverage, knowing he would be at a severe disadvantage trying to discover the reason for this "invitation" if his mouth was stuffed full of bread or cake.

'Then, if not your daughter, ma'am,' he said, 'I have to assume this matter, as you call it, concerns the fellow O'Donnell.'

'And I, Mr Palmer,' said Lady Olivia, 'had assumed, first, that Inspector Wilde would have told you that Connor O'Donnell was in my employ and, second, that you would have deduced that this was the obvious reason for your invitation here.'

'Your employ, ma'am – a known Fenian?' said Palmer.

Reverend FitzPatrick looked up at him sharply, in the act of knocking the dottle from his pipe into the fireplace.

'Rather, a family connection,' Lady Olivia replied. 'And Frederick,' she scolded her husband, 'shall you not be seated? You hover about like some…'

Palmer wasn't certain whether her agitation stemmed from the discussion or whether her apparent loathing for her husband, her obvious irritation with the fellow, was simply a natural state of affairs. But at that moment a man glanced in through French windows – a man carrying a shotgun – before sauntering down the steps onto the lawn.

'Gamekeeper?' said Palmer.

'It seems we may be plagued by poachers,' said Reverend FitzPatrick, with more than just a hint of irony in his voice.

'But still,' Palmer turned back to Lady Olivia, 'this O'Donnell – a Fenian?'

He sipped at his tea, while the woman appraised him for some seconds and her husband, obedient as a hound, followed the command to sit, though on a straight-backed chair near the glazed double doors.

'Mr Palmer,' she said, finally, 'I would have thought from our previous involvement that you would, at least, know I am loyal to the Crown. You must take my word that I would not employ any person who was not similarly faithful to queen and country.'

Palmer was about to repeat Superintendent Wilde's assertion about O'Donnell, but she held up a hand to stop him.

'And Mr Palmer,' she said, 'I also have to assume from our previous involvement that you, too, are loyal to the Crown. I believe you were sworn to secrecy. To protect the integrity of – well, I need not say.'

It was a good question. Her Majesty's director of military intelligence had, indeed, caused him to swear a vow of silence about those events. A matter of national security. Every detail of Palmer's involvement to vanish. A cleansing, the man had said, such that there should be no remaining record of Palmer ever having even been in Wrexham. Nor anybody else associated with the case. Palmer – and Ettie, of course – had taken the oath seriously, only returned quietly to Wrexham four years later and carefully avoided every potentially difficult question. Four years, and after the man himself, Sir Patrick MacDougall, had become commander-in-chief of the British forces in Canada. Yes, Canada. Palmer fleetingly thought of Jackson.

'Loyal, ma'am, naturally,' he said. Though he was not entirely certain. In his heart, he knew he leaned rather towards the republican tendencies of his late-lamented friend George Reynolds.

'Besides,' said Lady Olivia, 'given my family's history, how could I not believe that Ireland belongs to the Crown? An independent Ireland? Fenians? Do you seriously imagine I should have tolerated one of those murderous zealots within my household?'

It was so ferocious a statement that he could not help but believe her. Though he was about to diplomatically suggest there might indeed be supporters of an independent Ireland other than vile assassins. Or even that there might be dogmatists so intent on preventing Irish independence that they might kill for their own cause as well.

'Perhaps one does not...' he began, as Ettie gasped, her fingers jerking up to touch her lips.

'Oh, my goodness,' she said, staring at the French windows. 'Another?'

At first, Palmer assumed that the gamekeeper had returned to the terrace, but then realised that this was, as Ettie had surmised, an entirely different fellow, though also bearing a shotgun.

'We are blessed with a considerable estate,' Reverend Fitzgerald explained, without any great conviction. 'Are we not, my dear?'

'Our retinue of staff, Frederick,' she sneered, 'is not Mr Palmer's concern either.'

'Yet, I am keen to know,' said Palmer, 'what *does* bring me here, ma'am? You say I should have deduced that it's connected to the murdered man – but I fail to see…'

'Put simply?' Lady Olivia replied. 'I remember your tenacity, Mr Palmer. A talent for dogged investigation. It was once irksome to me but now, I believe, it may be useful. I need to know the truth – about Connor O'Donnell's killer.'

'But the police…' Ettie murmured, though Reverend FitzPatrick's snort of derision prevented her making the obvious point.

'The police,' he said, 'are incompetent nitwits, my dear. They, too, it seems, believe Connor to have seditious connections – and this, somehow, makes his murder of no consequence. A falling out of thieves, as they've put it.'

'And we understand, Mr Palmer,' said Lady Olivia, 'that you are already involved around the margent of these events, in any case.'

'How so?' he asked, though he already knew the answer.

'Please, do not obfuscate, sir,' she said. 'The other murder, of course.'

'Tobin,' he said. 'And the connection?'

She hesitated.

'I must tell you a story, I fear. Though some of it will already be familiar to you. The rising in '67 and the Fenians' planned attack on Chester Castle?'

'Of course,' he said. 'Yes, indeed.'

Palmer turned towards Esther, aware that she already knew the tale and simply wanting to give her the chance to speak for herself. However, as usual, she was already several steps ahead of the conversation.

'They were both involved, I assume,' said Ettie. 'Though if O'Donnell, as you say, was not a Fenian…'

'Back then, in his younger days, he almost certainly shared their views. Yet, he saw the light, as they say, when he finally understood the evil nature of the man they followed. The leader of these self-proclaimed Invincibles. A devil in disguise, Mr Palmer. And such was the epiphany that, at the last moment, O'Donnell knew he must do the correct thing, and inform the authorities about the scheme.'

'Tobin, too?' Ettie asked. 'One of the informers?'

'All told,' said Reverend FitzPatrick, 'four of them. Tobin, Connor O'Donnell, Michael...'

'Stop, Frederick!' Lady Olivia commanded, those hooded, Gorgon eyes blazing as though she might turn her husband to stone. 'It is not necessary for Mr Palmer to be burdened with our mere speculations about the rest.'

The fellow was cowed into silence, turned upon his chair and began to play once more with the Meerschaum, cleaning the bowl with a small pocket-knife.

But burdened? Palmer still had no idea what she might want from him.

'I believe I must explain,' he said, 'that my involvement, as you call it, in Francis Tobin's demise, has been little more than providing a chemical analyst's report to Superintendent Wilde.'

'And accompanying the superintendent in his investigations. Conducting your own visit to Farndon?'

'Madam...' he began to protest.

'I must admit that when I first heard your name mentioned, it troubled me greatly, but...'

'Wait,' said Palmer, believing he might finally have an answer to, at least, one of his conundrums. *Let sleeping dogs lie.* 'The note. You sent me the note.' He felt Ettie's fingers clench within those of his own hand. 'Do you not see, my dear?' he said to her, and was surprised to see the somewhat pained expression upon her face. Was she not delighted at this revelation?

'Note, Mr Palmer?' Lady Olivia was saying. 'I have absolutely no idea what you mean. But now, with O'Donnell...'

She had accused him of obfuscation – but was it not she who might now be dissembling? He had no idea.

'O'Donnell had seen the report,' she went on, 'about Francis Tobin's death and insisted on attending the funeral. It was ill-advised. We warned him...'

'Indeed, we did!' Reverend FitzPatrick had taken a renewed interest in the discussion. 'Warned him of the perils.'

Palmer felt Ettie's fingers slip from his grasp, and she folded her hands into her lap.

'O'Donnell,' she said. 'He was in hiding here?'

'Feared them,' the reverend replied. 'The Invincibles. Believed they would seek revenge for betraying them.'

'After all this time?' said Palmer. 'Why now?'

'Because it seems, Mr Palmer,' said Lady Olivia, 'that this fiend who leads them – this Number One, a wretch by the name of McCafferty, we believe – wherever he has been all this time, is now back.'

Chapter Fifteen

'The place was like an armed camp,' Ettie murmured, and Hatchet-Face nodded her understanding.

'Ach, no surprise there,' said the woman. 'Not in the circumstances, like.'

The Monday Market. Whenever she ventured here, she was reminded of the excursion train they'd taken to Holyhead, then the perilous trip by dog cart up and around Holyhead Mountain to view the South Stack lighthouse perched on its tiny island far below, at the lip of a wide sea-washed inlet in the cliff-face. When she had peered over the vertiginous edge, the harsh screams of countless nesting seabirds had exploded up to suddenly assault her senses. Here, though, it was the cries of the market's street vendors.

"Muffins! Crumpets!" or *"Bay Pots! Each a pretty penny!"* A hundred more besides.

As usual, Hatchet-Face had materialised from nowhere, trailing along behind Esther from stall to stall but pretending they were not together, only speaking when there was no risk of their conversation being observed or overheard. Or without needing to shout above the vendors' cries.

'The circumstances in which,' Ettie snapped at her, when she was able, 'neither Tobin nor O'Donnell were, in fact, Fenians at all. Rather the reverse.'

'Once a Fenian, always a Fenian, don't ye think, Mrs Palmer? An' maybe just tell me what it was – that the FitzPatricks were after.'

Ettie paused at Mrs Buckland's haberdashery wagon to examine the bolts of lace – for the new antimacassars on which she planned to make a start. But she also wanted to keep an eye on the ruffian in the bowler hat, constant but distant shadow to Hatchet-Face, currently loitering twenty yards away at the next junction in the market's maze of lanes.

'It seems,' she murmured, when Mrs Buckland – Paradise as she preferred to be called – was busy wrapping her purchase, 'that Lady Olivia also believes my husband might have sufficient detectivist aptitude to uncover the whereabouts of the Invincibles' mysterious Number One.'

'Ye don't think so yerself?'

'I certainly hope so. She has offered Neo a reward for information leading to his capture.'

'Reward? How much, Mrs Palmer?'

It was a good question, but Ettie simply moved on, glancing round to get her bearings. The Beast Market's street and open ground beyond was like that wide South Stack inlet in more ways than just the noise, for it was enclosed on all sides by the dark red or brown brick walls of housing terraces, substantial industrial buildings and chimneys, and the bulk of the National School. Within the confines of these soot-stained cliffs, this roiling sea of shoppers breaking upon the rocks of traders' carts and caravans, striped awnings and grey tarpaulins.

'I think,' Ettie told Hatchet-Face, 'that I should never have agreed to this subterfuge in the first place.'

She hated it – the deception. And any idea that it might somehow be in Neo's best interest now seemed absurd. Yet, she could think of no way to break free of the hook which would not threaten the harmony between them. How could she now confess?

'And why, precisely,' she continued, 'given the interest of Superintendent Wilde, yourself and now the FitzPatricks in finding this fellow, can you not simply collaborate without the need to involve my poor husband?'

They had passed the pot mender, the Messham's travelling show and Bethan Thomas selling copies of *Y Frythones*.

'FitzPatricks?' Hatchet-Face snorted. 'Believed her, did ye? About O'Donnell being a convert, like?'

There was no mackintosh today, just a simple outdoor coat of brown wool. However, she still wore the flat-crowned riding hat. Ettie had to admit that the woman blended perfectly with her surroundings.

'He's dead, is he not?' she said. 'And beyond even the help of Clarke's Miraculous Salve.'

She gestured towards the regular quack mountebank, now in full flow about his ointment's curative properties for ulcerated legs, boils, pustules, carbuncles, eruptions of the skin…

'And gatherings of all kinds!' shouted the rogue, but then froze when he saw one of Superintendent Wilde's constables among his audience.

'An' this, Mrs Palmer,' Hatchet-Face whispered in her ear, 'is about as much as we might expect from Wilde and his men.' For the constable was now making a fool of himself, challenging the self-proclaimed doctor to produce his medical certificates or other *bona fides*.

The Monday Market had become a magnet for those seeking bargain buys, or those who saw the weekly market as a social occasion – the place to share news with family and neighbours, to swap family information. A magnet for traditional hawkers and street sellers, as well. Or local smallholders and producers with only limited quantities of their wares to sell.

'But yes,' Hatchet-Face went on, 'at least that O'Donnell fella's dead.'

They moved on once more, Ettie wading through the crowd, shouting a greeting to acquaintances here and there, above the cries of the closest vendors.

"Mutton pies! Hot mutton pies!" and *"Matches! Buy a poor girl's matches!"*

'So, what is it?' said Ettie. 'That causes the FitzPatricks to require so many guns for their protection?'

Neo had spotted two more fellows with rifles in the grounds as they'd been leaving Warren Hall.

'Ach, Mrs Palmer. Did they seem like they were keenin' for the man? Ye've no idea, have ye? Folk like them, noses in the air. Aristocrats, claimin' to be loyal to Queen and Country – but really, only loyal to keepin' themselves rich and safe, no matter how they do it. Happy to stoke up a bit of war here an' there – but then find that war's landed on their own doorstep.'

'War?' said Ettie. 'You are serious?'

There was no answer, for the crowd was now especially dense and they were separated yet again. Ettie wrinkled her nose as today's breeze carried the stench of hides from the tanneries to mingle with the ever-present stable smells from the horse repository; the ordure of the nearby animal pens; the sickly vapours of the town's maltings; and, at her side, the sweet aroma of potatoes baking in Mr Hamble's portable oven.

'Yet, Superintendent Wilde has an admirable record as a policeman,' said Ettie, when they were reunited, and feeling the need to defend the man's reputation, though Hatchet-Face plainly did not intend to waste breath arguing with her. And Ettie could see that, if the woman was right – war, in the form of a stone-cold killer like this Number One – well, perhaps this would indeed be just a little beyond even Wilde's capabilities.

She stopped to give herself time to think, pretending to examine some very elegant willow fishing creels.

'But if the superintendent cannot help – then, my husband...?'

'Sometimes, Mrs Palmer, it's us little people who can make a difference – if we do the little things really well, an' all the time. An' that's yer husband, is it not? He has gifts – uses them so well, he can't help himself. Born great, like that Shakespeare fella says, even if he doesn't know it. I told ye, I read the file, so I did – about what happened eight years ago. Reward or no reward, mystery to be solved. He'll not be able to help himself. You, too, Mrs Palmer.'

Ettie flushed with embarrassment. Though, Neo? She knew exactly what this strange woman meant. He did, indeed. have a talent. It often seemed that he merely stumbled upon solutions. Yet, she had come to learn that it was never simple serendipity – more like some sixth sense which steered him towards discovery.

She stopped to put a few pennies in the jar of a one-legged banjo player, a veteran of the country's pointless wars from the medals on his chest.

'And you, perhaps?' she said, suddenly wishing to understand this woman better – a woman who, apparently, shared the rare ability to see beneath Neo's outward simplicity and see the complex character beneath.

'Me, Mrs Palmer? Just a simple agent of the Crown.'

'There are more of you, then – women agents in this Special Irish Branch?'

The woman laughed – a genuine laugh for the first time. It was a strange counterpoint to the new sounds filling the air where the market stalls began to thin and give way to the first animal pens – the distressing grief of calves and lambs separated from their mothers and, perhaps, somehow aware of the fate awaiting them.

'Yer Scotland Yard,' said Hatchet-Face, 'they have this fella, head o' their Criminal Investigation Department. His idea, so it was. Special agents to keep an eye on the Fenians. Maybe act as bodyguards for anybody they thought might be on the Fenians' list for...'

She drew a finger evocatively across her throat. An ironic gesture, Ettie considered, given their proximity to this place of imminent death and, as often happened, she remembered Neo so frequently telling her the story of that Tudor Catholic martyr butchered with such barbarity for his faith just yards from where she now stood.

'Anyway,' the woman was saying, 'brings himself all the way to Belfast to recruit the right people, so he does. An' me, I follows him about for a few days. Then confront him while he's eatin' his dinner one night. Show him the notes I'd taken. How I could have popped him there an' then. Proved how close I'd got to him, an' how he'd not even noticed me. Told him about my husband, an' all. The rest – well, here I am, Mrs Palmer. Not easy to persuade them.'

'The only woman they've got?' said Ettie.

'The only one. An' yes, Mrs Palmer, perhaps me, too. You, me, an' yer husband. Little people, all on the same path, to find this devil before he does any more harm.'

Ettie opened her mouth to speak, but Hatchet-Face cut her off.

'But no, Mrs Palmer, you still don't need to know my name. We have a single wee footprint to follow. Maybe two. One of the men who helped plan that raid on Chester Castle – ye remember, we talked about it?' Ettie remembered. 'Well, this hallion – McCafferty – they caught him. Supposed to hang, but somehow...'

Ettie remembered the name – from their meeting with Lady Olivia.

'Escaped?' she said.

Ettie leaned against the iron bars of the nearest animal pen, where a young Jersey heifer pushed her with its cream-coloured muzzle, so that she turned to scratch the creature's forehead.

'Banished,' said Hatchet-Face. 'To America.'

'Do we not send our felons to Van Diemen's Land any longer?'

'Oh, this fella was born there. Ohio. Fought in their civil war. Irish regiment. Then with a bunch of murderin' raiders. That's somethin', don't ye think?'

Ettie watched a dozen ewes being herded into the nearby auction sheds, a black and white sheepdog snapping at their heels.

'Sent back there – to America?' she said.

'That was in '71. Since then, nothing. Only rumours. That he might now be the Invincibles' Number One. That he might have been behind the Phoenix Park killin's. Other things.'

'If he's in America...'

Ettie glanced along the railings, to where the ruffian with the bowler hat was lighting a cheroot.

'How could we know?' said Hatchet-Face. 'Hallions like him. Forged papers. Come and go as they see fit. And seems he swore a promise – in the court. Revenge against the fellas who betrayed him. This could all be coincidence, but...'

'No such thing as coincidence. That's what Neo – my husband – says. Superintendent Wilde, too, as it happens. Do we know what he looks like – this McCafferty?'

From the auction sheds, the auctioneer's voice carried loud and clear, the bid calling on the sheep so fast it was impossible for Ettie to understand.

'Back then – like this,' said Hatchet-Face.

She produced a folded paper, greatly faded but still just legible. *Special Memorandum*, it said. *Metropolitan Police*. A sepia *Wanted!* notice. Beneath the heading, a wood-engraved illustration of a fellow in a broad-brimmed hat, moustache and the merest hint of a goatee beard. Ettie took the poster and read the words.

Captain John McCafferty: age 27, height about 5 feet 8 inches;
dark hair; dark, small sunken eyes, sallow complexion, scowling
visage, served as Captain in General Morgan's Confederate
cavalry. Wounded above the right knee.

'Twenty-seven?' said Ettie, searching for a date when the thing might have been printed. She searched, as well, for anything familiar about the rogue's features but it wasn't even a clear image.

'That was just after the raid, Mrs Palmer – well, the raid that never happened. Before they caught the devil, then let him go again. He'd be – what? Forty-four now. Maybe forty-five.'

'I still don't understand. The river...'

'The Dee, ye mean? Why the Dee? Good question, so it is. Again, coincidence? The fact is, the Fenians, like all fanatics, driven by myths and legends, they are.'

'And the Dee,' said Ettie, recalling tales told both by her father and by Neo, 'is a holy river. Sacred. The name – it means "goddess" to my people.'

The recollection sent a shiver down her spine, conjured up her recurring dream again – Neo drowned in the Dee.

'There's a River Dee where I come from as well, Mrs Palmer. But it also has an older name.'

Hatchet-Face gazed at the jersey cows here in the pens. They were restless, lowing and pushing each other around in the stinking filth, as though they sought some way to flee the future.

'Fine, they are,' she said. 'An' strange, this is.' She smiled ruefully. 'To be tellin' this tale here. For our Dee's famous all over Ireland. An' because o' these lovelies – or beasts like 'em.' She jerked a thumb towards the cows. 'You know the story – the Cattle Raid of Cooley?'

Ettie shook her head.

'Ach, well this cattle raid, it's famous, too. An' caused a fight in the olden times. Right there, at a ford on the Dee. The Chariot Ford, we call it. An' the river became known, back then – in Irish, mind – as *An Níth*.'

She saw the puzzled look on Ettie's face.

'Put simply, Mrs Palmer, it means "combat", or "fight". But like your Welsh tongue, the Erse has many depths. So, to me, I'd understand it as "challenge" – "challenge to combat", maybe. See now, do ye?'

'That if there's a meaning, a message in all this, then it's one meant only for Erse speakers – the men who betrayed McCafferty. And the FitzPatricks, perhaps?'

'An' for me, Mrs Palmer. Ye forgot about me – and the sergeant there, of course.'

She nodded her head towards Bowler Hat.

'Here's what I think, Mrs Palmer. That this McCafferty tracked down Tobin, met him and killed him. But wanted to flush out the other two, took the body across the border into England – so it would hit the newspapers. An' so it did! Then? The FitzPatricks were right, I figure. O'Donnell sees a piece in the papers, goes to Tobin's funeral, and McCafferty follows him back to Saltney. Two down, two to go – well, only one now.'

'One?'

'The main one who blew the whistle – Carr – dead of natural causes. Five years ago. But Carr's three friends, who all gave up details of the scheme, two of them killed and now just...'

'Michael something-or-other?'

'Cutter,' she said. 'Michael Cutter. But how...?'

'Reverend FitzPatrick,' said Ettie. 'He was about to let the fellow's name slip and...'

Ettie caught a movement from the corner of her eye, the gate to one of the pens swinging open just beyond where Bowler Hat still smoked his cheroot. She saw him move to close it again. But as he did so he was greeted by a snort of rage from inside the pen where, previously hidden from their sight behind bales of straw, an enraged bull charged forth. The biggest bull she had ever seen, a demonic shade of yellowish brown, and while its horns might not be enormous, they seemed wickedly sharp.

The bowler-hatted sergeant pushed against the gate just as the bull hit it from the other side. It sent the fellow tumbling backwards.

And with a speed which belied its great bulk, the beast was free, turning its head this way and that, snot and white froth dripping from its nostrils and bellowing, pawing at the stony ground. The sergeant was almost beneath its black front hooves but he was either knocked senseless or had the presence of mind to seem so, lying motionless in the dirt.

The bull span about, crashed its broad skull into the railings of the pen, wild in its fury. It made the iron rods ring like the bells of

St. Giles and all who heard it turned their own heads. There were screams, people running. Running for all they were worth.

From inside her coat, Hatchet-Face drew forth a small revolver. A useless toy, Ettie considered, in the face of such a monster. The bull seemed to think so, as well. It swung its bulk towards them. Or, rather, it swung towards the woman and her small daughter who stood, petrified, between them.

It all happened so fast. Hatchet-Face fired her pistol. The bull went for the mother and child. It lifted the little one on its horns and tossed the infant into the woman's outstretched arms. They both went down, shrieking and bloodied.

Ettie saw – or thought she saw – a man vault over the farther side of the pen. But, by then, the beast had turned its attention in her own direction. Towards herself and Hatchet-Face. It thundered forward. Hatchet-Face raised the revolver once more. She fired. Yet nothing would stop this solid mass of flesh and frenzy.

She heard herself scream, but watched helpless as men in white coats and flat caps came running from the auction sheds. By then, the bull had knocked Hatchet-Face to the ground and pierced her, again and again, with its horns, tossing her about as though she were a rag doll. A blood-soaked rag doll.

Chapter Sixteen

'Your wife was there?' said Viscount Broughton. 'When it happened?'

There had been a brief account in the *Western Mail*.

The unfortunate woman, named as Mrs Elizabeth McBain,
was visiting relatives in Wrexham from her own town of Cavan
in the province of Ulster. An inquest will be held in Belfast.

That was all. Though, at least, it mentioned the mother and child who had also been attacked – and miraculously survived with only minor injuries. And some other fellow, seemingly knocked senseless. Mention, as well, of shots being heard. Yet this must have been unconnected to the incident since Esther insisted she had no recollection of any such thing.

'Indeed,' said Palmer. 'Witnessed the whole tragedy.'

It had terrified him, the idea that she should have been so close to such peril. It terrified him still.

'Terrible accident,' said Jackson. 'Lord yes, terrible, indeed.'

Except, thought Palmer, Ettie had brought back that strange tale of having seen somebody in the creature's pen. But not running to help. Rather, seeming to flee the scene. She was mistaken, surely. There was no doubt the incident had shaken her considerably. And she had entirely broken down yet again when the *Mail*'s account had brought home to her once more the tragedy she'd witnessed. Poor, sweet girl.

'And Doctor – this woman?' said the viscount. 'Beyond salvation?'

Edward Davies seemed justifiably offended.

'I can assure you, sir,' he snapped, 'had she not been, we would hardly be having this conversation.'

A maidservant came to collect the empty soup plates and Palmer asked her to express his appreciation to the cook, for he believed strongly that the efforts of honest working folk should always be properly acknowledged. Besides, the soup – a concoction of celery and Welsh leeks – was delicious.

It was many years since he'd last dined here, in the well-appointed and private front parlour of the Wynnstay Arms Hotel – his Wrexham friends still refusing to call it anything but The Eagles, its former name – though little had changed. Except the reason for him being there – the viscount's personal invitation.

'I must congratulate you, also, sir,' he said to the viscount. 'If the rest of the dinner meets such an exacting standard, I might indeed consider attending in future.'

'You are not committed to a subscription, Mr Palmer?' said Sir Watkin's nephew, son-in-law and heir, young Herbert Watkin Williams-Wynn. Young, but already a captain in the Montgomeryshire Yeomanry.

'If his lordship will forgive me, Captain – and while I am myself passionate about history – a dining club with its partial purpose to commemorate such forgotten politics is perhaps not quite my cup of tea.'

Viscount Broughton had welcomed them here with a speech – a lecture, more accurately. A lecture about how this very room, for almost a century and a half, had been the venue for similar gatherings of diners.

'Herbert's great-great-granduncle,' he had said, beaming a smile at the young fellow. 'Third Baronet. A notable and worthy Jacobite who supported both the Old Pretender and the Young. Raised subscriptions for them both. His Cycle of the White Rose dining club. And it operated, remarkably, from the year 1710 until – well, only a dozen years ago. All that time. And what finer thing to do than invigorate that concept afresh? The concept of a gentlemen's dining club for Wrexham, I mean, naturally.'

But following the lecture, and as the first course was brought, grace having been said, the viscount proposed a toast.

'The Queen!' he had said. And there had been a bowl of water, strewn with white rose petals, placed in the centre of the long table, over which many of them, though not all, had dutifully raised their glasses – wine for the others, water itself for Palmer.

He had looked around at his fellow diners, several of them gazing back at him smugly, and he knew he might have missed something here. Yet, as the subsequent conversation centred so heavily on the allegedly admirable qualities of the long-exiled Stuart dynasty, he began to see, at least, a glimmer of their own zealotry.

'Do you not agree, Mr Palmer,' said the captain, 'that our poor nation has somehow lost its way in the world?'

Palmer thought he had taken, perhaps, a little too much from the wine bottles circulating so freely around the table, and was about to respond when Jackson, the Canadian fellow, cut across him.

'Herbert,' he said 'in all my born days. I've never met a man so intent on causin' me a colic. Politics and dinner make poor companions. Do you know, Mr Palmer, that our young captain here is an aeronaut? Balloon ascents. Should you like to try such a thing, sir?'

Palmer could think of nothing he would like less.

'Are you quite alright, Mr Palmer?' said the viscount. 'Bless my soul, you have turned perfectly pale.'

'Alfred,' said Edward, 'what ails you, old friend?'

'It is nothing,' said Palmer. 'But the very thought caused me to feel suddenly nauseous.' An irrational sense of vertigo, even though he remained firmly seated on his dining chair.

'But does that mean you have no interest in politics, Mr Jackson?' It was the viscount's emaciated cousin, another Morgan, all the way here from St. David's, with an accent to match. A lawyer, with some financial interest in the family's quarrying business, he had already been at pains to remind them of his blood connection with that same David Morgan of Penygraig – hanged, drawn and quartered for his part in Bonnie Prince Charlie's insurrection. 'A man with no interest in politics has no interest in the lifeblood of civilisation.'

'Bless your heart, Mr Morgan,' said Jackson, 'I'm Canadian.'

It seemed to serve as a satisfactory explanation and Morgan had, in any case, now turned his sour gaze upon the captain.

'And you know, do you,' he snarled, 'that this great-great-granduncle of yours betrayed the whole cause? Promised to raise North Wales for the prince, he did. But then...

'Gwilym, my boy!' said the viscount. 'One can hardly blame the distant descendants for the sins…'

He stopped as the door opened. A procession of hotel staff brought silver platters of meat and vegetables and began to serve.

The viscount had welcomed Palmer to the gathering, introducing him as "a gentleman of local substance with a passion, like our own, for the reign of King James the Second." It was far from the truth – for Palmer had only included mention of the *first* King James in the title of his paper on land tenure simply to set his studies within a given context – an important period due to the social changes taking place in that segment of the seventeenth century but not connected to King James the Second at all. Far from it.

'And you, my lord,' said Palmer, having thanked the maidservant yet again – and received an extra slice of meat and a cheeky smile as his rewards, 'how interesting that you chose to name your daughter in honour of the Old Pretender's wife.'

Maria Clementina Sobieska, Polish wife to James the Second's son – in whose name yet more blood had been shed. Another and earlier Jacobite rebellion. 1715. And Palmer's studies had shown him how some of that violence had spilled over even to here, in Wrexham. It seemed that his understanding of the fellow's eccentricity grew with each mouthful of roast beef presently sitting upon his plate.

'Gracious,' said Edward Davies, 'is that true?'

'Indeed,' said the viscount. 'Though I am always reluctant to use the word Pretender. It conjures the concept, in our less enlightened age, of dissembling, of impersonation, don't you think, sir? I prefer the French use of *prétendant*, which so better retains the original sense of a legitimate claimant.'

Further round the table, poor Edisbury the pharmacist wore a permanent troubled frown, as though his fellow-diners might be speaking an entirely unfamiliar tongue. He had, on several occasions, opened his mouth as though to ask for clarity but then, each time, thought better of it, perhaps not wishing to seem the fool.

'Fear naught, James,' Palmer shouted to him. 'I believe we are all on similarly unfamiliar ground. But here, at least,' he smiled, picking up the bowl of sauce from the table, 'we have an old and trusted friend – one which we may always relish.'

His little jest was greeted with several guffaws. Indeed, there could be no mistake. While the recipe was an Edisbury family closely guarded secret, the taste of grapefruit peel and cinnamon alone marked it out as the world-famous Wrexham Sauce, a relish uniquely and universally prized for both its fine flavour and its digestive efficacy.

'Edisbury's sauce is its own reward, gentlemen,' said that red-headed fellow, Mr Steward, from the Broughton Brewery, whose acquittal Edward Davies, in his capacity as chief magistrate, had been unable to prevent. Poor Edward was almost incapable of containing his rage each time he heard the Scotsman's voice. And for Palmer – perhaps for Edward, too – it was impossible to avoid the connection here, for it had been one of Edisbury's bottles which had contained the contaminated yeast with which this entire saga seemed to have begun.

But reward? Palmer flinched at the word. He had decided that this evening he would put the entire puzzle aside. Yet, Lady Olivia's offer. Two hundred pounds? It would set them up nicely, allow him to continue his business for the foreseeable future. Though a reward for what reason?

'Damn that fellow's eyes,' Edward murmured into Palmer's ear. 'And what, in Heaven's name, are we doing here, Alfred?'

'Let us simply enjoy the food,' said Palmer, as one of the servants toured the table yet again with the claret bottles.

Lady Olivia had given an explanation, but he was not certain he believed her. If, as she'd said, this Fenian – the Invincibles' Number One – had, in fact, killed Tobin and then O'Donnell in revenge, why should the FitzPatricks believe themselves to be in danger? By simple association, the reverend had insisted. Truly?

But no, he thought, I must simply try to set aside my fears for Esther.

Might she be called upon to attend the inquest in Belfast? And though only three days had passed, this being Thursday evening, he had expected perhaps some word from Wilde on the matter.

For now, Palmer determined, it was intriguing to observe his lordship's calculations about who might, and who might not, receive further invitations to this White Cycle Dining Club.

Not Sir Robert Cunliffe, he believed. Most definitely not. For that most Liberal of local landowners was presently locked in verbal combat with the lawyer, Gwilym Morgan – pressing the fellow, without success, to at least condemn the terror caused by the Fenians' infernal machines, their bombs, the murder of innocents, even if Morgan himself supported the concept of Irish independence.

'I understand, Mr Morgan,' said Palmer, 'you similarly believe that Wales itself should be independent of England...'

'Scotland, as well, Mr Palmer,' shouted Steward from the farther end of the table. 'Scotland as well.'

'Yet you would, surely,' Palmer pressed on, 'not support the use of bombs against train stations to further *that* cause?'

Morgan mumbled one of those trite answers so frequently favoured by politicians and lawyers alike – which was not, in fact, even closely approximating to the question.

Palmer decided not to waste further breath on the rogue. Instead, he turned again to the young captain, as the servants cleared the table and explained the options for dessert.

'A shame, Captain, that your uncle remains indisposed.'

'He would not have been here, even had he been well, Mr Palmer. Sir Watkin seems to have made it his life's work to distance himself from any mention of our venerable ancestor. He was a great man, sir. A man of vision.'

Palmer confirmed to the maidservant his preference for home-cooked apple pie.

'Perhaps...' he suggested, once she had moved on and he himself had swallowed his amazement at this young man's apparent total lack of gratitude, Sir Watkin having so recently named him as heir. 'Perhaps your venerable ancestor may have been somewhat lacking in vision to support Bonnie Prince Charlie's ill-fated adventure.'

'Ill-fated?' The captain seemed shocked.

'To be honest,' said Palmer, 'in relation to that particular episode in history – truth be told, in relation to many similar episodes – I tend more towards a "plague upon both thy houses" approach. It is always the duped innocent who provide fodder for the cannons of war, is it not? And, usually, in the name of some prince's vanity.'

Now the captain seemed simply disgusted.

'And your earlier question,' Palmer went on before the fellow could respond, 'about our nation losing its way. Is that not frequently because we have chosen the wrong side in disputes within which we should never have become embroiled in the first place?'

It was his own fault, therefore, that he now had to endure a further lecture – about the captain's view that, had Britain acted more decisively in the Sudan, General Gordon would not now be under such deadly threat at Khartoum. Or about the government's misguided approach to Spain – his view that there should have been support for the staunchly Catholic Carlist faction. This was, of course, an issue with which Palmer was intimately knowledgeable, but he refrained from responding, taking solace instead within the depths of his delicious apple pie.

'I must admit,' he said to the Canadian, by way of disentangling himself, 'that the title caused some confusion in my household. Or perhaps you were deliberately practising upon poor Esther, sir. The White Cycle Club?'

Jackson laughed amiably enough, the dark eyes twinkling wickedly.

'I could not contain myself, Mr Palmer. As soon as she mentioned at Dr Davies's that she was fond of cyclin' – too good an opportunity to miss. My pretence that we shared an interest. And shall we see you tomorrow, sir?'

Tomorrow. Good Friday. The Rhos Eisteddfod. Palmer was looking forward to the event. Though, he was unsure whether Ettie would be similarly enthusiastic about making the journey up into the hills. Besides, he rather feared that the fellow who'd accosted him at Farndon, the Irish ruffian with the bowler hat, might make a further appearance there. Indeed, Palmer was surprised he had not seen him recently.

He confirmed that, yes, he hoped to be there – even if he was far from happy about having to endure Jackson's company once more.

'Can't wait!' said the Canadian. 'And isn't there some connection with today's business? Some legend about Welsh Jacobites takin' refuge in this – you know, Mr Palmer, I can never quite get my tongue around the name...'

Palmer pronounced it phonetically. Rhosllanerchrugog.

The Canadian tried and failed to imitate Palmer's lesson.

'Seriously,' said Palmer, 'everybody here just says Rhos for short. *Rhoce...*' he said, rolling the 'R' for all he was worth. 'And yes, the inhabitants tend to favour their nickname for the very reason you've stated. Jackos. But that is plainly not your own connection, Mr Jackson – though, I suppose we could easily adopt the same foreshortening of your own name, if you chose. Mr Jacko Jackson.'

Jackson smiled, nodded his head with an expression of admiration.

'That's a neat suggestion. But my real shared interest? It's said my forebears were first transported to Canada's wild forests from prison hulks, in the wake of the Bold 'Forty-Five.'

Viscount Broughton overheard their conversation, straightened in his chair and twisted one waxed end of his moustache.

'We have forebears who suffered the same fate, Mr Jackson,' he said. 'Friends of my father in the Oxford Movement conducted some research for us. Years ago, of course. Dispatched as indentured slaves to the Colonies. America, of course. But still, I rather admired the Movement's appreciation of King Charles – the First, God rest his soul.'

It was before Palmer's time but somewhere he had read that the Oxford Movement not only viewed the king as a Catholic martyr and campaigned for the Vatican to beatify him – as had occurred with Wrexham's own Richard Gwyn – but also promoted a return, even now, to Catholicism as the state religion for this nation.

It was the turn of the dessert dishes to be removed, for ruby-red *porto* wine to be served. And cheese – both of which Palmer politely declined. He needed to think and think hard. And here came the Scotsman, Steward, trying to force some of the alcohol upon him so that Palmer had to set his hand firmly on top of his glass.

The water, he thought. The water with the white rose petals and that business about raising their glasses all holus-bolus above the bowl like some Masonic ritual. And he gripped Mr Steward by the wrist.

'Am I right in thinking, Mr Steward, that there may still be a Jacobite claimant to the throne of this United Kingdom of Great Britain and Ireland?'

'How could there not be, sir?' the fellow drawled, barely able to remain standing. 'Aye, laddie. Lawful descendants of King James the Third.'

Palmer was about to correct him, then recalled that, for Jacobites, the Old Pretender, James Francis Edward Stuart, had seen himself as James the Third of England and Ireland – and, what? James the Eighth of Scotland? It was all somewhat confusing.

'And this present *prétendant*,' said Palmer, 'he would be...?'

The greatly inebriated Mr Steward offered him a self-congratulatory smile.

'She, Mr Palmer. *She.* Princess Maria Theresa of Bavaria – or, as many see her, our own Queen Mary the Fourth.'

And, of course, Palmer finally saw the penny and picked it up. That toast, at the dinner's start – perhaps it had not been for Her Majesty Queen Victoria at all!

Chapter Seventeen

She feared this place. Not the populous village, because the Welsh-speaking folk of Rhos were generally kindness itself, but the haunting wilderness of the area all around. Something outside her ken. For, though her father, John Francis, God rest his soul, had been raised beyond the mountains of Snowdonia – *Eryri* in their own tongue – Ettie herself had been born and bred in Manchester, where her *tada* had become that smog-smothered town's City Surveyor. She had never known the rugged ridges, pale peaks, mysterious moorlands and haunted hollows of *Yr Wyddfa*. And though these uplands surrounding Wrexham might not possess the same grandeur, the thought of them held the same terrors.

This was another world, entered far below, at the horse tram's terminus, the New Inn in Johnstown. Until then, all had been familiar enough: the short walk from their home and the High Street's corner, where they'd stopped for a cup of tea and a celebratory hot cross bun at Kendrick's. Then along the High Street itself, dropping down Town Hill and over the bridge for the haul up Pen-y-Bryn to catch the tram at the Sun. There was always talk of the service being extended further into town, but even with carriages on rails, no horse would ever haul a fully laden tramcar up those ferocious urban inclines, and the best of braking mechanisms could hardly constrain an excessively precipitous descent. But it was civilisation, all the same. Whereas, beyond the cemetery, beyond the farmlands, beyond Rhostyllen, beyond Johnstown…

'The distance may be minimal in miles…' she murmured to Neo as the packed waggonette made its snail's pace climb from the tram terminus around the tree-shadowed twists and turns and through this Good Friday drizzle.

'Yet, like travelling back through centuries,' he replied.

Her father had regaled her with tales of those Hollow Hills, the dark, secret and sacred places of her bloodline. Dark. Though, today, a darkness to match the secrets within her soul.

Last night, Neo had returned from his strange dinner appointment and he had attempted to lighten her mood with tales of the viscount's absurd and amusing beliefs. He had a theory which he would check as soon as their fine Free Library – now in its new home within the Guildhall – opened again on Tuesday. A theory that all this nonsense about holding their wine glasses above the bowl of water might be a coded way of making the loyal toast to the person those deluded fellows believed should actually be upon the throne, the Jacobite claimant in exile, a monarch "over the water."

Ettie had been surprised such a person even existed. And how convenient for them that this current Pretender, this Princess Maria Theresa of Bavaria, was a woman. For, how more foolish would they have looked making a toast to "The King!" in these years of Victoria's reign. But "The Queen Over the Water"? Clever, he had told her, if somewhat obvious.

Afterwards, they had shared their customary week's end intimacy – earlier than usual this particular week due, she assumed, to the Easter holiday. But in the warmth of its wake, Neo had talked once more of raising a family. It had taken all her power not to weep, yet again – not to succumb to the ache in her belly.

Then, as he had snored in his frequently raucous fashion, she had lain awake half the night contemplating all those other deceptions from which she could not now escape. She knew, of course, that the simple thing would be to tell him the truth on all counts, including her involvement with Hatchet-Face – to whom she could not quite bring herself to give even more substance by thinking of her as Mrs McBain. But, in the way of such things, the simple option may sometimes be the least possible.

'You know, my dear,' Neo said now, as they alighted from the waggonette outside the recently rebuilt red-brick chapel, 'if there is anything more which troubles you…'

She shook her head, and shook open her rain napper as well, making straight for the temporary stalls outside this Calvinist

Methodist Capel Mawr on Brook Street, chosen venue for this year's Rhos Eisteddfod. *Capel Mawr*, the Big Chapel, to distinguish it, of course, from the town's *Capel Fach*, the Small Chapel, which stood just around the corner. But that was simply two, for it was reputed that Rhos boasted more chapels and churches per head of the population – and of every possible denomination – than almost anywhere else in North Wales.

The stalls were selling programmes for the day's events as well as all manner of hand-crafted goods, and the proceeds, announced a large billboard, destined to feed the families of unemployed miners. Forty or fifty pits in this immediate area alone, but these past years had seen collieries and brickyards closed, thousands out of work and left to starve.

'In this age of so-called enlightenment,' Neo raged and spent more than she knew he could easily afford on a pair of beautifully painted clogs.

'No, they are very good,' he insisted, lapsing into his easy *Cymraeg*, as he often did when they were in company of others for whom Welsh was their natural language. And that was Rhos. All those families who had moved here seeking work when the mining industry boomed – families from further west where English had remained a foreign tongue. From *Cambria profundus*, as he liked to call it. 'I have wanted to buy a pair since – well, since…'

They paid for their entrance tickets and took the stairs to the upper gallery, an organ recital in progress below to a packed house.

'I should have liked to be here for the Welsh translations,' he whispered, still in Welsh, and Ettie felt her soul marginally lifted by the wonderful harmonisations echoing around the chapel's pure white interior – a variation upon Charles Wesley's own *Come, Thou long expected Jesus!*

And how she wished that the Second Coming might be this very day – to deliver her from her woes. Though, how might she be judged? Not favourably, she imagined. The deceits which made her struggle with her own place in the world, her failings, somehow made even more acute on this day when the Lord Jesus had been crucified.

After the organ recital, the choral competition, and an outstanding performance by the Rhos United Choir, following which Neo begged leave to slip away, leaving her with the clogs, keen to purchase copies of two papers written by the village's own Mr Hooson, and on sale below: *The English Presbyterian Cause in Rhos*, and *Methodism in Rhos.*

'Back so soon…' she said, for it seemed he had been gone only a moment. Though she bit her lip and started in trepidation as she turned her head and saw that it was not Neo at all, but Superintendent Wilde.

'There's not much time, Mrs Palmer,' he hissed. 'And I need to know.'

'Know what, sir?' she whispered.

'Everything, ma'am.' He spoke quietly as well, behind his hand.

'I already told your constable everything, Superintendent.'

The very same evening. Monday evening.

'No,' said Wilde. 'Everything. That was before I knew who she was. Before my superiors even bothered to tell me. So, each damned detail of what you were doing with that woman.'

She was shocked. Cursing on this most sacred of days she might have expected from a different class of fellow. But for Wilde… She had never seen him so agitated, and it frightened her.

'Woman?'

'No games, Mrs Palmer. I know you for an intelligent lady. And you were at the Monday Market with McBain. I'm guessing you knew fine well she was with the Special Irish Branch long before I did.'

The next choir, down on the temporary stage, the Lodge and Bronygarth, began a spirited rendition of a madrigal, *O Happy Fair.*

Happy? Ettie thought. Fair? How had she come to this?

'There was a man…' she began, more loudly than she'd intended, and a gentleman sitting close to them harrumphed loudly, begged her to have some respect for the choristers. She apologised. Guilt upon guilt.

'Her sergeant, Mrs Palmer.' Hushed tones again. 'Badly injured. Shipped off to Liverpool, I'm told.'

'Not him.' She stupidly wondered whether they'd managed to recover the fellow's bowler hat. 'Another. I did not see clearly, but I think he may have set that beast loose.'

The neighbouring gentleman glowered at her again.

'Better if you start at the beginning, ma'am, don't you think? What were you both doing there at all? And what did she want with you?'

'You can't guess, Superintendent?'

He smiled at her.

'I think so, yes. It would just have been good to hear it from the horse's mouth, so to speak.' He turned his head. 'But I'm guessing that will have to wait for another day.' And he stood.

She followed his gaze, saw Neo making his way back down the gallery's steps towards her. But then Wilde quickly lowered his head again.

'Perhaps one more thing though,' he whispered. 'McBain's revolver?'

'Great Heavens,' said Neo, 'I thought somebody was shooting at us.'

There was a break in the proceedings, food available in a marquee set up on Brook Street – with, once again, any profits destined for the unemployed miners' families. They had shared a pie but were now wandering among the outside stalls again, Neo staring up at the sky where a hot air balloon floated across the April sky and the aeronautical showman – some fellow from Llangollen, it seemed – entertained the crowds by dropping pyrotechnic devices, rockets-sticks and firecrackers: filling the air with flashes of crimson; green sparks; clouds of rainbow smoke.

'And I am by no means certain,' he went on, 'that such a display is quite in keeping with the traditions of Eisteddfod.'

'Not natural, it isn't!'

It was Bethan Thomas, carrying her shoulder sack, bulging so much with copies of *Y Frythones* that it bent her frame even more than usual.

'Another modern obsession, I fear,' Neo replied as he handed over his penny for this month's edition. The newspaper might be produced primarily for women readers but her husband claimed that no study of the Welsh language would be complete without an admiration for its poetry, stories and religious articles. 'And it seems,' he continued, 'no event is complete anymore without, at least, one aeronaut on display.'

They watched as the red and yellow globe was wafted in a generally eastward direction towards Wrexham town itself. But Ettie was thinking of other matters. What *had* she seen, there in the animal pens? Was the woman's death truly more than a tragic accident? And where had Hatchet-Face left her now?

'An' where do folk think it will get them?' Bethan sneered, glowering up at Neo. '*Duw Annwyl*. Flyin', like. All the fault of you *science* men, it is.'

She spoke the word "science" as though it were the eighth deadly sin – one which Pope Gregory the First and Thomas Aquinas had somehow carelessly omitted from the lists.

'I can assure you, Bethan…' Neo began but, as was her custom, she moved on without giving him the chance to respond. It was a game she played with him.

'But saw that policeman, I did,' she said. 'Think he'd have better things to do – today, like. Birkenhead? Not far from here, is it?'

They moved on, Neo now anxious to return to their seats in time for the afternoon's prize awards.

'It *was* strange, don't you think, my dear,' he said, as they strolled arm in arm back inside the chapel, 'that Wilde should have run off the way he did? Though, not because of Birkenhead, I hope.'

The *Western Mail* had devoted three entire columns to the story. Another Fenian conspirator, John Daly, arrested at Birkenhead train station with a whole consignment of illicit dynamite.

'You see, Ettie?' he went on. 'I may have misjudged Lady Olivia, after all.'

'You intend to accept the reward?'

They began to slowly climb the stairs, in the midst of quite a crowd, and it seemed to Ettie that the word "Birkenhead" was on everybody's lips. One could almost taste the fear.

'I can only accept the reward if I am able to apply myself to discovering the whereabouts of this Number One fellow.'

This McCafferty, she thought. And if only she could find a way to tell him this much, at least.

'The alternative?' said Neo, when they finally reached the landing. 'More bombs at more stations. More innocents at risk. It could be us, my dear. It could, so easily, be us.'

'And do you not fear, husband, that your investigation of the puzzle might, itself, put your own life at risk?'

It was another thing she could not escape. Hatchet-face's convincing argument that Neo's only source of protection might have rested with this Special Irish Branch. But now?

'At risk?' he said. 'My dear, how? If I am able to put together any pieces of the puzzle, I would simply convey them to the superintendent. Or perhaps...'

He took her hand as they descended the gallery's steps towards the balcony and their previous seats.

'Perhaps?'

'You remember, Ettie, I mentioned that ruffian in the bowler hat?'

Of course, she remembered.

'Though,' he went on, 'he seems to have lost interest in me, I'm pleased to say.'

She tugged at his arm, stopped him at the lowest step.

'I was so keen for you to accept that work at the outset – analysing the samples for the police. But now, Neo...'

He patted her hand, a gesture of reassurance, and she was forced to sit through all the next two hours of prize-giving – and the reprised winning performance by the Rhos United Choir – contemplating the way she had been dragged into a conspiracy – one in which she now had to accept that Neo would find it impossible not to pursue the truth about McCafferty.

She just desperately wanted to get home, to work this all out. But Neo was engrossed in the session, the astonishing duet by Miss Hughes from Birkenhead and Madame Grieve from Liverpool. *Che soave zeffiretto.*

'That reminds me, my dear,' he whispered. 'Liverpool. The National Eisteddfod there in August. We should go, don't you think? Second city of the Empire. Why, it's said that there one may rub shoulders with all the nationalities of the world. And every creed – even Mahometans.'

She knew he had, in reality, already been there, though it had been a fleeting visit.

'Indeed, we should go, Neo.' She tried to sound positive even though she was beginning to doubt whether they might survive those four months intact. 'But would you mind if I take the air?'

'Sweet girl,' he said. 'Are you quite well?'

She whispered the magic monthly words in his ear.

'Feeling poorly.'

'I see,' he murmured, and patted her hand. But she wanted to hug him – the look of disappointment on his face. How long before she must tell him this also? 'But do you mind if I stay? This is so very good.'

She assured him she would be fine. She assured him she would be back soon. His turn, now, to look after the clogs.

Ettie made her way along the row, apologising as she went, then climbed the steps yet again to the rear of the upper circle. Down the red-carpeted stairs and through the front door, praying for divine guidance outside, under the wonder of the Almighty's mysterious firmament.

But she had scarce set foot outside the doors when she felt a hand upon her shoulder. Not for the first time today, she was startled fair out of her wits, and turned to find Mr Jackson following her through the exit.

'Mr Jackson,' she cried. 'I had no idea.'

'Heavens, Esther,' he said, 'I've been sittin' right across from you both, all this fine livelong afternoon. I thought you'd seen me – and, well, I fear I have now embarrassed myself. I kinda waved, in the expectation…'

He held up his hand and wagged two fingers, a fairly obvious gesture accompanied by a conspiratorial wink of his eye.

'Wait,' she said, finding it hard to believe that she should not have spotted his enormous beard within the audience, 'you were signalling that I should leave?'

'And here you are, dear lady. But now you say you hadn't seen me at all. I am mortified – all my hopes dashed, Esther.'

'Hopes?'

She went to return inside, but he gripped her arm. How dare the fellow? She enjoyed Jackson's company, that was true. And there had been innocent fanciful daydreams. Even, on one occasion, a troublesome nightmare. But – hopes?

'Oh, Esther Palmer, I see what's goin' through your mind. Lordy, sure I do. But that's just gettin' ahead of ourselves, if you don't mind me sayin'. See? I was just hopin' for a word.'

He came a step closer. There was something about the gaslight outside the chapel doors. It seemed to both bathe them each in shadow yet, at the same time, also in a curious sepia glow which, in Jackson's case, lit only certain of his features. Above the beard, the highlighted cheekbones, ears, brow and bridge of his nose, the deep dark eyes – were a perfect duplicate for another image she had seen recently. The *Wanted!* poster shown to her by Hatchet-Face.

Chapter Eighteen

'A theft?' he said. 'But only one item?'

Bethan Thomas slammed a wrinkled and arthritically deformed hand down upon the museum's wooden counter and winced with the pain.

'Good thing, that is – only one. First time, too. An' not in charge now, you're not!'

'But when I *was* in charge, Bethan, it was not entirely unknown for items to mysteriously disappear. You remember? Sadly, something about human nature, this propensity for theft. And all those folk then visiting from out of town. So, now somebody local, I suppose we must assume. A glass?'

It had, in fact, been Palmer's recommendation that Bethan should take up the curator's position when he, himself, was due to return to Manchester eight years earlier. There was not much of the museum left now, but it still occupied the two sides of the Westminster Building's archway, the Argyle Arch, as everybody now named it.

'Remember it, do you – the glass?'

He did. A single Order of the Garter wine goblet. Perhaps the last of what once must have been a complete set. Old. Though why anybody should wish to steal the thing was quite beyond him.

In truth, he had only ventured forth this morning to give Esther some respite. Since their return from Rhos the previous evening, she had been irascible. Something to do with her monthly condition, he decided – or so she had hinted. Something, though not that alone, he knew. His rheumy eyes, his frequent susceptibility to pulmonary infirmities, or simple sniffles, often created the impression that he was somewhat lacking in wits – and perhaps, at times, this was true. But he was no fool – not where Ettie was concerned. They were close, with no secrets between them. At least, not until recently. Yet, since the babe, and since this whole business with Tobin, all had changed.

'Shall I report the theft?' he said, glad to have a further reason to stay away from both his house and his office.

He had left the work behind. Samples of Mr Beecher's patent disinfectant to be tested for the strength of its carbolic acid. The dissolved animal bone manure – the stench itself intolerable – for which the courts required a report by Tuesday in some sort of fraudulent transaction case. And the respective nitrogen, phosphorous, calcium and potassium contents of the Peruvian *guano* sent to him for a second opinion by an importer of Palmer's acquaintance from Liverpool.

And the income from all his present workload hardly sufficient to keep food on the table. It could have been so different had he succeeded in his application to become Denbighshire's second County Analytical Chemist. But he'd been beaten in a vote at the Quarter Sessions last October. Eighteen votes to Palmer's eight, despite considerable lobbying on his behalf by Edward and others. Adding insult to the injury, the position went to a fellow from Chester, indeed. Not even within the county.

All of which made Lady Olivia's offer of the reward just so much more attractive. If only…

'Report?' Bethan smirked. 'To that useless…' But she used the phrase *dim gwerth rhech dafad*, a phrase which always made Palmer wince. Something to do with sheep's flatulence.

'I shall report it to Superintendent Wilde in any case,' he said, for he needed to speak with the policeman anyhow. 'Though, perhaps, without your character reference, Bethan.'

She grinned up at him.

'And the exhibition?' he asked, glancing around at the new paintings. For the museum now regularly served as a venue for such displays of local amateur art – and frequently, as now, the work of Wrexham's apparently numerous lady artists. Oils and watercolours. On canvas, China, and textiles. Needlework samplers and wood carvings, as well.

'Thinking about you, I was,' said Bethan and beckoned him to follow as she hobbled across the passageway to the farther side of the archway, the other half of the museum. She stopped in front of a garish picture. It could so easily have been the Virgin Mary, rising from raging waters, arms outstretched as though to embrace all who looked upon her, a broad golden halo about her reddish locks. But this figure was garbed in emerald green and sapphire blue, vines entwined about her limbs, her eyes blazing brown. It had something of Rosetti or Millais about it.

'Aerfen the goddess?' he said.

'See? The river, like. Told you, I did. About curiosity.'

'It was a fair warning, Bethan. But interesting. This, the way Miss…' He paused to read the name on the small card label once more. 'The way Miss Williams has painted the water…'

The waves, exaggerated, like mountain peaks.

Superintendent Wilde set down the revolver as well as the cleaning rod and its tow pull-through.

'A glass, Mr Palmer – you are serious, sir?'

'I am, Superintendent, yes. But the…' He waved his hand towards the lethal weapon. 'You're expecting you might need that, here in Wrexham?'

Wilde stared around the walls of his office, then invited Palmer to sit.

'Let me see,' he said, and held up a thumb. 'One. We have a man murdered by drowning. Almost certainly a Fenian.' Then the index finger of the same hand. 'Two. A second Fenian, this one with his throat cut at Saltney.' His middle finger. 'Third. An agent of the Special Irish Branch is gored to death…'

Palmer felt as though he had been slammed into a brick wall.

'Wait…' he managed to say.

'Please, Mr Palmer, I should by rights be speaking to your dear lady wife, this morning. Though I needed to first check some facts.'

'The woman,' said Palmer. 'The woman Ettie saw at the St. Patrick's Day parade. The woman you denied even existed?'

'I told you, sir, that if there *was* a woman, you should not interfere with her business.'

'And I did not, Superintendent. I have never even seen this person.'

'But *Mrs* Palmer – what was her connection to McBain? What was she doing with her at the Beast Market?'

'It was nothing but…' he began, then stopped in his tracks.

'You were going to suggest a coincidence?'

Palmer stared down at the crimson leather inlay of Wilde's desk, remembering the report he'd left there the last time he was here, his idiotic conviction that Ettie must simply have imagined the mysterious woman at the Overton Arcade. He shook his head.

'No,' he said, 'not coincidence. Of course, not.'

Wilde still had his hand raised, and now added his ring finger to the other three.

'Four. McBain's sergeant as good as dead, as well.'

'You are losing me, Superintendent. Her sergeant?'

'Devlin. You were acquainted, I think – complained to me he'd accosted you in Farndon, I believe.'

"And immediately there fell from his eyes as it had been scales: and he received sight forthwith."

'You refused to listen when I reported the thing, did you not?' said Palmer.

Finally, the superintendent's little finger.

'And five,' he said, 'the small matter of yet another Fenian, this Daly, just arrested in Birkenhead with enough dynamite to blow up half of Liverpool – or the whole of Wrexham. Chester, maybe. Thirty miles, Mr Palmer. Thirty miles only to here from Birkenhead. So yes, I'm expecting I might need this.'

He picked up the revolver again, opened his desk drawer and brought forth an ochre cardboard box of ammunition with fancy black lettering: *.442 Calibre, Twelve Cartridges.*

'Yesterday,' said Palmer, still trying to make sense of his remaining confusion, 'at the Eisteddfod, you spoke to Esther about all this?'

He pulled the snuffbox from his pocket and took a pinch, while the superintendent slid five of the cartridges slowly into the cylinder. A cautious fellow, Palmer thought, to leave the sixth chamber empty. A safe sixth chamber. Yet, somehow, it punctuated and emphasised the danger. The potential imminence of life-threatening peril. Palmer shivered at the thought – though, he was surprised to find that this felt like a tremor of anticipation as well as trepidation.

But then the office door opened and Wilde's wife entered, to offer tea – and a cheery greeting for Palmer. Martha Jane, he remembered. He would have declined, recollecting the strong brown brew from last time, thick enough that he could have stood the spoon upright in the mug. Yet, there was no refusing her and he finally succumbed to her hospitality.

'You see?' said Wilde when she had gone again. '*That* is the right place for women in the force. Barracks matron. But McBain…'

Palmer determined that the superintendent might not have been so free with this opinion in the face of Mrs Wilde herself. Though, he still had no clear grasp of the role the McBain woman might have played.

'This Mrs McBain,' he said. 'I hate to admit this, though…'

'Your wife, Mr Palmer, she has not…?'

He felt a fool, looked up towards the whitewashed ceiling without answering the silent question. And what did this say about himself and Esther? What was it? An hour – since he'd boasted to himself about their closeness, their lack of secrets? But, at least, Wilde seemed happy to spare his further embarrassment.

'You want to know about the FitzPatricks, I imagine,' said Palmer, by way of trying to salvage some remnant of his dignity.

'No, Mr Palmer, I want to know whether your own analysis of all that's happened so far might possibly match with my own.'

'I believe, Superintendent, that in this case all roads lead to Rome.'

And he summarised, so far as he was able.

Somehow, this leading player for the Fenians' so-called Invincibles, their Number One, this McCafferty as she named him, had emerged from hiding – wherever that may have been – to wreak vengeance on the men who'd betrayed him and his cause all those years before.

One of those men was already dead. But Francis Tobin had settled in Wrexham, eventually working for the Lager Beer Company. He had almost certainly been involved in trying to damage that company's business – the contaminated yeast – but, some way or another, he'd come to McCafferty's attention and been lured to the Pant-y-Golfen spring where he'd been drowned, his body then dumped, some miles away, on the Dee at Farndon.

Wilde had put away the revolver by now and taken up his pipe, tapping the stem against his teeth.

'And we're agreed, are we, Mr Palmer, that this was a deliberate act – the body left at Farndon? England. Attract more newspaper attention?'

'I believe so. The outstanding question, of course...'

'How it got there.'

'Indeed,' Palmer agreed.

'And O'Donnell?'

The second part of Palmer's summary, while the tea arrived. Though Mrs Wilde quickly made her exit again.

O'Donnell had, indeed, seen the newspaper report. Yet simply working for the FitzPatricks? Something more than that, surely? Otherwise, why their own armed camp? Why so keen to offer a reward? But, be that as it may, O'Donnell attended Tobin's funeral and McCafferty was able to follow him from there – later butchered the fellow at Saltney. Or, at least, dumped his blood-drained body there. Again, on the Dee. Why? That, too, was still to be established. But there was some connection with the river he needed to explore further – though he sensibly omitted any mention of the Corpse Dog.

'How many fingers is that, Superintendent?' said Palmer.

'Only two, I'm afraid,' Wilde replied, as he relit his tobacco.

'But your agent – Mrs McBain? And the sergeant – we surely cannot believe this Fenian rogue may have some devilish command of God's creatures that he could engineer their misadventure?'

'Merely an untimely accident, then,' said Wilde, puffing several clouds of irony into the room.

Palmer remembered Esther's insistence that there had been somebody in the pens. The bull's gate opened deliberately.

'Accident in the sense that it could have all turned out very differently. Fortuitous for McCafferty. Arrange for the beast to be released and then let fortune follow?'

And turned out differently? What if it had been the mother and child? What if it had been Esther? And Esther...

'You're thinking, I gather,' he said, 'that McCafferty must, anyway, have known about Mrs McBain and arranged to have her followed. So, her covert activities, no secret at all?'

'Nor, therefore, Mr Palmer, your lady wife's liaison with her – whatever that might have been.'

His dignity destroyed yet again. Indeed, he thought, whatever liaison that might have been. And the terrible, unspoken implication. If McCafferty knew about McBain, he must also know about Esther.

'So,' he said, 'your fifth digit, Superintendent. Daly and the dynamite?'

'I pray God, sir, there's no connection. The past is already written and the future may be a blank page. But a page may still hold only a fixed number of words. It's this way, Mr Palmer. If it had simply been McBain's death, Scotland Yard would have been crawling all over this by now.

'As it is,' said Palmer, 'all eyes are now on Birkenhead – not here?'

Wilde nodded his head, then waved the pipe at him.

'Still, I'm glad we had the chat. And I trust you'll speak with Mrs Palmer? No need for me to do so now, I don't believe. Though I hope I may have contributed something towards her safety. Or your own, sir.'

Palmer was puzzled. What did *that* mean? Yet, his calculating brain had turned full circle, back to the start of the equation. Curiously, as well, to that painting Bethan had shown him in the museum.

'Indeed,' he said, 'I shall speak with Esther. Though I may need to consider one or two matters first. And I wonder, Superintendent, do you still have that *post mortem* photograph of Tobin's tattoo?'

Chapter Nineteen

She had never known Neo so distant and yet, at the same time, so concerned for her safety. Since he'd eventually come home yesterday, she thought – wherever he had been. Certainly, she decided, not just at the museum with Bethan, fussing about some missing piece of glassware.

'I am obliged to be at chapel, Esther. And, just for once, might you not swallow your Baptist beliefs and come with me?'

In truth, she desired nothing more. It was a fair way to Talbot Road and Neo's own chapel. The weather was dry, and she imagined them walking arm in arm as they did on happier days. Arm in arm, and she, whispering all her secrets to him, unburdening her soul, while Neo – in that admirable way he had always possessed – would perfectly understand her predicament, comfort her with warm words, assure her that all would be well, and suggest the perfect solution. Just as she, when the roles were reversed, would do for him.

Yet it was never going to happen. Not this time.

'And you,' she heard herself snapping at him, 'might you not swallow your meaningless Methodism and simply step across Chester Street with me?'

But that would not work either. A word, Jackson had said.

Jackson? Why was she still thinking of him as Jackson, for pity's sake?

A word, and a warning.

'I shall know, Esther,' the wretch had said. 'If you say just one word to Alfred – or anybody else, I shall know. Just as I knew about you and McBain.'

She had believed him. Those eyes. They had still smiled. Though in a way that suggested pure evil.

'It is not possible,' said Neo. 'The lesson. I am responsible for the lesson. Easter Sunday. And I do not want you alone. All this danger. Fenians – that fellow at Birkenhead.'

It seemed the whole town had been infected by the story. Yesterday, at the shops, it had been the word on everybody's lips. Palpable fear. And little did they know that the devil himself was already among them.

'I shall not be alone. I told you already – Mr Jackson is visiting the Sunday School this morning.'

She hoped she had smothered the tremble in her voice.

'And meeting you at Howell's, did you say? Another of his jests?'

She supposed it must be. For Howell's had only recently opened just along the road, on the corner of Holt Street. A bicycle and tricycle depot. Singles and tandems for hire, as well. And there had, indeed, been a stupid grin on the rogue's face when he had suggested a *rendez-vous* there. Cycling. Did they not have a shared interest in cycling?

'And you will come alone, Esther,' Jackson had said. 'For I have eyes everywhere, my dear. I shall know. Believe me, I shall know.'

She had believed him. And where else could she turn? Nowhere.

'Sunday School?' said Neo, with that same coldness in his voice. 'Does he still pursue that nonsense? Socialist Sunday Schools?'

Their last whist party at Alison's house.

'I seem to recall you rather sympathised with his view. An idea shared by Mr Reynolds in London?'

Neo looked up from the table where he was busy with yet another chapter for his new book. He had settled on the title, confirmed now, this *History of the Ancient Tenure of Land in the Marches of North Wales*. And at least he seemed to have given up the idea that its content might be a threat to them. How right he was! A few irate landowners? Compared to the hell which had now descended upon them.

'It sat comfortably with Reynolds's commitment to the Chartists. A secular paradise. But since the movement fizzled, hardly relevant, don't you think? Though, perhaps for the Canadians…'

And so they continued to bicker, through breakfast and beyond, until it was time to leave. Together. They left together – though not arm in arm. A hundred paces along Chester Street towards town, and there on the farther corner of the junction, outside Mr Howell's, was

140

the monster, wearing his double-breasted mustard-coloured overcoat, his right hand entirely hidden beneath that absurd expanse of beard.

'Alfred!' he shouted. 'A fine good mornin' to you, sir. A pleasant Easter Sunday, is it not?'

'You would have been perfectly welcome to join us for breakfast, Mr Jackson,' Neo replied. A terse response – but no more terse than the tone her husband usually reserved for the fellow.

She saw Jackson smile – satisfied, she thought, that he detected no hint of unusual behaviour, no sign that she might have informed upon him, no indication there was anything abnormal for him to worry about. Satisfied that she was under his spell.

Ettie had the feeling that, had he sensed anything amiss, he would have made his escape, like Spring-heeled Jack, leaping prodigiously over the rooftops.

'I have eaten,' he said. 'But I thank you, sir, for your generosity. And for allowing me the pleasure of Mrs Palmer's company. At least, for this brief time.'

Neo sniffed, as though there were something with an unpleasant smell on his moustache.

'Socialist Sunday School?' he said. 'Truly?'

'I rather admire the concept. A very different Ten Commandments were they not? *"Help to bring about the day when all nations shall live fraternally in peace and prosperity."* Is that not a fine ideal? And when I return to Canada, and then Arizona…'

'Where in Canada, sir?' said Ettie. 'Ohio, did you say?'

If looks could kill, she thought, as he stared back at her.

'My dear,' said Neo. 'I fear you are somewhat lost. I believe Mr Jackson is a native of Alberta. Ohio, for its sins, finds itself in the United States. Is that not so, sir?'

She remembered the evening very clearly. At Alison's. Neo had quizzed him endlessly about the Alberta province. The rogue remembered it, as well, she could see, but merely flicked his head to one side and made a clicking noise from the corner of his mouth. Some sort of affirmative expression.

'And when is that to be, Mr Jackson – your journey home to those wide Alberta skies?' Neo pressed him.

'Soon, I fear – my business here almost complete. I have met some interestin' potential investors and learned a great deal from several of the mine owners hereabouts. But now, time to head back – though I'll miss dear Wrexham and all its attractions.'

He leered at her quite openly. However, Neo appeared not to notice. And she wondered what fiendish business he was truly about. Another murder to plan, at the very least.

'Not immediately, then?' Neo couldn't quite mask the regret in his voice. Yet, he bade them farewell politely enough and left them – left without any further word to Esther herself.

'He's annoyed with you,' said Jackson, and he offered her his arm.

She had no intention of obliging him, but the street was busy with people she knew, and Ettie could not be certain whether or not it might create a scene should she refuse him. So, she set her fingers as formally and lightly, as inconsequentially, as she was able upon his raised elbow.

'He fears for my safety,' she replied. 'For all our safeties. Though he can have no idea how close is the risk, can he?' She scowled up at him, afraid, yet refusing to be entirely cowed. She had no doubt that this man was attracted to her, though how much latitude might this provide her?

'For both your sakes, Esther, I hope that's true. Lord, I sure do. But shall we take the air?'

He turned in the same direction Neo had already taken, past the fire brigade's small depot, but only so far as the towering might of the Congregational Chapel, where he swung them into the tree-lined cobblestoned driveway to the Guildhall Square.

'They shall expect to see me in my normal place at chapel,' she protested, but he assured her they would be finished by the time Sunday School was done.

'And what is it you expect of me, Mr Jackson? Or would you prefer Captain John McCafferty?'

'It's all one to me, Esther. And brings us to the point, I guess. He's a smart man, your husband. And *he* might not know who I am, not yet, but how long, until he works it all out?'

'Perhaps you credit him with a skill he does not possess.'

The bells of St. Giles tolled in chaotic disharmony with the town's several other bell towers and steeples. There were folk in the square, couples and families hurrying to their respective places of worship. Some of them knew her, exchanged knowing looks, seeing her in this other man's company, whispering behind their gloved fingers.

'Let me tell you, my dear. I spent a lot of years bein' hunted, one way or another. Many a-time durin' our War Between the States. Then, your police, after the Chester raid. A dozen times since. You know what, Esther? I can *smell* it now – smell when there's somebody on my tail. Smell *who* it is. And I tell you, girl, the hunter I can smell, taste almost – it's your man.'

'That's nonsense,' she said, then found herself also sniffing at the air. Firewood burning and coal smoke, Sunday the only day of the week when those domestic fragrances might overpower the stronger odours of Wrexham's industry.

'Nonsense is it?' he drawled, and pushed her down onto a wooden bench beneath the trees, across from the Guildhall, so recently converted to this new purpose from the old Grammar School buildings. 'Let's talk about Agent Betty McBain, shall we? Let me see. She promised that if you told her everythin' your husband managed to learn, she'd keep him safe. She and her Special Irish Branch. You see how well that turned out, Esther? And you see how easily our everyday lives can turn to tragedy. But why do you think she'd have wasted her time that way? Unless she was able to see the same thing in him that I can smell and taste.'

Ettie relived the scene afresh. The bull's snorting frenzy. The yellow-brown of its ugly bulk, the blackness of its mighty head and the tips of its ivory horns, the dark switch of its tail. The screams of the mother and child. The silent, twisted suffering of Hatchet-Face.

'You killed her husband,' she said, staring at the red brick of the Guildhall's walls.

He moved to sit next to her, winced in pain and rubbed at his knee.

'Old war wound, Captain?'

She hoped it hurt him. A lot.

'It sometimes warns me when a storm is brewing,' he said. 'Or when I feel the noose tightenin' about my neck. But not personally, I didn't – kill her husband, I mean. No.'

'One of your so-called Invincibles, then.'

'It's important you remember it, Esther. We have a long reach. So, what do I expect from you? Simple. The same thing McBain needed done. You pass on to me any intelligence your husband might gather. Then I set him a false trail – and he lives. But if you don't warn me, and he gets much closer...'

Ettie stared up at the branches above just coming into bud.

'You are a killer, sir. Surely, what you intend is that I should betray my husband and you will kill him anyway.'

'I like you, Esther. I like you a lot. In one way it might suit me, was you a widow, but...'

'You seriously think I should even contemplate such a thing?'

The thought of his hands upon her made her want to vomit.

'You'd soon learn to see another side of me. And no children, Esther? Is that Alfred?'

'You disgust me, sir. A killer of innocents?'

'Innocents die all the time. And in your name, Esther. Want to know how many have died so your precious British Empire can sell its opium to Chinamen? How many thousands upon thousands you slaughtered in India after the Mutiny? How many Zulus you killed so you could grab their land and drive the rest to work in your diamond mines?'

'You've forgotten to mention Ireland.'

'Have I? Didn't think I needed to, my dear. You know that story as well as I do. Potato crop fails and there's a famine. It's brutal enough but then London sends out Trevelyan. He's supposed to oversee relief work but he's a good Christian – thinks the famine might just be God's way of punishin' the lazy Irish. And Heaven forbid that anybody should intervene when market forces and an act of God combine. No handouts for the Irish, therefore. No, he forces them into hard labour building roads that go nowhere so they can earn money to buy grain. Only – well, those market forces, they've pushed up the price of grain so nobody but the rich can afford to buy it. A million people starve to death, Esther, while the warehouses sit stuffed with grain. A million innocents…'

He paused, seeing one of Wilde's uniformed constables walking towards them. On patrol. She watched as Jackson – McCafferty – slipped a hand inside his coat, and his eyes narrowed. But the policeman simply saluted and strolled past. Still, she had no doubt that this murderer was armed and deadly.

'So,' she said when the constable was beyond hearing range, 'you kill innocents with bombs at train stations in the name of other innocents. You may mock my faith, Captain, but I believe in the word of the Almighty. *"Do not kill the innocent and righteous, for I will not acquit the wicked."* Would that not be plain to anybody?'

Innocents. She could not help thinking of her sister Lucy. Last year's tragedy in Sunderland.

'Exodus, 23:7, Esther? I learned my scripture too, girl. But nobody is innocent who allows their leaders to govern another man without that other's consent.'

'My father used to quote that same phrase, more or less, to condemn the way we Welsh folk are governed by London. Yet, he never would have employed it to justify murder, sir. Besides, were those words not first spoken by President Lincoln? I am surprised to hear them upon your lips.'

Her father again. She had been no more than a young girl, but he had been appalled at the sixteenth president's murder, read them the accounts and later often shared with them extracts from his many obituaries – finally even acquiring a copy of Lincoln's own *Speeches and Writings*.

'Lincoln was a hypocrite, Esther. He deserved to die, as well.'

'Yes, you must explain that to me.'

'I must?'

'Born in Ohio, were you not?'

'I was.'

'An anti-slavery state? I sometimes confuse the history of your civil war, Captain, I fear. Yet, you ended up fighting for the Confederacy.'

'I was in the south when it all started, Esther. You think everybody gets to pick sides in a war like that? When there's war, you just get sucked into the side where you happen to be.'

'To fight without conviction, then? But born in Ohio – and before the famine in Ireland, I suppose. You speak of it as though it gives you a cause for your mayhem and murder.'

'Born in Ohio makes me no less Irish, Esther. I chose a cause. Irish independence. It's in my blood. And I seek only justice for those who've been so wrongly killed in its pursuit.'

'I understand revenge, Captain – though no decent Christian would condone such a thing. I suppose I must acknowledge the fact that, at times, those crazed by the need to avenge their own innocents might murder other innocents in their name. But that makes it no less a sin. No less barbaric. And you have no such excuse, sir. None.'

'Do I not, ma'am? Do I not?'

'Or do you mean those so-called Manchester Martyrs?'

He eased himself to his feet, rubbing at the knee again.

'Well, this is pleasant, Mrs Palmer, but I think we both need to be about our business. My own's nearly done here. In Wrexham, at least. Next few days and I'll be gone. But I won't be gone far, Esther. So just you remember, if your husband finds out anythin' I need to know about, you send me a message. Just say it's for Mr Jackson. Leave it at the King's Head in Chester. They'll get it to me. But if I smell him still on my trail, girl – he dies, and you die, too.'

She had felt the storm brewing. All the way through their meal and the afternoon's weekly letter-writing hours.

It had been hard to concentrate, but Ettie had tried to distract herself within these many pages to her sister Lucy, thirty now. She should, of course, have stayed with them here in Wrexham but the offer of the post as a governess in Sunderland had been too good to miss. Then the disaster at Victoria Hall last summer had claimed the lives of two of the children in her charge, the little girl, just three years old, and the boy, Jonathon, fourteen, the apple of Lucy's eye. Only a couple of the almost two hundred innocents crushed to death in that terrible tragedy. The family, naturally, was damaged beyond comprehension, their surviving three infants riven by dark emotions. But poor Lucy. How could anybody be expected to deal with such burdens?

'Send her my love,' Neo called to her from his own writing slope.

It would have been more usual for him to find some comforting piece of scripture that she should include by way of closing, but today just those four short words.

'And as soon as I finish this note to John,' he said, 'I think we should commence our walk a little earlier than normal. There are matters to discuss, Esther.'

Indeed, there were.

'Yes,' she said, simply. 'Perhaps. And send John my love also.'

Her husband's younger brother, John Neobard Palmer – like her husband, retaining the mother's maiden within their own – still in Thetford and now a well-established Methodist preacher. A bachelor. Had he not been, she wondered, would some woman have called him Neo as well? As she had done with Alfred? She felt a tear well up in her eye and drip onto Lucy's letter. Just too many raw sentiments. The grief of her sister's situation. The lost babe. The web of lies in which she found herself entangled. Her love for the husband she wanted so desperately to protect.

'And to your father,' she said. 'Grandmama Jemima, as well.'

Old Jemima Neobard, matriarch of the family. Ninety now. An enviable target of longevity – and one to which Ettie felt she could not herself aspire, not with this devil McCafferty casting such an evil shadow upon them both.

He grunted some inaudible response.

'Though, to be honest, Neo,' she said, 'I should greatly prefer that we discuss those matters here, at our own hearth. Our walks upon Acton Hill are too precious to spoil with whatever troubles our affections.'

She watched him carefully set down his pen, draw a deep breath and exhale an impatient sigh before turning to her.

'Very well,' he said, 'then perhaps we should begin with an explanation. About your involvement with Mrs McBain, this agent for the Special Irish Branch – and how it could be that you never saw fit to share the information with your husband.'

Chapter Twenty

He had lain awake for much of the night, convinced there must be more to Ettie's story, though not wanting to believe she was still keeping things from him. But he'd decided he must let it pass – simply be satisfied with the dear girl's insistence she'd been trying to protect him. Yet, here they were. The Annual Pleasure Fair and Edmond's Menagerie in town. Surely, for today at least, they could set aside their troubles and enjoy the festivities. In any case, the McBain woman was dead in that terrible accident, was she not? Let sleeping dogs lie. Indeed, he would – and leave the investigation of Fenians to Superintendent Wilde.

'I merely remain surprised, my dear,' he said to Esther, upon his arm once more and an uneasy truce brokered between them, 'that you should have set such store by her tale. That my life should be at risk from this McCafferty?'

Truth be told, he remained somewhat touched by the depth of her fear on his behalf – angered, yes, that she had not shared the thing with him, but touched, all the same. Yet, she plainly chose not to reopen the wound – not directly, anyhow.

'So different today,' she murmured instead, 'from last Monday.'

Palmer followed her gaze around the Beast Market.

Dydd Llyn Pawb, he thought. Everybody's Monday – Wrexham's traditional Easter Monday celebration. Though, he had never known one quite so dull.

'I wonder,' said Palmer, patting her gloved hand, 'whether the woman's spirit has entirely departed the place.'

The sky was overcast. Some almost imperceptible sense of gloom. And everything about the entertainment seemed destined to draw them back into the same equally depressing atmosphere.

The Waxwork Exhibition, for example, contained nothing but the ill-fashioned forms of the notorious: Burke and Hare; Palmer the Poisoner – no relation, thank goodness; the Australian outlaw, Ned Kelly, complete with iron helmet; the evil female Chinese pirate, Ching Shih; and the villain responsible for the Black Hole of Calcutta, the Nawab of Bengal.

The Peep Show was dominated by a penny-slot automaton cabinet displaying the protracted hanging of Mary Ann Cotton, the child killer, while the noxious nursery rhyme played from a scratchy polyphon disk somewhere within its depths.

Mary Ann Cotton – she's dead and she's rotten.

The Ghost Show was ghastly. The boxing booth bloody. The shooting galleries grim and strident. Even the itinerant photographers seemed able only to produce images so out of focus that they also resembled phantoms.

'It is strange, indeed,' said Esther, 'to still feel her presence here.'

Ahead of them, a small crowd had gathered to observe two youngsters being bandaged outside the small medical tent erected for precisely such a purpose by the sawbones and his orderlies from the Denbighshire Militia, in town today to support the Constabulary and maintain the peace. Nearby, two policemen were interrogating the owner of the swing-boat which had collapsed and caused the injuries.

In the midst of the crowd was the Canadian, Jackson, apparently offering advice to the medical team.

'The nerve of the fellow,' said Palmer. 'And how did he fare with the Sunday School? Did the experience inspire him, d'you think?'

'I have no idea, Neo,' she replied – a little sharply, he thought. 'I simply left him there to his own devices.'

'So many children here,' he observed, watching a whole bunch of them – far too many for their own safety, he decided – spinning wildly, screaming with mixed joy and trepidation, upon a roundabout. 'But I keep meaning to ask him – Jackson, I mean – about his knowledge of the Fenians.'

He felt Esther stiffen at his side, looked down to see fear upon her face.

'I'm sorry, my dear,' he said. 'These murders. This business with the McBain woman. Dynamite in Birkenhead. All the rest of it. A little too close to home, is it not? But I intended only to discover whether the fellow might have been at all affected – when those devils invaded his homeland. Not Alberta, I know, but still...'

Less than twenty years earlier. The immediate aftermath of the War Between the States. Arms and uniforms a-plenty available to the raiders. And what had the battle been named? Ridgeway? Yes, he was certain. An army of seven hundred Irish Republican soldiers had invaded across the American border into Canada – and been confronted by a somewhat superior force of Canadian militiamen. The Fenians victorious as well. These and other raids only stemmed when the British and Canadians sent in reinforcements.

'Had you not determined to leave the investigation to the superintendent, Neo?'

'This is no more than idle curiosity, Esther.'

'I had hoped,' she whispered, 'we might simply enjoy the evening's entertainment, for whatever it may be worth.'

'Yes. Of course, yes.'

Well, he would wait until he had a moment of privacy with the fellow – before Jackson departed Wrexham, naturally. Soon, then. Or so Palmer hoped. But, at least, Esther seemed to have lost interest in the man.

They wandered around the Pedlar's Market for a while, remarking upon the thousands here today, apparently with money to throw away on every imaginable useless item of bric-a-brac, flotsam and jetsam.

'So many of these beardless boys,' he remarked. 'Chappies with cheap cigars. And the girls on their arms...'

'Please, do not tell me again, Neo,' she laughed – and he was pleased to hear it, 'that they all dress like strumpets in this day and age. Were we ourselves not once young like them?'

'Once, yes. But not like them. Raucous and irreverent. Lacking in good manners.'

But he instantly experienced guilt. Once young? For Heaven's sake, Ettie was still two years shy of thirty. Was he responsible for making her old before her time? He studied her face, relieved to see that, despite the frown she now so frequently wore, the young girl who had so smitten him still remained. The dark eyes seemingly spaced just a touch too wide apart, the raised eyebrows giving her that permanent expression of astonishment, the sharp nose and pursed lips. He hated to admit it, but his own sallow skin, his bloodhound's eyes and his sparse beard must make him seem ancient by comparison.

'And, my dear,' he said, 'I have not seen you in that walking dress for more time than I care to remember. It so becomes you. Indeed, it does.'

All beige silk and wool trim, a smart matching bonnet. She made some comment about needing to economise, about how she had carried out some modest repairs, more *à la mode*.

'But I should not wish to miss the Menagerie,' she told him. 'Is it time?'

He consulted his pocket watch.

'Indeed, it is!' he said, and led her through the merrymakers towards the huge twin blue and white striped circus tents set up in the farthest angle of these wedge-shaped grounds towards Farndon Street. They queued to pay their entrance fee, Palmer grumbling that they should be forced to pay two shillings each as Tradespeople and Gentry.

'I do not understand it,' he said. 'Are we not also Labouring People?'

The price list made it plain that Labouring People would only be charged one shilling apiece, rather than two.

'And if only we had an unwanted horse,' Ettie sighed. A pantomime sigh. A painted board invited those with horses no longer fit to work to contact Mr Edmond himself, for he would pay good, honest prices that such beasts might be slaughtered to provide fresh meat for his carnivorous collection.

A second sign announced that, as part of tonight's performance, Sargano the Lion Hunter would perform prodigious deeds of daring.

'You remember, my dear, that night when Hancock put his head inside the lion's mouth?'

Again, eight years earlier. Hancock, a journalist for the *Advertiser*, had been the willing volunteer from the audience and had lived to tell the tale.

'Where is he now?' she said. 'Birmingham?'

So, he believed, yes. But now they were through the turnstile – the entrance fashioned like some red-lacquered oriental temple

– inside the first tent where the wheeled cages had been arranged around the perimeter so they could be viewed and admired before the performance itself. A wondrous collection of snakes and other large reptiles, antelopes, camels, elephants – these had paraded through the town earlier in the day – hyenas, bears, leopards and, of course, Sargano's lions. And the equally wondrous collection of feral essences which accompanied them.

In the centre of the space, a brass band was playing Rossini's Overture to *Tancredi*. The big bass drum announced that they belonged to the Rossett Church Choir.

'They are good, aren't they?' said Edward Davies, coming to join them, Alison upon his arm and, just behind them, James Edisbury the pharmacist, with his own wife, Minnie. They all exchanged cordial greetings.

'Well,' Edisbury smiled, 'this promises to be more entertaining than the viscount's White Cycle Dining Club.'

'It was interesting enough,' said Palmer, 'though I suspect none of us will either be invited again or would accept even should that unlikely thing occur.'

'That much is certain,' Edward laughed. 'Absolutely certain.

'Death and taxes?' It was Jackson. He had come up behind them unnoticed.

Without Palmer realising, Ettie had slipped from his side and was standing close to Alison, staring intently at the bandsmen, while Jackson seemed to be struggling not to stare at Ettie. There was an awkward silence. Not a word from anybody.

Palmer broke the silence by reaching inside his coat and his jacket's inner pocket. He produced the now somewhat crumpled photograph he had borrowed from Wilde on Saturday.

'As it happens, Mr Jackson,' he said, 'we were talking about the viscount's charming *soirée* at the Wynnstay. I think, sir, you may just have been more familiar with the eccentricities than we newcomers.'

'The Jacobite toast, you mean?' said Jackson.

'Indeed, the toast. And Edward, you may also be interested in this.' Palmer showed the photograph to the doctor. 'You remember?'

Edward Davies took the picture and then recoiled, held it close to his chest and looked around quickly at the three women.

'Alfred,' he said, 'for pity's sake...'

'May I?' said Jackson, but hesitantly, plainly uncertain about what the photograph might show.

'Ladies, you must forgive me.' Palmer took the picture back from his friend and passed it to Jackson. 'Perhaps not for those of a delicate disposition. Though it is no more than a *post mortem* image of the tattoo from the arm of the fellow Tobin – the poor deceased fellow found at Farndon.' He turned to Jackson. 'Do you see, sir?'

'See, Mr Palmer?'

Palmer had the distinct impression the fellow sniffed at him.

'Yes,' he said. 'You see – here? Plainly a crown, is it not?'

'Without doubt. A crown, yes.'

'But these, below the crown. I had taken those for mountain peaks.' He turned to Edward Davies. 'We both did, I believe, Edward?'

The doctor nodded his head in agreement.

'May I see?' said James Edisbury, and moved to look over Jackson's shoulder. 'Mountains,' he said. 'Indubitably.'

'But might they not equally be the crests of waves?' said Palmer.

Jackson's teeth showed pearly white within the expanse of his great beard.

'The toast,' he smiled. 'You're an astute fellow, Alfred Palmer. I always knew it.'

Palmer had the distinct impression, however, that he directed the compliment rather towards Esther than himself.

'The bowl of water upon the table,' he said. 'The glasses raised above it.'

'Indeed,' said Jackson. 'The viscount was kind enough to share the secret with me. A toast to the king – or queen, in this case – *over the water*. So, you think this tattoo...'

'What in Heaven's name,' said Edward Davies, 'is this all about, Alfred?'

'No more,' Palmer replied, 'than another small piece in the puzzle. Though, to be fair, it is a puzzle I shall now place firmly in the hands of Superintendent Wilde. But it must be plain, must it not? That the poor victim, Francis Tobin, may have been both Fenian *and* Jacobite.'

He was pleased with himself, looked to Ettie, hoping that she might concur with his conclusion, perhaps even be amused by his acuity, while also being pleased that he'd be leaving all this to Wilde – although there was still the small matter of Lady Olivia FitzPatrick's reward to consider. But he was shocked to find that she was not paying him any regards whatsoever – instead, staring intently at Jackson. And his heart sank.

Chapter Twenty-One

'No, Neo,' she tried to reassure him. 'It was a masterful conclusion. Simply that, in the very moment when you made the revelation, I was trying to recall something Mr Jackson mentioned in passing yesterday.'

It was difficult to have the conversation, for they were still in company with Edward and Alison, as well as the Edisburys.

'Something?'

Yes, she thought. The killer's assertion that he'd soon be gone, his business nearly done. But only his business in Wrexham, and that he would not be gone far. Chester? Why Chester?

'Only that he will be gone within a few days. I think we shall not miss the fellow, my dear. Neither of us.'

She stressed these final three words – perhaps more strongly than she'd intended.

'Truly?' he said.

She forced a smile as they made their way towards the crowd around the lions' cage, holding the small silver tussie-mussie to her nose. It was a well-known fact that diseases bred within bad smells and she had rarely experienced any as bad as these. But her real fear was for Neo. She had seen the way Jackson – McCafferty – scrutinised him, and it terrified her.

The band had now moved on to a rousing medley of popular marching songs, *Men of Harlech* and other obvious choices, and Ettie began to conceive a plan. Only the beginnings of a plan, but...

There was a shout. A shout of alarm.

The crowd around the cage parted, and there was an old fellow in a white shirt, sleeves rolled up to the elbows, a two-pronged pitchfork, a pikel loaded with a small bale of straw, in one hand, while the other

– well, the other arm seemed to be reaching into the cage itself. At shoulder height, of course, for the carriage cage was raised from the ground by its wheels. Beyond the man, the biggest lion she had ever seen, its mane and much if its body, black as pitch.

'Christ, help me!' the man yelled. An Irish accent? Almost certainly.

The crowd parted still further.

'Heaven help us,' said Edward Davies. 'That creature has the fellow's hand.'

There were screams from the spectators now, and mothers dragging their children away from the scene.

'Go no closer,' shouted James Edisbury, holding his arm in front of Minnie and Alison.

'Nor you, Esther,' Neo said to her. 'You must not...'

But she had already broken free of him.

'Did you see?' she heard another woman gasp. 'The fool reached in to scratch the creature's nose, and...'

'He did?' said the man at her side. 'I could have sworn I saw that bearded fellow lean against him and...'

Ettie did not hear the rest for the renewed screams of the onlookers, though she could see now. It had the keeper's fingers gripped in its fangs, traces of glistening blood running down into the dark beard beneath its chin. The beast made no noise, though the fellow himself whimpered with fear.

It seemed to her that he was, all the same, trying desperately not to pull away, to remain calm and still, hoping the lion would, perhaps, simply release him again.

He was wrong. Perhaps it was the screams, perhaps the band's symbols clashing behind her – for the bandsmen must still be oblivious to the unfolding horror – but the lion suddenly started, lifted itself from its crouching position and lifted one of its huge paws, claws extended, as though to slash the poor fellow's arm. Yet, it did not do so. Rather, it snapped sideways with its jaws. So fast. Oh, so very fast.

And such a bite that it entirely severed the hand at the wrist. Still, the lion retained its grip on the fellow's forearm. She watched the hand fall. It bounced upon the cage's wooden, ordure-smeared planks.

The keeper's howl of pain was pitiful, and Ettie felt the bile rise in her gorge, turned away as the bandsmen's instruments fell silent, one by one, in discordant terminal notes.

'My dear,' said Neo, back at her side. 'Come away, my dear.'

'There must be something…' she sobbed, and looked over her shoulder, saw Edward with Mr Edisbury running forward.

But she saw McCafferty, as well. She'd not noticed him before. Yet he was there now, already alongside the cage.

The pikel had fallen to the floor at the keeper's side, and McCafferty stooped to retrieve it, shouting for people to remain composed, collected. Then he pushed the twin forks through the bars of the cage and stabbed at the beast.

'No!' she heard Edward Davies yell. 'That will only…'

The lion spoke for the first time. Neither growl nor roar. But a deep coughing noise from somewhere within its belly.

As the tines pierced its flank and drew yet more blood, it snapped forward yet again, swallowing the remaining arm up to the elbow, before raking its fangs back down towards the severed wrist.

Ettie saw bone and purple sinew and crimson gore. She spun away and was sick upon the ground.

She was aware of Neo's arms about her but little else, the noise of it all echoing in her head and the whole world spinning. Spinning fast. She did not quite lose consciousness, but almost. There were women – and, indeed, one man, poor Mr Edisbury – on the floor, fainted quite away.

Beyond them, the lion had its victim by the upper arm, though he too now seemed entirely and mercifully senseless. It played with the fellow, raising the limp body up and down, up and down, as though he were some inconsequential plaything.

Up and down – until the arm came away entirely.

The keeper fell to earth, and the lion settled to gnawing upon its prize.

Edward, however, was at the man's side, ripping away the keeper's shirt with powerful surgeon's hands. James Edisbury crawled towards them, shaking his head to clear it.

'I must help them,' said Neo. 'Shall you…?'

She looked up into his ghostly white face.

'I shall be fine, Neo,' she whispered. 'Go!'

She waved him away, just vaguely aware of Edward stripping off his own best tweed jacket and balling it against the frightful wound, while Edisbury applied strips of the linen shirt to bind it tightly into place. There was blood everywhere.

'For God's sake,' she heard Edward shout, 'somebody get a cab here. Fast!'

'I'll go,' she cried, turning towards Alison and Minnie. 'I shall go!'

She would fetch a cab, certainly, she hoped. But she would also pursue McCafferty – for he had now miraculously vanished from the scene.

She would have run towards town but remembered the Militia medical tent just in time. And did they not have an ambulance cart with them? She was certain she'd seen one.

'They need to get to the infirmary – and fast,' she cried as the sawbones raced for the Menagerie and the orderlies hitched up the covered cart with its red cross.

And now, she thought, where has McCafferty gone? She remembered that snatch of conversation she'd overheard – the fellow who thought he'd seen somebody press the keeper against the bars of the cage. Could it be? Though, as she gazed about, seeking any sign of the wretch, she heard fresh cries of alarm.

It was a moment or two before the shouts took shape.

"A lion is loose! A lion is loose!"

All through the Pleasure Fair and its attractions, all through the Beast Market. She imagined for a moment some great herd of antelope out upon the wild plains of Africa, one of their number raising an alarm and every head turned as one towards the predatory danger. A single moment of stillness. Then, stampede.

"Lions on the loose! All the lions are loose!"

'They cannot be loose,' she yelled. 'I was there only minutes ago. It's not…'

There were too few such voices of reason. Even members of the Denbighshire Militia, calling for order, were ignored.

She glanced back at the oriental entrance to the circus tent and saw it collapse as the crowd poured forth, falling over the lacquered frames and each other – and she could not help but think of that disaster in Sunderland.

Pure panic, stalls knocked down by the press of people – people clambering over everything in sight. Screeching women and their children, the very old and the very young. The weak, the crippled, the exhausted, all went down and were trampled upon. One of Wilde's constables was almost knocked to the ground in his efforts to turn back the tide.

"The lions are loose! Run for your lives!"

She found herself carried along by the flood, fighting to keep her footing as she was swept towards Charles Street.

Ettie passed houses where folk hammered frantically on strangers' doors seeking sanctuary, and shops whose proprietors were busy pulling down shutters.

On Charles Street itself, a mixed unit of police and red-uniformed militiamen pushed their way in the opposite direction, again calling in vain for order. But at the farther end of Charles Street, where the flood flowed out into High Street, she managed to disentangle herself, swinging right, around the corner into Chester Street. There she took breath, panting, tired beyond belief, her back against the wall of the Feathers. And there he was, a dozen yards away and smiling broadly.

'Changed your mind, Esther?' he laughed, and strolled towards her. 'Coming with me, after all?'

'You made that happen,' she said, standing her ground. 'That man...'

'Cutter,' he said, his face so close to her own she could smell his breath. 'Michael Cutter. Or so he calls himself now. I knew he was with the Menagerie – could have took him anywhere. But when I found out they were comin' to Wrexham – just too good to miss.'

She turned her head towards the corner, where foolish folk were still pushing and jostling each other, shouting and screaming.

"Lions are loose!"

'But the lion...' she said.

'I had plans for Cutter later – with this...' He drew from his pocket a spring-blade knife and pressed the button to release its wicked stiletto, pressing the cold steel close to her throat. But still she held his gaze, terrified, though refusing to give him the satisfaction of seeing it. 'This,' he whispered, 'and the river. But there I was, alongside him, saw him reach in to scratch that creature's nose. Can you believe it, Esther?'

'I believe it, sir. You pressed him against the bars so he could not pull back his arm.'

He smiled at her and flicked the knife's blade closed again as customers began to emerge from the door of the Feathers to see what all the fuss was about.

'The last of them,' he said, taking a step backwards. 'All the traitors, Esther. But that husband of your'n. He knows, girl. He might not *know* he knows – not yet. Soon, though.'

'You'll kill him too, Captain?'

'If he gets just one step closer – yes, you can bet your sweet life I'll kill him. And who's to stop me? You, Esther Palmer?'

Yes, she thought. Me, Captain McCafferty.

Chapter Twenty-Two

Life, Palmer decided, was wasted upon whist. Rather, they would not allow him to play anymore. It was not simply that he and Ettie could now read each other's hands to perfection. Nor was it the other tricks they each employed to *win* tricks. No, it was more the uncanny way his brain could read the flow of cards itself, as though some mathematical formula instructed him that, when the cards were shuffled between each game, there remained only a fixed number of permutations to dictate how the cards would be dealt – and as soon as the first hand was played, the first trick taken, he could calculate with remarkable accuracy the precise remaining boards held by each player around the table.

His place at the green baize this evening, anyway, had been taken by Ned Owen, only arrived from London a couple of hours earlier and hardly had time to draw breath before they'd dragged him off here, to Plas Darland, and Alison's usual Friday hospitality – though, tonight, only the five of them.

'So,' said Ned, as he dealt the next hand, 'it's all been happening in Wrexham. And the poor fellow died.'

'Cutter,' Palmer told him from the leather armchair next to the fireplace, his copy of today's *Advertiser* spread like a blanket across his knee. 'Originally from Dublin, it seems. Been with the Menagerie ten years.'

'Must we?' Ettie snapped at him.

The whole affair had taken its toll upon her, and little wonder. He'd warned her to stay away but the stubborn girl must have seen everything. The horror of it all. Though, four days gone by, and she refused to even acknowledge her part in fetching the ambulance. Not that it had done any good, in the end.

'You must forgive me, of course,' said Ned in that tone which let Palmer know some amused thought was shaping in his friend's sometimes inappropriate head. 'But – Cutter? Really? Considering his fate...'

'We couldn't save him, sadly,' said Edward Davies. 'Two hours upon the operating table, and then all those hours dealing with the injuries from the panic...'

'Edward, please!' Alison murmured, and Palmer saw her glance in Ettie's direction, concern upon her face.

'Yes, quite,' said her husband, more loudly than was necessary. There was a moment's silence as they each recalled the shame of that day, the whole town – or so it had seemed – run amok in fear that the lions might be loose. Incredible, Palmer thought, that so many could be so easily beguiled.

'Not what we're here for,' said Edward, at last. 'And hearts are trumps,' he declared, as Ned turned the pack's final card face up on the table.

From the armchair, Palmer could see Ettie's hand perfectly, as she arranged the fan of cards to her best advantage. He could almost hear the calculations she would be making. Still, it troubled him that her fingers trembled so. He had hoped this pleasant company would help to take her mind off the tragedy, but it seemed there was no way to escape it.

'Michael Cutter,' said Edward. 'And if that fool Jackson had not prodded the beast with the pikel...'

'I'm sure,' said Alison, taking the first trick, 'he can only have intended to chase the creature away.'

'And he has gone, you say?' Ned asked. 'No longer your neighbour. Oh, and that reminds me, Alfred...'

There was a knock on the library door, Alison's young maidservant asking what time she should serve supper.

'Yes, gone,' Edward remarked. 'Though Blanche – Madame Morrel – says they saw little of the fellow. Always up at the ironworks. Or working on designs of some sort.'

'Designs?' said Ettie, and Palmer was shocked to see her play entirely the wrong card. Your two of clubs, he thought. Why did you not play the two of clubs?

'Quite the draughtsman, she says,' Alison told her, having dismissed the serving girl. 'Some new industrial scheme.'

'You have a fine house here, Alison,' said Ned, but he was frowning at Esther. And yes, thought Palmer, Ned knows she's given the game away as well.

'My father built it.' Alison smiled. 'A wedding present. Both houses, of course. He'd hoped my sister would move in next door, but she had other plans. Still, the Morrels are good neighbours.'

And not only the house for a wedding present, Palmer knew. But William Low had built the whole of his Westminster Building so the rents would provide her dowry. Yet, he was thinking also of the Irishman, Cutter. Something niggling in his brain. Michael Cutter. Michael...

'Do you miss him, Esther?' Ned's frown had disappeared as he took the next trick, his confidence returning. And yes, thought Palmer, studying his wife's remaining cards. Still *just* possible!

'Miss him?'

If Ned had slapped her across the face her reaction could hardly have been so vexed.

'The Canadian,' he smiled. 'I just meant – well, Alfred said he was sweet on you. But look, I was only teasing.'

'Might we not simply concentrate on the game, Ned?'

Her reply was like iced water thrown upon a flame.

'Of course.' Ned was contrite. 'My apologies. But Alfred, you must remind me – oh, never mind, it will keep until later.'

Palmer decided it was probably about the book. For they had come to something of an *impasse*. A technical difficulty about how they should present details of the survey for the Lordship of Bromfield and Yale undertaken as early as 1391, to which they had found many references, though for which the Public Records Office could not produce the original. Ned was already talking about the possibility they might need to produce a second edition in the future, should the document eventually come to light.

'And the Lager Beer Company,' said Ned, plainly deciding this would put him on safer ground. 'No more poisoned yeast?'

'As you once remarked, Ned,' Palmer replied, determining to steal Ned's inevitable thunder, 'it did, indeed, prove to be the yeast of our problems.'

There were groans from Alison and Edward. Though, nothing from Esther, except the loud and irritated slap as she laid down her queen of diamonds.

'Stole my jest!' Ned cried. 'You are a scallawag, Alfred. A knave, sir.'

Palmer was pleased with himself. He could hold his own in conversations about most subjects, but he considered himself rather a dull fellow when it came to wit and *répartie*. A rare thing, for him to be amusing – even though the *bon mot* may not have been his own.

'But they are in trouble, all the same,' said Edward. 'Is it not in today's paper, Alfred? Having to reduce the capital of the company? Reduced share values. And they say that, if the business were to be put on the market today, there'd be a loss of at least twenty thousand pounds.'

He passed the cards to Esther to be shuffled, and Palmer heard that pitch to her voice as she tried to get back into the conversation, to overcome her dark humour.

'They are likely to have a strike on their hands, as well,' she said. 'Are they not? This question of the allowance?'

'Allowance?' said Ned, and he flicked the marker on the scoring board for another trick taken.

'The demon drink, as usual,' Edward replied. For here they were, all five of them for temperance. 'All brewery workers receive their daily allowance of beer, of course. And the Lager Beer Company, no exception. Like all the other breweries in town, their workers are entitled to eighteen pints each day.'

They'd had the conversation before. At least, they all acknowledged that eighteen pints of lager were an improvement on eighteen pints of other stronger beers and ales. All things were relative, of course.

'But now,' said Palmer, 'some trouble-maker has alerted the Lager Beer Company workers to the fact that, in the German and Bavarian breweries, their allowance is no less than twenty-four pints!'

'You'd think,' Ned laughed, as he cut the cards, and passed them back to Esther for a second shuffle, 'that the trades unions might negotiate some international parity agreement on the matter. But, you know Alfred, I was thinking about the breweries and your little conundrum.'

'Which would that be, Ned?'

'The Farndon mystery, of course. How that poor fellow Tobin could have been transported to Farndon.'

'For Heaven's sake,' said Ettie. 'Might we have no respite?'

'But, my dear,' said Palmer, 'I should like to hear Ned's solution.'

'Why, is it not obvious? What is the one vehicle upon the roads so numerous that none of us ever even notice?'

'The brewery dray,' said Edward Davies, taking the shuffled cards and dealing the next hands. 'But surely...'

Palmer was only vaguely aware of the next exchanges, for there were shapes coming together, patterns similar to those he saw when analysing the flow of playing cards – or, indeed, the chemical samples in his work. He needed to speak with Wilde again – though the superintendent had not been seen since Monday's chaos.

'And speaking of Farndon, Alfred,' Ned was saying, 'that rogue in the bowler who accosted us – did you ever see him again?'

Palmer glanced at Esther, and she turned her head to stare back at him. He noticed she was stroking again at that small but troublesome wound upon her neck. Scratched upon some brickwork, she'd said, during Monday's crush. Yet, it was a very precise wound. No grazing. She must have caught it on something very sharp, surely. A protruding nail, perhaps?

'I did,' he replied, and stood to stretch his legs, to better observe the game.

'Diamonds,' said Edward, turning over the final card, the five of that suit.

'The fellow knocked down by the bull?' said Alison.

'Knocked down by...' Ned was incredulous, and opened with the two of trumps. 'Might somebody...?'

'I meant to put it in my last letter to you,' said Palmer. 'But it's a long story. Perhaps later...'

'And the Corpse Dog,' said Ned. 'Are you still seeing it?'

'There's a mention in the paper, this very day,' said Alison, and played the four. Esther was forced to lay down the king, a bad but unavoidable move. 'Where was the sighting again, Alfred?'

Palmer heard himself click his tongue in disapproval and Ettie turned sharply towards him with her most withering look. So, he settled to turning the pages and found the relevant paragraph. It sent a shiver down his spine to read it again.

'Here,' he said. 'At Erbistock, it seems.'

'Corpse Dog, indeed!' said Edward, and triumphantly slapped down the ace. 'I posted the cutting, just this afternoon, to a colleague in Portsmouth. He has a passion for such tales. Interesting fellow, though – another advocate of compulsory vaccination.'

'And, like yourself, Edward,' said Ned, 'this fellow…'

'Doyle,' Edward replied. 'Arthur Doyle.'

'And has Doyle, like yourself, also been attacked by those anti-vaccination fanatics?' said Palmer.

'He has, indeed,' said Edward. 'But he has been working with the police on the matter, to uncover the rogues responsible. He has quite a passion for detective stories, Alfred – inspired by your old friend in London, he says. And your deal, Ned, I think.'

Reynolds, thought Palmer. *The Mysteries of London*, Reynolds's own penny blood. A wonderful literary requiem.

'Perhaps, one day,' said Palmer, 'Doctor Doyle's stories will sit among your fine collection, Alison.'

He waved his hand towards the leather-bound volumes which lined the library's walls.

'My father's collection,' she replied, with her gentle Scots accent. She took the pack from Ned and began the shuffle. She had the professional gambler's skill of riffling the cards. Learned from her father, Palmer decided.

Close to him were titles by Low's favourite Scottish writers. Jane Porter's *The Scottish Chiefs* and *Thaddeus of Warsaw*. Mary Brunton's *Self-Control*. Walter Scott's *Waverley*. Dozens more.

'And, Alison,' said Ned, 'I am right in thinking there is yet another River Dee in Scotland? Alfred – am I correct?'

'To the best of my knowledge,' said Palmer, before Alison could reply, for he had studied this, 'there are *two* River Dees in Scotland: one in Aberdeenshire, rising in the Cairngorm Mountains; the other in Lowland Galloway.' He raised a finger to indicate he was not yet finished. 'And then...' He paused for effect. 'A further River Dee in Westmorland. In addition, of course, to our own Welsh Dee, and a fifth, in Ireland. Each of them holy.'

'And, perhaps, equally cursed,' murmured Esther.

The room fell silent as the cards were dealt yet again.

Palmer coughed into his closed fist and reached for his snuff box.

'Your father, Alison' said Palmer, choosing to ignore Ettie's gloom, 'did he ever have Jacobite leanings?'

'You know my father well enough, Alfred,' she laughed.

And indeed, he did. Palmer had lodged with the family at Roseneath those eight years earlier.

'I imagine he would also have set a curse upon both their houses – Stuart and Hanover alike.'

'Only the innocent suffer,' she replied. 'Only the innocents.'

Now the cards were played fast. Another trick to the Davies team and with that trick the game.

'Speaking of which,' said Edward, and waved his free hand towards the newspaper, 'that other piece – about the telescopes. What is your scientific opinion, Alfred?'

The door again. Supper in five minutes, announced the serving girl.

'I have tried to persuade my husband,' said Esther, coming to stand beside him, 'that he should have no further opinions on anything concerning the police or their investigations.'

She peered up at him when nobody else could see, and silently mouthed the word "Sorry" to him. He saw there was a tear in her eye and he hugged her.

'And Esther is quite right, as usual. Arming the police with telescopes? They may be beneficial for spotting poachers from a distance, but...'

'What if the constable in question happens to be a prying individual?' said Edward, tidying the cards. 'Imagine? A Peeping Tom policeman? Would that not be a social nuisance? To have those in authority prying into our private lives? And how much was the stake again?' He reached over and gently punched Ned's arm. 'But Fenian bombers like Daly – this Dynamite Gang?'

'By my reckoning,' Ned replied, 'we owe you seven shillings, sir. And, for the Dynamite Gang, nothing will serve except a good revolver, I fear.'

The Dynamite Gang, Palmer thought. Here in his hands, in the *Advertiser*, an entire page. More details of Daly's capture in Birkenhead last week. Two tickets, one for Chester, one for Birkenhead. In his bulging pockets, infernal clock-pattern devices, the same as those used at Victoria Station in London and elsewhere.

Yes, he thought, only the innocent suffer.

And Daly, himself? Now confirmed as part of that Dynamite Gang from America. Like Daly himself, all Irish-Americans. They had traced him to a hotel in Liverpool, to which he had arrived with a suitcase – though the suitcase now disappeared.

'But, at least,' said Edward, as they filed out of the library for supper, 'the police seem satisfied that they put a stop to yet another murderous conspiracy – some further outrage they must have planned for the Midland Counties over Easter.'

'Americans,' he murmured, as they entered the dining room.

'Yes, quite,' said Ned Owen, 'I've been trying to tell you all evening. My friends at the India Office, you remember?'

'I do,' said Palmer. 'You reminded me that there were, indeed, Indians in Arizona – though not your sort of Indians, I collect. So, your colleagues – anything interesting to tell us about our Canadian friend?'

Ettie was just a pace or two ahead of him, about to take her seat at the dining table. But he saw her spin around.

'Neo...' she said, and he foolishly almost thought it was a warning. But by then his curiosity was piqued.

'Jackson?' he said.

'There's the thing,' Ned replied. 'Our friends at the appropriate desks in the Foreign Office tell me they can find no trace of anybody by the name of Jackson with mining interests in Arizona. But they thought I might be interested in some cove who made his money in the big Arivaca mining boom. But not Jackson. They hinted at some Fenian link, as well. Some fellow by the name of McCafferty.'

Chapter Twenty-Three

Damn Ned Owen!

The curse went through Ettie's head one more time as she bustled, early, to the telegraphic office.

'To – your own address, Mrs Palmer?' said Mr Edgar, as he took the details and her money.

'Indeed. Simply a prank, as you might say. Practising upon my husband.'

She almost managed to persuade herself that it was true, that she was merely engaged upon some harmless escapade from which her terrified soul could withdraw at any moment she chose. Neo would discover the deception, of course. Wrexham was not a place where you could expect to keep a secret for long. But, by the time he learned the truth, she would likely be past caring, one way or the other.

Half an hour later and she was back at the house, Neo coming out of the front door on his way round to the office as she was coming up the lane.

'They did not bring the milk, my dear?' He planted a kiss upon her cheek. 'We shall need to complain – make sure they adjust the bill accordingly.'

'These things happen,' she lied. Yes, of all things, she lied – again. 'And the dairy is usually so reliable.'

Well, this was one blessing, anyway. He had not discovered the jug filled with this morning's delivery – the jug she had so carefully hidden, giving her the excuse to be out so early. She brandished the white enamel can she'd carried back from Sunter's on her way home. And now it was simply a matter of waiting.

'I still cannot believe it,' he cried over his shoulder as he headed down the lane. 'That wretch, hiding in plain sight all this time.'

Damn Ned Owen! she said to herself, yet again. Not lies alone, but profanities as well.

Neo had kept her awake half the night, playing over the events time after time, on each occasion with a minor variation as he added one new ingredient, then another, into the mix, calibrating the calculation afresh.

As she'd listened to him, she had become ever more convinced that each variant of the calculation led him closer to McCafferty's deadly blade and that she had no choice in the matter.

'Reverend FitzPatrick,' he had said, at one point. 'Michael – he spoke the name Michael. Esther – the lion keeper. Michael Cutter. His third traitor? Do you think it's possible? For him to have engineered such a thing?'

And later, his questions about how long she had known, and his embrace when, dear fellow, he had been afraid for *her*. But none of his permutations led him to a satisfactory conclusion about how Jackson – McCafferty – could possibly have sent him that note. *Let sleeping dogs lie.*

Guilt, guilt, guilt.

'Yet, come hell or high water,' he said now, halting before he turned the corner, 'I shall find out where Wilde is hiding.'

Then he was gone, and she stepped inside, alone again with all the demons calling upon her to give up this foolishness. Yet, in some way, her trepidation simply caused her resolve to strengthen and, while she waited, she prepared for the day ahead, though still fearful that there was every chance she might not survive. In that case, she decided, a note for Neo. Not a farewell note, for she could not bring herself to such a task. Even the suppressed thought of it caused her to choke back tears. But a confession, at least. And an outline of her intentions.

Beyond that, there was her attire to be considered – and considered with care. Her cycling skirts and matching jersey bloomers were the obvious choice, as well as her green rain cape. She could not, after all, afford to be encumbered with an umbrella. Not today.

Finally, there was just her bag to pack, the leather shoulder bag – in truth, a decently sized round box purse, which she also frequently carried on her cycling expeditions. And she packed it with equal care today.

After the preparations, more waiting until the telegram finally arrived – though, in the hands of Neo, rather than the boy from the telegraphic office. She heard her husband open the front door.

'My dear,' he shouted. 'There is – well, you should come and see.'

The boy had delivered it to Neo's office, rather than the house. An easy mistake to make. But he held it out to her, and she opened the officially printed red-brown envelope with all the trepidation one normally reserves for the arrival of a telegram.

'Is all well, Ettie?'

She pretended to read, then breathed a theatrical sigh of relief.

'Yes,' she said. 'And no.'

She spoke the words.

APOLOGIES STOP ARRIVING THIS TWO PM CHESTER STOP
WILL EXPLAIN STOP LUCY STOP

'Great Heavens,' he said. 'Some trouble, do you think?'

She feared she had no idea, as Neo pulled out his pocket watch.

'If we hurry,' he said, 'we can just catch the next train.'

'Neo,' she said firmly, 'I shall not hear of it. More important that you find the superintendent. Besides, you have the appointment with Mr Edisbury. If he is happy to offer you a contract – my dear, we cannot afford to miss the opportunity.'

James's Aerated Mineral Water Company at the Horse Market, his thriving trade in quinine tonic, lithia and potass water, seltzer, and lemonades. In truth, he wanted to employ his own analytical chemist, but Minnie Edisbury had persuaded her husband it might be economically preferable to seek an outside contractor. And who better?

'No, of course,' said Neo. 'But report to Wilde? Last night, you forbade me to have anything further to do with the matter.'

'True,' she said. 'But now I have thought better upon it and there *is* Lady Olivia's reward to consider. It is significant, is it not? Knowing precisely what this McCafferty looks like. But now I must go.'

'In your cycling clothes? And I did not know you planned on cycling today.'

'It was a whimsy, husband. My intention to hire one of Howell's tricycles. Though no time to change if I'm to catch the train. It is so like Lucy to behave impetuously like this. But, after all she's been through...'

The fire in the hearth was naught but embers now, though enough to consume the telegram, which she balled and threw upon the coals. She could not, after all, allow Neo to see the time or location at which it had been dispatched.

She remembered that verse from Psalms: *He that worketh deceit shall not dwell within my house; he that telleth lies shall not tarry in my sight.*

At every station halt along the journey, she forced herself to remain in her seat, and at every station they approached she was convinced she must surely flee, take the next train back to Wrexham – especially when, at Saltney, she realised she had not, after all, left her confessional note. Still, she reasoned, Neo would work it all out for himself. Poor, dear man.

But when she finally stepped down onto the platform at Chester General, Ettie found she had steeled herself afresh for the task ahead. She felt simply a surprising sense of calm, as she sought directions for the King's Head, worried that there might be more than one establishment of that name in a city of this size. And, indeed, there was. But the most likely candidate, she decided, must be the hotel at the junction of Grosvenor Street and Whitefriars – though she was not sufficiently familiar with the geography to find it without directions.

Easy, she was assured.

From here, the General Station's main entrance, straight ahead, City Road, over the canal bridge and, at the farther end, a right turn onto Foregate Street. Then keep going until she reached the Cross and St. Peter's. At the Cross, left down Bridge Street and, at the next major junction, across from St. Michael's, there she would find the King's Head.

It was a wet and windy twenty minutes from the clock on the station's main façade to that which adorned the sandstone tower of St. Peter's, and with each step she took, her surroundings became more recognisable from her few previous visits. On Foregate Street, along the upper gallery of the Rows to keep out of this thin drizzle. The bustle of Saturday afternoon wealthy shoppers. And she turned heads. Perhaps, the cycling clothes. Perhaps, the purposeful stride. Or, perhaps, the grim determination in her eyes.

And, of course, she knew the King's Head as soon as she saw its bullnosed bulk on the rounded corner. It was not exactly what she had imagined. This place had a distinct air of respectability. But McCafferty…

'No, my dear,' said the licensee, Mr Parry, when she was finally able to speak with him. 'Mr Jackson does not reside here. A travelling gentleman, is he not? But he pays me a modest fee to receive his correspondence.'

'How collected, sir?' she asked him. 'For I have a message to deliver.'

She received the information that a serving fellow – and American – visited most afternoons for that very purpose. At about this hour, as it happened, and yes, she was welcome to wait. Indeed, if she wished to avail herself of one of the armchairs here in the lobby, Mr Parry would make sure a pot of tea should be served to her – with his compliments, naturally.

'And your cycle, madam?' he said, peering at her attire, then towards the doorway. 'Safe outside, I trust?'

It would have been too complicated to explain, so she simply thanked him for his concern, assured him that it was, indeed, safe. Then she slipped out of the rain cape, hung it to dry on the coat stand, and settled herself in the armchair. It was comfortable, warm near the lobby's log fire, and a lack of sleep. By the time the tea arrived she had fallen into a troubled slumber. But she started, suddenly awake again, with the prod at her arm.

'Lady! Hey, lady, you got a letter for Jackson?'

The accent was entirely different from McCafferty's. Nasal. Harsh and uncouth.

'A message,' she said, rubbing at her eyes and straightening her bonnet. 'Just a message.'

'Then, go ahead. Tell me.'

He wasn't tall, but his bearing spoke of concealed nervous energy, like a coiled spring. Something Germanic about his features – the square jaw, his moustache and cropped hair the colour of dried straw. He had a coat of light-coloured canvas and, in one hand, a visored, braid-bound shipboard cap.

'My message is for Captain McCafferty's ears only.'

The fellow straightened, suddenly alert to danger. He looked all around, his free hand reaching inside the coat.

'I think you got the wrong place, lady.'

'In that case...' She stood, steeling herself to hold his gaze, reaching for her rain cape. 'When you see him, tell him Mrs Palmer was looking for him – though I dread to think how he'll take the news that you turned me away.'

She walked through to the reception desk, shouted her thanks to Mr Parry for his hospitality and apologised for letting the tea go cold. She could not recall ever having been so anxious. Though her fears now seemed tempered by a certain sense of animation, her pulse racing.

Ettie was out on the street and heading back up Bridge Street before the man caught up with her.

'Hey,' he shouted. 'Hold up there!' He grabbed her arm and she glared at him. 'Could be I know the name, after all.'

She looked down at his hand and he released her from his grip.

'Then, if you know what's good for you, you will take me to him.'

'The captain don't take kindly to visitors, lady. He sure don't.'

'Your choice, Mr...'

He grinned at her, some of his teeth blackened and several missing.

'You the woman?' he said. 'The goosecap's woman?'

'Goosecap?' She had no idea what the word meant. Though it was spoken with such contempt that she could guess. Was that how McCafferty viewed her husband – as some sort of simpleton? If so, how did this stand against his alleged fear of Neo's investigative skills?

'Sure,' said the American. 'But maybe he'd wanna see you, still an' all. Just keep yer bone box shut and follow me.'

He strode off, setting the seaman's cap upon his head and crossed the junction. He stopped in the middle to take a cupped handful of water from the drinking fountain. Over the way, a wine merchant. Beyond this establishment, across another short and narrow street, the Falcon, first of a bewildering number of hostelries on both sides of the road all the way down to the Bridgegate's broad arch and balustraded parapet. And, at least, the rain had stopped.

Beyond the Old Edgar, through the domed footpath passage to the ancient bridge and the Dee, they turned right, away from the old weir and its white water. But she glanced in that direction anyway, her attention drawn by the steam whistle from one of the many pleasure craft plying the waters upstream.

The American had still spoken not a word but he led her past the Dee Mill and its churning paddlewheel, to a small jetty, a wherry with an oarsman tethered beneath its wooden ladder. He was wrapped in a long, waxed coat and, upon his head, a broad-brimmed hat.

'This is it, lady,' said the American. 'Get in.'

'Down there?'

'Or stay. I ain't tight about it, one way or the other – you bet I'm not.'

This was it – her last chance to turn around. Just for a moment, she did indeed take a step back. But then she found herself climbing down the ladder, glad that she'd chosen the trousers beneath the skirt.

'Who's the gal, Sarge?' shouted the oarsman, as Ettie balanced precariously on the unsteady thwart. Another American, stubbled chin, an evil eye. Yet a different accent again. 'Pretty li'l thing.'

The light was just starting to fade and the slowly ebbing muddy waters murmured sinister secrets to her. Sarge? Another former soldier from their War Between the States, she assumed. This oarsman as well? But she kept her lips tightly closed, wondering where in Heaven's name they would take her.

'There!' said the first fellow and pointed to the bow, where a small foredeck offered her just enough room to sit. She moved unsteadily forward as he vaulted down behind her and slipped the mooring rope. 'Cody,' he said to the oarsman, pushing them off from the jetty and settling himself in the stern. 'Just row.'

Ettie looked over her shoulder as they followed the river's bend and the broad span of the Grosvenor Bridge came into view. There were no other boats, though they scattered a family of ducks and their young, sending them splashing and squawking into flight. She thought the boat must be heading further downstream, and was surprised when, just minutes later, they swung across to one more narrow jetty – though it barely justified the name – this side of the bridge itself.

On the other side of the river, the sandstone bulk of Chester Castle stood proud upon its mound.

'Would it not' she said, 'have been quicker to walk?'

'Less eyes, lady,' said Cody the boatman, lifting his oar and easing the wide, overhanging side of the wherry alongside the planks, which half-rested, half-floated upon the stinking quagmire of the riverbank.

Ettie would have ended up pitched in that morass as well, she knew, if the American had not guided her up the flimsy and precarious pathway, anchored at its upper limit, she saw, to a tree stump so it would float, rising and falling with the tide. And she breathed a sigh of relief when they reached the solid ground of a rutted lane with, beyond, the wall of Chester's newest cemetery.

'Here?' she said.

'Here,' said the American, and led her to a wicket gate.

Inside the grounds of the Overleigh Cemetery, the shadows were already long and sombre from the winged angels, black marble monuments, chest tombs and white grave markers scattered all up the slopes away from them and interspersed with yew trees – so many yew trees. In the bowl between the slopes, a substantial lake overhung by willows and alders.

A winding path brought them across the width of the burial ground, parallel to the river, over a stream flowing from the lake, then up a ridge with great stone urns: tall obelisks; sculpted temples and Celtic crosses on either side of the path; and woodland beyond. The ridge was capped by a table tomb with a recumbent white effigy beneath an open arched canopy and, through the arch, another glimpse of the Grosvenor Bridge before they passed a chapel and then dropped down some steep, slippery steps to a large house, set in another broad hollow, a natural amphitheatre with higher ground all around. The house seemed deserted, but Ettie's American guards led the way around to substantial outbuildings, a coach house and stable.

'Wait!' she was instructed, left in the charge of the oarsman while the other fellow entered the coach house through its large wooden double gates. 'Captain!' he yelled. 'Captain...'

Minutes passed and, yet again, she thought of running. Though, she knew, she'd not get far. Not now. And when McCafferty finally came to the gateway, at first glance, she would have failed to recognise him had it not been for his customary double-breasted yellow Ulster. The beard was gone, only a moustache remaining, almost as his younger self appeared in that *Wanted!* poster Hatchet-Face had showed her. But, where the beard had been, there now remained only white flesh, mottled red, which contrasted strangely to the tanned high cheekbones and forehead.

'Why, Esther,' he smiled. 'Here, after all. Salome, come to deliver John the Baptist's head?'

He stood aside, jerked his head towards the interior.

'Neo?' she said as she passed him. There was no carriage inside the coach house, only a couple of spare wheels and shafts hanging upon the whitewashed wall. 'He would be flattered,' she murmured, making her way through an interior door. 'He's a great admirer of the prophet, Captain. And you were right, of course. A simple revelation from his friend Ned Owen that there is no Arizona mine owner named Jackson – only a fellow called McCafferty at a place called Arivaca.'

Beyond the door, the room which must once have been the living quarters for stable boys or coachmen. The interior was simply furnished. Cold and cheerless. Three campaign beds, chairs, and a table, the latter strewn with maps and drawings. On the opposite side an open door, leading to the stables.

'I miss the place,' he said. 'Old Arivaca. You, Sergeant? Sitting out on the boardwalk in the warm shade of the *ramada*, watching the world go by.'

The fellow leaned against a ladder, leading up to what must have been a hay loft.

'It ain't the Bronx,' he said. 'An' too many *Mexicanos* up in Spanishtown. But sure, good to get back.'

'Soon, I suppose?' said Ettie. 'Now all your work's done here?'

'We ain't nearly done yet, lady,' the sergeant sneered.

It was pretty much what she'd expected, but she was more worried about the oarsman, still behind her in the doorway.

'So, now,' McCafferty drawled, perching himself on the edge of the table, 'what do we do with you, Mrs Palmer? I'd be flattered if I really thought you were here for me, Esther. But we both know that's not the way of things. The big question is, how many more people has he spouted his mouth off to?'

'You promised, did you not? That if I passed on whatever I know – whatever my husband knows – you'd not kill him.'

'I'm afraid, I lied. And now Sergeant Kelly will need to deliver a message to him. If he wants to see his lovely wife again – that sort of thing…'

'I thought so,' she said and put her hands to her face and sobbed loudly, turning slightly and walking further into the room until they formed almost the four corners of a square: herself, the oarsman, the sergeant and McCafferty.

'Please, Esther, console yourself…'

But he stopped abruptly as she reached into the shoulder bag and pulled out a small revolver. Mrs McBain's revolver. Shining, nickel-plated. She moved still further into her own corner of the room, waving the pistol from one to the other.

Yet McCafferty simply laughed.

'Why, Mrs Palmer. You do surprise me! What's that toy you got, now? A woman's piece. McBain's, I guess. A Bulldog?'

She had no idea, but Ettie saw the sergeant's hand slip towards his coat.

'Do not!' she yelled, and swung the revolver towards McCafferty. 'For myself, I care not, but whatever you do, Sergeant Kelly, your captain shall surely die.'

She was aware that her hands quavered but she was certain that, at this range, both hands tight about the chequered wooden grips, she could not miss.

'Now, Sergeant, let's be easy here.' McCafferty half-raised his hands, while Kelly had frozen, his fingers poised in front of his chest. 'And, Mrs Palmer, I asked you, did I not, who might stop me? But I never guessed. You've got grit, girl. Tenacity. I like that.'

She thought about her father. His favourite saying. *Dyfal donc a dyr y garreg.* Persistent blows shatter the stone. Perseverance pays in the end. Yet she now realised she had exhausted her plan. She had easily imagined herself confronting the wretch, using the pistol she had concealed so carefully since picking it up at the Beast Market two weeks earlier. But beyond that point? She had rather assumed that matters would then proceed in whatever direction fate might decree. Though, she had not foreseen this gaping paralysis, the entire scene temporarily petrified.

It was the oarsman who shattered the stillness.

He roared and ran towards her.

She span and pulled the trigger. It was harder than she'd imagined. She squeezed, watched the hammer come back, then squeezed some more, surprised when it went off, the noise deafening in that confined space. The fellow cried out, went down. There was a wisp of smoke, the stink of sulphur.

At the same time, the corner of her eye caught the sergeant reaching inside his coat and pulling forth a revolver of his own.

She fired again, this bullet hitting the ladder near his shoulder, wood splintering while, behind her, the oarsman groaned on the tiled floor and cursed.

The sergeant levelled the gun's long barrel towards her as she pulled the trigger for the third time, watched in amazement as the rogue's cap flew from his head but left him apparently unhurt.

'No, Sergeant!' yelled McCafferty. 'Hold your fire, man.'

Kelly looked at him as though he was mad. Ettie's gun exploded yet again, this time causing a hole to appear in the skirts of the sergeant's canvas coat.

McCafferty was advancing towards her, his hand outstretched and now holding that wicked spring-blade knife, so that she felt a sudden pulse in the half-healed scratch upon her neck.

'Give me the damned thing, Esther,' he said, as she swung towards him, the pistol pointing straight into his face.

'You won't shoot me, girl.'

He grinned at her as, without hesitation and driven by her terror, she pulled the trigger one last time.

Chapter Twenty-Four

'It seems there can be no doubt.' Wilde studied the note for what felt like the tenth time.

'Seems?' Palmer shouted at him, more because the fellow at this early hour, still wearing his red paisley dressing gown, his smoking cap, and carpet slippers, cut such an absurd figure. 'Seems?' he said again.

He had gone to bed worried beyond his wits for her but assuming she had chosen, for reasons of her own, to overnight in Chester with her sister. Worried, but angry at the same time. He had slept fitfully, then been awakened before dawn by the sound of a horse in the lane and, by the time he was down the stairs, only the note trapped beneath the knocker.

Overleigh Cemetery. Old chaplain's house. Riverside. Alone.

The message was eloquent in its simplicity. Simple and menacing. No need for the sender to attach his name. No need for him to spell out the threat.

It had brought him, as soon as he was dressed, hurrying to Regent Street and the police barracks, where he had finally persuaded the duty sergeant – Hugh Jones, the police team's goalkeeper, as it happened – to send for the superintendent, though again, only by raging at the fellow.

'Mr Palmer, you must understand,' said Wilde, there in the guardroom, 'I have spent the past few days in Birmingham – and I am instructed to keep my nose out of this whole Fenian business.'

'Good, Superintendent. Good. Then you should have no qualms whatsoever about helping me recover my wife – a victim of abduction by some person or persons unknown.'

'Or so you surmise, sir. So you surmise.'

'I surmise nothing! Is this note not clear enough? And did nobody during your sojourn in Birmingham mention this killer, McCafferty?'

Wilde coughed and rubbed at his eyes.

'Yes,' he said, 'McCafferty was mentioned. But the authorities believe him to be there, in Birmingham. Yet, you say he has been living here under our very noses? The Canadian? I suggest you come to my quarters, while I get dressed.'

'I have no time to wait.' Palmer glanced at his pocket watch. 'Do you not understand? I must get to Chester.'

'Mr Palmer,' said Wilde, 'this is Sunday morning. There is no train until eight o'clock – unless you intend to fly, sir?'

'Eight? Yes, I suppose...'

'And it is not yet seven.'

'But if you do not intend to help me, Superintendent...'

'I did not say so. I did not.'

Wilde folded his arms, tapped his foot on the terracotta tiles while he gave the matter consideration.

'But you must appreciate,' he said at last, 'that I have no jurisdiction in Chester, Mr Palmer. None, sir.'

And thank the Lord Jesus for this small blessing, thought Palmer. For the first time since he'd discovered the note, he felt the beginnings of hope.

'You're certain, Superintendent – about Saltney?'

Palmer rubbed at the carriage window as they passed the level crossing and eased into Rossett station, with the bells of the village's Christ Church peeling joyfully in the distance.

'Closer to the cemetery, Mr Palmer, I believe. And shall give us the advantage of approaching from a direction this McCafferty might not expect.'

It was all Palmer really cared about – Ettie's safety. Her freedom. But he was nervous, his knee shaking uncontrollably. He needed this conversation to keep his mind from all the unthinkable possibilities lying before them.

'I still do not understand,' he said, steadying himself on the seat as the train came to an unusually abrupt halt, 'why they believe his target will be Birmingham – when it is plain he's still here in Chester.'

'First, because Daly, the fellow arrested in Birkenhead, had a ticket for that destination. Second, because an informant has revealed that Daly's missing suitcase – more dynamite, it seems likely – has been dispatched there as well.'

'Though not discovered,' Palmer mused.

He peered through the window again. A grey and dreary day. And nobody, it seemed, either alighting or disembarking here.

'As you say, sir. It could be anywhere.'

'Then, their instruction that you shouldn't concern yourself – nothing more than the authorities not wishing a witness when, inevitably, they fail to prevent McCafferty's next atrocity.'

The carriage remained empty as the stationmaster's whistle blew and the engine chugged back into action, obscuring the view with steam and coal smoke. Wilde reached into the pocket of his worn brown overcoat and set about lighting his pipe.

'At least one murder on my own patch. And I am instructed to sit upon my hands. What about my duty to the victim, Mr Palmer? My oath, sir – to keep the peace. Prevent breaches of the peace. Though you cannot be correct about the Menagerie fellow – this Cutter.'

'I imagine, Superintendent, you are about to tell me that your superiors in Birmingham believe he has no obvious connection to McCafferty. That the other man who betrayed him had some different name?'

He helped himself to a pinch of snuff.

'How in Heaven's…?' Wilde began.

Palmer considered the policeman for a moment. Overall, he liked the fellow. But he represented that class of person he had encountered on only a few occasions. Generally, he understood, different folk possessed varying degrees of intelligence. But in a consistent way. The highly intelligent remained so, at least for most of the time. The broadly least intelligent blessed with the occasional flash of brilliance. And then there were those rare specimens who seemed to display great intelligence for perhaps half of their existence, and rank stupidity for the rest. Yes, he liked Wilde, but…

'Taylour, perhaps?' he suggested.

'Well, indeed – but…'

'I think I began to see the light as soon as I first learned his name – his alias, anyway. Cutter. Another word for a tailor, of course. Though, in antiquity, it was frequently written thus... T.A.Y.L.O.U.R. You see? Taylour.'

'And...?'

'And Taylour was the married name of the woman we now know as Lady Olivia FitzPatrick. Unless I miss my guess, this fellow Cutter was some distant relative. Under her protection, perhaps. Even, it is possible, in her employ in some way. She is, after all, a fearsome opponent of Irish independence. And, as I know to my cost, with connections to the military intelligence services. Their whole estate at Warren Hall, an armed camp. And I can only assume she may have believed McCafferty would also come after her. Indeed, might that not be the reason he's still here, rather than in Birmingham?'

'The Menagerie?'

Palmer nodded. They were travelling at speed now, through the fields and woodlands between Pulford and Dodleston.

'As good a place to find employment,' he said, 'and hide himself away, I suppose.'

'He would have believed himself safe, you think – Cutter? Coming to Wrexham?'

'Why not? He would have seen the newspaper report about Tobin, I suppose. But seventeen years passed since the betrayal. He would have changed considerably. Though, obviously, McCafferty must have recognised him – or been informed, more likely. He is a spider, is he not? A whole web of other Fenians at his disposal. Informants. Spies. These Invincibles.'

'Then it could be that, at the cemetery...'

'Precisely, sir. We have no idea how many of these wretches he might have at his disposal.'

He saw the policeman's hand touch the bulge in his coat.

'I assume, Superintendent, that you took the precaution of bringing your revolver?'

Palmer felt himself a hypocrite. How many times had he admired the articles by both his old friend George Reynolds *and* Reynolds's rival, Dickens – perhaps the only thing upon which they would ever have agreed – about the need for increased restrictions on gun ownership. But with the bombings, and the Phoenix Park murders, the mood of the public seemed somewhat altered. He had even joked with Ettie about the matter – this new obsession with cycling, the recently reported incident of the lone lady cyclist who had been the subject of a most despicable attack.

'Perhaps, my dear,' he had said to her, 'if you insist upon this new pursuit, you should at least go armed.'

She had scolded him, of course, and quite correctly, for treating the case with such unacceptable levity.

But where was she now? How much in peril? He trembled at the thought. He recalled the last time they had travelled this way together. The sign for Balderton – the duke of Westminster's private station. Their summons from Lady Olivia.

'I have a licence for its use, Mr Palmer.'

'Licence?' said Palmer. He'd almost forgotten about the revolver, realised that Wilde must have misread the frown upon his face. 'Yes, of course. The licence. Yet I had assumed that, as an officer of the law...'

'Only on duty, sir. And, as I have told you, I am neither on duty nor within my jurisdiction. Besides, this is my own weapon.'

'A reliable one, I imagine.'

'A Webley, sir. The best.'

'But capable of dealing with a whole squad of McCafferty's henchmen?'

'You have some other plan?'

'I'm not certain we have a plan at all. And I am anxious to secure Esther's release as soon as may be. But, perhaps – Saltney...'

Incongruously, Palmer was taken back to St. Patrick's Day, the evening performance of *The Castle Spectre*, and Angela's imprisonment by evil Earl Osmond.

Sing, Megen-oh! Oh! Megen-ee!

The words kept bouncing about his brain.

'For Overleigh,' Wilde repeated. 'Saltney will be faster – providing we can find a Hansom on a Sunday morning. And from there to the cemetery...'

'I believe, Superintendent,' said Palmer, 'that we shall not be going straight to the cemetery after all.'

'I decided,' he told the woman, 'that there might be an accommodation to be reached. The reward for McCafferty in exchange for one or two of your seemingly plentiful gamekeepers.'

One of those same gamekeepers, shotgun cradled in the crook of his arm, watched from the far side of the overgrown pond below them. Palmer and Wilde stood, hats in hand, beneath the branches of this spreading chestnut tree at the centre of Warren Hall's sloping lawn. There was a bench built about the trunk, though they'd not been invited to sit.

Lady Olivia's face was an empty canvas as she adjusted the blanket around her knees, while Reverend FitzPatrick, standing behind her bathchair, offered him a wistful smile.

'You are somewhat outside your jurisdiction, are you not, Superintendent?' she said.

'Lady Olivia,' said Palmer, before Wilde could respond. 'Time is of the essence. And since we were here last, the agent, Mrs McBain – at least,' he stammered, 'I assume some sort of agent... Dead, ma'am. And Michael Cutter - Michael Taylour, should I say? A cousin, I assume?'

She looked as though he had slapped her and he saw the reverend's knuckles whiten as he gripped the back of the chair, the smile disappearing entirely from his lips.

'And now,' Palmer pressed on, 'my wife is McCafferty's prisoner.'

'Are you so certain?' she hissed, and the Irish accent was more pronounced in her ire. 'A prisoner – or a willing accomplice?'

'What?' Wilde protested. 'For pity's sake...'

It was preposterous. Absolutely preposterous. But Palmer was stuck for words to express his anger.

'Yes,' she said. 'I met McBain. Once or twice. But I had the clear impression she did not entirely trust your wife, Mr Palmer. She had observed her closeness, her *familiarity*, as she described it, to this Canadian fellow, Jackson – the same man, sir, you now claim to be none other than McCafferty himself.'

Closeness, thought Palmer. Familiarity. Yes, a little. And he was ashamed of the envy he'd felt. But accomplice? How dare the woman!

He opened his mouth to speak. However, the policeman threw his arm across Palmer's chest to stop him.

'Met Mrs McBain, ma'am?' said Wilde. 'In what capacity, may I ask?'

'No, *Mr* Wilde, you may not. And Frederick...' She did not even deign to turn her head. 'The bible, if you please.'

'Must I?' her husband whined. But he plainly knew it for a rhetorical protest and did not wait for an answer. He nodded to them briefly and returned back up the garden towards the terrace and its French windows. It was dry today and the call of crows rose up towards them from the poplars beyond the pond.

'In that case, Lady Olivia,' said Palmer, biting back on his anger, 'we shall trouble you no more. But I tell you, ma'am, that it shall be upon your own conscience if...'

'Mr Palmer,' she spat at him, 'spare me the amateur dramatics.' She waved her hand as if to dismiss him. 'If you choose to leave, be my guest. But if you would care to have me add a few pieces to those you seem to have so admirably already joined together, please, sit a while.'

'Sit?' Palmer raged. 'Sit? My wife...'

'You will sit, sir, or leave and be damned – for, be assured, the two of you will never...' She broke off, seemingly thinking better of whatever else she was about to fling at them.

It was enough, anyhow. Palmer felt Wilde tug the sleeve of his coat, nod his head towards the bench, and they both sat.

'I believe you deserve to know, gentlemen,' she said, in more measured tones, 'a little of my history. You see, until I reached almost the age of twenty...'

'Part of Her Majesty's household,' Palmer growled, still annoyed, 'were you not?'

He saw a nerve twitch in the side of her jaw and he doubted she would often tolerate such interruption – though she did so this morning, perhaps understanding his impatience. At the same time, her husband reappeared on the patio, a large black bible in his hands. Palmer was already guilty about missing chapel and the sight of the holy book served only to stoke his anxiety. The guilt was made worse by the first cautious peal of bells from the local church they'd passed on the way from Saltney.

'My father, Mr Palmer,' Lady Olivia proceeded, with slow deliberation, 'was a Knight of the Order of St. Patrick. We had some intriguing connections in military intelligence – even after I left Her Majesty's service.'

Left? Palmer smiled to himself. He could not be certain of its veracity but he recalled the story he had once been told, all those years ago, about Lady Olivia's dalliance with none other than the queen's consort himself, her beloved Prince Albert.

'That was before I married Frederick, of course.'

Forced to marry, more like, Palmer recalled. To help hide the shame of it all. To help bury the embarrassment for her aristocratic family.

'And, soon after,' she went on, 'this so-called Irish Republican Brotherhood formed in our homeland. Fenians. In America, the Fenian Brotherhood. Both dedicated to the dual principles of Irish independence – but independence achieved through violence.'

Reverend FitzPatrick was back behind the bathchair, bible pressed close to his chest. And now there were yet more church bells, this time from the opposite direction.

'Frederick preached from the pulpit against those troublemakers, naturally,' said Lady Olivia.

'In the town,' said Reverend FitzPatrick himself, 'there were disturbances. Scuffles. Almost riots. And on one occasion…'

'There was a shot, gentlemen,' said his wife. 'From the crowd. I saw my husband fall.'

'Great Heavens.' Palmer and Wilde each spoke the words in unison.

'Wounded, sir?' asked the superintendent.

But the reverend smiled at them and turned the bible about. There, in the centre of its black leather cover was a neat round hole and, just visible within the hole, a piece of dull grey metal.

'A miracle,' he said.

'You moved to England?' Palmer suggested.

'And all was peaceful,' said Lady Olivia. 'For a while, at least. American Fenians like McCafferty busy with their War Between the

States. Fenians on both sides, of course. Well, what else would you expect? But then, only a year after that conflict came to an end, their first attacks against Canada.'

'I remember,' said Wilde. 'Suddenly, everybody here on alert. If there was a threat to Canada...'

'A possible threat here, as well,' Palmer replied.

'And those of us with positions in Irish society,' said Reverend FitzPatrick, 'approached by military intelligence and encouraged to grow our own networks, help gather useful information.'

The rest was pretty much as Palmer had surmised and shared with Wilde. Lady Olivia's impoverished cousin Michael Taylour, several times removed, had successfully infiltrated the Fenian rings in both Chester and Liverpool. And he had recruited two other associates, Tobin and O'Donnell. After exposing the plot to attack Chester Castle, and following McCafferty's threat to be revenged, Tobin had fled to Wrexham - where he'd initially had family links – and O'Donnell had taken refuge working for the FitzPatricks, while Michael had changed his name and run off to work for the Menagerie.

'And now,' said Palmer, 'you believe he will be coming for you, ma'am.'

The bells rang more urgently now.

'That may be so, Mr Palmer,' she said. 'But do you hear? St. Mary's on the one hand.' She waved her hand from left to right. 'St. John the Baptist on the other. Each calling us to prayer. And whichever of these we choose today, gentlemen, you may rest assured I shall be taking my protection with me. You understand?'

Palmer stood from the bench and clamped the hat back upon his head. He was furious, felt betrayed. All this time wasted. He had cause to believe that Lady Olivia might – just might – have been responsible, eight years ago, for an attack upon himself and Ettie by some drunken drovers on Wrexham's High Street, and then by a rogue who'd nearly killed him at Chislehurst. All to protect – well, that was another story. But to toy with him in this way...

'All this?' he raged. 'Simply to waste our time?'

'Perhaps not entirely,' she replied. 'I owe you nothing, Mr Palmer, regardless of what you might believe. But my man down there at the pond...' Palmer turned to see the fellow still there. 'He has something of a score to settle with Captain McCafferty as well. You may take him if you choose. My phaeton, as well. And may God go with you.'

Chapter Twenty-Five

Four bullets! She cursed herself for the hundredth time. Four! How could she not have worked that out for herself? Hatchet-Face – the McBain woman – at the Beast Market. She'd fired at the bull twice. Of course, she had. And Ettie had not checked the revolver since then. She had simply used the thing, down there, below. Yesterday? Only yesterday? Four times. And when McCafferty had come at her, when she'd had the chance to destroy the monster, when she had pulled the trigger for the fifth time – nothing.

She stared through the filthy window of this cramped cobweb-strewn storage room up in the coach house loft – the coach house, it transpired, belonging to the now abandoned chaplain's manse. She shivered again, remembering the number of times during the night when she'd felt the frightful touch of spiders running across her face. Ettie had been forced to bite her tongue so she would not scream. In the end, fumbling in the dark with the vesta and its parlour matches, she had lit the oil lamp they'd left her, determined to stay awake and watch for the creatures.

Even now, kneeling at the window, wrapped for warmth within her rain cape, she couldn't prevent herself scratching at the red bite marks inflicted upon her by whatever other vermin lived in the straw palliasse. The window looked out, past the eaves of the main building, through the branches of a spreading yew, onto a driveway leading upwards to disappear among more trees. Above the trees, a roof and chimneys, perhaps a hundred yards away.

The sound of a key in the door's lock. She sprang to her feet and span around.

'Boss says to bring you food.'

'Bread and cheese, Sergeant?' She peered at the enamel plate. 'Delightful.' And she knocked the plate from his hands, some of the contents splashing into the bucket they'd provided for her use as a privy.

In truth, she was famished, the ache in her belly caused more by hunger now than anything else. But she'd sworn to herself, when they forced her up here to this dismal cell that she'd eat nothing from the hands of these killers. Nothing.

'Are you dumb?' he snarled. 'Need to eat. Pretty girl like you.'

He came closer. Too close. But she stood her ground and laughed in his face, watched as he raised a hand to strike her.

Am I frightened by this man? Yes, she thought. Beyond just frightened. But she was angry too. Perhaps more angry than she'd ever been in her life before. Over his shoulder, through the open door, the bales of hay past which she'd squeezed last night. Now, as then, her eye was drawn to the tall loft door – beyond which, she knew, lay freedom. A dangerous drop, yes – but freedom.

'Were you so brave in your war, sir? In the way you treated your slaves, perhaps?'

'Slaves?' he laughed. 'In the Bronx? Don't be dumb, lady.'

She had no real idea where the Bronx might be, but at least the wretch had lowered his hand.

'Wrong army,' he said. 'You think me an' the captain was both on the same side? Woulda thought, no? But you'd be wrong, see.'

'And you think I care?' she said, turning her back to him, folding her arms across her chest. Angry? Yes, she was angry. But she was ashamed, as well.

Now, in the cold light of day, everything seemed so turned upon its head. Her journey here had been full of trepidation in all its forms. Yet her passion for Neo had driven her. It had driven her to the point of firing the pistol. Even for that useless fifth time. The time when, had it functioned, she would have killed a man. A man like McCafferty, indeed, but a man, all the same. Another human being. So that her waking hours during the night had been filled with thoughts of how God would punish her for this most heinous breach of His Commandments.

She felt Kelly's fingers touch her uncovered hair.

'Want me to bring more food, lady?' he said, and she shuddered as his hand slipped down to her upper arm. She shook herself free.

'Leave me alone,' she hissed. 'Or the captain shall hear of it.'

'No disrespect, but if you think him bein' sweet on you is gonna save your soul – well... But me, lady – if you talk to me nice...'

She turned to face him again, fighting back tears with her fury.

'Where is he?' she said. 'I would speak with him.'

'He'll be back. Gone to check our pickets, you might say.'

His square face had settled into an expression she found hard to read, his lips pressed tight together, the muscles of his cheeks stretched taught, the pale blue eyes grown cold. But he was backing out through the doorway, at least.

'You want cheese,' he whispered, 'you just shout. I'll know what you mean, lady.'

'Wait,' she said, and she saw a flicker of expectation upon his face, quickly dashed. 'The man I shot – how is he this morning?'

They had been binding his wound while McCafferty interrogated her yesterday evening but then, later, after she'd been brought up to the loft, she'd heard the rogue's screams from below as they'd extracted the bullet.

'Cody?' said the sergeant. 'He'll survive. But I'm guessin' when it comes time, he'll have somethin' special in mind for you. See, old Cody, before he joined the army, he was a skinner – a good one, too.'

He slammed the door leaving her with this fresh nightmare.

Ettie had been determined not to sleep. For a while it had been easy. She'd tried to press her ear to the floorboards, in the hope she might be able to overhear their conversation, to know their plans. But the sturdy oak made that impossible. Then, later, there had been the sound of one or more of them on the ladder and she had suffered badly, imagining they were coming for her, imagining a dozen unspeakable fates. Yet it had become clear they were simply moving things – boxes, perhaps – from downstairs up to the hayloft. And, somehow, the dancing shadows cast by the oil lamp's flickering flame had lulled her softly into slumber.

On each occasion, however, there had been bad dreams. The first, still vivid, was a strange concoction of images from the St. Patrick's Day performance. *The Castle Spectre.* Ettie now in the role of poor

Angela, imprisoned by McCafferty until she might agree to marry him. McCafferty playing the part of wicked Earl Osmond. And, all the time, Evelina's ghost hovering above her, smothering her, while Easter Monday's Peep Show tune played over and over in her head.

Mary Ann Cotton – she's dead and she's rotten.

The second, more visions of the Corpse Dog gnawing at poor Neo's lifeless corpse. She trembled at the memory but, back at the window, Ettie could see McCafferty coming across the cobbled yard.

'Oh, Neo,' she murmured to herself, 'where are you, my love?'

She had no doubt he would come. None. After all, McCafferty had talked to that awful Sergeant Kelly about taking a message and, in the middle of the night, she had heard a horse – though she had not heard its return.

Yes, he would come. He was Alfred Neobard Palmer, was he not? In truth, for the most part, she hoped he would have the sense to stay away, but she knew he could not. He would come. And the fault was hers. How could she have been so foolish?

But in what manner might he come? He would have caught the first train, surely. Perhaps gone to the castle and roused the garrison.

Earlier, there had been the church bells. Somewhere near. And now, as the bells finally fell silent, the church clock tolled the hour. Ten. Ten o'clock. Surely, soon...

She heard the creaking of the ladder's rungs, footsteps outside, the turning of the key. McCafferty, of course.

'Pickets, Captain?' She forced herself to laugh at him as soon as he stood in the open doorway. 'Pickets? You think my husband such a threat?'

He shook his head and smiled at her.

'Nice try, Esther. Kelly told you that? He has a tendency to exaggerate, though. Just one, as it happens. One picket. Pierce. Watchin' the bridge. It needs watched. Though I'm beginnin' to think he might not be comin' for you, after all.'

Before she could answer, there came a terrible whinnying from the stables, one of the horses kicking at its stall.

'Sergeant!' yelled McCafferty. 'That horse needs fed and watered. Keep it settled, man.'

He listened for a moment until the commotion died down but the interlude had given Ettie time to compose herself again.

'He'll come,' she said. 'Alfred, he'll come.' But she could hear the doubt and the fear, both at the same time, in her voice. For she was certain now that, when Neo did come, they would, most likely, both die. She looked McCafferty in the eye and saw there the cold killer behind the affable drawl. How had she not seen it earlier, all those weeks when, indeed, she had felt some fondness for the fellow – or, at least, the fellow he'd pretended to be.

'Will he?' said McCafferty. 'Will he come? I guess we'll have to see. Though it's gettin' late, don't you think? And Kelly says you won't eat.'

He leaned casually against the doorframe and stared down into the night bucket.

'I'll take nothing from you, sir.'

'Then maybe you'd do me the honour of answerin' another question.'

She turned her back on him as she'd earlier done with Kelly.

'Was last night's interrogation not enough? I told you, I've nothing more to say to you.'

'I guess I'm goin' to ask, anyhow. About the pistol, Esther. When McBain had her little accident, did nobody realise the Bulldog was gone?'

'It seems they did not.'

In truth, she was certain, Wilde had known. He had known about McBain. He had asked what she was doing there with the woman, and though she had been evasive, she guessed he must have seen through her obfuscations. And then his final question.

'Perhaps one more thing, though,' Wilde had said. 'McBain's revolver?'

Ettie had simply shrugged her shoulders, but he'd perhaps understood she might be in some danger. No, she *knew* he'd understood. There was more depth to Superintendent William Wilde, sweet man, than Neo gave him credit for. The policeman was right, of course. For, here she was, trapped in this filthy hole with a despicable assassin.

'And you kept it hidden?' said McCafferty. 'For what purpose, Esther Palmer?'

'A souvenir, perhaps.' She spat the word at him over her shoulder. It was a good question. But did she really know the answer? At the time, it had simply lain upon the ground and she had picked it up with no clear intent. She had known that Neo would not have tolerated its presence in the house and, initially, she had fooled herself into believing that she simply needed time to decide what to do with the weapon. So, she had hidden the gun. But afterwards...

'Perhaps a better question might be,' she said, turning slowly back towards him, 'how did you know the beast would kill her?'

'That?' he smiled. 'Why, it woulda been Cody's way. He worked the stockyards before the war. Learned a thing or two about animals.'

'Yes. Sergeant Kelly informed me.' She felt the same familiar nightmare and shivered, hugged herself tight to still the shaking. Cody the skinner. 'And Cody was following her?'

'Saw the chance and, like a good soldier, he took it.'

'The poor man at the Menagerie, too. Or so you said. Chance, then?'

'Fortune smiled on me, I guess. There he was, hand inside the cage, ticklin' the beast's nose. You gotta laugh at that, don't you, Esther? Ticklin' a lion's snout? Must have done it a hundred times. But I pressed him hard against the bars – and then he knew me. Cried out. Frightened the beast, and it snapped. But if it hadn't been the lion...'

He pulled the spring-blade knife from his pocket and there was no need to say more.

'My turn now, Captain?' she said.

'I shall miss you, Esther.'

He took a step towards her, and she felt the terror of imminent death's inevitability. Overwhelming sadness, a fathomless gulf of emptiness. Neo, she thought. Oh, Neo...

'My husband,' she whispered. 'Tell me, when Kelly delivered your message, did he – did he see him?'

'Playin' for time, Esther?' said McCafferty. But he halted there, just a few feet from her.

'Do I have anything to lose by doing so?'

'I suppose not. But no, Kelly didn't see him.'

'And do I die without even knowing the cause?'

'If it's a consolation, Esther, it's the cause of Irish independence.'

Think, girl. Think!

'I mean your real cause, Captain. The reason you're here – in Chester.'

He laughed at her. The creature laughed. But she was determined to buy every second of life. Every chance.

'Bigger than anything you can imagine, Mrs Palmer. Much bigger.'

He stepped forward again and she closed her eyes, stretched her head high, knowing she should pray but imagining only Neo's sweet face, feeling nothing but the tear rolling down her cheek.

Then, in the distance, a sudden report, a hollow crack.

Gunshot? Surely...

She opened her eyes in time to see McCafferty running through the doorway, slamming it closed behind him.

But no sound of the lock.

Now or never, she thought. Now or never.

She tried the door. It opened.

Ettie could hear McCafferty below, shouting at his men, then running out through the coach house gates. But who was left below? Cody, she supposed, the devil she'd wounded. She couldn't take a chance on the ladder. But there was the hayloft door.

She ran those few steps – her boot heels loud upon the floorboards – lifted the bar holding the door closed and tossed it aside.

A shout from below, then a curse. Yes, Cody – but with the wounded leg, the ladder wouldn't be easy. Her bonnet and bag were both below as well. But they'd have to stay there.

She turned back to the storeroom, knelt at the oil lamp and the vesta case. With trembling hands, she struck one of the two remaining matches. But it guttered into smoking impotence as she lifted the glass chimney and turned up the wick a notch.

Cody was still shouting, telling her to stay put or, by God...

Let there be oil, she prayed, as she fumbled for the final match. Let there be oil. The Lord Jesus be praised, a flame, and the flame applied to the wick. The chimney back in place.

Outside again, and there was the top of Cody's head in the opening, the fingers of one hand gripping the edge as he tried to haul himself up with one useless leg. She went to the bales, lamp in hand, and shouldered a couple of them down onto the boards near the ladder.

She smashed down the lamp, saw little tongues of blue fire leap and catch at the scattered wisps of hay, then feed upon the broken bales.

Cody cried out and she heard him fall. A scream of rage.

Now she had the hayloft door open, but jumped back when she saw the drop.

Above the opening, there was a hoist and, hanging from its outstretched rusted iron arm, a pulley with a large hook below, the rope secured to a cleat bolted to the brickwork. She unfastened the rope and lowered the hook until she could set a foot into the bend, the hook's throat. And then, keeping the rope taut to slow her descent, she began to drop, spinning round slowly as she fell.

Her last glimpse of the hayloft's interior was the burning hay, billowing smoke and, on the farther side, small crates – and a single suitcase.

Chapter Twenty-Six

They heard what sounded like a gunshot. And, soon after, an explosion. A loud explosion.

Palmer stared along the narrow iron footbridge ahead of them. It spanned the wooded ravine – this "Dingle", according to their guide – on the far side of which stood more trees, then the road and the cemetery beyond.

'Wilson?' he said. 'But what…?'

Wilson, the black-garbed, sour henchman lent to them by Lady Olivia, had driven them in the phaeton from Warren Hall, through Saltney to the lodge of Curzon Park, where they had abandoned the carriage in the care of the lodgekeeper, an associate of Wilson's. Perfect timing, for they had arrived just as the occupants of those fine houses above the river's cliffs were taking to their own vehicles and heading to church. A mass exodus, almost, which allowed Palmer, Wilde and Wilson – the latter with his shotgun hidden beneath the skirts of his long, dark Inverness cape – to pass through without attracting undue attention.

By that time, Palmer's nerves were entirely frayed. The closer he came to their destination, the greater his fears for Esther. He had been almost beside himself when Wilson insisted on going ahead alone.

'Scout the ground,' Wilson had said. 'There's a lodge. Main entrance to the cemetery. But the keeper's new. Strange cove. Keeps himself to himself. But I'll go ask him about the old manse.'

That had been ten cruel minutes ago. And now, the shot, the explosion…

'I believe we should wait no longer,' said Wilde, and he set off across the footbridge.

Palmer followed, but doing his best not to look down, for the drop was vertiginous. His concern for Ettie, however, overcame the acrophobia, and he quickly found himself among the lichen-boughed silver birch, oak and chestnuts, all coming into leaf. As Wilson had suggested, they provided an approach to the burial grounds at least somewhat under cover of their unfurling foliage and freshly sprung or evergreen undergrowth.

They halted briefly at the road beyond – this main road carving a passage through the surrounding woodland, away south and eventually to Wrexham, a dozen miles away. A tunnel with a canopy veil of green lace. There was little traffic, a cart in the distance and a carriage coming towards them over the Grosvenor Bridge to their left, but Wilde urged Palmer to be cautious as they crossed towards the broad cemetery gates. There, they sheltered behind one of the sandstone gateposts and surveyed the scene.

Inside the gates, the lodge, at the junction of two internal lanes, the broader of the two heading straight across, sloping down towards trees and a lake, perhaps two hundred yards away. Galloping along that path was a frantic riderless horse. Wilde and Palmer exchanged puzzled glances but said nothing, while Palmer could not keep that annoying line from his brain.

"A horse, a horse, my kingdom for a horse!"

The other, more narrow way, also ran downhill, to the left, almost parallel to the road. There were treetops, the chimneys of a house and, from somewhere at the back of that building, a shroud of smoke rising into the breeze.

'My wife,' he murmured. 'You do not think…?'

It was not possible, surely? That Ettie could somehow be anywhere near that conflagration?

'Of course not,' said Wilde. 'Else why would they be there?'

For, it was the path itself which drew their attention.

Upon it, four men struggled to carry something between them. A dark shape with dangling arms and legs, black, flapping skirts. Wilson's Inverness cape, Palmer had no doubt. They were arguing among themselves, gesticulating wildly towards the billowing black cloud.

'Great Heavens,' he said, 'they have him.'

He moved to follow, but Wilde stayed him.

'Wait,' he said. 'They are too many.'

'We have your revolver, do we not?'

'Do you not see they are similarly armed, sir? And do you know those men, Mr Palmer?'

Palmer had expected to see Jackson – McCafferty – and his absurd beard. But no. There was a fellow with a brown tweed jacket and cap, another in shirtsleeves, raw-boned and short in stature. The final two then ran from the group, towards the smoke – to the obvious annoyance of the pair left behind with the burden of Wilson's slumped and inanimate form, as well as the shotguns each of them carried. One of the runners was a square-headed hatless rogue in a light-coloured canvas coat. But the fourth...

'I don't recognise any of them,' said Palmer, 'though, that fellow in the mustard-coloured Ulster...'

Ettie hauled herself up the steps she'd descended the previous afternoon. She was injured. Badly, perhaps. The explosion had blasted her face – and blasted the rope from her hand. She'd fallen the remaining six feet or so – enough for her to twist an ankle. But, worse, the pulley had come crashing down upon her shoulder.

She stopped at the top to look back.

The coach house was now entirely afire, smoke and flames spiralling from the roof. Only moments before, she'd seen the horse either escaped or released from the stables, charging off along one of the paths.

But how? How had it happened – the detonation? She couldn't think. Not clearly. Dazed and a little dizzy.

Behind her, Cody, yelling and cursing, limping up the first of the stone steps but carrying a naked blade.

Where now? she thought. She didn't know the place and had decided that retracing the route by which she'd been brought here yesterday was the only viable option. After that? The river, perhaps? In any case, McCafferty and Kelly had gone off in the opposite direction. That's it, she decided, keep moving. Away from them. Away! But where was Neo? And the gunshot she'd heard? She prayed to Lord Jesus he was safe.

At her feet, along the path's edge, lay some ornamental rocks. She picked one small enough for her to manage and pitched it with all her might down towards her pursuer, but it bounced harmlessly past Cody. He grinned up at her and brandished the knife.

'I'm gonna gut you, lady. Then peel you like a peach.'

She turned and hobbled away, pain jarring through her shoulder, as well as her ankle.

Could she make it to the river ahead of Cody? She wasn't sure. But there was closer possible sanctuary. Below her, on this reverse slope of the ridge, was the mortuary chapel, standing proud above the lake with its overhanging willows, its island, its pair of gliding swans, and its raft of quacking ducks taking to the wing and stirring the water. Their flight drew her eye to the cemetery's high ground beyond, and to a distant funeral cortège. Sunday burials were not exactly unknown, of course. Although, personally, Ettie frowned upon the practice. Something strange about this one, however. The splashes of white mottled among the otherwise sombre smudge of mourners.

No time to ponder this mystery now, and she turned her attention back to the chapel. Past the Gothic bell-gable, the side of the building closest to her boasted three tall arched windows of stained glass and a porch with, it appeared, an inviting open door. Surely there must be some way to secure it from within. And, surely, even a creature like Cody would not violate the sanctity of God's House.

She slipped down the grass as best she could, always looking behind to see whether Cody would spot her destination, but when she reached the porch he was nowhere in sight. Yet, when she was inside, taking a final peep through the crack before she closed the door fully, there he was, up on the ridge and staring all about in his frustration. She carefully worked the ring handle to set the latch in place. Though there was no way to lock or bolt the door.

She began to scan the interior for a decent hideaway. There were few options. The walls were unadorned and whitewashed. A couple of wooden troughs held prayer books. Close at hand, down the gable wall, the bell rope passed through several rusting iron eyes with a triangular pull at its lower end and the upper section disappearing through a pipe in the ridge beam. Rows of pews, naturally. A font, always incongruous, she thought, in a mortuary chapel. At the farthest end, a lectern and a lattice-carved rood screen, with a loft above. Just beyond the screen, and framed by its wide archway, a simple but dominant altar, upon which stood a large brass crucifix, burnished so well that the light through the south-facing windows played about it in a rainbow halo.

A sign, she thought. It was, in any case, the only possibility. What better place to pray for her salvation? Perhaps, also, for some relief from her hurt? She moved as quietly as she was able, down the aisle, though the mahogany-polished archway, and eased herself down behind the altar. Once she was settled, she could see, at its side, the narrow stone doorway leading to the even narrower rood loft spiral staircase. Would she be able to climb up there? Absolutely not. But she decided to slip off her boots. Probably a mistake, for the ankle would swell. Though, more immediately, she had worse things to worry about.

A metallic click. The almost imperceptible scrape of another's boot on the stone slabs. Then silence. She held her breath. A minute passed. And another.

She heard a rhythmic scratching noise.

'Come out, little coney,' Cody whispered. 'Wherever you are.'

Ettie stole a glance around the corner of the altar. There he was, shuffling cautiously towards her, looking all around, checking each row of pews, running the tip of his skinning knife along the whitewashed stone of the wall beside him.

She pulled away slowly. Almost not daring to move. Hands and knees, inches at a time. She crawled backwards along her own side of the altar, her movement disturbing ancient dust. Ettie thought she must surely sneeze and clamped a hand to her nose.

The scratching stopped, the ensuing silence oppressive, and the world standing still.

'I'll make it quick, girl,' Cody sighed. 'Promise, I will.'

It began again, the knife scratching at the stone. Louder now, almost upon her. She reversed around the altar's flank, praying the Almighty would guide her timing. She wished that she might close her eyes, that the floor might swallow her. And, with the Lord's protection, she found herself crouching behind the other side of the altar. Cody, it seemed, now stood in her former hiding place.

'Left your boots?' she heard him mutter.

She edged still further, completing almost the full circuit. Slowly, she raised her head. Cody had his back to her and he was staring at the rood loft stairway, then up at the underside of the loft itself.

'Clever coney,' he laughed, while Ettie silently lifted the heavy crucifix from its place upon the altar and swung it back.

Oh, my Good Lord Jesus, she said to herself. Forgive me!

Palmer found himself in the embrace of a deadly dance.

It had all happened so fast, Wilde stepping resolutely forward and pointing the pistol. His stance had reminded Palmer of a duellist, ramrod straight, feet together, arm outstretched, the revolver already cocked.

'Now, gentlemen,' the superintendent had said in that rural Salopian tone which almost made it sound like *gentle-mon*, 'let us not do anything foolish. And I'll thank you to release your prisoner.'

Palmer had praised Heaven that Lady Olivia's henchman was, at least, still alive, Wilson having stirred, trying to struggle free. The two men had already half-dropped him, one of his legs dragging along the gravel. But when Wilde had spoken, they'd both spun around in surprise, so that Mr Wilson fell completely onto the path.

'Not one of them, I'm not,' the fellow in shirtsleeves had screamed, raising both arms and holding his shotgun aloft. 'Don't shoot, sirs. Don't shoot. They forced me, so they did.'

Irish, without a doubt. But the other cove, in the tweed shooting jacket and cap, had seized poor Wilson around the neck and, levelling his own weapon at them, begun to drag him backwards down the incline.

'Keep your distance,' he'd shouted, the accent American. 'An' you...' he had turned his attention to Shirtsleeves. 'You get back here!'

But for every step the American took, Wilde had moved as well, and that Webley revolver unwavering, aimed at the rogue's head.

Palmer himself had been paralysed with fear, assuming foolishly that at the sight of the policeman's weapon and daunted by the presence of such evident authority – even though they might not know his precise position nor even his lack of jurisdiction – they would simply surrender. Yet, all these guns. These terrifying guns. As always at such moments, he'd felt his chest tighten, the coughing begin.

'Take that fellow's weapon, would you, Mr Palmer?'

There'd been the merest movement of Wilde's head in the direction of Shirtsleeves.

'Me, Superintendent?' Palmer had said, hoping that naming the policeman's rank in itself might expedite a non-violent conclusion. Still, despite his better judgement, he'd stepped towards the wizened rogue, looking into the man's face. 'And my wife,' he'd said, stretching out his hand. 'Where is my wife?'

Wilde had now been several paces past them, still slowly pursuing the American and a struggling Wilson and repeatedly calling on the villain to submit. It was the moment when Shirtsleeves, the duplicitous dog, had shown his true colours, turning quickly and levelling the shotgun at the superintendent's back, ignoring Palmer entirely.

Had he assumed that Palmer's reluctance was a sign that he had nothing to fear from him? That Palmer's evident terror would prevent his intervention? If so, it was a serious error of judgement, for Palmer had jumped forward, more by instinct than any sense of bravado, gripped the shotgun's barrel with both hands and thus had begun this bizarre fandango.

Indeed, there was a certain symmetrical rhythm to their struggle. Shirtsleeves, snarling into Palmer's face, tried to step and swing the shotgun in one direction, and Palmer followed. Then the other way, followed by a writhing pirouette. The man's finger caught the trigger, and the weapon fired, Palmer feeling the blast perilously close to his head.

A ringing in his ears and, as it cleared, the noise came again – or so he thought.

But this was no problem with his hearing. It was the jangling bell of a fire appliance in the distance and, from the sound of it, coming fast.

With a final effort, Palmer succeeded in pulling the shotgun's stock from the man's hand, then swung it back into the fellow's face. He heard the crack as it connected with the man's cheekbone. Shirtsleeves staggered back. For good measure, Palmer struck him again. And now the little wretch fell – dazed, but quickly struggling to get up again.

Palmer turned in time to see Wilson, still in the American's grip, but also holding that other shotgun's barrel. He pushed it down and across, twisting his captor around. It fired. Shirtsleeves was hurled forward with a scream of agony, buckshot slamming into his side at close range. Though, he had not hit the ground before there was a second retort.

A curl of smoke rose from the Webley. Wilson finally released, crashing to the ground. The American, his cap spinning through the air, a look of simple astonishment on his face – a neat dark hole in the centre of his forehead.

All this time, as the sound of the shot echoed away, the fire engine's bell came closer. Palmer could even hear its wheels now, the horses' hooves, as the machine thundered towards the Grosvenor Bridge, only hundreds of yards away to their left, though beyond the cemetery's boundary and its entrance gates.

Then, another bell. It tolled loud and insistent as a tocsin alarm. But this one from beyond the trees to the right.

'Ask not…' Palmer muttered.

Ettie heaved on the chapel's bell rope one last time and glanced back at the altar. Had she killed him? She had no idea. There had been blood, but she could not bear to look closely. Blood on the heavy base of the crucifix, as well, which she had simply set back where it belonged. Perhaps later if, God willing, she might be spared…

Still, she'd had the presence of mind to pick up Cody's knife and set it down on the book trough while she rang the bell.

'What have you summoned, Esther Palmer?' she said. 'Hell or salvation?'

She had no idea, but she was determined that, by this evening, she would lie once more, either in the arms of her husband or in those of the Lord. Yet she would bring an end to McCafferty's torment of her, one way or the other. So, she picked up the knife and threw open the chapel door.

Ettie stood within the porch in her stockinged feet, the damaged ankle hurting like the devil. But defiant, knife in hand, as though –

armoured by God and righteous indignation – she might defeat entire legions of her foes. Yet, for a moment, she was disorientated. The light. The illusion – that, somehow, the chapel bell still rang. But no, this was different. Urgent and raucous, in harmony with the *caw, caw, caw* of crows startled into the cloudy Sunday sky. A fire bell, surely. Salvation, then? she wondered.

Yet, her courage slipped away like beach sand between her fingers as she saw her enemy's approach. Slipping and sliding down the slope towards her. McCafferty and Kelly, the latter with pistol in hand.

McCafferty saw her now. He stopped his descent, venom in his eyes, then looked back over his shoulder to where, above the ridge, soot and smoke still climbed within the swirling smoke. His hands were empty. She remembered the things she had seen in the coach house. The papers. The plans. The crates. The suitcase. Whatever they had concealed, it must all be gone now. It caused her to smile ruefully.

Though, when the Fenian turned back, it was not in her direction, for Kelly was yelling, pointing past the chapel. Somewhere beyond her vision. Somewhere to the left. Somewhere in the direction of that fire bell.

Ettie fought the urge to head that way. There was, at least, some cover within the porch whereas, out in the open, and Kelly's revolver, a vengeful McCafferty...

Some altercation between the two Fenians – McCafferty trying to urge Kelly towards the river, but Kelly pulling away from him.

'Go, Captain, go!' he yelled and pushed McCafferty away from him.

Then he checked his revolver and came straight for her.

The picture, Palmer decided, might have been composed by some absinthe-crazed painter. Daumier, perhaps. He took in the entire canvas in a single moment of time. The ridge, the trees, the smoke. Coming down the slope, two men. One of them – the fellow in the yellow Ulster, McCafferty surely – heading for the chapel to Palmer's right, from whence the bell no longer chimed. The other, the square-headed rogue they'd also seen earlier, a flapping canvas coat, running towards Palmer and Wilde. This fellow held a pistol.

More closely, emerging from the trees on another path at this right hand, a funeral procession. A funeral among the obvious fraternity, Palmer noted. A Sunday? Well, these were Freemasons. All men. All with covered heads. All with the sashes and the white lambskins of their order. The coffin draped with the white apron of the deceased and littered with yew sprigs. The coffin carried by pallbearers, each of them similarly attired.

Palmer's instinct was to remove his Derby, but when these funeral-goers remained bowler-hatted…

In that frozen instant, the cortège had stopped, the mourners gaping in astonishment, muttering one to another, as Wilde and Palmer shattered the scene and rushed past. Wilde still brandished the Webley. But both of them paused briefly to doff their hats in respect. How much more shocked might the mourners have been, thought Palmer, had they passed Mr Wilson, left behind to guard the American's dead body and the seriously injured lodge-keeper? For, at least, there'd been time for Wilson to briefly gasp out how he'd knocked at the lodge, enquired about the chaplain's manse and been assured by the Irishman there was nobody there. Certain, he'd said. But, walking away, Wilson had heard a horse from the direction of the manse itself. He'd returned to the lodge, asked whether there were stables down there – and been clubbed for his troubles.

And now, behind them, the thunder of the fire engine and the fireman still slamming the bell's clapper rope back and forth. They both jumped out of its way, stopped in their tracks on the path's verge and Palmer turned in time to see the moment of its passing. Four snorting horses at the gallop, all flying white manes and frothing spittle, jangling harness and slapping leather reins, gravel like grapeshot from beneath their hooves. The long red cart with the slogan in gold along its flank: *The Earl of Chester's Volunteer Fire Brigade.* The ladders, the hoses, the crew – part-fastened tunics of blue, buttons and helmets of brass, one of the men clutching a yapping mongrel dog. And, clinging to the side of the appliance, a policeman, aghast at the revolver in Wilde's fist.

Palmer was desperate to reassure the fellow. 'Friends!' he wanted to shout. 'Friends in pursuit of law and order!' But the moment and the fire engine had already passed. Instead, he simply tipped his hat by way of acknowledgement.

'There, Mr Palmer,' Wilde shouted. 'That one, at least, is making a break for it.'

'McCafferty,' said Palmer.

Sure enough, the fellow – still some distance away – was running across the lower section of the slope and heading, Palmer guessed, for the river. McCafferty's companion, however, was now making for the chapel.

Palmer and Wilde loped towards the chapel, as well. For it was plain, was it not? If all the other players were accounted for, the chapel's bell-ringer must surely be…

Ettie, he thought. My dear girl. And still in danger. Immediate danger from McCafferty's henchman.

Yet, he was breathless, his chest tightening once more. He was forced to stop, to catch his breath, hands on his knees, though Wilde raced on. As the superintendent ran, that other Fenian wretch looked up, saw Wilde – or, more likely, Wilde's Webley – and changed direction. Towards Wilde himself. Towards the junction ahead, at the bottom of the slope. Towards the junction where the fire appliance was about to make its turn to the left, towards the manse.

Palmer observed one final scene. The Fenian raised his pistol as he ran, aiming at the superintendent. Wilde's own revolver coming up.

Then Ettie, his beloved Ettie, coming into view from the far side of the chapel. Ettie limping. Ettie with something shining in her hand.

Everything exploded together. A shot from Wilde. One from the Fenian. Both missed.

And Ettie crashing into the Fenian's back – the wretch stumbling beneath the stamping, trampling, pulverising hooves.

Chapter Twenty-Seven

Ettie winced as Edward Davies dabbed at the yellow stains upon her cheeks.

'It stings,' she told him, sunlight bouncing from the ribcage of the skeleton dancing in the corner of his private consulting room. Yes, sunlight. Spring, it seemed, had finally arrived. Or perhaps, after the darkness of yesterday, and the past weeks, it simply seemed that the warmth spreading through the window was especially intense. All things were relative, were they not?

'Ammonia, my dear,' said their friend. 'I need to clear away the Carron oil and make sure these burns and abrasions are clean. They treated you at the Chester Infirmary?'

'It was mercifully close to the cemetery,' Ettie replied.

'No lasting damage, I trust?' said Neo, flapping like a mother hen.

'I cannot believe, Alfred,' said the doctor, with some annoyance, 'that you allowed this sweet girl to face such dangers. And you, sir, what in Heaven's name were you thinking?'

Neo blustered for a reply which might mask the gulf which had sprung up between them. Still, she decided to rescue him as he, yesterday, had attempted to rescue her. Ettie's own Earl Percy, hero of *The Castle Spectre*. Though, if he had his time over again, might he not simply have abandoned her in that place.

'We kept the infirmary busy all afternoon,' she said, trying to trivialise the situation but her legs still trembling with the delayed shock of it all and the ankle still vexing her.

'It sounds like a bloodbath,' Edward scolded them both.

'I still shudder at the thought.' She forced a smile, but the doctor looked down at her shaking limbs.

'In a moment,' Edward murmured, 'I shall give you something to calm those tremors, Esther. Those vermin bites, as well.' She couldn't help scratching at mention of them. 'But two dead, you say?'

The bites – or maybe they were more symptom than cause – had kept her awake most of the night. The bites, and Neo's endless questions. Two sleepless nights, therefore. Yet she felt entirely invigorated. Strangely and excessively animated.

'Two, yes,' said Neo, rubbing angrily at his beard. 'Two more at death's door. Still, the police surgeon believes they shall both survive. At least...'

Yes, Ettie thought. They shall survive long enough to stand trial and, most likely, to hang – as accomplices to McCafferty's murders.

'But Jackson – McCafferty, I mean,' said Edward. 'Dead as well?'

'They detained us all afternoon and well into the evening,' she told him, with bitter memories of how they had been interrogated first at the infirmary, then at the police headquarters on Foregate Street. Their questioning had been punctuated by a series of telegraphic messages, apparently bouncing back and forth. The incoming telegrams coming from where? It was never made clear. Though, with each break in the proceedings, with each subsequent waving of yet another cable – and never the courtesy of the contents divulged – the Chester City constabulary's attitude towards them hardened.

'But by the time they saw fit to release us,' she went on, 'they had found the boat.'

'Smashed upon the weir with the flood tide,' said Neo. He stared into her eyes as though this, too, might be another of the deceptions she had practised upon him.

Ettie looked up at the doctor.

'And this?' she said, touching fingers to her singed and frizzled hair.

'I fear I cannot do much about that, my dear.' He stood back and admired his handiwork, fresh oil applied to the burns, a camphor salve to her cuts and scratches. 'But it will grow again. And the rogue himself?'

Ettie had wept openly when they'd finally returned home – Mr Wilson having himself been released and gone to collect the phaeton and driven them to the station, leaving them with an assurance – or, perhaps, a threat – that he would report to Lady Olivia. It transpired that Wilson's sister had died in the Clerkenwell Outrage all those years before and, given McCafferty's prominence among the Fenians, now considered his score against them settled.

'Almost certainly drowned,' Neo told him. 'His coat found caught in the undergrowth at the river's edge. And the tide running something fierce.'

There had even been a witness who'd seen him go into the water. The Handbridge side. Watched him thrashing in the swirling waters, one of his mustard-yellow sleeves snagged in the branches and, at the end, the man sinking down, the Ulster left empty and afloat.

'There,' Edward smiled down at her. 'Good as new. Just this...' He poured a greenish tincture for her to drink. 'For your tremors, your phlegm and to help you sleep. And let's hope McCafferty's demise is an end to the matter.'

She exchanged glances with Neo. This was almost the least of the things which had troubled them through the night. Neo the optimist, certain that McCafferty must indeed by dead. Dead, regardless of her foolishness. Her deceits. But her own instincts screamed at her that her husband – her poor frightened husband – might be wrong. And in some strange and despicable corner of her brain, she did not want it to be true.

'Thanks to my wife's presence of mind,' said Neo, his words laced with unaccustomed sarcasm, 'I believe you are correct, Edward. Good gracious, such mettle! Cracked one of the devils over the head with a crucifix, of all things. Doing the Lord's work, indeed.'

Cody, she remembered. Cody and the skinning knife.

She stood carefully, testing the ankle. At least the swelling had subsided and she'd just about been able to get back into the boots recovered from the chapel.

He helped her into her coat. Though she could sense his distance, the stiff formality of it all. She tied the ribbon of the casquette beneath her chin, pulling down the pink tulle veil, chosen for its ability to cover most of her poor face.

'And Friday?' said Edward. 'Shall we see you for cards? Or a music night, perhaps?'

They both said yes, even if it was half-hearted, to say the least. And she saw the disappointment on Edward's face.

'Of course we shall come,' she said, now with too much enthusiasm, rather than too little. 'For Heaven's sake, I cannot wait to hear what Alison might have to say about our little adventure.'

She tried to laugh, but it was a hollow, foolish little sound.

Back on the street, heading for the police barracks, she limped beside him and linked Neo's arm.

'My dear,' he said, brusquely, 'I must ask. When they brought the news about that wretch and the river, it seemed to me – well, that the news saddened you?'

'Saddened?' she said. 'No. We cannot be certain, can we – what might have happened next? To me. To you. Yet there, in that place, McCafferty seemed the least of my perils.'

'Merely a murderer?' That sarcasm again.

'Of course. I know that, Neo. I suppose that pretence of affability made him the most evil of them all. Though – well, he succeeded in creating some illusion that I was under his protection. Kelly, on the other hand, or Cody...'

Ahead of them the sandstone turrets and gateway to Wilde's domain, the road busy with traffic. Another Monday, though the Beast Market held too many uncomfortable memories. Besides, she had not told Neo the whole truth.

'And this,' said Neo, 'brings me to my second question. About that Cody fellow.'

'Cody?'

'The police surgeon. Was I mistaken? I thought I heard him say that, apart from the fellow's crushed skull, the wretch also had a leg wound. Bullet wound, of all things.'

'Did he say so, my dear?'

She heard the note of chemical gaiety in her own obfuscation, felt herself floating almost. Whatever had Edward given her?

'He did,' said Neo, stopping before the entrance gate. 'And, in all your descriptions of the events, I do not recall you mentioning how the rogue might have received that gunshot injury.'

'A mystery indeed,' she laughed without any sense of guilt. 'Perhaps I shall recollect matters more plainly after some sleep.'

'Of course,' he said, 'there is also the small matter of that poor woman killed at the Beast Market. Did you not say she fired a pistol at the creature?'

'Recovered by the police, I imagine.'

'Or perhaps…' he snapped, but then plainly thought better of whatever might have followed. 'Esther, I cannot ever recall a single dishonest word between us.'

'I told you, Neo. I only sought to protect you.'

'But do you not see, my dear – how little sense that makes? Protect me, how? With what? You expected to march into their midst and persuade those wretches from their vile turpitude?'

'I suppose this must have been the case,' she murmured, recalling the night's other accusations. About the spurious telegram from her sister Lucy. About her failure to understand how delivering herself into those evil hands had provided McCafferty with precisely the lure he had wanted. About her clandestine involvement with McBain and the Special Irish Branch. About so much more. Would the Lord Jesus ever forgive her? And for the worst dishonesty of them all?

They announced themselves at the guard room, asked to speak with the superintendent, and Ettie could not help noticing the frown, the hesitation, with which Sergeant Jones greeted them. And, though they were ushered up to Wilde's office, it was not Wilde himself they were destined to encounter.

They both knew this tall gentleman – by sight, at least – though they'd never been introduced. His face was weather-worn, though he could not yet be fifty, and it was graced with a drooping walrus moustache, already turned grey.

'Expecting you,' he said, his accent Lowland Scots, pointing peremptorily to the two chairs in front of the desk. 'Leadbetter. Major Leadbetter.'

He stressed the rank. *Major* Leadbetter, she thought to herself, in the same internal pompous voice. For some silly reason, she found his rudeness amusing. She grinned at the man. And he frowned back at her.

'Good morning, Chief Constable.' said Neo.

Well, of course, the Chief Constable. His name in the newspaper often enough. And it was hardly possible to attend any of the town's amateur concerts without hearing him perform one of his favourite renditions. *Impossible to Tell*. Or *Knocking*. The last time she'd heard him sing this latter ditty – the town's Music Festival back in February – he'd been accompanied by some fellow on a banjo. In post here for a few years now. But before? A distinguished career in the army. Some mention of service in Canada?

Ettie had not been here before. Though the office certainly had Wilde's stamp upon it. Family photographs among the *Wanted!* posters. The lingering smell of his pipe tobacco, despite the open window. Only the cuspidor at the side of the desk seemed out of place.

'And Superintendent Wilde?' Neo gently enquired.

'Confined to quarters. Suspended from duty.'

'But, my dear sir…'

The major stopped him with a raised hand as surely as he would have halted traffic at Bridge Street.

'Please, Mr Palmer. I believe you have interfered enough in this case.'

'Case?' Ettie repeated, the smile still affixed to her lips. 'Major, I was kidnapped and in mortal danger.'

Kidnapped? She remembered using the same word during the night, and Neo correcting her. How could it possibly qualify as kidnapping, he'd said, when she had so foolishly walked into their waiting arms.

'Without my husband's immediate action,' she pressed on, 'without the actions of Superintendent Wilde…'

'The authorities in Birmingham, ma'am, will be sending an artist to sit with you. A new description of McCafferty needed.'

'To identify the body?' said Neo.

'If he is, indeed, dead – yes. Though with John McCafferty, one can never be sure. And since my deputy has somewhat prejudiced their observation of the man…'

Neo raged at him for a while about his use of the word 'prejudiced'. But Ettie could not help thinking about William Wilde confined to quarters. She had no idea how large or small their living accommodation might be. Yet, she recalled seeing the family all together once, at the circus – the wife, Martha Jane, and an entire brood of children. Children of all ages. Lucky woman, she thought, when I would have given anything for just one. Though she imagined them now, cramped together in their meagre rooms. And she remembered yesterday, the look of defeat upon Wilde's face when he'd been required to surrender both his gun licence and his revolver. All her fault, as well, of course.

'The suitcase, madam,' she heard the Chief Constable say with some annoyance, and loudly. He had obviously already asked the question – perhaps more than once…

'Suitcase, Major?' She wasn't sure she understood.

The man picked up a typed sheet.

'Your statement, Mrs Palmer. You say that you started a fire to help you escape but noticed a suitcase. Then the explosion.'

Outside, a very different sort of commotion. The constables being paraded in the central courtyard, the sonorous voice of Sergeant Hugh Jones setting them to their drill. Marching boots. *Left… Left… Left, Right, Left.*

'Yes,' she said, raising her voice above the sergeant's shouted orders. An epiphany. 'Green. Normal size, I suppose. Brass corners. Battered. Well-travelled, I thought.'

The major picked up another paper, stared at it through a lorgnette.

'And crates,' he said. 'You mentioned crates.'

'Small. About so wide…' She held her hand perhaps a foot apart. 'Maybe a yard in length?'

'For tubing,' said the major. 'India rubber tubing. We found the remains.'

'The suitcase has some significance?' Neo asked.

Chief Constable Leadbetter seemed to be calculating – whether he might be divulging some state secret before he replied. He stood from the desk, went to the window, his gait betraying the slight duckwalk of a man who'd spent too many years in the saddle. He slammed down the sash. Then he stopped to hawk into the cuspidor before murmuring an apology to her, before settling again in Wilde's chair.

'You know about the arrest of Daly – in Birkenhead?'

Well, of course they knew!

'Your description, Mrs Palmer, matches the one we have for the suitcase he was carrying. And the explosion...'

'Then why, in the name of Heaven,' Neo himself exploded, 'is the superintendent suspended from his duties. Why? The man deserves a medal. McCafferty and his machinations, no longer a threat. A service to the entire nation!'

'Perhaps. Perhaps not. But certainly no affair of your own, sir. Had Superintendent Wilde not been so precipitate we might have discovered the entire scheme. But now...'

He held up Ettie's statement again.

'Did I omit something?' she said.

'Two details, perhaps,' the major snapped. 'The first, did you hear any mention of the castle – Chester Castle?'

'I did not,' she replied. 'I could hear them arguing at times, but it was all very indistinct.'

'The relevance, sir?' said Neo.

There was another long pause. Leadbetter took a kerchief from his pocket and dabbed at some spittle from his lower lip.

'I suppose it can make little difference now. The newspapers are already making enquiries. Witnesses, Mr Palmer. Funeral cortège. Reports of gunshots. And the inevitable speculation – about whether it might be true that Daly is now incarcerated at Chester, waiting to stand trial.'

'Chester?' said Ettie. 'We had read that he is remanded at Birkenhead.'

'He was transferred secretly to Chester last week,' said Leadbetter. 'Reasons of security.'

It all made sense, she thought. McCafferty's hideout at the cemetery, literally a stone's throw across the river to the castle itself. But she had no time to consider this further, for the Chief Constable was stabbing his finger at the page.

'And this intriguing note, ma'am. You say here you had seen some plans. Designs, perhaps?'

'And so I did, sir,' she replied, the memory making her smile yet again.

'But your description,' he said, using the eyeglasses to peer more closely at the typeface. 'What was it? Yes, here. "Like a cow's udder". What did you intend by that, Mrs Palmer?'

'Precisely what I said, Major. I did not see them clearly. No more than a glance. But what I saw brought to mind a drawing of a cow's udder.'

Chapter Twenty-Eight

It nagged incessantly at Palmer's brain. Where had he seen such a thing? The shape of a cow's udder? Infuriating. It caused him to pause in his breakfast, his search through the columns of the *Western Mail*.

'Well?' Ettie nagged at him. 'Is it there?'

There was still a cool distance between them. Though he was pleased she had virtually slept the clock around, and her poor face at least seemed less raw this morning. But she still limped a little, and she scratched through her blouse almost continuously at the bites beneath. She had awoken somewhat more irascible than he, himself. His anger at her deceptions and the lack of reasonable explanation for her actions had diminished in seemingly equal proportion to the way her own vexation with his questions had increased.

Palmer resumed running his finger through the articles on page three. A letter from Gordon Pasha still besieged at Khartoum. Questions in Parliament about the whole Sudan affair. Infanticide in Austria. A duel between two Fenians in Paris. And immediately after…

'Here,' he said, finding the piece. It was shorter than he'd expected.

DISTURBANCE AT CHESTER'S OVERLEIGH CEMETERY
On Sunday afternoon at the Overleigh Cemetery, Chester, there was a serious disturbance. Witnesses reported a fire and explosion in the stable block of the house once occupied by the cemetery's chaplain. Soon after, shots were heard and, allegedly, a Masonic funeral procession was disrupted. Officers of the local lodge have been unavailable for comment, though it is understood that arrests were made. An appliance from the Earl of Chester's

Volunteer Fire Brigade, an ambulance from Chester Infirmary, as well as local constables, were soon upon the scene. There has been considerable speculation that the Fenian John Daly, arrested recently in Birkenhead, may have been transferred over recent days to Chester Castle and that the disturbance may have been connected to his new incarceration in Chester. Later in the morning, a runaway horse was subdued in the vicinity of St. Mary's Church at neighbouring Handbridge.

'Kelly's horse,' she murmured, sipping at her tea. 'I hope the poor creature was unharmed.'

'I fear it does not say.'

Mention of the horse reminded him of the other matter troubling him. He had asked her several times about that same fellow – Kelly – being pushed beneath the hooves of the fire appliance. Yet, she seemingly had no recollection of playing any part in the rogue's death. She had virtually laughed at him when he had dared suggest such a thing might even have been possible. Well, it would wait. At least, she was safe. And McCafferty, he was certain, must be dead.

Palmer made her promise she would rest and assured her he would be back as soon as his work was done – and, perhaps, after another attempt to meet poor Wilde.

Down in his office-cum-laboratory, there were more yeast samples from Mr Wassmann to be tested, as well as stinking Ammonium Alum from the Leather Company's new supplier. Stinking, but nowhere near so foul as the softening solution they produced on the premises from the excrement produced by those vicious mastiffs – creatures kept tethered for the primary purpose of devouring offal from any poor beasts butchered on the premises.

With the various reports written and ready for delivery, he removed his apron and put on both hat and coat. He must meet Ned at the station, make sure he appraised his friend of the weekend's events – at least, so far as he understood them himself. What had Esther been thinking? The more he dwelt upon her actions, the more perplexed he became. In truth, it put him in no mood for tonight's talk at the library though, with Ned already on the way, he would have to make the most of it.

Palmer thought about going back into the house – and then thought he might not. Instead, he set off through town, chin lowered onto his chest in quiet contemplation. And, in this way, he failed to notice Bethan Thomas, strutting about the archway like an ancient peahen, until too late.

'Yes, I know,' he said defensively in Welsh, and briefly doffing his hat, before she even had a chance to open her mouth. 'The glass. But no news, I fear.'

'To be expected,' she replied, to his amazement, as though it were obvious.

'Really?'

He glanced about. A busy day. A lot of traffic, more horse dung on Hope Street, he decided, than usual. Bethan also glanced about, lowered her voice and turned her head up towards him. Close. Very close.

'All right, is she? Only, there's rumours, like. Papers, see. An' you missin' chapel – goin' off with the police. Two and two, Palmer *bach*. Two and two.'

How much did she know, for pity's sake?

'I thank you for your concern, Bethan – though, I'm not really at liberty...'

'*Hisht nawr!*' she urged him. Hush now. 'Just tell her old Bethan was asking for her.'

'I shall, Bethan. I shall. But now...'

He tried to leave, but she gripped his wrist.

'Got something for you, I have.'

She limped back to the museum, leaving him fumbling in frustration with his watch chain and exchanging greetings with passers-by familiar to him. But Bethan returned quickly enough, brandishing a rolled piece of paper, which she spread to show him a design in pencil. A design of the missing glass. It was beautifully rendered.

'Bethan, did you...?'

'Thought it might help, see.'

So precise. The goblet itself on its knopped stem and domed foot. The complete etched design of the nearer side, the large **WW** he remembered so well. Alongside the initials, the badge and emblem for the Order of the Garter. And then a cleverly sketched hint at the same motif – initials and emblem – being repeated on the farther side as well.

'Just as I recall it,' he murmured. 'All this from memory?' Palmer was full of admiration. 'But this?' he said. 'Of this I have no recollection.'

There was a continuous line of decoration above the stem, around the base of the goblet's bowl. A series of crowns. And beneath each crown, three small peaks – waves, of course.

'Think old Bethan's got it wrong, like?' she barked at him, and snatched back the scroll.

'It is myself being a fool, I fear. I showed it once to Sir Watkin, for it was plain the goblet must once have belonged to the Williams-Wynn family. But he would have none of it. A part of his family's history best forgotten, he said. You know, of course, that his ancestor was a noted Jacobite?'

Of course, she knew.

'But who'd steal this one, like?' she said. A good question. 'Still, with all these killin's. Bombs everywhere – well, only an old glass, isn't it? It's those that have died I feel sorry for. Who ever cares about *them*, like? Hunt the killers – of course. But those they've murdered? Forgotten about, they are.'

He was about to protest. But then he remembered that, in this case, at least, she may be correct.

Tobin, he thought. What do I actually know about Francis Tobin? Little enough, it seemed.

He looked again at his pocket watch. Still an hour before Ned's train arrived and he hurried on, to deliver his report for Mr Wassmann. And while the Lager Beer Company's manager wrote him a welcome cheque, Palmer put just one of his many questions.

'Can you tell me, sir,' he said, 'whether Mr Tobin ever had business – professional business, I mean – at the Pant-y-Golfen spring?'

'Tobin?' The German looked up quickly. 'Still questions about Tobin?'

But yes, he said. *Natürlich*. They must check the waters often. There had been occasions when creatures had been found dead there.

Two dogs. A sheep. Hence it had been part of Tobin's duties to visit weekly. How easy, therefore, Palmer decided, for somebody alerted to the fellow's routine and follow him. Somebody? McCafferty, of course.

Bethan had been right. Who had even given poor Tobin a second thought? Despite their own good intentions, he and Ned had only ever made the most cursory of pilgrimages to the probable scene of his actual death. Their focus had been on that fateful journey to Farndon.

The watch told him there was still time, so he headed out along the brewery's own new access road and left down Caterall's Lane under the railway, the just discernible ghost of Wat's Dyke, and onto the narrow track beyond. Up to his left, the Union Workhouse – and, to the north, the site where Edward Davies hoped work would soon begin on the town's own fever hospital – beyond the tree-lined Gwenfro. The rutted path meandered through a virtual wilderness of thick woodland, of birdsong-filled ivy and undergrowth, of bluebells in profusion, until the track came to an end at a bubbling, narrow stream. He followed the flow thirty yards uphill to the place where it sprang from a small sandy pool beneath a natural rock-bound fountain.

He crouched and ran his fingers through the cool water. He felt guilty – that he had only made his calculations from his own studies for the paper he'd written, or from the available herbaria. Yet, he felt somewhat vindicated when, just to his left, grew a thriving example of the rare Stag Spring Hawkweed.

Palmer muttered a short prayer for Tobin's soul, then scrambled over the remains of some ancient walls to more open ground. The walls industrial? Perhaps. For this area, he also knew from his studies, was named Maesgwyn – *whitefield* – for its historic limestone quarrying. He imagined the kilns which may once have stood nearby, where the crushed limestone could be heated to produce quicklime for mortar. But now only the empty fields remained, four of them, bordered by a still more ancient sunken pathway.

He picked his way along the track for ten minutes and emerged on the main road, not far from Mr Tench's house – which he had also named Maesgwyn. He turned right, past the Racecourse and the Turf, arriving at the station, just in time to meet Ned.

'Dear friend,' cried Ned, hastening to embrace him. 'I trust I find your Wrexham haven as tranquil as when I was last here!'

'Well...' Palmer began.

'I told you, Alfred, we should simply have cancelled!' Ned scolded him.

The evening had not ended well. Ned had gone to such trouble, and Palmer had so much affection for the younger man. Far beyond his appreciation for his assistance with the book and the regular visits to Wrexham which must take him away from his important role at the India Office. A certain notoriety, as well. Yes, the first Welshman ever to enter the Civil Service by public examination. Ten years ago, at the tender age of twenty. But also his extracurricular and antiquarian renown with the British Museum.

He had, at the Museum, used the pages Palmer sent him – the three maps: of Erbistock's Quilleted Fields; of Allington Meadows; and the Lordship of Bromfield and Yale – and arranged for a friend to have them photographed and the images etched onto magic lantern slides. A fourth slide had been created in the form of a green cloth book cover image, the lettering picked out in scrolling gold: *A History of Ancient Tenures of Land in North Wales and the Marches*. Beneath, his name in matching font: *A. Neobard Palmer*.

Beautiful and expensive, though Ned had brushed the cost aside. After all, the Wrexham Free Library – being alerted to the forthcoming book – had been kind enough to invite Palmer to speak on the subject. Flyers about the town had announced the event using precisely the correct title for its headline.

'Your name should be there as well, Ned,' Palmer had said, and Ned had laughed.

'Perhaps for the second edition, Alfred.'

He had also taken the trouble to hire the necessary apparatus – from Mr Price Jones.

But when they had arrived at the venue, the Free Library itself, the lamp had refused to function, rendering the projector entirely redundant.

Or perhaps it was poor Ned's distraction which cast such a cloud upon their efforts.

'Do you hold me responsible?' whispered his friend as they packed everything away and the librarian waited for them to finish, arms folded and his foot tapping a monotonous rhythm on the parquet.

'For alerting me to McCafferty's identity? Of course not.'

'And Esther assumed it would be enough to set you on the rogue's trail – put you in danger?'

'It seems she believed my life already at risk – some threat the fellow had made which she believed. Believed it with all her dear soul.'

Ned slid the magic lantern carefully down inside its mahogany case, while the wall clock ticked loudly in time with the librarian's foot.

'But whatever possessed her?' he said. 'To beard the beast in its lair?'

'A trap,' murmured Palmer, packing his papers into the canvas satchel. 'Yet, one she decided to spring – to confront him. Perhaps more than just confrontation.'

'More?'

Palmer shook his head. There was still that small matter of poor Mrs McBain's revolver, the other fellow who'd been shot, still without explanation of how he'd been wounded. And then there was a persistent anamnesis. What was it Wilde had said to him? *'I hope I may have contributed something towards her safety. Or your own, sir.'*

Ned laughed quietly.

'All so hard to credit,' he smiled. 'Our Esther. The Fenian's dynamite destroyed. McCafferty himself drowned in the Dee.'

'I try to avoid tempting providence,' said Palmer. 'And, somehow, I feel our world shall never be the same again. The whole business has left a rift, Ned. And we are still no closer to knowing how McCafferty intended to use his cache.'

'Whatever its purpose,' said Ned, 'you may be certain more innocents would have died.'

They took their leave, Ned still repeating the same questions, time and again. Yes, it had cast a shadow, his bewilderment – but not so dark as that brought to the meeting by the audience itself.

Few in number, but troublemakers plain from the outset. Three of them, dispersed about the room despite having arrived together. The same stern faces. The same clenched fists upon their knees.

Palmer's introduction had been lively enough, he thought. He had thanked the Free Library for the chance to speak about his forthcoming book. The title needed little explanation. *A History of Ancient Tenures of Land in North Wales and the Marches.* Self-evident, was it not? Yet, how easy, he had asked, to take for granted the location within which we spend our lives? How greatly enhanced, if we understood even just the etymology of our location's name? How utterly magnificent, when we can trace its entire history? For, the localities in which we spend our own years are themselves living entities.

One of the awkward squad had guffawed and Palmer had ignored him.

'Anybody here from Maesydre?' he had asked, hopefully.

There was not, but he explained anyway.

'Maesydre,' he repeated. 'Town Field in English. Because, in ancient days, so it was. Common land. For use by our townsfolk collectively. A common treasury, as Gerrard Winstanley might have named it.'

Blank faces. But he had persevered. About the old common fields, common land, common meadows, common quarries – like the Maesgwyn whitefields – and the common woods. An explanation of commotes and hundreds. Though, with the loss of the Welsh manorial system, all had changed.

'It seems clear,' he'd said, 'that those kings and princes ruled with a more common touch than could be said for those later imposed upon the people under the English Crown.'

One of the men rose from his seat. The other two had tutted and shaken their heads.

'Is that not disloyal to the Crown itself, sir? Are you not proud to be British?'

'I think, sir,' Ned had finally been unable not to intervene, 'it is possible to be proud of those things our nation has done well – yet still be critical of those it has not. It is called objectivity, I believe. But blind loyalty to Queen and Country, warts and all, simply because an accident of birth did deposit us here – well, sir, that is the epitome of foolishness.'

Ned had launched into a lecture.

'Have you so easily forgotten the Treason of the Blue Books?'

He reminded them. Forty years earlier, and the British Government Commissioners' Report on the state of education in Wales, the Welsh language and the morality of the Welsh people held to be the principality's greatest flaw. The report had sparked the Tredegar, Merthyr and Rebecca Riots, among others – and raised the entire question of Welsh tenants' rights. Or lack of them. Land tenure. The powers of the great landowners – and the very issues which inspired Palmer and Ned to their respective writings.

The other audience members – twenty of them – had been appreciative enough, despite the failure of the magic lantern. But, with the frequent interruptions of those three trouble-mongers, the meeting had broken up in disarray.

'Who sent them, do you think?' Ned asked, once they were out in the darkness of the square.

'There are enough big landowners out there, my friend. But perhaps Sir Watkin's nephew and heir. He seems to have me marked as a rabble-rouser. And Heaven alone knows what he'd make of you, Ned. But come, let's take a brew at the Cocoa House, shall we? To celebrate the success of the evening.'

Ned laughed.

'Why not?' he said. 'And you can tell me how your business may be faring. New contracts, Alfred?'

And there it was – the one contract he'd forgotten about. Designs, plans and the like, upon a table, hastily covered. An image. Like a cow's udder.

Chapter Twenty-Nine

'I spoke to the fellow just yesterday,' Neo told them, as Lady Olivia's barouche trundled towards Chester's Grosvenor Bridge. 'Mr McDermott.'

The invitation had come, as she'd known it must, to visit – but also to accompany the FitzPatricks, as their guests, to this afternoon's event. And this she had not expected. Hardly her personal cup of tea, either, but a distraction, she hoped – if only they would all forget their obsession. It was over. Why could they not let it rest?

'He had offered me a contract some weeks ago,' Neo went on. 'And during my visit to his foundry he'd been at pains to hide some plans. The shape, you see? Whatever the purpose, it resembled a cow's udder.'

'He built it, d'you know?' said Reverend FitzPatrick, dressed today in his best clerical frock coat and silk topper. 'For what purpose – did you deduce, Mr Palmer?'

What was her husband thinking? Since when had they become so close to the FitzPatricks? Did he not remember?

'McDermott insisted,' Neo told him, 'that he'd refused the work – that he had not asked too many questions. He could not, of course, recall anything of the fellow who'd brought him the plans.'

'How very convenient,' said Lady Olivia.

'Though, he managed to remember some of the internal moving parts – the teats, as he called them. Springs. Other mechanicals.'

'An infernal device,' said Lady Olivia. 'Without doubt.'

'Indeed,' Neo replied. 'And McDermott knew it. I suspect he was also well aware who it was that wished him to complete the work – though he denied it, naturally. Poor man was terrified.'

They turned towards the bridge, sunlit fingers groping through the spreading green canopy, the cemetery off to their right. A fine Saturday afternoon, the last in April. Summer very soon and she prayed the new season would bring better fortune. How much more acceptable was the world when God's grace shone upon it!

'Then, do we know whether the device will have been made elsewhere?' said Lady Olivia, her breath stirring the rose-pink veil.

'It seems unlikely any of the other foundries would admit to it.' Neo turned to Ettie herself. 'Do you not think so, my dear?'

Ettie knew she had been silent too long – and this was Neo's way of asking whether all was well.

'I am certain,' she said, 'that plans for such a device must have perished with McCafferty and his henchmen. Do you not repeatedly tell me, Neo, that he is indeed dead?'

She heard Lady Olivia's less-than-polite cough, but she turned her head back towards the Overleigh Cemetery.

Reminders everywhere. Wilson, behind her, up on the high box-seat, next to the coachman. The occasional crack of the whip. The *clop, clop, clop* of the two grey mares. And over there? The nightmare memories. Visions of Cody – the skinners' knife. Still alive, it seemed, and bound for the next Assizes. The lodge keeper, Lawson, as well. Lady Olivia had unravelled that one, at least. For Lawson – a Fenian sympathiser – had admitted he'd been bribed to play his part.

'Those bites still trouble you, Mrs Palmer?'

She looked sharply at Lady Olivia.

'Your pardon...?'

Ettie realised she'd been scratching at her arm, through the red and green paisley shawl. But then they were on the bridge, the town before them, the castle proud on its mound, the river and the Roodee Racecourse below to the left.

'The Dee,' she murmured.

'Yes,' said the reverend. 'A natural border, is it not – between the old and the new?'

Another world, she thought, as she glanced at the other guests beneath the grandstand's upper-level canopy with its ornate and gloriously painted ironwork. Monocles, whiskers, high beaver hats and curling cigar smoke. Voluminous silk skirts, parasols, bonnets and opera glasses. Below them, crowds of the merely modestly rich but, up here, only those – except herself and Neo, of course – with some claim or connection to aristocracy. And Neo had left her entirely alone with them, taken himself off to the conveniences.

'Thank Heavens for our veils,' Lady Olivia leaned across to whisper surreptitiously in her ear with those honeyed Irish tones. 'Mine to hide my age, yours to mask your wounds, yes?'

'They heal,' she replied, studying the older woman through her own lemon-yellow gossamer. Lady Olivia must have turned many heads in her day – and most men, Ettie decided, would still find her captivating. Perhaps, to some, her age would merely add to her allure. And was it true – a dalliance in her youth with the queen's own late-lamented consort? It seemed entirely plausible.

'Do they?' said Lady Olivia. 'Heal? Wilson told me about that day – about the fellow you...' She made a pushing gesture with both hands. 'Those things may leave their own scars.'

'I think he must be mistaken, ma'am,' said Ettie.

She was sick of the memories. Last night – Alison's musical evening: Edward at the pianoforte, normally with Alison singing at his side; their daughter Gwendoline, only eight, yet already a fine fiddle player; Joseph, the surgery boy, and his tin whistle; and Ettie with her concertina. Though, it was Neo's performance of *A Bandit's Life* which had touched a raw nerve. Some absurd connection she'd made between the bold bandit's hidden cavern and that hayloft. Then, that thunderous chord towards the end. Like the explosion. She should have been expecting it - she'd heard him sing it often enough – but it had caught her unawares, frightened her afresh.

After the music, there'd been the ritual sharing of the letters they'd each received during the week – news from here, there and everywhere. Yet, Ettie's contribution had been lacklustre, her mind too cluttered with recollections of her captivity – confused recollections of McCafferty. And when the evening had closed with a couple of heated debates – about the Colchester earthquake and about Khartoum – she had been unable to summon any enthusiasm for either issue.

'Well,' said Lady Olivia, leaning back in her chair, 'now we shall have some amusement.'

Out on the track, the first hooves thundered, the first sabres flashed and hacked. Quite a spectacle. The Earl of Chester's Regiment of Yeomanry Cavalry – their Grand Military Tournament and a tribute to their commander-in-chief, the earl himself, who had died earlier in the year. The opening event? A contest to see which of the immaculate horsemen – dark blue tunics with white braiding, black fur headgear – could slice open the most post-mounted coconuts at the full gallop. Mildly entertaining, though the entire grandstand was distracted by the arrival of familiar faces, the duke and duchess of Westminster – the duke's second wife, of course, and only married these past two years. The duke wore a black armband, still in mourning for the earl, his eldest son, Victor. And, remarkably, they were accompanied by somebody else she recognised instantly, with a jolt – and brought back still more unpleasant memories.

The fellow offered Ettie a brief salute, touching a finger to the brim of his bowler hat, though with no other expression upon his ruffian's face. He took up his station at the white wrought-metal railing, never once taking his eyes from the duke. Ettie stood, went to stand at his side, though looking down upon the cavalrymen.

'Sergeant Devlin,' she said, while the duke paid his respects to Lady Olivia and received her condolences. 'I hope you may be fully recovered.'

The last time she'd seen Devlin, he'd been laid out on the Beast Market's concrete.

'Ye can't keep a good fella down, Mrs Palmer.'

He pronounced her name precisely as Hatchet-Face would have done, harsh and protracted.

'And I'm sorry,' she said. 'About Mrs McBain.'

Yes, Mrs McBain. Another victim. It was Neo's present obsession. That the victims in all this should not be forgotten. It had been the main reason, he'd said, for so readily accepting the FitzPatricks' invitation. And earlier, at Warren Hall, they had pooled their knowledge of what had happened to the others. Ettie had repeated the confession from McCafferty – not that there was any doubt about his involvement.

'The last of them,' McCafferty had said to her. 'All the traitors, Esther.'

Francis Tobin? Undoubtedly followed to the Pant-y-Golfen spring. But who had divulged his routine to McCafferty? And how had Tobin's body been conveyed to Farndon. Had news of his funeral drawn Connor O'Donnell to leave the safety of Warren Hall's protection? Of course. And, at least, the FitzPatricks had been more forthcoming about their part in providing a refuge for him. A reminder that those with some status in Irish high society had been persuaded to develop their own intelligence networks and, in her own case, Lady Olivia had nurtured the role of her distant cousin Michael, as well as those of Tobin and O'Donnell.

Indeed, for the first time, Ettie had discerned some modest emotion from Lady Olivia about the loss of her cousin Michael Taylour – or Cutter, as he'd chosen for his alias – though she'd cursed him for his stupidity with the lion.

Meanwhile, Sergeant Devlin simply shrugged.

'Jest yer line o' duty, ma'am. An' she's at peace now – beside her old man.' It sounded less than respectful. 'They tell me ye went after them – McCafferty's gang. She always said you was the very devil.'

Ettie smiled. She would never have normally taken that for a compliment. But *went after them*? It was hardly the way she saw things. Heavens, it almost implied she had some plan to avenge poor Hatchet-Face. Imagine!

'And you, Sergeant? Here?'

'Protection duty, ma'am. For his grace.'

She looked over her shoulder. The duke had aged. Bushy sideburns extending right to his throat but white with tragedy now. And that absurd beak. They spoke of people having their noses in the air, but with the duke it was literally true – as though he needed to keep it there lest it should otherwise do somebody an accidental damage. His top hat was pale grey, luxurious like the absurdly oversized bow tie. At his side, the duchess, younger than her husband by far – actually younger than most of the children from the duke's first marriage. All summer silk of delicate blue to match the cloudless sky.

The FitzPatricks stood with them now, accepting flutes of champagne from a passing flunkey, just as Neo made his return.

'And, your grace,' said Lady Olivia, 'you will remember Mr Palmer, of course.'

It sounded like an instruction.

'Palmer...?' said his grace, as Neo offered him a respectful nod of the head.

Ettie watched the duchess murmur in his ear.

'The *Lady Constance*, Hugh. You told me the story.'

'My yacht?'

'You said she was run aground, my dear. Remember?'

'What? The rogue who...?'

'No, your grace,' said Lady Olivia. 'Mr Palmer was – well, on board. And here,' she extended her hand in Ettie's direction, 'is Mrs Palmer. Our guests for the day, sir.'

Courtesies were exchanged. The duke and duchess continued their progress, though Ettie saw that her grace continued to whisper in her ageing husband's ear and, with every sentence, he glanced back, each time more sharply, each time with his mouth hanging open ever further.

Eight years, Ettie thought. And for all the terrors of that day, they do not match those of these past weeks.

The duke and duchess vanished among the crowd of fawning admirers, and Sergeant Devlin followed them, passing Neo, giving her husband a salute, as well – and Neo's turn now to stand with gaping mouth pointing at the Irishman's back.

'Was that not...?' he said to her. But, by then, the FitzPatricks had joined them at the rail, Lady Olivia and her husband each sipping at their champagne.

'You are not partial to the French grape, Mrs Palmer?' said the clergyman, raising his glass to her.

Ettie pulled back the lapel of her coat, displayed the blue ribbon pinned to her blouse.

'Did I not tell you, Frederick?' said Lady Olivia, then turned to Ettie. 'Your husband, too?'

'We are for temperance, ma'am,' Neo replied, taking instead a pinch of his snuff.

Below, the cavalrymen had switched to a new contest – tent pegging, the horsemen attempting to spear small red ground targets, leaning right down out of their saddles and using the tips of their swords in lieu of a lance. Indeed, one of them reached so far that he fell entirely from his mount. A gasp from the spectators, lurid excitement at the possibility of blood, as the poor man barely managed to roll clear of the trooper coming up behind.

'In any case,' said Lady Olivia, 'there remains the small matter of the reward we discussed.'

'I believed, ma'am,' Neo replied, 'we had agreed to trade – the reward in exchange for the services of Mr Wilson and his shotgun.'

'Indeed, I had forgotten. But, even so, I intended to say simply that I do not believe your side of the arrangement to be fulfilled.'

'Not fulfilled? Information leading directly to McCafferty's capture, was it not? Surely, the fellow's death…'

'His coat discovered in the river? I fear you do not understand McCafferty, Mr Palmer. But now, if you will excuse us…?'

And they swept away in the duke of Westminster's wake without another word.

'Is that it?' said Ettie. 'Are we dismissed? Abandoned here? I trust you are now properly reminded of your station, husband.'

'We can get to it easily enough, my dear,' he told her with that air of mischief which sometimes could be so irritating at such inappropriate times.

'To what, precisely?' she replied, knowing she would regret it.

'Why, the station,' he beamed. 'Either here or Saltney.' Yet, he looked so crestfallen when he failed to draw even a smile from her. He began to stammer an apology, poor man. And then: 'But was I dreaming, Esther? The fellow in the bowler hat…?'

'Sergeant Devlin? Indeed, it was.'

Speak of the devil and doth he appear, she thought to herself, reminded of Devlin's own earlier comment. Her father, on the other hand, had been fond of another phrase. Name the wolf and he'll be at your door. For here came the man himself, once more, swaggering towards them like a prize-fighter.

'Mr Palmer,' he said. 'Her grace at least knows the service ye once did her husband. Quite the story. If I'd known about it earlier myself…'

'Is that an apology I hear?' said Ettie.

Devlin offered her a formal nod of the head for acknowledgement.

'Simply, ma'am, that her grace says to tell ye, if you'se need anythin' – transport or the like – I'm to arrange it for ye both.'

'The Special Irish Branch providing personal protection, Sergeant?' said Neo.

The sergeant removed his bowler and, taking his kerchief, wiped sweat from the inner band.

'Dangerous times, are they not? Those hallions not done yet, to be sure. An' the duke's a likely target. Hired an extra ten watchers of his own, he has. Each of them handy at what they do, if ye get my drift?'

'You do not believe McCafferty to be dead either?'

'We have his coat, Mr Palmer. An' in the pocket, his safe passage. Mr William Jackson,' he quoted from memory. 'British subject and mining proprietor. Requirement for him "to pass freely without let or hindrance". Signed by the marquess of Lansdown himself.'

'Governor-General of Canada,' Neo found it necessary to remind her. Did he think she did not know? 'But if he has no passport...'

'Sure, that's so. The point? A man like McCafferty, he comes and goes as he sees fit. A dozen identities. Nine lives, like.'

'I cannot believe he still lives.' Neo rubbed at his beard, a sure sign he was worried, not so certain as he had pretended to be.

'Hope for the best but be ready for the worst.'

'Your motto, Sergeant?' said Ettie.

'Betty McBain's. Funny, though. The Branch was never able to work out a rank for the woman. So, none of us ever knew where she stood – above us, or below. Not that it mattered. A woman? Imagine. To us she was just always Matron McBain. Seemed to fit the bill.'

It almost sounded like sarcasm. He turned to go while, out on the paddock, the regimental band struck up a rousing medley of martial tunes.

'Wait, sir,' said Neo. 'You have military experience, I think. Might I ask you one thing?'

He took from his pocket an envelope and his propelling pencil. He quickly made a sketch.

'This, sergeant. Have you seen such as this before?"

'Ach, now where did you see a thing like that, Mr Palmer?'

'A long story, Sergeant. But an infernal device of a particular sort, I gather?'

Devlin hesitated, as though deciding how to respond.

'Orsini bomb,' he said, at last. 'The fellow had it designed for an assassination attempt against the French emperor. See these pins?' He pointed at the "teats". 'Each filled with mercury fulminate. When they sense contact with an object, whatever the angle... BOOM!'

Ettie was scared almost out of her wits, jumped back with the shock – and fear.

'Apologies, ma'am. But deadly.'

'Yet, the French emperor lived to tell the tale,' said Neo.

'He did. But ten others killed. And nearly two hundred crippled. Interestin', too. Seems the Confederacy used them in their War Between the States. Throw one of those things anywhere near yer target, or bury one in the road yer enemies are going to pass over – well, ye cannot really miss.'

'But here?' said Neo. 'For what purpose?'

Devlin grinned at them both, in a most unpleasant way.

'I suspect by the time ye solve that mystery, Mr Palmer, it will be too late.'

Chapter Thirty

It hit him like an express train.

'My dear,' he cried. 'This is it. Great Heavens, this is it!'

Palmer had worked his way through today's copy of the *Western Mail*, as he had done since last Saturday at the Roodee. Page one: the shipping notices; sales by auction; public appointments; tenders and contracts.

Page two's editorials – Khartoum still besieged and plainly now doomed; Sunday Closing; and results from the Spring Assizes. Page three, with more about the Sudan and news that the Prince of Wales – the debauched and dissolute Prince of Wales, as Palmer knew only too well – had been installed as Grand Master of England's Freemasons. It caused him to think about the funeral cortège at Overleigh. Had the mourners all been sworn to secrecy, somehow? Well, it was, after all, the thing at which Freemasons excelled. And plenty of Palmer's friends were members of the local Square and Compass Lodge, meeting at the Corn Exchange.

But, on the back page, below letters to the editor and Welsh football news, there was this…

MR JOHNSON AND HIS BALLOON

Mr Frederick Johnson, the renowned Midlands aeronaut, has written to confirm that he will, indeed, be attempting a balloon ascent and pyrotechnic display as part of the Duke of Westminster's May Day summer fête at Eaton Hall. As we reported yesterday, the event will be attended by Prime Minister Gladstone and by His Royal Highness the Prince of Wales. Mr Johnson's balloon has a capacity of 24,000 cubic feet of gas, to be supplied by Wrexham's Gas Works, where the ascent shall begin should the weather and prevailing winds be favourable.

Ettie read the piece from over his shoulder, mouthing the words. 'You think...?' she said.

'I do.'

'But Mr Johnson. I have read accounts of his aerial exploits many times.'

'His *bona fides* will have been checked and checked again for an event like this. But I can smell it, Esther. McCafferty. An attack from the air? They could have an entire brigade of watchers guarding the estate and it will not protect them.'

'And all eyes on Birmingham, Neo.'

He checked his pocket watch.

'What time did Lady Olivia tell us it begins?'

'Midday, I believe.'

'Then, we shall divide our forces. You must try to find Wilde – or even Major Leadbetter. Warn them, my dear.'

'You are no longer certain he is dead, then? And why should either of them pay me any heed?'

'I do not believe either of them could afford to ignore such a warning. They have men on the ground, after all. They simply need to be alerted to the skies, as well. Nobody else seems to believe we are rid of McCafferty and I am happy to observe the same precaution.'

'Perhaps it might have more force if we went together.'

'You fear for my safety, Ettie. But you worry for no good reason, sweet girl. I shall, of course, do nothing but observe, and then join you post-haste at the barracks to confirm whether it is, indeed, McCafferty.'

He could see her doubt but, each attired in their summer coats, they walked briskly together to the bottom of Lambpit Street, where they kissed briefly but with some renewed affection. They parted company, Ettie for the centre of town and Palmer himself down Yorke Street, around into Mount Street and up the Salop Road towards Hightown.

But the closer he came to his destination, the tighter grew his chest with the tannery's stench and the rotten egg miasma from the

Gas Works itself. And the tighter his chest, the greater his doubts. How could such a thing even be possible? The conveyance of a balloon and all its paraphernalia – from Birmingham? The men required to assist in the ascent? All managed clandestinely? It was absurd.

He almost stopped and turned about. Yet, he was now part of a gathering stream of other folk, word having spread and everybody anxious to see the spectacle. Thus, it was more curiosity than duty which drove him on, to the offices of the Wrexham Gaslight Company, left along Rivulet Road past the public urinal, past the town's more venerable gasholder, as well as past the modern and more substantial telescopic gasometer. It was, he had long ago decided, the town's physical class divide – whether one lived upwind or downwind of the Gas Works and its surrounding stink.

Still, he could see it now, the huge netted dome of the scarlet and amber balloon rising above the open meadows and that pleasant riverside valley beyond – the scene of two fine summer concerts last year. Upon the balloon, the name *Empress* in large white letters.

Once past the Gas Works wall and standing upon the grassy knoll overlooking the broad green valley, he could see precisely the scale of the undertaking. A half-circle of onlookers, perhaps five hundred strong. Beyond them, one of the longest flatback lorries he'd ever seen. A team of eight horses. Snaking across the open ground, beneath feet and hooves alike, the India rubber tubing by which the balloon, it seemed, had been entirely inflated. For it was now become a living thing, a creature striving to rise into its natural environment and tethered to *terra firma* only through the efforts of two dozen strapping fellows. In the car, a square wicker basket, the aeronaut himself, helping yet another team to stow small wooden crates.

'Mr Palmer, what a pleasure to see you again,'

Viscount Broughton and in company with that parsimonious lawyer, his cousin, Gwilym Morgan.

'My lord,' said Palmer, 'I would have expected you to be at Eaton Hall for the duke's festivities.'

'Another engagement, I fear.'

'And you, Mr Palmer,' Morgan sneered, 'from your reaction to the very mention of aeronautical activity last time we met, I should not have thought to see you here, either.'

'A strange thing,' Palmer replied, 'but I rather believed I might need to be here. But if you will excuse me, gentlemen...'

'Of course, dear fellow,' beamed the viscount, as Palmer touched the brim of his hat in salute and began to walk away. 'But I hope,' Palmer heard him shout, 'that we might see you at the dining club?'

Palmer waved his hand above his head, an indeterminate gesture which Viscount Broughton might interpret in any way he wished. But catch me, he thought, in that confederacy of fools again? I think not! Yet, no mention of Jackson – McCafferty. No enquiry about him. I wonder why.

Though the question had no sooner sprung to his mind than he spotted another acquaintance of that evening at the Wynnstay – the ballooning enthusiast himself, Sir Watkin's nephew, Herbert, the yeomanry captain. There was a young woman on his arm, pretty, auburn curls, lace and feathers.

'Captain,' said Palmer, and doffed his hat to the young lady. 'I might have expected to see you make the ascent yourself.'

Embarrassing. It was plain the fellow did not recognise him.

'Forgive me...?' said the captain.

'Palmer, sir. We met at Viscount Broughton's *soirée*. The Wynnstay?'

'Ah, indeed.' The fellow seemed less than pleased at the renewal of their acquaintanceship. 'The scourge of honest landowners, are you not? But no, Mr Palmer. I am perfectly competent at the ascent and the landing, but such precise navigational skills required by this particular event is the preserve of only a few men. Men such as Mr Johnson. Though I was at least able to organise the thing for his grace. My contacts within the Balloon Association, you see?'

'Skills,' said Palmer. 'Yes, I suppose so. To steer the vessel, you mean? I had never given the matter much thought. But to change direction when one is entirely at the whimsy of the winds...'

The captain regarded him as he might a simpleton and Palmer took his leave, moving right down to the front of the crowd, where he stood just next to one of the carters, a bewhiskered dark-skinned man in an oversized cap, stroking the muzzle of his lead horse.

'Difficult journey?' Palmer asked him.

'The usual, sir. The usual. Three days on the road from Birmingham.'

'Is this Mr Johnson's usual conveyance for his balloon?'

'It is, indeed. We've served the gentleman twelve years now.'

'And the team holding those ropes?'

'Bless you, no, sir. Recruited yesterday at some of the local hostelries. All Wrexham boys seeking a few extra shillings. Mr Johnson pays well for the service.'

From here, Palmer could see the aeronaut himself more clearly. Sunlight glinted upon the glass and brass instruments mounted on the rigging rails. The fellow himself was dressed in a seaman's smock of dark oilcloth, its broad collar like a perimeter wall, high around his nose and mouth. On his head, a sou'wester of the same stuff. He reached down over the coiled ropes and grappling iron hanging from the basket's side and lifted the final crate from one of the ground crew's outstretched arms.

'That is Mr Johnson?' said Palmer.

'Sadly, no, sir. He was taken ill last night – at the Wynnstay. Fortunately, his associate is also a competent aeronaut.'

'Associate?'

'They met recently, in Birmingham. And Mr Johnson was pleased to have him for his companion on this flight.'

'He has a name, this associate?'

'Indeed, sir. A pleasant American gentleman. Mr Jefferson Davies.'

Ettie suffered a sense of impending doom. A dark cloud descended upon her as she bustled through the townsfolk also making their way in the same direction. Along Rhosddu Road and up through Argyle Street. Yet, the further she walked, the greater her doubts. It was unlike Neo to be so lacking in analysis. She had seen the modest scale of McCafferty's recent operations at uncomfortably close quarters. The abhorrent murder of individuals, of mindless revenge, might be one thing. But she had observed no evidence that he still possessed sufficient resource for an operation such as her husband now feared.

And the dark cloud, she knew, had as much to do with her memories of their previous dangers associated with this very location.

Blood among the threads, she said to herself.

There was little left here to remind anybody of the great Art Treasures Exhibition which, eight years ago, had filled the now derelict land to the right. The grand pavilion of timber, glass and zinc sheets had not been of the best construction and, within six months of the exhibition's end, it had been entirely demolished. Still, the elegant four-storey Westminster Building, commissioned by Alison's father for his daughter's dowry, still stood proud before her.

But the archway beneath the building's centre – back then, the entrance to the exhibition itself – was packed with people. The May Day parade, she should have realised sooner.

She began to ease her way through the crowd, squeezing herself against the pale-yellow brickwork of the archway's wall, then banging her elbow against the padlock of the first high door on this side of the passage. She winced with the pain, noting that the two matching doorways on the farther side – normally housing the works of local amateur lady artists – also remained firmly bolted today. But at the second nearside door she encountered Bethan Thomas standing guard, arms folded defiantly beneath her bent body, upon the museum's threshold.

'*Calan Mai hapus, Mrs Palmer.*' Happy first day of May.

Normally, Ettie preferred to think of this as the first day of summer, *Calan Haf,* but she had no time for the annual May Day debate. Not like the old days, Bethan would usually complain, recalling the *coelcerth* – bonfires – of her childhood: the straw men; the willow wands; and the garlands.

It had all begun with this. Bethan might now be the museum's curator, but it was the death of her predecessor, poor viper-envenomed Rose Wimpole – as well as the exhibition – which had first brought herself and Neo to Wrexham and their subsequent perils. Was Neo right? Had returning here been a tragic mistake? The babe? Another brush with death – this time at McCafferty's hands?

'And the glass?' said Bethan, still in the *Cymraeg.* 'Found anything, has he?'

It took Esther a moment to remember but, by then, she was out upon Hope Street.

'I think not,' she yelled back over her shoulder, over the cheers of the crowd, and over the strains of a military band leading the parade.

The pavement was crowded here but she bobbed and wove her way northwards, against the shop fronts, past the savings bank, along the front of the Seion Chapel. She caught occasional glimpses, between the backs of onlookers, of James Edisbury's Aerated Mineral Water Company's green vans rolling past, one after another, nine in total, vehicles and horses decked in May Day flowers and ribbons.

By the time she finally managed to cross the road – behind a strictly disciplined gaggle of joyful schoolchildren, all dressed like diminutive druids and singing *Cyfri'r Geifr*, the Goat Song – she no longer had any confidence that Neo's assumption merited even the least consideration.

As she crossed, friends from the following contingent urged her to join them, or demanded to know where Alfred might be. For, normally, they would indeed have been there, Ettie playing her concertina among the serried ranks of the Blue Ribbon Army with their glorious temperance banners and placards. Today, of course, as usual, they were taking abuse from those among the bystanders with an unhealthy attachment to the demon drink. She would, on any other occasion, have confronted the poor, foolish wretches. But, by then, she was at the gatehouse.

Neo must surely be mistaken, she thought. And should I waste police time in this way? She turned to watch more of the procession winding its way around the corner from Grosvenor Road. More lorries, this time from the Cobden Mill, laden with brand new sacks, stamped with the company's mark, and filled with grain. Horse harnesses polished bright and jingling merrily. The crowd cheering.

Of course, I should! Esther Palmer, she scolded herself, whatever are you thinking?

But as she approached the gate and its guardroom, she could not help glancing back the way she'd come. And there, in the middle distance, rising slowly above the rooftops, was the red and yellow globe of Mr Johnson's aeronautical machine.

Palmer's brain screamed at him not to do it. Find Ettie, he told himself. Find Wilde. Find Major Leadbetter. For pity's sake, find *anybody.* Yet he found only himself – entirely beyond control, unable to constrain himself. He was running, wheezing, towards the balloon, and shouting like a madman.

'Stop!' he cried out. 'Stop that man. Impostor!'

The balloon began to rise. Gently. One foot from the ground. Two. Oh, so gently did the ground crew begin to play out the ropes at the aeronaut's commands. Several of them turned their heads in Palmer's direction. He pointed as he ran – or, rather, he stabbed in the direction of the balloon with his finger – though no more words would form in his breathless mouth.

The car had risen to shoulder height, and Palmer grabbed for a coil of rope as though he could, alone, defy the very laws of science and nature he worshipped almost as staunchly as his Methodism.

He hauled upon the coil and heaved downwards with all his might, half-turning and flapping his free arm like a vulture attempting to fly. And all the time he mouthed the silent words at the astonished ground crew watchers.

'Down! Down!'

Silent words.

Somebody laughed.

Palmer's feet lifted from the ground and he kicked his legs, uselessly. And now the laughter spread.

How wonderful! That the aeronaut should have arranged this amusement for them.

Palmer found his voice. He screamed, scrabbling to get a better purchase on the ropes, twisting his arm through the coils. The derby flew from his head and the laughter wafted it, spinning, into the crowd. Somebody caught the hat with a cheer.

'Lord Jesus, help me!' Palmer shouted, now twelve feet above the ground.

Beyond salvation. Too high to leap for safety. Too nauseous for his brain to function further.

His entire body trembled. Pure paralysing terror. He knew that, soon, he must fall. His eyes turned towards the handrail of the basket above his head. And there he saw the aeronaut playing to his audience, the face – McCafferty's face – now exposed.

A pantomime exaggerated grimace of confusion. A clown's wide-open mouth, the small eyes now large with feigned surprise. The two gloved hands raised from the bent elbows, fingers spread wide, questioning. What, he seemed to ask, was to be done?

Then he reached down over the side.

And Palmer knew he was about to be cast into oblivion.

Chapter Thirty-One

'Mrs Palmer,' insisted Major Leadbetter, 'there can be no cause for concern. The Fenians have lost their Number One. McCafferty is gone. Dead, ma'am. And the credentials of Mr Johnson, the aeronaut, are impeccable. Sergeant Jones is watching the ascent as we speak.'

'Nobody seems quite certain anymore, Major,' she said. 'About McCafferty.'

But she was flustered. Having arrived here, she was caught between two stools. Foolish not to follow Neo's wishes and, at least, share his suspicions – even though she now thought them groundless. Foolish to waste the Chief Constable's valuable time. Still, he had the courtesy to speak with her – even though she'd been forced to wait ten minutes for the audience.

'Well,' she murmured, pushing herself up from the chair in his office, 'I have taken quite enough of your day, sir.'

'Not at all, dear lady.' He smoothed the extremities of the walrus moustache. 'Not at all. And, please, allow me to escort you to the gate.'

Now, as he came to join her from behind the desk, stood at her side, Ettie realised just how tall he must be – ramrod straight and a good foot more than Neo, she decided. And that horseman's gait as they descended the staircase. She could picture him, out on the vast wilderness of Alberta's prairies or some such. She had a sudden urge to ask him about the buffalo – Ettie had always been somewhat fascinated by the creatures.

But as they reached the gatehouse, there was Sergeant Jones. He'd been running. Yet, in that instant he was bent almost double, trying to catch his breath, his face glistening with sweat and red as a ripe cherry. For a moment, it was almost comical. The police team's goalkeeper? No wonder they lost so frequently.

'Well, Sergeant?' said the major. 'Explain yourself, man.'

The sergeant stared up into Ettie's face. She saw fear there, and her amusement fainted quite away.

'Your husband… ma'am…' he gasped.

'My husband?'

'What about her husband?' demanded the Chief Constable.

Sergeant Jones looked from one to the other, and when he spoke it was to each in turn.

'Looks, ma'am… looks, sir… as if… he's made… the ascent… as well.'

'What nonsense is this?' said the major. 'Mr Palmer *and* Mr Johnson?'

'That's… the point, sir. On the way back… I was stopped… at the Talbot. Seems Mr Johnson – well, drugged, sir. An associate…'

Ettie felt the blood freeze in her veins.

'McCafferty,' she said, simply, though within her, some new form of chaos had taken hold.

'McCafferty?' said the major. 'Can we be sure?'

Yet, he knew it for a rhetorical question.

'Not sure, sir…' said the sergeant. 'But made enquiries at the hotel… and seems this associate – well, an American gentleman.'

There, she thought, no room for doubt. But Neo, up there? How? Why? He could not bear even to stand upon a small ladder.

'And made the ascent? Mr Palmer?' The major was incredulous.

'More likely, tried to prevent it,' she said. 'But now…'

It was all too preposterous. All too terrifying. But the Chief Constable seemed to take it seriously enough. Instructions for his gig to be readied, his revolver and binoculars to be fetched.

'Do not fear, Mrs Palmer,' he cried. 'However your husband has become embroiled in the affair, and wherever this fellow – McCafferty or whoever else it might be – shall make his landing, we'll be there to take him. Your husband shall be safe.'

Safe? What *was* he talking about? Neo with that stone-cold killer and, she was certain, an entire cargo of infernal devices. But there were already more instructions – to Sergeant Jones.

'I believe,' said the major, 'the estate office at Eaton Hall may have a telegraphic service. Alert them. And our colleagues in Chester. The Castle as well. Oh, and fetch Inspector Wilde. I may have need of him. You, ma'am,' he turned to her, 'may remain here under police protection, should you wish, and...'

'You're going to Eaton Hall, I gather?'

'It seems the sensible destination.' He glanced at his watch. 'We can be there in an hour. And as soon...'

'Then I'm coming with you, sir.'

The argument lasted only so long as it took for the sporty cab-fronted gig and its bay stallion to be brought from the stables. Long enough, too, for a disgruntled Superintendent Wilde to join them, in company with the sergeant.

'Am I to understand I'm no longer suspended from my duties, sir?' he asked.

'We may have something of a national emergency on our hands, Wilde,' the chief constable snapped at him. 'I cannot deny you might have some part to play.'

'And if you don't mind, sir,' said Sergeant Jones, handing Leadbetter the revolver and binoculars he'd sent for, 'I also took the liberty...'

The fellow reached back onto the gig's seat, brought forth a cloth-covered bundle, unwrapped it to show a second revolver, presumably the one surrendered by Wilde in Chester.

'Yes, very well,' said Leadbetter, and motioned for the superintendent to take the weapon. 'Now, climb aboard, if you please.'

A fine conveyance, open to the weather, but fast – the major's personal means of transport to commute back and forth between barracks and home, wherever that might be. And, within ten minutes, Ettie and Wilde, with the Chief Constable at the reins, had hurtled at breakneck speed down Grosvenor Road – where they'd passed an open-mouthed Edward and Alison. They swung along the Chester road and crested Acton Hill. And there, taking the turn into Box Lane, they saw it again. That red and yellow globe. Perhaps a mile distant. And high in the sky.

*

247

Palmer's brain could make no sense of it. His head hurt so much that it allowed no function other than dealing with the pain itself. And the head was lolling back and forth upon his neck, each movement multiplying the pain a hundred-fold. He tried to hold the head still. Though there was some other force at play here: his arms, extended upwards. No, not extended. Being pulled upwards. A secondary pain. Burning about his wrists. The stretching of his armpits, his whole body hauled upright, or very nearly. He tried to open his eyes, but they would not obey his command. For as soon as light flooded against the irises, the agony cut him like a knife. And the voice – one he almost recognised.

'Up we go, Alfred. Up we go. A bit more height and this south-westerly should freshen nicely.'

Palmer heard a grunt and the rope burned him yet again, his arms now pulled to full stretch. His right eye opened just enough for him to see a pair of hands below him, tying off the rope to a belaying pin, one of several in a rack.

He imagined himself back aboard the duke of Westminster's yacht. The *Lady Constance*? Yes, that must be it. For, without doubt, he was somewhere at sea. The same gentle motion.

'I once had the honour,' said the voice, 'of navigating the *Gazelle* for General Alexander. Artillery spotting, Alfred. Can you hear me, sir? Gaines Mill. Great victory for the Confederacy.'

Gazelle? Another yacht?

'Hear you?' he murmured.

'Had to hit you harder than I'd planned, my friend. But couldn't very well just drop you, Alfred. Not then, anyway. But later…'

'Drop?'

The curtain of fog in his brain began to part. Just slightly. Ever so slightly.

'You!' he said. Though the name would still not quite come to him. Even so, he knew this much. It was about Ettie. Danger. And this man…

'McCafferty,' he said.

And now, regardless of the agony, his eyes opened. Slowly, they opened. Yet, not entirely focused. Rigging. Definitely rigging, the man in his oilcloth smock and sou-wester checking instruments.

The oilcloth smock…

'Oh, God preserve me!'

It came back in a sudden squall. He'd been running. Towards…

Above his head, a series of valves – and above the valves, the red and yellow fabric of the balloon, constrained within its rope netting and secured by a web of cordage. To that cordage, above his head, Palmer's hands were tightly lashed. But if he turned his head, his aching head, just a little, he could see…

His stomach turned a somersault. He couldn't be certain whether the nausea was the result of vertigo or the blow to his head – or both. He closed his eyes again. He closed them tight. He heard McCafferty's laughter.

'That's right,' he said. 'I forgot. That night at the Wynnstay. Just the mention of a balloon trip. And here you are. What the hell did you think you were doing, Alfred?'

Where were they? He breathed deeply. In and out. In and out. The hammering inside his head would not subside, but he could feel now the precise spot where he'd been clubbed, just above his right ear. It stung, and he could sense blood there. Yet, a strange thing. As he inhaled and exhaled, tried to calm himself, he realised that his lungs, at least, were functioning perfectly. Their usual tightness gone. The air, he decided. Cleaner at this altitude.

He opened his eyes, and the vertigo had disappeared, as well. How bizarre. Palmer had, on occasions, been persuaded to climb to dizzying heights. Church towers. Castle battlements. And always that stomach-wrenching giddiness. He had made a fool of himself times without number. But here…

Palmer decided to keep this astonishing fact to himself. Perhaps it might, at some stage, give him an edge.

'Where are we?' he croaked.

McCafferty consulted a map, folded carefully within a wooden frame and hanging by a chain from the basket's handrail. Then he took a hand compass from his pocket, flicked it open, spat over the side, carefully observed the bearing upon which the spittle drifted away on the wind.

'Just past… Borras,' he said, and tapped his finger against the map. 'Good progress, Alfred. Good progress.'

He went to the instruments, mounted upon a board, a channel platform, through which the lower rigging passed, like the shrouds of a sailing ship. A simple barometer, Palmer saw, with a circular gauge to help measure height. A chronometer. A familiar Daniell's hygrometer, with twin glass tubes and balls, as well as a thermometer, to measure humidity. And a hooter, a brass trumpet with a black India rubber squeeze-ball.

'Is this… necessary?' he managed to say. 'My arms? Feels like… crucifixion.'

'What's that now?' McCafferty smirked. 'For a Holy Joe like you, Alfred, would that not be just dandy? Though I got other plans for you, sir. Plans, indeed. You won't believe it – but we need each other.'

Palmer looked around the rest of the balloon. Ropes everywhere, of course. The mooring ropes, all neatly coiled and brought inboard, hanging from cleats. The heavier hawser, the anchor rope, just visible over the side. Bags – of sand, presumably. Close to where Palmer himself was tethered, a roll of material – silk perhaps – with something resembling a milkmaid's yoke and a broad leather belt, the whole thing attached to the rigging with a careful arrangement of slipknots. He'd read of such things, of course. The parachute – a highly questionable piece of safety equipment, if recent newspaper reports were to be believed. And in each of the car's four corners, a wooden box. The same as he'd seen the aeronaut – McCafferty, as it turned out – lifting aboard earlier, each box about two feet square.

'You survived… the river,' he said. A useless comment. He'd meant to ask *how* the wretch had survived, but his aching brain and his desiccated tongue seemed to be lacking coordination.

'Only just. And would that not have been an irony, Alfred? Me, dying in the Dee.'

'It has some purpose… in your plan? The river?'

'Call it a whim, my friend. Just a whim. And Esther – how is dear Esther? You should have seen her, Alfred. That pretty little piece in her hand. Pulled the trigger, too. How about that? Grit, Alfred – that girl's got… Hey, wait now. You *do* know, right?'

Palmer tried hard to assimilate all this. To make himself remember. Ettie. Dearest Ettie. Yet, pulled the trigger? What is he talking about, my love?

She must be wondering, surely? Had anybody observed what had happened to him? Might Viscount Broughton, or Sir Watkin's nephew, Herbert, or one of the ground crew, have reported him being taken aboard? But he looked back on McCafferty's pantomime. Wasn't it possible the entire crowd had taken it for a dumbshow, for simple entertainment?

'So, secrets, eh? Well, I guess it doesn't matter much right now. But what d'you think about this beauty, Alfred?' He glanced up at the globe above them. 'Good stout calico. Horrocks's A-grade strong-cloth. Rendered gas-proof, naturally. Needs town gas, of course. Coking gas. Can be a drawback. Know how many gasworks poor Johnson had to have on standby just so we could launch in the right place today?'

'Depending on the wind,' said Palmer.

'Depending on the wind, Alfred. Sure thing. Give that man a cigar!'

Palmer risked another glance over the side of the basket. Great Heavens, it was like looking down upon the map he'd recently hand-drawn to include within the book's appendices. This northern section of the Lordship of Bromfield and Yale. To their right, the serpentine bends of the Dee. Below, a farm and field enclosures. Just to the left, thick woodlands with a substantial house at their heart – Horsley Hall, surely. And, further to the left, more than a mile away, the village of Gresford, easily distinguishable simply by the remarkable size of its parish church.

'Fine view, is it not?' said McCafferty. 'And you seem to be coping with it better than I'd expected.' He glanced up at the wispy clouds above them, as he'd done several times already, ever vigilant for signs of a change in the wind's direction.

'India rubber tubing,' said Palmer, remembering something Chief Constable Leadbetter had said.

'You never know whether any particular gas company's going to have enough available – or willing to let you use it. So I had some spare supplies at Chester. Only – well, your Esther again. That and Daly's dynamite. Poof!'

McCafferty made an explosive gesture with his hands.

'But you acquired more.'

Palmer nodded his head down towards one of the boxes.

'In this business, you need friends, Alfred. Friends with mines. Friends with foundries. Friends with inside information. Know what I mean?'

'Friends like Mr Johnson?'

'Took me a while to cultivate Johnson. But he swallowed my stories well enough. He had to admit, after the first few ascents, that I'm the better aeronaut. Good man. I didn't enjoy doing what had to be done this morning, but...'

Palmer shook his head to try and clear the miasma, but it served only to reignite the fires of his pain. Was it true – Johnson innocent?

'Friends you lost at the cemetery, as well?' he said.

'Kelly,' said McCafferty. Was that a hint of sadness? 'Good soldier, sir. Fought on opposite sides, back in the day. But a good soldier. I saw what she did, Alfred. Your Esther. Like I said – grit!'

Palmer assumed there'd be some hint towards revenge. But no, it sounded more like respect – one soldier for another, albeit an enemy.

'Friends, then,' he said, 'who can help you plan the assassination of both the Prime Minister *and* the Prince of Wales.'

'Peradventure, Alfred. Peradventure. And you, sir. Imagine, playing your part on behalf of not one great cause – but two!'

Ettie clung to the gig's side rail for dear life as they took the bend at the bottom of Marford Hill, past the Trevor Arms and down into the start of the Cheshire levels – the full glory of which had been spread, away to their right, all the way down the steep gradient – and past the estate houses, where the afternoon light glistened on blue Berwyn roof slates.

Major Leadbetter had not spared the whip all this way and she'd been mildly impressed by his skill, his light touch on the break lever just enough to keep the conveyance from impeding the bay stallion's steady downhill trot.

'Are they going faster?' she cried, pointing up at the balloon, when they were back on the flat, the road here straight and tree-lined.

'Then, we shall match them,' said the major, spurring the horse to still greater speed which, in turn, brought tears to Ettie's eyes.

'Certainly higher,' shouted Inspector Wilde. 'They say a good aeronaut knows how to catch the fastest winds by adjusting the balloon's height.'

'But if this *is* McCafferty,' she said. 'How could he be – a good aeronaut?'

'Seems to know what he's about, all the same,' said Leadbetter. 'I just hope they got the message at Eaton Hall.'

She hoped so, as well. Though she knew in her heart there could be no happy outcome to any of this. And Neo – how had he been so foolish? Up there – with McCafferty. He could be no willing passenger, of that she was sure. But what devilry had been at play here? And Wilde's next words chilled her soul.

'But if the Castle has been alerted, and they believe the Prince of Wales to be in danger, might they not simply send a marksman to bring it down?' He turned to her, and Ettie saw how much he must have regretted what he said. 'Mrs Palmer, I'm certain that will not...'

'Between the devil and the deep blue sea,' cried Leadbetter. 'What facts do we actually possess? Only that the actual aeronaut is taken ill and an unknown assistant taken his place. This fellow may – or may not – be American. If they *did* decide to force the balloon down, Mrs Palmer, and all was innocent – well...'

But if they do not, she thought, and this *is* McCafferty with a cargo of infernal devices, and he is allowed to drop them...

Then she saw Leadbetter haul on his reins and she was almost flung along the seat.

'No, boy!' yelled the major, swinging past the junction with a lane off to their left – the road to Llay and beyond. 'This way.' And they were back on course. 'Damned brute – begging your pardon, ma'am – knows his way home. Up there. Burton!'

Ettie settled her bonnet back in place – and settled herself on the bench seat. She forced a smile and looked once more for the balloon. But the gig swayed violently yet again as they narrowly avoided collision with a phaeton just turning from Trevalyn Hall's driveway – the coachman screaming abuse at Leadbetter and the major returning the curses blow for blow, his Scots accent becoming distinctly more pronounced with each blasphemy.

Past Rossett Mill and the Alyn's millstream, then the tight bridge over the Alyn itself. She had no idea of the speed of their headlong journey, but she could not recall any which had ever seemed faster. The gig shook and rattled, so that she gave thanks for its springs – *triple* springs, Leadbetter had proudly announced.

Thus, on they raced, through Rossett village and Lavister until, at last, they came in sight of Pulford's newest wonder, the rebuilt St. Mary's Church, all red roof and two-tone brick, and she knew the worst of the journey was behind them. But as they approached the narrow bridge over Pulford Brook, her hopes were dashed. Disaster struck.

A huge haywain had shed one of its wheels and slewed sideways across the lane, blocking the bridge entirely.

'For pity's sake!' Leadbetter shouted at the farmer, who stood in the centre of the calamity, hands on smock-shrouded hips and shaking his head in despair.

'What?' said the fellow. 'Got some magic wand, have thee? Silly bugger!'

But Ettie was not about to allow this minor setback to stop her. She jumped from the gig and ran for the bridge.

'Follow me when you can!' she called back over her shoulder, ignoring the two policemen's demands for her to stop.

For, while St. Mary's stood proud on one side of the road beyond the brook, on the other was the farm and hotel – the Grosvenor Arms. She lifted her skirts and hurried past the haywain and its perplexed farmer, certain that, at the hotel, there must surely be another vehicle which could carry her the final couple of miles to Eaton Hall.

Yet, before she even reached the red-brick sprawl of the hotel, another opportunity opened itself before her. Divine intervention, she was certain. Two familiar faces, halted in their own journey. From the Chester Cycling Club, were they not? And abroad today on the very latest models.

Chapter Thirty-Two

Two noble causes? Palmer was still trying to fathom the rogue's meaning. Friends with a mine, he'd said. Friends with a foundry. Who?

McCafferty had spent the past ten minutes, the past mile or more, recounting his further exploits with the Confederacy, whether or not Palmer wanted to hear them. As an artillery spotter.

'Of course,' he'd said, 'much of the time it wasn't free flight, Alfred. No, sir. Men to hold the ropes, keep us at a fixed height, steer us to wherever we were needed. The *Gazelle* could lift five hundred pounds – so, two of us, like today, and a whole mess of sandbags.'

'But today you've different ballast, Captain.'

He had glanced at the boxes and McCafferty touched his foot to one of them – but gently. Then he'd bent down, unfastened the brass catches and lifted the lid.

Palmer had seen it clearly, a half-ball of iron, a wooden handle above and attached to a gimbal while, below, the detonator finger teats protruded at various angles.

'Why?' he'd said. 'Irish independence won by bloodshed? By the bomb? You believe it will answer?'

There'd been a lecture. About Ireland being a sovereign nation occupied by a foreign power. Lessons to be learned. By the occupiers. That the bombs had the power to hurt them, wherever they might be. By the occupied, that the occupiers – or even their more peace-loving opponents – had no answers, were powerless by comparison and could not be trusted to offer a settlement. By the occupied without the spirit themselves to fight, that it was those with the bombs who had the power to rule once the occupiers were driven out.

Palmer had argued with him – at least, as much as his aching head, his pain-racked arms, shoulders and wrists would allow.

'Believe me,' McCafferty had said, 'the Irish will be happier once they're freed from the English.'

But now he consulted the map once more, a set of dividers to measure the distance.

'Exactly a mile, Alfred,' he said, and peered over the side. 'Aldford, down there.'

He pronounced it with a soft 'A' at the beginning, a bit like *Alfred*. Palmer corrected him. This was England, however – Cheshire, and apart from Neo's sense of pronunciation, his detailed geography was less acute in this part of the world.

'A mile?' he said. 'And then what?'

McCafferty watched him for a moment, then lifted the oilcloth hem. There was a holster, from which he drew a long revolver.

'Is that what you hit me with?' said Palmer. He could almost feel the shape of the weapon etched into the side of his skull.

McCafferty lifted a shoulder and smiled.

'I could manage this bit myself, Alfred – though, it's tricky. So, here's the deal. I let you down from there. You help. All you gotta do is let them go when I tell you. The bombs. You do that, you go back safe to Esther. If not, I shoot you and do the job myself – like I woulda done if you'd not joined me. What d'you say?'

'Hobson's choice,' said Palmer. He did his best to sound calm, knowing that, one way or the other, McCafferty could not, would not, allow him to live.

'What's that now?'

'Rock and a hard place.'

McCafferty nodded.

'I guess so.'

He approached cautiously, the revolver's muzzle pressed to Palmer's temple while he slowly unfastened the rope keeping his prisoner hanging from the rigging. As the rope loosened, Palmer began to feel the blood surging back into his arms, the very worst of cramps. Agonising.

'We got time,' said McCafferty, once Palmer was sitting on the wicker floor of the car.

'A mile,' said Palmer.

'Wind's dropped,' said McCafferty, glancing up at the sky.

Palmer got to his knees and finally stood. He looked over the side, astonished that he felt no fear. Neither the height, nor McCafferty's pistol. Almost – well, the opposite.

Below and to the right, the circuitous River Dee and a village. Aldford, it must be. To their left, in the distance, the smoky, rolling grey folds, the hills and mountains of Wales. Ahead and below, a carpet of dark green trees, an occasional glimpse of fallow deer, of sheep, of cattle. Cloud shadow, but almost motionless. And the beginnings of a broad serpentine lake. Far below, at the lake's edge, two men, barely visible, but fishing. The staggering revelation that, despite the distance, he could hear their every word, their exclamations of wonder at the balloon passing above their heads.

This, he decided, must be how one feels in Heaven. And, the Lord Jesus protect him, Heaven was precisely where he thought he might soon find himself. That was, of course, should he be deemed worthy.

'And,' he said, 'a mile from the destruction you must bring to so many innocents.'

'Innocents?' said McCafferty. 'I had that conversation with Esther, sir.'

It stung. Still too many things hidden from him.

'Yet, your own fate, Captain. How many times have you, yourself, been close to death in pursuit of your causes? You have some hope of going to a better place, perhaps?'

'Those willing to die for a cause, Alfred, simply have little to lose in this life.'

'To kill the Prime Minister? The Prince of Wales? Do you not see, sir, that such infamy will gain you nought, except global opprobrium?'

McCafferty laughed. He seemed genuinely amused.

'Well,' he said, 'there endeth the lesson, I fear. You see? The way we've drifted off our course.' He checked the compass bearing again. 'Need to be precise.' He reached up into the rigging. 'But if I pull down on this…'

Palmer felt the balloon tilt just a little, and he gripped the handrail.

'And then open this…' McCafferty reached, with his revolver hand, for the thick cord attached to the gas valve. The escaping gas hissed.

The science was obvious and, precisely as McCafferty had planned, they changed direction. Not by much, but enough.

'But releasing the gas…' said Palmer. 'We're going down.'

'Then I guess, when we're done, we'll just have to lighten the load, some. Don't you think?'

Ettie was furious with herself. She had badly underestimated the uphill slog north from Pulford. She had badly underestimated the distance from Pulford to the nearest entrance lodge to the Eaton Hall estate. She had badly underestimated the inadequacy of her normal outdoor clothing for the purpose of cycling. And, once at the lodge, she had badly underestimated the length of the duke's driveway.

Yet at least they had, indeed, been alerted. The telegraphic warnings must have been sent. Armed watchmen and a brace of police constables – their horses tethered to the wrought-iron gates – as well as two soldiers from the local Yeomanry. Hard men, who refused to believe she had legitimate business there.

'I would strongly advise you,' she said, with as much authority as she could muster, 'to check with her grace. But be assured, Lady Katherine will want to see me – urgently!'

'From Wrexham, Mrs Palmer?' one of the soldiers sneered. 'On your bicycle?'

'By bicycle, only from Pulford, as I have already twice explained. But somewhere close behind me – though somewhat delayed, I fear – are Chief Constable Leadbetter and Superintendent William Wilde. Perhaps you might direct some of your foolish questions to them, when they arrive.'

She was in no mood. It had been difficult enough to requisition the bicycle in the first place, "in the name of the law", she had said – and she fully expected to be arrested for theft, for physical assault due to the brusque way in which she'd finally been forced to seize the machine. That was all, of course, apart from the rigours of the subsequent journey, the perspiration, the screaming leg muscles, the renewed pain in her ankle, the gathering exhaustion, and the dishevelled state in which she'd arrived there.

'A good friend of her grace, then?' The younger policeman had looked her up and down, a smirk on her face.

Ettie made an attempt to straighten her clothes, to tidy the hair, to refasten the bonnet's ribbon. But the second constable – older and perhaps marginally wiser – told her to follow him. He mounted his horse and waited. She hesitated, not sure she could go the distance. Another mile to the hall itself? It must be. There, in the distance, with its tall clock tower. Yet, she had no choice. She almost fell, twice, as she tried to set the bicycle in motion once more, eliciting laughter from the soldiers and scowls from the watchmen.

The longest mile of her life. Past the howling hunting hounds in their kennels. Past the deer park. Past the obelisk. Thick woodland on either side of the driveway's carefully manicured grass verges but, for the final few hundred yards, she could see the balloon. It seemed to be perfectly still, almost impossible from this distance to discern what might be happening. Yet, the most worrying thing? She could only make out one occupant. It surely could not be Neo – so where was he?

Panic gripped her, and her arrival at the driveway's farther end was less than graceful. The bicycle was flung aside upon the gravel, near those astonishing Golden Gates, and another guard post. The mounted policemen instructed the gatekeepers to inform the duchess that Mrs Palmer wished to see her. And another anxious five minutes passed before her grace appeared, and all that time the balloon hung almost motionless in the sky. Five minutes during which Ettie's only distraction was watching the activity from the enormous white marquee erected away to the right, beyond the trees and along a broad paved path. It seemed to fill an open field – a sports field, of some sort – and a team of workmen carried tables and chairs to some destination she could not see.

'Polo field,' said one of the watchmen. 'Spent all that time erecting the tent,' he complained, 'an' then decide to shift the whole shebeen.'

The warning, she decided. If McCafferty had bombs in the balloon, what a target the marquee would have made. But shifted – to where? It was a question for the duchess, who arrived at the gate, remarkably, in a rickshaw, hauled by a liveried driver. Two further armed watchmen for her bodyguards, loping alongside. By then, Ettie was so distressed that she did not even offer a greeting.

'My husband, ma'am,' she cried. 'He is supposed to be up there. But now…'

'Have faith, my dear. Your husband, so far as I know from the tales I've heard, is resilient in the extreme.'

The duchess dismissed the policeman, who trotted back towards the lodge, and she bade Ettie join her in the conveyance.

'And let me show you, Mrs Palmer, how we have thwarted the rogue's plans.'

At these close quarters, it was plain that Lady Katherine was no older than Ettie herself. And the duke? He must be sixty, surely.

'The staff have been remarkable,' explained her grace. 'All our catering and entertainments moved to the Camellia Walk. Sergeant Devlin's recommendation. He believed the marquee makes too easy a target. And is it true, my dear? The bombs?'

'We cannot know.'

'Then Sergeant Devlin's advice makes perfect sense. My husband was all for shooting down the balloon.'

Ettie gasped.

'Never fear, my dear. I persuaded him it would be folly, indeed. If the balloon proves not to be a threat, how foolish should we all look. But if it does carry some awful device and they dropped through our actions on Pulford or Aldford – well, you may just imagine the outcry. Yet if your suspicions are correct, and this Fenian rogue believes we are all in the marquee, he may drop as many bombs there now as he might desire, and no harm done. Except to poor Hugh's polo field, of course.' She laughed, gaily. 'You see? We shall all be safely elsewhere.'

'But the Camellia Walk?'

'Beyond the house. Come, I shall show you.'

'I regret, your grace, that I'm hardly dressed…'

The next ten minutes were entirely overwhelming. First, the rickshaw ride around the nearer portion of the oval carriageway, a statue at its centre, before Eaton Hall house itself – and the carriageway lined with phaetons, growlers and landaus.

Second, Ettie's trepidation, her eyes ever skywards.

'I'm sorry, your grace,' she said, 'but the balloon does not seem to be heading for the marquee in any event.'

'Indeed, it does not. Perhaps it is the wind shall ruin their schemes.'

Their schemes? Who did she mean? Ettie wondered whether the balloon was even moving at all. But by then the flunkey in the shafts had begun to run them along the drive which fronted the imposing facades: red brick and sandstone; columns, turrets and archways; mullioned windows; past the tall clock tower and past the chapel.

'Your grace,' she said, 'the senior officers of our Wrexham constabulary are somewhere behind me. Can word be sent to admit them?'

The shotgun-armed watchmen had kept pace alongside but now the duchess instructed one of them to return to the lodge, while the rickshaw turned through the wide archway entrance to the half-timbered stable block, trundled across the broad courtyard – busy with horses being groomed and fed – and out the other side of the manure-heaped quadrangle. Rattling onto brick-paved pathways past walled kitchen gardens filled with scents of rosemary and buzz of bees. Past cooing dovecots, orchards and blossoming terraces.

'There,' said Lady Katherine, 'the Parrot House!' It looked, at a quick glance, like a round Grecian temple, from which came a chorus of chirruping chaos. 'Though it sadly accommodates only budgerigars.'

In truth, Ettie was more interested in the balloon. Moving again, and seemingly in their direction.

But there the rickshaw stopped and allowed them to disembark, the duchess leading Ettie across to a high-roofed greenhouse, from which spilled the strains of a string quartet. She paused in the doorway, looking up yet again. There was still only a single figure to be seen in the basket. Where in Heavens name was Neo? Yet, all seemed so peaceful, not a hint of danger.

'You seem remarkably calm, your grace,' she said. 'The balloon is distinctly headed this way, do you not think?'

'I imagine simply the wind changed direction. Still, we are safe here. Sergeant Devlin says we shall be invisible.'

'Invisible?' said Ettie, glancing into the glasshouse. 'Yes, I suppose so. But the music?'

Inside, shrubbery with pink, red and white blossoms everywhere. Long tables as well, light refreshments for the many guests. Servants aplenty to cater for their needs. And the guests were many, indeed, for the conservatory building was itself a thing of wonder, stretching on and on. In fact, she could not even see the farther end.

Many guests but, so far as she was able to observe, they were all…

'Your grace,' she said, 'I had feared there might be children.'

'Of course,' Lady Katherine beamed at her. 'A May Day fête without the children? But we had already arranged the maypole and other entertainments near the Tea House and the Dutch Garden. Should there *be* a threat, they will be safe there. Besides, my husband is still in mourning for poor Victor. The thought of so many boisterous youngsters…'

Ettie was somewhat awed to spot, ahead of her, the familiar figure of Prime Minister Gladstone, though she knew him best from the caricatures in *Punch* – Gladstone as Micawber, constantly confident that "something would turn up". Something ethereal about him. How old? Mid-seventies, Ettie reminded herself, yet walked with the grace and elegance of a trained dancer while, at his side, Mrs Gladstone seemed somehow more firmly anchored to the ground.

They were deep in conversation with the FitzPatricks, and Lady Olivia gave her a cursory nod of acknowledgement.

'Do they all know?' Ettie murmured, when the duchess had finished yet more greetings.

'Know?'

'The reason for being here, rather than the marquee.'

'Only the Prime Minister, my dear. And the royal party, of course.'

And there they were. Ettie was even more amazed by the size of this glass pavilion now than when she had entered, for they must by then have been a hundred yards or more along its length and still no sign of the opposite end. A maze of foliage – the refreshing fragrance of camellias – and catering arrangements, wine and *canapés* being served, the string quartet playing Strauss waltzes. It was all so gay, so hard to imagine any threat.

Except for the large elliptical shadow beginning to creep across the roof panes.

At the heart of it all, the prince himself, exactly as she'd seen his photograph so many times. Overweight, the jovial, bearded face, the chequered deerstalker, the matching Norfolk jacket and shooting trousers.

'Mr Gladstone?' she heard him say to some admiring *ingénue*. 'Generous to lame beggars, so I'm told.'

Those around him laughed. Fawning and sycophantic. All except Princess Alexandra. Her headgear matched her husband's, though it was deep rose-pink, the same as the long, tightly-buttoned tunic, pinched at the waist, above skirts of imperial purple. Even at forty, her clothes, it was said, set the fashion for every aspiring young woman of the nation – and beyond, to her native Denmark. And what was that absurd poem Lord Tennyson had penned, she thought – about us now all being Danes?

But no, the princess did not seem amused. How much did she know, Ettie wondered, about the rumours – the scandals to which certain of the newspapers so regularly alluded? Her husband's affairs. So many affairs.

The duchess was still at Ettie's side. She had even linked Ettie's arm, as though they were the closest of friends. And a constant stream of chatter, yet more introductions. And the inevitable questions.

'The pyrotechnic display?' asked one gentleman.

'We shall see nothing in here, your grace,' said another.

'The aeronaut himself,' the duchess told them, doubtless telling the truth, 'explained that we shall hear a short blast upon a hooter when he is ready to begin. At that point, we shall all move out upon the lawn. Otherwise the spectacle might be spoiled.'

Ettie admired her *sang froid*, but it was the princess she still found distracting – at least, until the commotion behind them. Chief Constable Leadbetter and Superintendent Wilde, now in company with another distinguished gentleman. Strangely, he could have been Neo's twin – and Ettie knew him.

'Ah, Mrs Palmer,' Lady Katherine began, 'allow me to name...'

'Chief Constable Fenwick,' said Ettie. 'We meet again.'

The duchess was surprised, it seemed.

'Mrs Palmer and her husband,' said Fenwick, a trace of Newcastle in his words, 'were involved in the incident at Overleigh Cemetery, your grace. I had the honour of interviewing them afterwards.'

'Good Heavens,' said Lady Katherine.

It had been thanks to Fenwick that all had worked out so well. For the Chester Chief Constable and her husband had established something of a rapport. The policeman, it transpired, had the same passion for Chester's history as Neo had developed for Wrexham's. But, more than that, one of his first tasks on taking up his duties in the city, almost twenty years earlier, had been to deal with McCafferty's planned raid on the castle. Then, just two years ago, he had become famous for his handling of Chester's Black Sunday riots, when the temperance marchers of the Salvation Army had clashed so violently with ruffians of the anti-temperance, anti-Salvationist, so-called Skeleton Army. It was Chief Constable Fenwick who had saved the day.

'A pleasure to see you again, Mrs Palmer,' said Fenwick. He looked up to the roof, now entirely darkened by the balloon's shadow. 'Though, the circumstances...'

'And if you would allow me to say so, your grace,' said Leadbetter, 'this place...' He glanced around, his voice dropping to the merest whisper. 'All this glass. If, God forbid...'

'Sergeant Devlin believed it is the perfect shelter.' The duchess smiled at him as though he were a simpleton.

'Devlin?' Fenwick seemed surprised. 'I was told the Special Irish Branch required his immediate return to London. Something about...'

'Well, Chief Constable...' Lady Katherine turned to scan her guests. 'No, there!' she said, and pointed back to the prince's party. The Prince of Wales now deep in conversation with her husband, the royal hand around the duke's black armband, an expression of sympathy upon the prince's face, quiet words being exchanged.

At the duke's side – at the prince's side – Sergeant Devlin.

Ettie saw the slow movement of the Irishman's hand.

It seemed to her that everything fell suddenly silent, that time itself stood still, but the silence shattered by an epiphany. By her own scream. By her single word.

'Assassin!'

Chapter Thirty-Three

'I fear the altitude has affected me more than I thought,' said Palmer, and he staggered a little, brushing a hand across his face, feigning dizziness. 'I believe I must sit again for a moment.'

He lowered himself once more to the wicker floor. Yet, McCafferty was unwavering in keeping the revolver pointed at him. Somehow, Palmer could not believe they had been allowed to get so far. Surely, Ettie must have raised the alarm? But then, what did she actually know? What if his suspicions had simply been ignored? After all, had his own fears not been allayed when he'd thought the balloon ascent to be legitimate? And if the authorities did have concerns, what could they do without some form of evidence?

'Get up, Alfred, You're fooling nobody.'

'Truly, it has all been a little too much.'

The sound of children laughing, singing, the raucous strains of a calliope playing *Yankee Doodle* rose up to meet them.

'A shame,' said McCafferty, 'it's not *Dixie*. And then, of course,' he touched the toe of his shoe to the nearest box, 'I've never been able to test one of these in person. I suppose here's as good a place as any. And right in our path. Don't even need you for this, Alfred.'

Palmer jumped to his feet and looked over the side.

There was a field, with caravans and striped awnings about the margents: a maypole with streaming, coloured ribbons of red, white and blue; carousel horses, up and down, round and round, steam billowing from the calliope cart; and a building which looked oriental, beside trees, and another lake. Children, of course. Many children.

'Very well, Captain. You've made your point.'

'Then, you'll play ball?'

'Do I have a choice?'

'I suppose not. But why are you here, Alfred? Seriously – why?'

'You left me without much choice in that regard also, did you not?'

But, as he glanced down yet again, at least he saw they'd passed the field, the wind freshening.

'Only after you left me with none. What could I do? Run the risk that you'd survive the fall? You're the only one who could have said, with any certainty, that this balloon and its contents genuinely pose a threat. As it stands, who knows? And yes, I suppose there was a risk they'd shoot us down in any case. But here? In England?'

'Wales,' Palmer corrected him, then realised that they were, in fact, presently in – or, rather, over – England. Since the border, at Pulford Brook.

'You know what I mean, Alfred. Wouldn't have been cricket, old boy.'

He laughed.

'So, you see, Alfred? Isn't this a waste? You could have stayed at home.'

'And so could you, Captain McCafferty. For, you see? Unless you can command the winds to bend unnaturally to your will, you have already missed your mark, sir.'

He pointed westwards, beyond a maze, beyond a neat orchard, beyond another lodge, to a great open space half a mile distant with, at its centre, a sprawling white marquee, plainly erected for today's fête.

'You are entirely ditched, sir,' said Palmer with triumph.

'You know what they say, Alfred, about the best laid plans of mice and men?'

'Gang aft a-gley?'

'Burns,' said McCafferty. 'I admire a man who knows his Burns.'

For some reason, Palmer thought of another Burns poem, which Ettie had reminded him about. *Ye Jacobites by Name*. A paean against war – and especially against internecine conflict.

'Nonsense, of course,' he said. 'For, does any decent plan not always have a fallback?'

McCafferty nodded his head enthusiastically.

'A Plan B?' he said. 'Isn't that what folk say these days? And mine? Well, I spent a long time on this one. Young Herbert was a great help. Introduced me to the Balloon Society, and through them I met Mr Johnson. We've become close friends, and he was happy to have me along for the ride. Of course, your sweet Esther rather spoiled things for a while. But dynamite you can always replace. And the foundry work? Well, it's always good to have friends in the right places. Friends who have their own cause.'

'Still, now off your intended route.'

'I am? All it needed, Alfred, was to plot a simple course and then make sure our target was somewhere along that line rather than where they'd intended to be. I may be good at aeronautics but even I couldn't have navigated our way over there.' He nodded towards the marquee. 'What was the story – about how, if the hill would not come to Mahomet, Mahomet decided he would go to the hill? And, even then – well, maybe that's all you need to know, Alfred.'

'Francis Bacon's story, I believe.'

'*Touché*, Alfred, *Touché*.'

The breeze carried them past the rear façade of Eaton Hall house, over long formal gardens stretching out eastwards toward yet another lake, or fish pond. The sun gleamed on a water-filled channel running along the centre of the parterres. Beyond the house, the clock tower, a chapel, and a large quadrangle. More trees and, in the trees, a round granite temple of some sort. Away to the right, along a bend in the Dee, an industrial complex with a gasometer. Did they supply their own coking gas for the estate? Why not? All this landowners' wealth.

Ahead, a glass structure, tall, almost hidden by trees. Not especially wide but it must be two hundred yards in length.

'There?' said Palmer. 'Is that your target?'

'In a way. But time for you to play your part at last.'

Palmer heard the familiar yet incongruous merriment of *The Blue Danube* billowing up towards them. He stared at McCafferty, saw the smirk of mutual recognition. The May Day guests were here, not in the marquee at all.

'So, here's what I want you to do, Alfred. Reach down into that box and unfasten the device from its gimbal. But carefully, Alfred. Carefully.'

Palmer looked down at the nearest box.

'If I don't?'

'I shoot you anyways. Then do the job myself.'

'You said earlier that, when we're done, you'll have to lighten the load. What did you mean, sir?'

'You don't need to worry about that, Alfred. Just do as I say. The device?'

Palmer crouched down beside the box, opened the lid and examined the clasps holding the bomb to its gently swinging gimbal. He gripped the handle with one hand, unfastened the clasps with the other. Then, gingerly, he lifted the device free and stood.

McCafferty looked over the rail of the car, and so did Palmer. They were just beginning to glide slowly over the glass roof.

'Now,' said McCafferty, 'carefully, hold it over the side.'

Palmer lifted the bomb, extended his arm. It was heavy. Painfully heavy. And it made him wonder – again.

'Tell me,' he said. 'Lightening the load – what *did* you mean?'

McCafferty laughed. He clapped his hands.

'Oh, my!' he said. 'You think I intend to toss you over into the abyss, Alfred. But you could not be farther from the truth. No, sir.'

But Palmer didn't believe him. Instead, he turned swiftly and held the bomb over the centre of the car. It seemed a madness had overtaken him. For, in his heart he knew that, one way or the other, McCafferty – for all his pretence at affability – did not intend him to survive this day. He thought of Ettie, choked back a tear and steeled himself.

'Alfred, what are you doing?'

McCafferty pointed the revolver at Palmer's head.

'Did you not say, Captain, that he who holds the bomb also has the power?'

'But that depends, does it not, on whether he who holds the bomb is willing to give up his life, as well? And does your church not condemn suicide, Alfred?'

'I am a Primitive Methodist, sir. We believe nothing – not even suicide – can separate us from the love of God. But how can this be suicide? To die for Queen and Country. Our soldiers do so every year, it seems.'

But he could feel the muscles in his arm and shoulder begin to tremble. Or was this his terror? How long could he hold the thing?

Palmer did not have to wait long to find out. For, below them, from within the conservatory came the sound of a shot. Then two more, in rapid succession.

'There!' said McCafferty. 'I guess we're done.'

'Done?' Palmer waved his free hand in the air. 'But all this? The balloon – the bombs?'

'Sleight of hand, Alfred? *Legerdemain*?'

Like a sudden light in the darkness, Palmer believed he'd enjoyed a flash of insight.

'Yes,' he said, 'I think I see now.'

He let the bomb slip from his fingers.

Ettie saw Devlin's hand reach inside his coat. She saw the pistol. She saw the prince's look of astonishment as the revolver came up towards him. She saw the bodyguard appear, as if from nowhere, to fling himself in front of the prince.

'Assassin!' she screamed.

Devlin fired and the bodyguard fell into the prince's arms. The Prince of Wales staggered back, holding the man.

She felt the blast of a second shot close to the right side of her head, and then a third near her left. Both ears began to ring. All the commotion around her turned to an echoing cacophony, the sounds all blurred and distorted as though in a faint, the smoke clouding her vision and stinking of rotten eggs.

As the smoke began to clear, Superintendent Wilde's face was pressed close to her own, one hand upon her shoulder, his lips mouthing words she could not hear, his eyes brimming with concern. But slowly...

'Mrs Palmer, are you all right?'

She nodded, glancing down to see the revolver in his other hand, a curl of smoke still circling from the barrel. She tilted her head to see past his extended arm.

Devlin was down, blood bubbling from the side of his mouth, Leadbetter kneeling at his side, his own revolver in one hand and a second pistol – Devlin's, she assumed – in the other.

Chief Constable Fenwick shouted orders, urged the Prince of Wales – with great deference, naturally – to set the wounded bodyguard upon the ground. But Lord Jesus be praised, at least the poor fellow still lived.

'All is well, my friends!' shouted Lady Katherine. 'All is well!'

Ettie was surprised there was no obvious panic. Foolishly, she remembered that day in Wrexham when the whole town, it seemed, had feared the escape of Wombwell's lions. Here, by comparison, in the face of real and present danger, there was simply unflappable self-assurance, everybody – from the prince downwards – acting as though this sort of minor inconvenience was an everyday thing. Upper class ice in their emotional veins? And what had Harriet Beecher Stowe called it – stiff upper lip? But no, these people simply believed they were immune to the perils and hazards of everyday life. Wealth their armour against all things.

Lady Katherine, she thought, understood this perfectly. She had taken charge, quietly ushering her guests back the way they'd come into the glasshouse, while her now dithering husband – as though in his dotage – was escorted towards the house. By family members, Ettie guessed. But then the duchess was at her side.

'It was him,' she said. 'Devlin. How can that be? His advice that we should come here, rather than the marquee...'

Ettie thought she understood the reason. Devlin would be more assured of opportunities at closer quarters than in that huge expanse on the polo field. But she had no time to explain. And the more important question? When had Devlin become an assassin in the first place? Yet, for now...

'Your grace,' she said. 'My husband...'

She waited no longer to explain further. Instead, she gathered her skirts and ran for the other end of the Camellia Walk. Out onto another brick pathway, a cluster of buildings to her left.

Directly over her head, the basket. How high? Neo, how high?

Five hundred feet? A thousand? Above the basket, the net-shrouded red and yellow globe.

As she watched, there was movement. It looked, for all the world, as though somebody climbed over the side of the car.

What was happening?

She took a few steps forward, following the direction in which the balloon travelled. But then she saw something come away from the side of the netting. A flag? She couldn't make it out. Yet, a moment later, she felt her heart stop.

There was a body. Falling earthward.

'Neo!' she screamed.

Chapter Thirty-Four

It had seemed to Palmer as though he'd held his breath for many minutes. All the time it had taken for the device to fall. And for McCafferty to catch the bomb, mere inches before those mercury fulminate-filled fingers reached the floor. The American had caught it and swung the iron hemisphere sideways, fear in his eyes – and Palmer knew, deep in his soul, that fear was a rare emotion for this wretch.

'God dammit, Alfred,' he'd panted. 'All that time playing whist. Impressive. But I never realised your real talent would be for poker.'

Palmer, however, had been thinking of a recent report in the *Western Mail*. From America, as it happened. Somewhere in Indiana. An airship wizard, it had said. Professor Baldwin. An exhibition in which he was supposed to drop sticks of dynamite in yet another pyrotechnic display. Only the dynamite had exploded in the car itself. Tiny fragments of the balloon, and of Professor Baldwin, had rained down on the horrified crowd – including Baldwin's wife.

'What have you done, Captain?' he'd said. 'The shots.'

'I guess you'll be needing a new Prince of Wales. New heir to the throne.'

Palmer had found himself shocked to the core. He rather despised the prince for his famed debauchery. Little time for the monarchy in general. But this? It was an assault upon their entire society. And, worse, there was this developing sense of failure, as though this fresh atrocity was somehow due to Palmer's own credulity.

'Who, Captain? Down there...'

'An old friend of yours, as it happens. Devlin.'

'Devlin?' Palmer hadn't been able to believe it, and his feeling of gullibility had grown yet stronger.

'Good man. Loyal to Ireland. So loyal he worked his way right into their Special Irish Branch.'

'The woman – Mrs McBain...'

'Positioned himself behind the gate when Cody set the bull free. Poor Cody. Another good man. And your dear, sweet, butter wouldn't melt in her mouth, Esther...'

Palmer had no intention of allowing him to pursue this particular line.

'He shall hang,' he'd said. 'And Devlin too, I hope.'

'We all know the risks. But given a fair wind, we'll spring them before that happens. Daly, as well.'

'But *two* causes?' Palmer asked.

McCafferty had still held the revolver, still kept it pointed at Palmer.

'No time for that, Alfred. Not now. We've work to do, you and me.'

'All this, Captain?' Palmer waved a hand towards the balloon. 'Simply a charade?'

'Means to an end. This end, Alfred.'

'But if I had dropped the bomb?'

'I'm no fool, Alfred. You'd never have dropped them. Not down there, anyhow. You'd have forced me to shoot you. Better this way. Just a few simple adjustments to make.'

Now he motioned with the pistol, so that Palmer was forced to back around the sides of the car until they had changed position. McCafferty's turn to crouch this time, to set the bomb upon its gimbal once more. He shook his arm in relief when it was safely in place.

'If not for here...' said Palmer, looking around at the four boxes.

McCafferty edged around to the instruments and checked them, tapping at the barometer's glass and looking up at the sky. Clouds were gathering, a chill descending. He spat over the side again.

'Not here, no,' he said. 'But time for us to say farewell, Alfred.'

He pulled on the valve rope, and they dropped suddenly by several feet, Palmer's stomach lurching as they did so.

'Farewell?' Palmer felt that frisson of fear once more, the certainty he would be thrown overboard. His mind raced. How to defend himself? McCafferty was stronger than him, despite their age difference. Stronger by far. And a soldier. A trained killer. There was the revolver, too. He cast about for a weapon of his own and thought about the contents of his pockets. Propelling pencil. Snuff box. Might he…?

More than anything, he needed to buy time. Time to think. Time – just time.

'The bombs,' he said. 'If Esther destroyed the dynamite…'

'The advantage of a resourceful business partner. But now…'

'Wait,' said Palmer. 'At least tell me one thing. The Dee – leaving the bodies along the Dee. Why?'

'What, Alfred? Think your Lord Jesus will find some way to save you if you keep me talking? That won't happen. But the river? That was Danny Devlin, as much as anything. That rat, Tobin – well, we needed him found somewhere the newspapers would take note. But after? Devlin had this thing about the river. Been brought up by the Dee in Ireland. Famous, you know? One of our Irish legends. He said it would send a message. That the name – in Irish – means something like throwing down the gauntlet. Ain't that what you say?'

But all this while, McCafferty had been busy at the rigging – the frame like a milkmaid's yoke attached to the folded roll of silk.

'What are you doing?' Palmer demanded, and McCafferty turned to explain.

'I only done this once before, Alfred. But it worked just fine. So, here's how it goes. I use the parachute to get away. And with this breeze – why, you get the ride of your life, old friend. The *last* ride of your life, I guess. If I got the calculations right, all the way to Chester, Of course, once you get there, with this chill, an' all – well, I reckon you should end up…'

He chopped with his hand in the direction they were presently headed. Palmer swung about and followed the indicated route. Sure enough, in the distance, maybe three miles away, beyond the intervening green countryside, beyond the sinuous glimmer of the river, lay the grey and sandstone sprawl of the city, its features indistinct except for the occasional tower or steeple.

'You cannot!' he said, though, when he span around, McCafferty was already perched upon the handrail – rather on the yoke, as though it were a trapeze – his legs dangling over the side and his hands, one of them still gripping the pistol, busy with the wide leather strap he buckled under his armpits and around his chest.

'I'm afraid I can, Alfred,' the wretch laughed, and reached up to the first of the slipknots holding the silk to the cordage. Then the second.

'Bon voyage!' McCafferty yelled as the parachute came free.

There was a moment when it seemed it must surely tangle in the rigging but then the American had dropped and gravity did the rest.

He fell, and the billowing silk followed, while Palmer, the balloon – its load so suddenly lightened – surged skyward.

Ettie saw the body fall. And she saw a cream canopy billow above.

'Parachute,' said Wilde, now at her side. 'I never saw one before.'

There had been her instant of terror. The thought of Neo plunging to his death. The relief as the parachute opened and the descent had been arrested, followed immediately by the return of terror with the realisation this was not Neo, after all.

'McCafferty,' she murmured, and watched as the silk mushroom drifted north away from them.

'And Neo...' She turned to the superintendent, tears now running down her cheeks.

'Your husband is resourceful, Mrs Palmer. The balloon must inevitably descend.'

'And if it *does* carry some device...'

'The Fenian would have used it here, surely? No, I believe the entire escapade with the balloon was intended as no more than a distraction. It served its purpose, did it not? And had you not brought us here – well, imagine if Devlin had gained just two seconds more.'

Ettie still struggled to understand it all. Devlin? Mrs McBain's shadow. Her loyal associate? Plainly, nothing was as it seemed. And there *had* been the incident at the Beast Market. How convenient he'd been safely behind the gate when the beast broke free. Or, rather, been set free. By Cody. Cody, who was now behind bars. Behind bars because she had – no, she buried the memory again. Buried it deep. And now, Neo...

'We must follow,' she said.

'The Chief has sent for his gig, and...'

The two chief constables joined them.

'McCafferty?' Fenwick pointed at the parachute. 'Are we certain?'

'It seems likely, sir,' Wilde told him. 'Though, with McCafferty...'

'Nothing ever seems certain,' said Leadbetter. 'And your husband, Mrs Palmer – have you spotted him? Do you even know he's up there?'

She did not. She had seen the balloon suddenly rise and then apparently gather speed. Perhaps change direction, at least a little. But still no sign of Neo.

'Well,' said Chief Constable Fenwick, 'we shall pursue both parachute *and* balloon, since they are inevitably carried by the same zephyr in the one direction.'

And so began the pursuit. In the case of McCafferty, it was mercifully brief. The gig had been brought close to the glasshouse and they were aboard, Fenwick mounted upon a phaeton two militia riflemen and a pair of constables clinging to the sides. Both vehicles swung around onto yet another driveway.

'Chester approach,' yelled Fenwick. 'A straight run, all the way to Overleigh.'

Not quite straight. It curved across an open deer park, then a further bend through thick woodland, occasional glimpses of the balloon but, closer, the parachute descending. Ten minutes, until they crossed a bridge above a lane leading, to their right, to a village.

'Eccleston,' Fenwick shouted from the phaeton. 'And where is the parachute?'

No sign of it. They came to a turning, also off to the right. They followed it, their horses snorting, spittle flecking and flying, past brick and half-timbered houses and down to the church. St. Mary's, the notice board announced. And there was the parachute. Hanging from the church itself. Not from the large square castellated tower, but from one of the pyramid pinnacles at the base of buttresses rising above the aisle. But where was McCafferty?

'Went that way!' shouted an old woman with a handcart. She pointed down the narrow lane between stone walls.

The gig and the phaeton were abandoned.

Within a minute, they saw him. He was limping badly, struggling out of an oilcloth smock, his head bare.

'Halt!' Fenwick cried. 'Halt, now!'

But he did not. He kept going until he reached the river. And there he turned.

'Why, Mrs Palmer,' he said, though gritted teeth, those small dark eyes creased with pain. 'I might have known. The bane of my existence, Esther.'

And from the belt at his waist, he pulled a revolver. But before he could even raise the weapon, the militiamen had him in the sights of their rifles.

Bang. Bang.

McCafferty span around, dropped to one knee. He staggered two steps, three. He turned and raised the pistol.

Bang.

The third shot lifted him from his feet and dumped him into the waters of the Dee.

Palmer thought he heard shots. Though he could not be certain. Somewhere back from the direction he'd come. And no sign of McCafferty's parachute anymore. But he had better things to worry about. Where was he? And could it be true – the Prince of Wales assassinated? A nightmare.

His course seemed unaltered, and the panorama below showed him yet more thick woodland of the Eaton Hall estate, the duke's private driveway to Chester angling away to his left. To the right, the river curving, disappearing into the middle distance. But beneath him a road, true as a die. He'd recently attended a lecture by a Salford antiquarian who was about to publish a study of Roman Cheshire. And this road, in particular, he had discussed in detail.

'Yet, the fellow,' he said to himself, 'will never have seen it so majestically.'

He had begun to experience some strange euphoria mingled with his sense of failure. He could not quite explain it. His situation was parlous, and he could see no way that he might survive. Yet, here he was, master of all he surveyed – more or less. To see the world in this unique way. He gripped the rigging, Ahab at the helm of the *Pequod*. He was Maryatt's Mr Midshipman Easy. He was Fenimore Cooper's pirate, the Red Rover.

He began to hum the tune to *'Tis so sweet to trust in Jesus*.
'Dee-dee dum-dum, dee-dee, dum-dum.'

There were some at the chapel who were less than fond of the hymn but, personally, he liked it and the words now seemed entirely apposite. He checked the instruments himself, and began to sing. He found that it helped.

"Tis so sweet to trust in Jesus
Just to take Him at His Word...'

The air was exhilarating. It filled him with a longing to survive, even though he was no longer certain he deserved to do so. But to survive, he needed a plan.

He estimated his rate of travel at about four miles an hour and he was steadily losing height. Over the side of the basket was the grappling iron and its considerable coil of rope. But how to deploy it? And surely he did not want to come down in woodland. Yet, this was precisely what would happen if he continued to descend at this rate. He looked around, loosened a sandbag and tipped the contents overboard. The balloon climbed immediately.

He sang the hymn's refrain, louder now.

'Jesus, Jesus, how I trust Him!
How I've proved Him o'er and o'er.'

In the past five minutes, the road had left the countryside behind and was presently lined on the right with expensive Italianate villas. And the left, red-brick terraces. Further still to the left, allotments and nurseries, growing fruit and vegetables to feed the local populus. And the wind was now blowing him off the line of the road.

Five minutes more and he could see Overleigh Cemetery and the Grosvenor Bridge away to the left. Beneath him was the road through Handbridge, a church immediately to the right. Directly ahead, a school and, at its rear, a playground full of children. Palmer thanked his Lord Jesus that the winds had not blown him straight onto the church steeple.

He made a quick trajectory calculation. At this rate, he would land on the castle itself, or somewhere near. Palmer would die. He looked down at the bombs. Others would die also. There was the river. But could he be sure to drop each of the devices in the short time it would take to cross the Dee? No, it would not answer. He

278

reached for the valve rope and tugged it – but gingerly, having no idea how much of the gas he must expel.

Not enough. He tugged it again, cursed as the balloon dropped like a stone, far more than he'd intended. He span around, jettisoned another sackful of sand.

From the playground, children screamed with excitement. He leaned over the side. They were twenty feet below him, no more, and he waved at them. They waved back.

He stared ahead and sang again.

'Jesus, Jesus, how I trust him.'

Though, at this precise moment…

Beyond the schoolyard, another nursery. Fruit trees. If he could snare one of them, anchor the balloon – yes, it might just work.

He cast off the cable lashing the grappling iron to the basket and began to play out its hawser. Palmer swung the rope, and immediately snagged a young damson tree, a sapling.

The balloon moved beyond the tree, then jerked to a sudden halt. He hadn't expected it. His heart missed a beat as two of the boxes slithered across the wicker floor. But everything steadied. At least, for a moment. There was a rending noise and the balloon began to move again, this time pulling the uprooted sapling behind. It dragged across the ground, all the way to the river's edge, where both sapling and grapple caught in the branches of a large weeping willow. Once again, the balloon moved on, only to be stopped in its tracks.

But this was better. It strained against its new mooring point, the willow angrily shaking its branches in an attempt to be free of the monster. Though, this time, it was held fast, hanging at an angle above the water. Safe. The bombs could do no harm here. But Palmer knew he was tempting providence if he stayed with them.

He looked down into the waters of the Dee. He was surprised to see the surface flecked with white. Some form of tree blossom. Further along the bank, folk were gathering. He hesitated. Was there no better way? He knew how to swim, of course. Those family day trips sailing on the Broads. The friend of his father's who'd insisted they must all learn. And inevitably, this caused him to think about his father, his family.

Perhaps, he thought, I should try to use the mooring rope. Hand over hand back to the shore. But he had never been especially good at that sort of physical exercise.

No, there was no alternative. Yes, he could swim. Though – well, it had been such a long time. And was it true, that once learned the body could never forget? He readied himself, but then froze.

A bloodcurdling howl from the river's bank and echoing across the waters. There it was. Huge. Black. The Corpse Dog. *Cwn Cyrff.*

The shock, the fear, caused him to loosen his grip. He fell, and plunged downwards. Though he had not allowed for the height of his fall – or for the depths to which he would disappear below the surface. Dark. Cold. He tried to kick towards the shimmering light above but his coat, his clothes, weighed him down, and the river's currents seemed to have him in their grip.

Palmer could see nothing in the murk, his chest aflame, fit to burst. But, at last, his head came up and he gasped for air.

'Help!' he tried to scream. Though it only served to make him swallow water, and the word was cut short in a choking, splashing burble.

In that instant, as he broke through the short, choppy waves, he saw little, only the balloon, though now a dozen yards away – and the hound. It was in the water, too, its monstrous head coming towards him.

He heard Ettie's sweet voice, the first time she'd told him the tale. '*Yr araeth marwolaeth,*' she'd said. The herald of death.

Ettie, he thought, dear Ettie. And the waters pulled him down yet again. Down and down.

Until he felt something clamp about his upper arm. It hurt. Oh, Lord Jesus, how it hurt.

Chapter Thirty-Five

By the beginning of June, Ettie began to feel as though life was returning to normal. Well, almost. Her husband's head wound healed. A more comfortable truce restored between herself and Neo, his ineffable rectitude a blessing to her once again, rather than an irritant.

'Yet, he is recovered?' said Alison as they waited for the auction to commence. A final wander around the items on display at Mr Aston's auction rooms on Regent Street. Ten minutes before the sale was due to start.

'Still troubled – guilty almost – by how close we came to the prince being killed.'

'Guilty – how?'

'That is Neo, I fear. And continues to profess it was the Corpse Dog which saved him from the river – though, not a single witness.'

There had also been his insistence that the river was strewn with white tree blossom. Like her vision, all those months earlier.

'Saved him from the Dee.' Alison ran her fingers across the crimson studded leather of an elegant chair belonging to a dining room suite. She glanced at the item number and checked for the catalogue's estimate. 'Always the Dee. Was there, indeed, some mystical connection?'

'Poor Mrs McBain believed so. That, for the Fenians, the very name of the river had significance. In the Erse tongue it signifies a challenge, a call to action. And so, after that first murder – of Tobin – they used this significance as a way of letting those they thought had betrayed them know that they were coming for them. But I never told Neo. There was so much, Alison, I did not tell him, about the things spoken between myself and Mrs McBain.'

'Alfred had not resolved the connection himself, then?'

Ettie admired four Brussels tapestry carpets. Beautiful, though far beyond her budget.

'He said McCafferty told him the same – though the wretch claimed it was Kelly, or perhaps Devlin, who had some superstition about the thing. Yet I'm not entirely sure I believe it. Something more. *Afon Dyfrdwy*. The Waters of the Goddess. Dangerous. The goddess and the river, as well. And if those devils chose to use the river for their own purpose, the goddess has paid them harshly for their heresy, has she not?'

'The phantom hound belongs to the goddess, then?' Alison laughed. She intended it for a jest, but Ettie did not share her humour.

'He's dragged me to Handbridge not once, but twice. And yes, we managed to find folk who'd witnessed the balloon coming down, but not one who recalls anything about a hound. Neo, of course, is now convinced the bite marks on the victims is evidence that the Corpse Dog may simply have been trying to save them also.'

'And all these folk blissfully unaware of the bombs, I suppose,' Alison whispered as she scrutinised some fine Oriental jade jewellery.

Ettie span about, praying that nobody had overheard.

'Alison! Please!'

Today, of all days. The newspapers were full of it. Three days earlier, the end of May. Ten people injured. London. Infernal devices exploded outside the offices of the Special Irish Branch in Scotland Yard. Another in the basement of the Conservatives' Carlton Club. And a third outside the London home of Sir Watkin Williams-Wynn – the old gentleman unhurt, though still suffering the effects of his present illness.

There had been a fourth, planted at the foot of Nelson's Column, yet failing to explode. McCafferty might be dead, but the bombs still spoke.

'I remain astonished,' said Alison, 'that your own adventures should have attracted so little attention. Though, Edward says, that's simply *naiveté* on my part.'

It was true. There had been plenty of coverage about the successful balloon ascent, despite the unfortunate illness of the aeronaut, Mr Johnson. His unnamed assistant, however, had accomplished the task admirably and made successful landfall near Chester Castle. The whole afternoon had added considerably to the duke of Westminster's May Day fête. His Royal Highness, the Prince of Wales, as well as Prime Minister Gladstone, it was reported, were especially appreciative of the spectacle.

'Hardly naïve,' said Ettie. 'I should barely have credited the power of the press – or, indeed, our intelligence services – had we not experienced their reach once before.'

Of the shootings, at Eaton Hall itself, and then at Eccleston, not a word. And here they stood, before a double-barrelled breech-loading gun. Exquisite. French. Ornamented with damascene work in blue-silver and gold.

'But these new bombs – Esther, it is not possible, surely...'

Ettie decided she would bid later, on a brace of handsome walnut duchess toilet tables.

'I saw him shot,' she said. 'Not once but three times. He went into the river.'

'Yet, would they not have found – well, the weir, for example?'

Ettie found the subject just a little distasteful. She wrinkled her nose and chose her words carefully.

'Chief Constable Fenwick was satisfied that the progress of such a thing downstream would not be impeded by the weir when there is a particularly high tide. A spring tide? And there was such a tide the very next night. On such occasion, the height of the water both above and below the weir are the same and a – well, an object, let us say – would simply continue its journey out to sea.'

She shivered at the very thought. How easily that could have been Neo's fate. If he chose to believe this harmless fantasy about the dog, it was a small price to pay. Bless him, it was not a bad characteristic, was it? His refusal to acknowledge his own resourcefulness? Still, he had persisted, repeatedly produced the rents in the sleeve and shoulder of his coat as evidence, the bruises on his upper arm. Were these not indicative of a dog's jaws? And yes, she'd said, with feigned amazement, it must be so, my dear.

'Still...' said Alison, but no more than that. And then, almost as an aside: 'But if you wish to use the tricycle at any time...'

Ettie laughed. She would rather not think of cycling again just now. There had been the painful interview about the machine she had appropriated at Pulford and only Leadbetter's intervention had made the matter disappear. It had been yet another matter of discussion between Ettie and Neo all these past weeks, and between Ettie and Alison during their rare encounters. And rare they had indeed been.

First, there was Neo's health to care for. The inevitable catarrh and cough. Mustard plasters. Alison's husband telling him he was lucky to have avoided more serious pulmonary damage.

Afterwards, there'd been Neo's reluctance to leave the house. There was work to be done, naturally. Contracts to be fulfilled. Income to be earned. But, in addition, he'd said, there were so many loose ends to be knotted together.

So, here she was, chasing just one of those loose ends, as Neo had insisted. Perhaps germane, perhaps not. And it was Bethan Thomas who'd brought him the news. A strange visit, the woman implying that she knew more about Neo's involvement than she'd care to admit. Almost admiration.

'Hero, he is,' Bethan had murmured to her. 'So they say.'

On the other hand, it was just as likely she'd come on a fishing trip and merely pretending at inside information. No, with Bethan you never knew. But she had spotted this item in today's auction catalogue.

Neo had wanted to know who might buy them, though he'd not wished to be there himself. And here they were. A final table, with fifteen new joiners' saws, a collection of musical boxes – and this set of seven early Georgian monogrammed drinking glasses.

'It was the number which attracted Bethan's attention,' said Ettie. 'Seven. Neither six nor eight. As though one was missing, she said.'

Ettie examined them. A comparison with the sketch Neo had drawn for her. And, indeed, they seemed to match. They sold, as it happened, for an astonishing maiden bit of twenty guineas. Twenty! For seven drinking glasses.

She did not recognise the fellow who'd made the bid – but she knew how to discover his identity. Having done so, she shared tea and macaroons with Alison at Maddock's on Hope Street. But when she returned home with her news, she found Neo excited with news of his own.

He waved a document at her.

'From Ned,' he shouted. 'And today, of all days. It could not be better timed, my dear. I've sent a note to Leadbetter.' He embraced her and kissed her forehead. 'At last. We can unravel all of this!'

'I trust, Superintendent,' said Palmer, sheltering beneath his rain napper and skipping around the street's many puddles, 'it's not your intention to confront them alone?'

'Our trusty sergeant will be along shortly, Mr Palmer. Never fear. But I was mindful of the time, sir, as you suggested.'

The first Friday of the month, and Palmer had received his usual invitation. He would have ignored it, naturally, his curiosity having been well and truly satisfied about Viscount Broughton's eccentric dining club at his last visit. But with Ned's telegram…

'And Daly,' he said. 'Committed to stand trial at Chester Assizes, I see.'

'So I understand from the newspapers, yes.'

They passed Howell's bicycle and tricycle depot on the corner of Holt Street.

'You do not believe it?'

'I did not say so.'

'You did not need to, Superintendent. I know that tone only too well.'

It was a tone Palmer trusted, however. Hard to mistrust a man who spoke with a Shropshire accent, he'd long ago decided.

'It's my understanding it will be Warwick,' said Wilde. 'And it'll be penal servitude for that rogue, Mr Palmer. He'll go down for life, unless I'm much mistaken. But, for the record, might we say that's only my opinion?'

'And your own differences with Chief Constable Leadbetter – all resolved, I assume?'

'They are, sir. And with His Nibs away visiting family in Scotland – well, here I am!'

They left coats, hats and umbrellas in the Wynnstay's cloak room and were directed to the familiar private dining room. Though

Palmer was surprised to find only three of them around the table. A maudlin affair, with Viscount Broughton literally in the act of raising his wine glass over the water bowl with its white rose petals. It reminded Palmer of those tree blossoms upon the Dee.

'The qu...'

His two companions stopped in mid-toast also – the brewery manager, Steward, and Sir Watkin's nephew, son-in-law and heir, Herbert. Palmer had last seen them all on the occasion of the balloon ascent.

'Mr Palmer!' said the viscount, and fixed a welcoming smile to his lips. 'Why, you are welcome indeed. Superintendent Wilde, also. A pleasant surprise. Yes, pleasant.'

The Van Dyke beard and the waxed moustache seemed marginally more unkempt than at their previous encounter.

'You will join us, gentlemen, I trust,' he said, though it was hardly a convincing invitation.

'I think not,' said Wilde, and Palmer smiled. He recalled that early meeting at the brewery when the man had seemed so diminished by the insolence of both Steward and the viscount himself. There, he thought, you are Inspector Bucket once more.

'The queen?' said Palmer. 'Let me see – Queen Mary the Fourth, I assume.'

Viscount Broughton looked as though Palmer had just struck him.

'I see no cause...' the viscount stammered, affrontery splashed across his face. But Palmer was in full flow.

'Ah!' he said. 'The glasses. You are not using those belonging to the hotel this evening.'

The maidservant arrived with a tureen of soup. But she did not make it so far as the table.

'You may take that away, miss,' Wilde instructed her and, despite Viscount Broughton's protests, she obeyed, while Palmer picked up one of the spare glasses.

'Twenty guineas, Lordship,' he said, and ran his finger around the familiar monogram. 'But, great Heavens, were there not only seven pieces at today's auction? Yet here we are – with eight.'

There was the obvious tirade from Steward, his already ruddy snub nose and bald head each now red with rage. Was Mr Palmer making yet another outrageous allegation? Was it not enough that the courts had dismissed the previous calumnies of which he was accused? That nonsense about the contaminated yeast?

Palmer was about to respond, but Wilde raised a hand to silence him.

'The possible theft of a toasting glass, gentlemen?' he said. 'We would simply have sent Sergeant Jones to deal with such a minor matter. But treason is the business which brings me here tonight.'

'Treason?' said his lordship. 'This is a jest, surely.'

'Although...' Wilde paused for effect. 'There's no denying that these goblets have a part to play in the story, I suppose.'

'Story?' Steward demanded. 'What story?'

'A good question, sir. But as I understand it from Mr Palmer, it all begins here.' He waved his arm around the room. 'A hundred and fifty years. What d'you call it, Lordship?'

'Cycle of the White Rose, Superintendent. But your point?'

Wilde picked up one of the glasses and waved it at Herbert Watkin Williams-Wynn.

'These? They belonged to your great-great-granduncle, did they not? And dining club? Just a pretty excuse for sedition.'

The captain looked mortally offended, a slight upon his family's honour.

'A simple belief,' he bristled, 'that there might be a legitimate alternative to our present monarchy? You call that sedition?'

'More than that, Captain, surely,' said Palmer, 'when Jacobites launched three armed rebellions and brought civil war to these islands, yet again.'

'History, Mr Palmer,' snapped the captain. 'Ancient history.'

'If only that were true, Captain,' said Wilde. 'But, you see, just a month ago, something very strange happened. It's not widely known but a Fenian by the name of Devlin tried to assassinate His Royal Highness, the Prince of Wales.'

'Hang it all!' exclaimed Viscount Broughton. 'Wait – not at Eaton Hall, surely?'

Palmer could not help remembering McCafferty's conviction, that he would somehow be able to secure Devlin's release before the rogue should face the gallows. And there he'd been, Devlin, already dead at Wilde's hand.

'Indeed, my lord,' said the superintendent. 'A shame you weren't there. Must have been the only member of our local aristocracy missing from the gathering.' Palmer saw the viscount purse his lips, though he made no comment. 'But that, I fear,' Wilde continued, 'is not the crucial part of the story. For the entire scheme was planned in collaboration with a second treasonable organisation. What did you call it again, Mr Palmer?'

'A relatively new scientific term, gentlemen. A symbiosis. A union of two different organisms based on mutual benefit. It occurs most commonly...'

Wilde stopped him again, his hand raised. And quite right, too, Palmer decided. He was in serious danger of digressing.

'A symbiosis,' the superintendent repeated. 'Two parties. Two beneficiaries. The one party happy to commit the crime and accept the credit for its execution, the other party happy to fund the deed, to provide a natural diversion, but with the absolute understanding that their own participation must never come to light.'

'And might you explain,' demanded the captain, 'precisely how any of this concerns myself?'

'Gladly,' said Wilde. 'But if you don't mind, it's been a long day.'

He picked up one the glasses, filled it from the wine decanter, and knocked back the contents in one swallow. Palmer had tried to persuade him towards the Blue Ribbon Army on more than one occasion – plainly without success. Wilde slammed down the glass with evident satisfaction before he continued.

'It is all connected to the balloon ascent on May Day.'

Palmer sought a reaction on any of the three faces but there he found only shared puzzlement.

'It was you, Captain,' Wilde pressed on, 'who introduced McCafferty to the Balloon Society and...'

'McCafferty?' said the captain. 'I know nobody...'

'Jackson, sir,' said Palmer impatiently. 'The bogus Canadian – Mr Jackson.'

'Bogus?' Viscount Broughton exclaimed. 'Bogus? Why, I have dealings with the fellow. You have evidence…?'

Palmer glanced at Steward, and saw a different expression there, as if a curtain lifted before his eyes.

'I suspect we shall get to the evidence in due course,' said Palmer. 'But, for now, suffice to say that McCafferty – Jackson, if you prefer – was none other than the leader of the Fenian Invincibles, their mysterious Number One. And through your introduction, Captain, he managed to inveigle his way into the confidence of Mr Johnson the aeronaut.'

'Yet I had no idea,' the captain stammered. 'And was it not you, my lord, who persuaded me to make the introduction for the fellow?'

'Business dealings, as I say.' The viscount made a leisurely play of opening a silver case and fitting a cheroot into an ivory holder before lighting it from a table candle. 'The fellow asked me if I knew anybody and…'

'Besides,' said the captain, 'you were eager enough yourself, Mr Palmer, to get aboard for the May Day ascent.'

It was now that Palmer saw pure shock on the faces of both Steward and the viscount.

'I was about to remark upon it when Mr Palmer came in,' the captain explained to the others. 'You recall his reaction at the mere mention of ballooning and yet, after you had both left, there he was, running to take part.' He turned to Palmer. 'And you did, sir – take part. Yet, no mention of you in the newspaper reports. Only of Mr Johnson's assistant.'

Steward got to his feet, pushed back his chair.

'If you'll excuse me, gentlemen,' he said. 'None of this concerns me, and…'

'Sit yourself down again, sir,' Wilde told him. 'We shall see whether any of this concerns you in a few moments. Now, if you please…'

Steward sat once more, grinding his teeth together. It gave Palmer considerable satisfaction to see the fellow so perturbed. Time for a pinch of snuff.

'It was necessary, Captain,' said Wilde, 'to keep Mr Palmer's name out of the newspapers.'

That was true. Yet, Palmer had already been asked several times by folk in town – including Bethan Thomas, naturally – about his part in the ascent.

'And other details as well,' Wilde went on. 'You see, the balloon was carrying four infernal devices.'

'Bombs?' exclaimed the viscount.

'Orsini bombs, to be precise. I'm sure, given the Captain's position, that we can rely on his integrity.'

'And my own, Superintendent,' said Viscount Broughton, blowing a pleasurable ring of smoke towards the ceiling. 'And my own.'

Steward said nothing. He gripped the edge of the table, his knuckles white. He almost looks, thought Palmer, like a man must when he has just been condemned to hang.

'The bombs,' said the captain, now gone quite pale, 'intended for His Royal Highness?'

'No, sir, they were not.' Wilde waited a moment for his words to penetrate. 'Though, we initially thought so. They were intended to destroy innocent lives in Chester – an evil prevented, in large part, due to Mr Palmer.' Palmer felt himself flush, the colour rising to his cheeks. 'But they were certainly intended as a decoy, to distract attention while this other Fenian attempted to assassinate the Prince of Wales. Thank Heaven, he failed.'

Ettie had told Palmer the story a dozen times. It was good of Wilde to give him the credit, but it was the Superintendent's pistol and accuracy – Leadbetter's as well, of course – which had saved the prince's hide.

'The culprit arrested, I trust,' said the viscount.

'Dead, sir. One of the culprits, at least. The very point, in fact. For, while the Fenian who held the gun may have had one motive for killing His Royal Highness, others involved in the plot had quite another. Did they not, my lord?'

Palmer was impressed with the way Wilde managed to infuse those two words, *my lord*, with so much contempt. And he knew the superintendent would call upon him now to play his own part.

'You see, sir,' Wilde continued, 'thanks to Mr Palmer – or rather, to his connections within the India Office in London – we have this interesting piece of paper.'

Palmer withdrew the document from his pockets, the one procured for him by Ned. He set it down on the table with a flourish.

'As you say, Lordship,' said Wilde, 'business dealings. To be precise, the contract by which you became an equal partner in a mining venture. The Arivaca mine in Arizona, yes?'

Palmer saw a weak smile upon Viscount Broughton's lips.

'Both signed on the same day, did you not?' Wilde pointed at the date. 'And here, sir, your own signature.' His finger stabbed down upon the page. 'And here,' he said triumphantly, 'the name of your partner. You see, my lord? Captain…John…McCafferty.'

'Hubris,' Neo explained, when they were each settled with a mug of cocoa upon their respective bedside tables – those fine walnut duchess tables upon which she'd bid so successfully during the morning. 'Arrogance, my dear. McCafferty would have been required to use his own name as the proprietor. And his lordship…' He tried to imitate the way Wilde had done it. 'Well, his lordship, with all the self-assurance of his class, would never have believed the document might see the light of day. Or cared if it did. They always seem able to be immune from justice, do they not?'

'But he is arrested now?' she asked.

He set down this month's copy of the *British Chess Magazine*. Too many distractions from today, she assumed, for him to deal with any of its challenges. In any case, the gaslight was spluttering and must not make reading any easier.

'Sadly, no. Steward, certainly. Sergeant Jones arrived with news that they had dug up the fellow's garden, as instructed. A quantity of mercury fulminate found buried there – the same as would have detonated the bombs.'

She saw the puzzled look upon Neo's face.

'Is that not sufficient evidence?' she said, as he picked up his cup and blew upon the beverage.

'Perhaps a little *too* convenient,' he said. 'Though I'm sure a jury shall have no such concerns. And, to be fair, Wilde has been busy. He managed to find a witness in Farndon who'd seen the Broughton Brewery's van on the morning Tobin's body was discovered. From the description, the driver was certainly Steward.'

'But what does that prove?' Ettie asked him.

It had been Ned, of course, all that time ago, who had first put the thought in his head – about how brewery drays were so common, nobody even noticed them.

'Precisely the point. I think we all *know* what happened, yet knowing is not enough.'

'So,' she said, 'Tobin moves to Wrexham, takes work at the brewery. He learns about their passion for the Jacobite cause and ingratiates himself with the tattoo?'

Ettie had been intrigued many times by the travelling showmen offering this service at the Annual Pleasure Fair. She had even been tempted. Perhaps a few words of scripture tattooed upon her shoulder.

'Certainly,' said Neo, and for a moment she foolishly mistook this for his concurrence that such a tattoo might be acceptable. But no, he was talking about the crime again.

'McCafferty – Jackson – follows a lead here in an effort to track the fellow down and strikes up an association with the viscount himself. A symbiosis. Regardless of the court decision, there can be no doubt Steward had arranged for Tobin to use the contaminated yeast to ruin the Lager Beer Company. Perhaps Tobin had threatened to expose them. Or simply refused to see it through.'

'In any case,' she said, and sipped at her own cocoa, then dratted as she spilled a few drops down the nightgown's bodice, 'they each had reason to see him dead.'

Neo shrugged.

'Symbiosis.'

'But this discovery in Steward's garden,' she mused. 'It is, as you say – well, convenient, is it not?'

'Incredibly so,' said Neo. He set down his cup and settled back on his pillows, adjusting his night cap. 'The rogue protested, of course. Claimed he knew nothing about the explosives. But it was enough to force a confession – though one could hardly call it such – from the viscount himself.'

'He confessed to the plot?'

'Hardly. I think I have never met such a competent – and charming – liar. No, he simply listed all the prominent members of parliament, of the aristocracy, who had assured him they would be happy to raise the constitutional issue of succession might some misadventure *actually* befall His Royal Highness. Or, indeed, when the time came naturally for succession with Victoria's demise. But he made it all seem so entirely hypothetical.'

'To put this Princess Maria Theresa of Bavaria upon the throne?'

'To be honest, my dear, the more he spoke, the more plausible it became. We have a history, of course, of making such changes. William of Orange. The first Hanoverians. It is, after all, simply a matter of politics. There is a process. And, as George Reynolds would have reminded us, the Prince of Wales is hardly a shining example of the Saxe-Coburg bloodline. When Victoria dies, as die she must one day, might the people not welcome another queen in her stead – and a queen who could be said to have stronger roots in British history than the Saxe-Coburgs?'

'But a confession of sorts,' said Ettie. 'And his proven link to a known Fenian. Yet, no arrest?'

'I believe Wilde to be under orders from above.'

'It would raise questions. I suppose that's plain. Uncomfortable questions. Bringing the aristocracy into disrepute. Oh, perish the thought.'

'Wilde implied that the viscount might be about to run into difficulties. His mining venture in Arizona gone wrong. Bankruptcy on the horizon. The brewery and his other businesses forced to close. He and his family moving abroad.'

'The superintendent knows all this for a fact?'

'Foreknowledge?' Neo laughed. 'More likely, he knows sufficient about the workings of the powers that be – the authorities' ability to make such things come to pass, as they require.'

'Exile?'

'I suppose so. I keep thinking about his daughter. Poor girl. Forced to spend her whole life carrying the name Clementina Sobieska – mother to that same so-called Bonnie Prince whose personal ambitions plunged this nation into yet another civil war.'

Ettie feared for a moment that this would lead him into still more reveries about their own children but, thankfully, his mind was elsewhere. And for Ettie herself? At least there had been no further pain for several weeks. No physical pain, anyhow. The waters of her life flowing almost fully again. As fully as they were ever likely to be.

'The glasses,' he smiled. 'You see? The hubris again. He already had plans to possess seven. It seems Sir Watkin himself had told him of his intention to put them up for auction – only too pleased to distance himself from his ancestor's seditious leanings. But it was unthinkable for his lordship that he would not own the entire set – and he knew the eighth was in the museum. What easier solution for a man of such privilege than to simply arrange its theft.'

'Impossible to fathom, is it not? That one can be so far removed from the realities of life that he would willingly pay twenty guineas for seven, and have no guilt about stealing number eight?'

'That, my dear, is the aristocracy in a nutshell. Yet the theft put something in the back of my mind, Ettie. Just the germ of an idea. The very beginnings of suspicion about the man.'

'And we'll need to report all this to Lady Olivia?'

'Will we, indeed? I think we might leave that on the warming plate for now, don't you agree?'

'Perhaps. But she has a long reach, Neo. And we still don't know for sure where the devices themselves were forged.'

'Nor from whence the explosives came. You may have destroyed the supply at the cemetery but they were plainly replaced with ease.'

'And for these latest London bombs, as well.'

'Yes, that is strange, is it not. The device at Scotland Yard I understand. But the one outside Sir Watkin's house? I have a dreadful feeling that the old fellow's open contempt for his ancestor, for the Jacobite cause as a whole...'

'Viscount Broughton?'

'How can we ever be certain? Wilde confronted him with several other allegations, of course. He'd admitted to me that he'd received an invitation to the May Day fête, so he would undoubtedly have had prior knowledge that the prince – and, indeed, the Prime Minister – would be there. So, plenty of time for him to alert McCafferty and hatch their plot. But he merely shrugged it all aside. He did not even have a word of farewell for Steward, taken away clapped in irons. Though he reserved a few for me, Ettie.'

'Hardly words of praise, I imagine?'

'Indeed, not. Rather an accusation that at least now I would be free to continue stirring trouble for honest Welsh landowners. Can you imagine? As I say, arrogance.'

'I suppose he's correct in a way. Time to finish the book, Neo.'

'First I need to redraw my map. In light of my aeronautical experiences, you understand?' Ettie smiled. 'It made me realise how distorted my view of the world had become.'

'I believe, husband, you intend more than just your view of its geography.'

'I had begun to wonder whether we'd made a mistake coming here, Esther. A tragic mistake. The babe, you know? And the difficulties of making ends meet. But we have made a difference, don't you think?'

'Somebody needed to care about those three victims of McCafferty's, Neo. To find some justice for them.'

She wondered whether to tell him about the note. *Let sleeping dogs lie.* Or her total lack of guilt about pushing Kelly to his death. Or the pistol. Or her doubts about whether McCafferty might, against all the odds, possibly have survived. But she decided that these Corpse Dogs were, themselves, all best left to their slumbers.

We must, she knew, plan when there are things we may change, and pray when there are things we may not. And how she had prayed, during her imprisonment by McCafferty. Though it all seemed somewhat like a dream now, somehow confused with the performance of *The Castle Spectre*, she in the clutches of wicked Earl Osmond, her rescue by Neo in the role of Percy.

'At least,' he said, 'young Captain Herbert is exonerated. Important, don't you think? That Sir Watkin's heir should be as blameless as Caesar's wife?'

She smiled. How much he had changed. How much she cared for him. How much she wished they could, indeed, have children together. But life was life, and we must delight in what we have, she knew, not that which we desire.

'Of course,' she said. 'He is in your debt now, is he not? I wonder whether he might be persuaded to take you ballooning again?'

'Well, bless my soul, Esther Palmer.' He beamed at her and blew out the candle. 'That thought had never occurred to me.'

Epilogue

'Thirty years, Neo,' she said, and patted the lid of his coffin for the last time. 'And you never once stopped believing he's still out there, somewhere.'

It was absurd, the number of times over those three long decades that they'd seen newspaper reports, the last of them only a month earlier, before Neo's final illness. A book review, of all things. A new poetic sensation. Nogales, Arizona. Captain John McCafferty, it had said, a former soldier of the Confederacy. It could not be, surely?

'Esther,' said Ned Owen. 'It's time.'

'No,' she said, choking on the words. 'Another minute, Ned?' She turned to Neo's brother, standing at Ned's shoulder. It was like looking at Neo himself. The beard as white as Old Father Time's. The wrinkles of old age and wisdom. 'John?' she wept. 'Another minute?'

She glanced around at the others packed into the chapel: the mayor; the aldermen; the town clerk; the entirety of the town's clergymen; representatives from the Pharmaceutical Society of London, from the Royal Commission for Ancient Welsh Monuments and from *Archaeologia Cambrensian*; the gentleman from Liverpool University, just too late to award him the honorary degree they'd decided to bestow upon him; and journalists galore. How proud he would have been. How amused.

'Ned is right,' said John. The same Norfolk accent. It could have been Neo's voice and it tore her apart. 'It is time.'

The pallbearers lifted the coffin to their shoulders with ease. He had grown so spectral this past year, his skin almost translucent. But how would she survive without him? Two halves of the same whole. And now just this great aching emptiness which she knew from friends would never be filled again.

John put his arm about her shoulders – shoulders wrapped in her widow's weeds – as they followed the coffin out of the chapel and around the path to the right, towards the plot Neo had insisted upon when they had lost the babe. A simple stone as yet, with no name – for the little one's name remained hers to know, and hers alone, even now.

'Is there not some comfort,' said John, as if he read her mind, 'in knowing they will now be reunited at last after all these years – father and child?'

She had thought the same herself. And it was a strange thing, that he had reserved this particular plot all those years earlier. For, when their financial circumstances had improved, and they were seeking a new and better home, it had been this very thing which had decided them.

She looked down now to Bersham Road, down to the house. Inglenook, they'd name it. Cosy. Warm. Yet, when they had first gone to see it, Neo had stood outside, looking up to where he knew the child's burial place to be.

'There,' he'd said. 'We can see it from here. Come what may, my dear, we shall all be able to keep an eye on each other.'

He had said it and laughed. She had laughed as well.

'I doubt,' she'd said, 'any couple has ever made a house selection in such a way.'

'Well,' he'd replied, 'there has never been a couple like ourselves, Esther.'

At the opened grave, John left her for a few words with the chaplain, since it was Neo's brother who would preside over the interment. It had been Neo's wish, and natural enough, John himself a Methodist minister all these years.

Ned's turn to care for her now.

'If there is anything, Esther,' he said. 'Anything at all.'

'Nothing I need, Ned. Except…'

She stared at the coffin and thought she would faint away. It was true enough. There was income from the books. Modest, but income all the same.

'He was so proud of you,' said Ned. 'The way you did so much to help the families during the protests. And more besides.'

She smiled. The Tithe Wars, they called them now. But back then? All across Denbighshire, tenants forced from their lands just as Neo – and Ned too, of course – had predicted might happen. Riots. So many injured. Families to be fed. Legal defence cases to be funded. The campaign for improved legislation – which had come, eventually. He'd been at her side all that time. And so, she thought with amusement, had Lady Katherine. Well, the money had to come from *somewhere*.

'More besides?' she said. 'You mean my feeble efforts to win us women the right to vote? They didn't get us very far.'

'But they will, Esther,' Ned told her.

It was impossible to think about Ned without also thinking about the pension. That had been Ned as well, of course. It had taken so many years and, in the end, it had been granted ostensibly on the basis of the Civil List Awards, paid from the Privy Purse of the monarch to those who had distinguished themselves in the arts or science. But the truth, as they both knew it, was that, ten years ago, the monarch in question, formerly the Prince of Wales, then King Edward the Seventh, had been reminded how her husband had risked everything to save his life.

'In the midst of life,' John began, 'we are in death…'

Then he stopped, looked skywards, and they followed the direction of his gaze.

'See, Ned?' she smiled. 'He did it.'

Drifting towards them, across the clear sky of winter's end and spring's beginning, was a balloon, a green and white globe.

'Herbert,' Ned smiled.

'*Sir* Herbert,' she said. The Seventh Baronet now. Retired from the army with the rank of Honorary Colonel. Service with distinction in that awful second war against the Boers. And, in retirement, he and Neo had shared this passion for the skies.

'Lucky to be retired,' said Ned, 'and not caught up in the madness.'

No, she thought, though running a munitions factory on the Wynnstay Estate was itself, she knew, making a contribution to the insanity.

'I believe it is the thing that killed him, Ned.' She looked again at the coffin. 'The horror of it all. This useless, awful war fought for nobody but the royal families of Europe.'

'He's at peace now.'

'Yes,' she agreed. 'At peace.'

She was startled to hear Neo's voice, spun about, then realised it was his brother John again, beginning the service of committal afresh.

'Behold, dear friends,' he said, 'what manner of love the Father hath bestowed upon us, that we should be called the children of God.'

Neo had spoken about children so many times but, with the passage of years, he had simply stopped asking about children of their own. Or, rather, he had come to look upon all the children of the town as though they *were* his own.

'You see that old fellow there?' their parents would say. 'He is the kindest man alive. One of the cleverest. And one of the luckiest. Why,' they would whisper, 'it's said he survived great perils on land, upon the sea, and in the air. You see the walking stick he carries? The one with the hound's head handle? Well, if you ask him politely, he will let you touch the hound's snout for luck.'

Yes, she thought. Luck! They had shared so much. Selfless companionship. All these years. And that was the luckiest thing of all.

The End

But if you enjoyed this story and want to know more about the author's other novels – or better still – to sign up for his monthly Inner Circle newsletter, visit his website:
https://www.davidebsworth.com/

Historical Notes

This is, of course, a work of fiction. But, as usual, much of the background against which the novel's set is purely factual.

I've sketched the geography of Wrexham (and Chester) in 1884 as accurately as possible from the available Ordnance Survey and other maps, as well as the Census records – though I may have taken an occasional liberty here and there simply to fit the narrative.

The same is true for many of the characters – Alfred and Ettie Palmer; Ned Owen; Dr Edward Davies and his wife Alison; the Edisburys; McCafferty; Superintendent Wilde and the Chief Constable, Major Leadbetter; the FitzPatricks; Mr Wassmann; and a host of others. The things that happen to them may be invented but I've tried to paint them as they appeared to me from the various newspaper and similar references in which they are recorded. The only entirely fictional characters in the book are, for example, McCafferty's henchmen and victims, as well as Viscount Broughton, Matron McBain and Sergeant Devlin, plus a few others – including Bethan Thomas, of course.

And the events? Again, many of those have simply been taken from the pages of the *Wrexham Advertiser* for 1884 and the years in question: the recent Anti-Salvationist Riots in Chester (for more on a related theme, read the brilliant novel by Alis Hawkins, *The Skeleton Army*); the St. Patrick's Day entertainment; the Blue Ribbon Army's temperance activities; the sudden upsurge in cycling as a pastime, and especially cycling for women; the awful incident of the lion during the visit by Wombwell's Menagerie, as well as the ensuing panic in town; and, of course, the general sense of terror engendered by the bombing activities of the "Fenians" seeking independence for Ireland.

In the aftermath of the American Civil War, Fenian activity increased dramatically and in an entirely new way. So, the several invasions of Canada by significant armies of Irish Republican soldiers; the 1867 raid on Chester Castle; the rising in Ireland during that same year; the Phoenix Park assassinations; the planting of bombs in public places – particularly railway stations; and the arrest of John Daly at Birkenhead in 1884 itself – all this and much more can be readily researched.

The mood was set by the Clerkenwell Outrage in December of 1867. Members of the Irish Republican Brotherhood – by then commonly known as Fenians – tried to set free one of their group from Clerkenwell Prison. The bomb they used failed to secure any release, but it killed twelve innocents and wounded over a hundred more. For the times, it was a crime of "unexampled atrocity" which outraged the whole country and caused a huge setback for the legitimate Irish Home Rule Movement. But, more, it created a sense of terror in the minds of the British public which would be prevalent for the next twenty years and beyond.

At the heart of much of this history, stands the real-life shadowy figure of John McCafferty. In brief, he was born in Ohio around 1838 and joined the Irish Republican Brotherhood in about 1855. He served the Confederacy as a captain with Morgan's Raiders and other units but, by 1866, there are records of his presence in Dublin. In February 1867, he helped to plan the Chester Raid. The plot betrayed, McCafferty managed to escape but was subsequently captured, convicted and sentenced to death. However, the sentence was commuted and he was banished to the USA in 1871 – though not before swearing vengeance on his British gaolers and those who'd betrayed him.

In 1874, McCafferty apparently had a plan – obviously thwarted – to kidnap the Prince of Wales, Albert Edward ("Bertie"). From 1876 until about 1880, he's back and forth, between Britain and his mining interests in Arivaca, Arizona. It's likely that, in May 1882, he was involved in the organisation of Dublin's Phoenix Park killings – when Lord Frederick Cavendish and Thomas Henry Burke were stabbed to death. In 1883, he was in Mexico and in 1884, as well as 1885, he was linked to yet more bombings, including those mentioned towards the end of *Death Along The Dee*, those on 30th May 1884, the three bombs exploded in London.

After 1884, the accounts of McCafferty's activities vary wildly – either claiming that he disappeared entirely or, variously… that he helped plan the Grover Cleveland presidential campaign; that he continued prospecting and mining, this time in Alaska; that in 1894, he was in Nicaragua campaigning for the rights of native Mosquito Indians; or that, in 1908, he was publishing poetry in Nogales, Arizona. Terrorist? Dashing freedom fighter? Fake adventurer? Nobody really seems to know, but my favourite account of McCafferty's life appears in a 2006 edition of the *Journal of Arizona History*. It's the article written by Mary Noon Kasulaitis, entitled *A Fenian in the Desert*. Well worth a read.

John Daly has already been mentioned a few times and the curious may wish to know that he did, indeed, appear before the Warwick Assizes, under charges of treason felony, at the end of July 1884. He was sentenced to penal servitude for life. In practice, he served twelve years and was released in 1896. He departed for the United States on a lecture and fundraising tour but on his return to Ireland he opened a bakery and was soon serving on the Limerick City Council. From 1899 until 1902 he was Mayor of Limerick. By the time of the 1916 Easter Rising, he was confined to a wheelchair and died at his home in Limerick on 30th June 1916.

For more on this particular aspect and a remarkable account of the entire Fenian story, see Julie Kavanagh's stunningly good *The Irish Assassins*.

Which brings me, I suppose, to the whole question of Jacobitism. The topic has cropped up with alarming regularity within the pages of my books. From the time when James (*Jacobus* in Latin) the Second went into exile with the so-called "Glorious Revolution", to be replaced by William of Orange, Britain was awash with plots and open armed rebellions aimed at restoring the Stuart monarchs to the throne. Their hopes perished, of course, with Bonnie Prince Charlie's defeat at Culloden in 1746. Perished? Well, not quite.

In Wrexham, from about 1710 onwards, Sir Watkin Williams-Wynn (3rd Baronet) had established the Cycle of the White Rose, basically a dining club dedicated to raising funds and support among

Welsh Jacobites. It was later resurrected by his son and ran, pretty much uninterrupted, until the 1860s. But then, in 1886, it was reformed, yet again, now as the Order of the White Rose, by Bertram Ashburnam, 5th Earl of Ashburnam – who broadly provided some of the inspiration for my Viscount Broughton. A believer that Charles the First was a martyr and that the Stuarts were the rightful claimants to the British Crown, he was also an agent for the Catholic fanatics of the Spanish Carlists and a fervent supporter of Irish Home Rule. Weirdly, there was – and still is – a legitimate Jacobite claimant. In the 1880s, it was, indeed, Princess Maria Theresa of Austria-Este, and there's some documentation to show that the Order of the White Rose included extremists (though Bertram Ashburnam wasn't one of them!) who planned a coup to put her on the throne, a scheme with which she would, herself, have absolutely no truck. But my storyline hence seemed not so outlandish after all!

In the 1890s, the Order helped to establish a whole artistic movement, with entire exhibitions dedicated to the House of Stuart. Mostly nostalgic and romantic, of course, but the movement sparked a couple of dedicated newspapers and new interest in the "political ideals" (whatever those were) of the Jacobite cause.

In 1926, the Royal Stuart Society and Royalist League was founded and continues to this day. Its members, at the time of writing, recognise the *prétendant* Franz von Bayern, Duke of Bavaria, as the current head of the Stuart Dynasty and, therefore, the rightful British monarch – a claim he does not himself endorse, naturally. But the society's members also see themselves as natural successors to the Order of the White Rose. It has many supporters.

But perhaps the most difficult research elements for this one were those relating to the Welsh Land Question.

I first read Palmer's *History of the Ancient Tenure of Land in the Marches of North Wales* a couple of years ago, when I was researching for *Blood Among The Threads*. At face value it was, and still is, a straightforward and not hugely exciting academic study delivering precisely what the title implies. Yet, as the plot for *Death Along The Dee* developed, and the research deepened, I began to see the book – it was popular enough for a second edition, this time with Edward (Ned) Owen as co-author, to be published in 1910 – through different eyes, and with a view to what was happening in relation to the Welsh Land Question at the time it was written. In 1836, legislation had been passed which forced tenant farmers to pay rent to the landowners in cash, rather than in kind, as they'd previously been able to do. Very often the "landowner" was the Anglican Church, which simply made the whole thing even more intolerable for the largely Nonconformist farmers. Then, in the 1870s, the agricultural depression created still greater hardship and even less ability to pay the steadily increasing rates.

Enter Alfred Neobard Palmer, whose book explains, without a single overt criticism of the new systems, how much better were tenancies and common lands handled under the more ancient regimes. Did he do so deliberately? Politically? It doesn't quite seem to fit, and yet there he was, writing at the very time when all this unrest was bubbling to the surface in the background.

And then immediately afterwards – literally a year or so after it was published – with yet another wave of enforced sales of land and property, of evictions, the whole thing erupted. Violent protests in Llangwm (Pembrokeshire), Mochdre (Conwy) and Llanefydd (also Conwy). Thirty-one of the Llangwm protesters were sent to court and the Mochdre protests resulted in eighty-four injured, including thirty-five police officers. Troops were deployed throughout Denbighshire. And these "Tithe Wars" only came to an end, with improved legislation, in 1891.

Coincidence? Probably. Relevance to the story? Very little, except it made me think differently about Alfred Neobard Palmer. Strangely (or not), almost exactly the same issues were occurring in Ireland, a residue from the famine and partly fuelling the calls for independence. Again, this is all neatly covered in Julie Kavanagh's *The Irish Assassins*.

For the more "technical" stuff – Alfred's analytical skills, balloon flights and the like – I've tried, as with the geography, to be as accurate as possible. Though I must admit to having taken some literary licence with the issue of the Killer Yeast – but not much – as well as the entirely invented Stag Spring Hawkweed.

Finally, there's Palmer himself. By the time he died on 16th March 1915, he'd written a whole batch of additional books, including *The History of the Parish Church of Wrexham* (1886); *The History of* the Older Nonconformity of Wrexham (1888); *The History of the Town of Wrexham* (1893); *The History of the Thirteen [Country] Townships of the Old Parish of Wrexham* (1903); his *History of Gresford* (1905); and his *History of Holt* (1910). In addition, there was an unsuccessful novel, *Owen Tanat* (1897). Finally, there would have been his *History of Ruabon Parish*, which he began in 1909 but never finished.

By the time of his death, he had inspected most of the ancient monuments of Denbighshire and Flintshire and begun on those of Merioneth, and from 1907 he took an active part in the excavation of the Roman site at Holt. He had, therefore, become an especially noted antiquarian and historian.

And Esther? She continued to live at Inglenook on Bersham Road for another fourteen years after Alfred's death. She passed away there on 24th February 1929 and was buried, with her husband, three days later in Wrexham Cemetery. There is, however, no record of a child and I hope readers will forgive this particular invention.

As usual, I owe an impossible debt to my "ideal reader", best friend and constant companion, Ann, who is also foremost among my literary critics as well as tolerating my endless ramblings about plot lines and character developments. I was especially lucky that both Pauline Vickers and Dylan Hughes agreed to act as further beta readers, supplementing the formal editing process by Nicky Galliers. My thanks, as well, to cover designer Cathy Helms at Avalon Graphics, plus Helen Hart and her team at SilverWood Books for assisting with the technical publishing processes. Finally, and most of all, my undying gratitude to all of you who read the story!

David Ebsworth
May 2024